He was on stage making a living as a singer – not quite up to West End standards, but a good living, way beyond anything he could have aspired to if he'd remained in Pontypridd. And if the impresarios and critics were to be believed, the world was poised, waiting for him to take it by storm. National success was around the next corner. And although he might not have a regular sweetheart – he glanced at Babs; by no stretch of the imagination could he apply that word to her – that was his choice. He had all the women he could handle and more throwing themselves at him, not because of his looks and talent, but because the ratio of girls to men on variety tours favoured men, which meant that he'd often found himself with five and sometimes as many as ten willing and able paramours to choose from. As his father would have said, 'He was in God's pocket.' So why had he felt so damned miserable ever since he'd come home?

Catrin Collier was born and brought up in Pontypridd. She lives in Swansea with her husband, three cats and whichever of her children choose to visit. Her latest novel in Orion paperback is *Finders & Keepers*, and her latest novel in hardback, *Tiger Bay Blues*, is also available from Orion. Visit her website at www.catrincollier.co.uk.

All That Glitters

CATRIN COLLIER

*For all those on the brink of life looking
to glittering horizons, especially my daughter
Sophie Watkins.
May they find the happiness they search for.*

An Orion paperback

First published in Great Britain in 1995
by Century
First published in paperback in 1996
by Arrow Books
This paperback edition published in 2006
by Orion Books Ltd,
Orion House, 5 Upper St Martin's Lane,
London WC2H 9EA

Printed and bound in Great Britain by
Clays Ltd, St Ives plc

The Orion Publishing Group's policy is to use papers that
are natural, renewable and recyclable products and
made from wood grown in sustainable forests. The logging
and manufacturing processes are expected to conform to
the environmental regulations of the country of origin.

www.orionbooks.co.uk

Acknowledgements

I continue to owe the people of Pontypridd a great debt of gratitude for their support and the assistance they so generously and unstintingly give me with my research.

The staff of Pontypridd Library, especially Mrs Morris and Penny Pugh for so many acts of kindness, and the staff of Pontypridd Historical Centre who are doing such sterling work to preserve Pontypridd's past in photographic form.

Mr Brian Hubbard and Mr Keith Woods of the Pontypridd Market Company for talking to me and allowing me to go into the Town Hall in Pontypridd. Sad, derelict and deserted, it is still the theatre of my childhood, and the same theatre where so many greats played as unknowns at the outset of their careers. Anyone who wants to see just how many, has only to go into the Market Tavern in Pontypridd and read the old billposters. My only hope is that it can be preserved before it goes the way of other institutions in Pontypridd that are no longer there to be seen; the New Inn, Coronation Ballroom, Co-op Arcade, White Palace, Palladium, Park Cinema, Fairfield, even Shoni's pond has shrunk in size from the lake I remember from my own childhood.

I also wish to thank my family, my parents, Glyn and Gerda Jones, my husband John, and my children, Ralph, Sophie and

Ross for their continued love, support and the time they so generously give me to write. Margaret Bloomfield for her friendship and practical help in so many ways.

And last but not least, my editor Mary Loring and her assistant Julie Stevens for their professionalism and helpful suggestions, and my agent Michael Thomas for his encouragement and continued belief in me.

Thank you.

I have again taken the liberty of mixing my fictional characters with real ones, especially the great boxers Frank Moody and Jimmy Wilde. Several of the events depicted in *All That Glitters* actually occurred, especially the sermons in the churches and chapels deploring the 'morally corrupting' variety shows in the Town Hall. However I would like to stress that all the major characters are creations of my imagination, and while acknowledging the help I have received while reasearching and writing *All That Glitters*, I would like to stress that any errors in the book are entirely mine.

Catrin Collier June 1994

Chapter One

Haydn Powell tipped his trilby over one eye, slouched back in his seat, and tried to look as though he was used to travelling first class. The performance wasn't up to the standard of his twice-nightly theatrical presentations. Nonchalant, debonair rakes were his speciality. They were easy to play when he was surrounded by an adoring female chorus, but here, in the company of a single glamorous companion, he couldn't help feeling that the guard was about to arrive in the compartment at any moment and shunt him down to third class where he belonged.

Turning his back on the corridor, he glanced out of the window. Terraces of houses straggled in untidy lines across the mountainside. Above them, ramshackle pigeon-coops and sheds balanced precariously on improvised foundations that looked as though they were ready to relinquish their loads at any second. A puff of grey-black smoke blotted his view momentarily before wafting past on the breeze. He suppressed a smile as the scene re-emerged from the fog. It was all so wonderfully, blessedly familiar. The scrubby mottled green and brown hillside. The glistening black slag heaps. The coal-grimed streets set with gleaming, sun-jewelled windows and billowing lace curtains blowing free from open casements. Summer and home! Radyr, Taffs Well and Treforest behind them, next stop Pontypridd. In less than half an hour he'd be in Graig Avenue. Returning in triumph, the way he'd dreamed of when he'd worked Wilf Horton's second-hand clothes stall on the market. Successful, with a season's work ahead of him starring in Revue and Variety on the stage of the Town Hall where he'd last worked as a callboy. Money enough in his pocket to live comfortably, and enough to spare to stand treats for all his family. A suitcase full of expensive clothes above him, a good watch on his wrist, and, his smile focused on Rusty, his co-star and bed partner of six weeks, a beautiful, if trifle mature, girl-friend to flaunt in front of his old mates.

'Is that a "I'm going to miss living in the same house as you Rusty" smile?' she enquired archly.

'No, that's a "Don't forget to stay behind in the dressing room every night after the show finishes" smile.' He left his seat and lifted their cases down from the string rack overhead.

'I wish we could stay in the same digs.' She reached up and tugged playfully at his tie.

'Don't do that. Not unless you want me to drop this case on your head. What the hell have you got in it?'

'Girl things.'

'Brick things, by the feel of it.'

'You sure there's no room for me in your house?' she pleaded.

'I've told you, my family are squashed in like cockroaches behind a skirting board. There's only three and a bit bedrooms. My parents are in one, my sister and cousin share another. Another cousin's in the box room, and the only way you can stretch out there is to leave your feet behind in the passage, and my brother and I are crammed into the fourth. As if that's not enough, there's a lodger in the front room. Once I get there, there'll be eight of us in the kitchen trying to sit around a table meant for four. The only place we could possibly put you is the ty bach.'

'What's that?'

'The little house in the garden,' he teased 'Every Welsh house has one, they're about two foot square . . .'

'You,' she pretended to hit him with her handbag, but not so hard as to disturb the crisp waves in her improbably red hair, or crease the extravagant applications of rouge, lipstick, powder, eye black and blue that proclaimed loudly and clearly to anyone who cared to look that she was 'on stage'.

'You'll be much more comfortable in digs.'

'Oh yes, in some lodging house run by an old biddy my husband knows, and approves of,' she added acidly.

'Which is in Tyfica Road, five minutes' walk from the theatre and just about the smartest street in town,' he said flatly, loath to listen to another of her tirades on the inadequacies of her comedian husband who was working on a Blackpool pier. 'There'll probably even be an inside bathroom.'

'You haven't got one?' Sometimes, like now, she found it difficult to determine when Haydn was joking.

'Everyone knows the Welsh don't wash.'

'If you move into my digs we could share the bathroom and the bath,' she murmured seductively.

'I'll visit some time.'

'And perhaps you won't be welcome,' she snapped, finally realising that for the first time in the six weeks they'd been together, Haydn wasn't prepared to allow himself to be persuaded.

'For a smile I'll see you off the train as far as the taxi rank.'

'I suppose you have a girlfriend meeting you?'

'Sister.' He was finding it increasingly difficult to keep his temper.

'Too good for me to meet?'

'Don't start, Rusty.' The train slowed. Haydn rose from the seat, shrugged his arms into his new, and very expensive camel-hair coat, and pushed their cases towards the door with his foot.

'Doesn't it worry you that I'll be lonely?' she wailed in a last-ditch attempt to make him feel guilty.

'How can you possibly be lonely with twenty other girls close by?'

'You know what I'm like, Haydn. I feel insecure without a man around. I get frightened.'

'I'll ask Billy and Norman to look in on you.' He picked up their cases.

'Billy's more of a girl than me, and Norman scares me to death.'

'Then go to bed early with a book,' he suggested impatiently. 'It's only for tonight. I'll see you in rehearsals first thing tomorrow.'

'And the day after you begin rehearsing for the Summer Variety, leaving me to spend every day in a strange town by myself. I'll be bored senseless. Not that you care.'

'If you let me wear you out every night, all you'll be fit for is sleep.' Secure in the knowledge that he'd be out of earshot in less than five minutes, he kissed her briefly on the lips before opening the door and stepping down on to the platform. Calling a porter, he lifted their cases out of the carriage, his two matching beige and brown leather grips and Rusty's three bags, and that was without the two cavernous trunks she'd stowed in the guard's van.

'Rusty?' Judy, the 'head girl' in charge of the static Revue nudes waved from further up the platform. 'Want to share a taxi to your digs? You are next door to Mandy and me, aren't you?'

'So you've told me a dozen times,' Rusty answered unpleasantly.

'Take those down for us, please.' Haydn gave the porter sixpence, and took secret delight when the man, known throughout Pontypridd as 'Dai Station' tipped his cap and went about his business without recognising him. It was good to be home, and even better to be mistaken for 'crache'.

'Haydn?'

He whirled around. A tall, dark, elegant woman waved to him from the top of the steps at the end of the platform.

'See you, Rusty.' He raced headlong towards his sister; gathering Bethan into his arms he whirled her around.

'Steady,' her husband, Andrew warned. 'She's pregnant.'

Haydn hadn't noticed Andrew John, but then he hadn't been looking for him. The last time he'd been home Bethan had been living there, alone. He looked into his sister's eyes. She was smiling, but he knew Bethan. The smile was superficial. It was hardly surprising; he remembered the baby she'd buried a few months before.

'It's good to see you back and looking so well.' Andrew held out his hand and Haydn shook it for his sister's sake. He, along with the rest of his family, wasn't enamoured of Bethan's choice of husband. 'The car's in station yard. Let's get your cases and go.'

'We thought you'd like to lunch in our house.' Bethan took his arm and clung to it. 'That way you can catch up on all the gossip before going home.'

'Lunch?' When he'd left it had been breakfast, dinner, tea and supper. Where had Bethan picked up 'lunch'? From her crache in-laws who resented her working-class background? They followed Andrew down the wide, steep flight of stone steps into station yard where Andrew opened the boot of a brand new Daimler. Haydn looked, but said nothing. He'd be damned before he'd praise anything that belonged to Dr Andrew John.

'Haydn, coo-ee.' Rusty blew him a kiss, the luminous pink, low-cut costume and feathered hat he had admired in Finchley appearing cheap and tacky in contrast to Bethan's well-cut navy wool coat and green felt cloche. 'Your cases!' she screeched, pointing to the porter's trolley that had emerged from the goods lift.

'I'll get them,' Andrew offered.

'Careful, those females are maneaters.'

'That didn't sound like a joke,' Bethan said as she climbed into the front passenger seat of the car.

'It wasn't meant as one.'

'There does seem to be an awful lot of girls.' She watched three crowd into the back of a taxi while the hapless driver tried to cram their cases into his boot to the accompaniment of suggestive innuendoes.

'Ten static, non-moving, non-dancing nudes,' Haydn said drily, 'plus ten fully experienced and trained chorus girls. One comic, Billy Bert, he's the short one on the end in the bowler hat, and one producer and impresario, Norman Ashe.' He indicated an imposing man wearing a black trilby and astrakhan coat. 'He tries, but usually fails to keep the circus in order.'

'You weren't joking about them being maneaters.' Andrew lifted Haydn's grips into the boot and slammed it shut. 'I was lucky to get away in one piece.'

'If your flies are still buttoned, count yourself fortunate.'

'I take it that's the voice of experience talking?'

'Me?' Haydn turned an innocent face to Bethan. They exchanged glances and both burst out laughing. 'So what's happening in Pontypridd?' he asked once Andrew was in the driver's seat.

'Nothing that can't wait until we eat,' Bethan replied evasively.

'Come on, I've been good until now, but I can't wait another minute. Tell all? What's it really like being one of only three men working in a Revue of predatory showgirls?'

Trying, and failing, to ignore the chill that seeped up from the concrete into her knees, Jane Jones bent her head over the grey stone steps of the Workhouse Master's house and scrubbed as though her life depended on the degree of cleanliness she acheived. Above the rasping of bristles on granite she heard the echo of footsteps moving from Courthouse Street, through the main gates of the workhouse behind her. She listened intently. Two sets were slow and heavy, one light. Two men and a woman? The brush slipped in her hand, and she stifled a cry as it dropped into the bucket of cold, scummy water. She examined her palm. An enormous splinter was lodged deep below the skin and she had no means of getting it out. Not until she was back on the ward with Nurse Davies after supper. If – and it always was an 'if' with Nurse Davies – she was in a good mood she might try to remove the splinter for her with a needle. Jane winced at the thought.

Since she had left the orphanage for the workhouse two years ago she had spent all her daylight hours scrubbing. And because she was one of the youngest, not even inside floors. Outside steps, paths, yards, and always with cold water liberally laced with a cheap soda that burnt into every crack and hairline cut on her fingers.

The bell on the lodgegate clanged, rousing the slow, measured tread of the porter. As she delved into the bucket to retrieve the brush she risked a sly peek from behind her raised arm. It wasn't two men and a woman, but one man accompanied by an enormously fat woman and a young girl dressed in the same coarse, grey flannel workhouse garb as herself. Despite the hint of summer warmth in the air the hem of the girl's dress was quivering. Surely she couldn't be cold? Not in this weather? Not unless she had been used to warmer temperatures than those of the workhouse, but if that was the case, why was she already dressed in the uniform?

By bending her head low and looking up at an angle as she scrubbed, Jane could see that the girl was crying. So that was it! She wasn't cold; just upset at the prospect of entering the workhouse. Any sympathy she might have felt evaporated. Only fools whined. Snivelling never won anyone anything. To survive life behind these walls you had to keep your wits sharp and be prepared to grab every opportunity as it came. They did come; not nearly often enough, but they came. A chance to cadge an extra bit of food from the back door of the kitchen, or earn a penny doing a nurse's or porter's personal mending.

The bristles of her brush lodged in a crack between the stone step and the wall. Pushing the brush aside, she peered at the obstruction, spying a small sliver of curved copper. A farthing? No, it was too big to be a farthing. A halfpenny, or even a penny. She looked around for something she could use to dig it out. A splinter of slate? There were none. Not even a shard of stone in the flowerbed. She forced the bristles of the brush deep into the crack. The brittle back of the wood dug painfully into her hand, but she persisted, pushing down and dragging the bristles towards her. The coin moved. It rolled. A few seconds later it was in the bottom of her pail. A penny. A whole penny. She would put it with the others she had scavenged and saved over the years.

She hadn't squandered a single coin that had come her way.

Not even the Christmas penny St Matthew's parish church gave all the orphans resident in Maesycoed homes. Every one of them was safe, knotted into a handkerchief her house mother had given her as a going-away present when she had left Church Village Homes on her sixteenth birthday. This would make it one and elevenpence she had hidden. And she defied anyone to find her secret place.

'Jones! Jane Jones!'

'Yes, sir.' Keeping her eyes lowered, she dropped her brush, rose to her feet and turned to face the porter who had called her.

'You're wanted in the ward right away. Here, I'll take your bucket.' He held out his hand, but she shook her head.

'No. I'm responsible for it. Sister said. She'll have my guts for garters if I lose it.'

'Have it your own way. Just run to your ward double quick, or you'll get us both into trouble.'

He walked away, Jane following at a slower pace watching as his broad-shouldered, athletic figure turned right at the inner gate and headed for the male wards. Struggling with her heavy bucket, she turned left. Pausing outside the door to the female ward she tipped the rim into the drain, straining the filthy water through her fingers until the penny dropped into them.

'Jane Jones, whatever do you think you're doing? Just look at yourself. Your hands and face are filthy, and your dress – fresh on only four days ago – is covered in mud.'

It didn't occur to Jane to protest that it was impossible to scrub outside steps and remain clean. Life hadn't been fair in either of the orphanges, or the workhouse; and having no other kind of existence to compare it with, she simply accepted injustice as an immutable fact.

'Get into that washroom this minute and clean yourself up. Six girls are wanted to line up for an employer who's offering a live-in position. Although what he'll say to the sight of a filthy ragamuffin like you, Jane Jones, I don't know.'

Jane walked through the door that led into the ward, past the twin rows of beds, each made with unbleached calico sheets and a single grey blanket, and into the tiled washroom. Three girls were washing at the row of sinks opposite the door. She walked past them to the toilet cubicles. Closing the door of the last one in the row, she listened hard. No one was close; she would have heard their breathing if they had been. The toilet in the cubicle was old and cracked. All the women avoided it, except Jane. Standing on the edge of the wooden half-seat she reached up to the cast-iron water tank high above her. The lid was heavy. Very heavy. But she managed to push it aside and open up a gap just wide enough to insert her fingers. Tied to a hook on the inside of the lid was her handkerchief, dripping wet, stained and filled with her precious hoard of coppers. Lifting it out, she returned the lid to its resting place and stepped down on to the floor. The cloth was soaking and slimy, difficult to untie. The sister shouted her name before she had slipped the first knot. She pulled down on the chain. There was no time to replace the handkerchief. She'd have to risk a search and the loss of all she owned. No inmate was allowed to keep money, not when the Board of Guardians needed every penny they could get to pay for the parish paupers' keep.

She pushed the new penny into the makeshift purse. Lifting her dress she looked for loose threads she could tie the bundle to. Finding a few at the waist, she heaved until they frayed, knotted the ends of the handkerchief securely to them and pulled her dress down. She brushed at the freshest mud spots ineffectually with her fingers as she walked out of the cubicle. The handkerchief banged cold and wet against her naked skin. One of the worst things about the workhouse, and one she hadn't got used to in two years, was the uniform: rough, wooden clogs, grey flannel dress and nothing else. No stockings, no petticoats, no bloomers, no underclothes. Unlike the children's homes where winter and summer she had been stuffed into scratchy, itchy flannel knickers, vests, liberty bodices and petticoats. She'd never thought she'd miss them. But she did. Especially when she had to cross the open yards in breezes strong enough to lift her skirt.

'Hurry,' Eira Williams, the trainee nurse, urged as Jane washed her hands and face. Jane rubbed a wafer of hard yellow soap vigorously between her hands in a vain attempt to produce a lather. The sister's voice echoed in through the open window from the yard as she commanded the girls who had already obeyed her summons: 'Square your shoulders, stand up straight, and get into line.'

'What's the job, Nurse Williams?' Jane knew that the trainee should be addressed as 'trainee' not nurse, but hoped that flattery would gain her a few crumbs of knowledge.

'Something you'll steer clear of if you've any sense.' Eira walked to the door. Sister was still talking to the Master and only three of the girls ordered to the line-up were in place. There were a few minutes to spare. 'It's a dosshouse over in Trallwn. Off Foundry Place. The couple who run it have taken two girls out of here in the last year and both have come back to the unmarrieds ward. They say it's the class of girl we supply them with, but I've heard different from the staff on unmarrieds. Poor girls didn't stand a chance.'

'Williams! Is that girl ready yet?'

'Coming, Sister.'

Walking clumsily in her heavy clogs, Jane stumbled outside and into line. She was the last to arrive. Keeping her head low she focused on the ground at her feet just as her housemother in Church Village Homes had taught her.

'They're all good workers and strong, healthy girls.' The Master extolled their virtues as though he were selling livestock. 'I appreciate you've been unlucky with your last two, but I guarantee you won't have problems with any of these. The first four – ' he nodded towards the end of the line where Jane was standing – 'are orphans. Born here, and bred in the homes. I can vouch for their religious and moral training.'

'What about this one?' The obese woman Jane had seen at the gate pointed to a girl in the middle of the line. The sturdily built fair-haired girl began to tremble. Jane had no time for her. The job might be hard work, the man someone no sane woman would want to be left alone with, the woman grotesque, but collectively they offered a way out – an escape route from behind the ten-foot walls that towered over every waking and sleeping moment. She was prepared to do whatever was necessary to gain her freedom after eighteen years lived out behind barred windows. Drawing herself up to her full height, which was barely five foot in her stockinged feet, she raised her eyes and stared at the man in the hope of catching his eye. He was at the other end of the line listening to his companion's observations on the fair-haired girl.

'The big ones are too slow,' he said dismissively. 'Remember the first one we took in?' His fleshy, ruddy face contorted as he spat a ball of phlegm on to the yard. Jane wondered if his high colour and broken veins came from too many beers, or too many hours spent toasting in front of a hot fire. She'd had no experience of beer and very little of fires or men, but she had once overheard two porters discussing a third. Perhaps the man had simply gone red and fat with age. His suit had evidently been made for a thinner man, possibly even himself at a younger age. Now, the cloth strained, tighter than skin across his shoulders, and the buttons on his jacket wouldn't even meet the edge of the cloth let alone the buttonholes. Even his thighs looked like two bloated sausages ready to burst out of the rind of worsted that held them in check. He was big – weightier than any man she'd seen before. It certainly wouldn't be as easy to knee him in the groin and push him away as she had the boys in the homes. But that was a bridge she'd cross when she came to it. After he'd taken her out through that gate. Wearing her most determined smile, she glanced coyly at him from beneath lowered lashes.

'What about this one?' He lumbered towards her, his eyes focusing on the bodice of her shapeless smock. Jane breathed in, and pushed out the small, plum-sized breasts the other girls teased her about.

'Too skinny.'

'The skinny ones are generally quick and strong.'

'I can vouch for that one being a good, hard worker,' the Master interposed. 'And she's not that long out of Church Village Homes.'

'It doesn't take long to pick up bad habits, and this place must be rotten with them if our last two girls were anything to go by,' the woman commented tartly.

'She's used to working on her own initiative. Give her a job to do and she'll see it through without too much supervision.' The Master looked to the man, sensing that the decision would ultimately be his.

'We'll take her. With us right now, if that suits.'

'It suits.' The Master gave a rare, tight smile. The Board of Guardians were always pleased when a pauper was taken for outside work.

'Salad, steak and chips for Sunday dinner, and no husband in sight?' Haydn looked enquiringly at Bethan as a girl in maid's uniform carried loaded trays into the dining room.

'We eat dinner at eight, and you heard Andrew, he has to work.'

'On a Sunday?'

'People don't stay well just because it's a Sunday. He and Trevor Lewis take it in turns to cover for emergencies, and it's easier for them to work out of the surgery they've opened in town. And then again –' she pushed the plate of steak across to her brother – 'he's trying to be tactful. He thought we might like to talk.'

'Last time I saw you I didn't think you'd live with him again. Not even in a place like this.' He glanced around the large, beautifully proportioned oak-panelled dining room.

'I love Andrew, and he loves me.'

'You could have fooled me.'

'It hasn't been easy, Haydn, for either of us. There are times, even now, when I think that if we'd known what we were getting ourselves into when we danced together for the first time at that hospital ball, we would have run in opposite directions. Marriage is hard enough when the husband and wife are from the same world. We might have both been born in Pontypridd, but Dad was right when he said there was a lot more than distance between the Graig and the Common.'

'But you want to live with him now, Beth?' He laid his hand over hers as she reached for the salad.

'Most definitely, yes.' She smiled at him and this time the smile wasn't strained.

'So, you decided to kidnap me on my way home to gloat about your new-found happiness, and ask me to be nice to Andrew?'

'Not exactly.' She helped herself to a large portion of salad and a smaller one of beefsteak. 'I wanted to talk to you about the changes at home.'

'Eddie's married?' he joked. There was an edge to his voice. His brother Eddie had filched and, he suspected, slept with his childhood sweetheart Jenny, just before he'd left Pontypridd, giving him good cause to stay away – until now.

'Of course not. Eddie's the same as ever.'

'Boxing?'

'Every spare minute. And he and William are both working full time on the meat stall and in the cooked-meat shop Charlie's opened.'

'Good to have an affluent lodger.'

'Charlie doesn't lodge with Dad any more. He married Alma Moore a couple of weeks ago. They're living on top of his shop.'

'Charlie married Alma? You've got to be joking?'

'I'm not. They seem very happy together.'

'Good for Charlie. I never thought he had it in him.'

'William and Diana are still lodging with Dad of course,' she said, referring to their cousins. 'Diana's working for Wyn Rees in his High Street sweet shop.'

'So I heard the last time I came home.' He put down his knife and fork and stared at her. 'You're building up to something, Beth. Come on, out with it. Has Dad done something to get himself put back behind bars?'

'I don't think he'll ever swing a punch at a policeman again.'

'Then it has to be Mam. Despite all the names she called Dad when she walked out on him, now he's been released she's come back from Uncle Bull's to give him a hard time?'

'Mam won't come back. Not now.'

'That's not so terrible is it, Beth?' He heaped his plate high with chips, sprinkled them liberally with vinegar and began to eat. 'It's not as if they were ever really happy together. When we were kids . . .'

'That's just the point. They never were happy together. Not for one minute. But they are now. Or at least Dad is. Haydn, there's no way to tell you this except straight out. Dad wanted to write, but he kept putting it off, so when we got your letter saying that you were coming back I offered to tell you for him.' Taking a deep breath she looked her brother squarely in the eye. 'He's living with Phyllis Harry. They share the same bedroom,' she added, making sure there could be no misunderstanding.

'Phyllis? But she had a baby a year or so back . . .'

'It's Dad's, Haydn. Our half-brother.'

'Half-brother?'

'His name is Brian. He's the image of our Eddie when he was small,' she continued, taking advantage of his stunned silence. 'You'll like him. Phyllis too, when you get to know her. She's good for Dad. They suit one another. They're happy.'

'Happy!' He threw back his head and laughed. A brittle, mirthless laugh that set Bethan's teeth on edge. 'That's absolutely bloody priceless.'

'You just said he was never happy,' she protested, allowing his swearing to pass without comment. 'And neither was Mam. Well now they've both got what they want. Mam's back teaching, and he's – '

'He's living in sin with his bit on the side and his bastard.'

'It's not like that!' she exclaimed angrily.

'Then what is it like? My God, when I think of all those lectures on clean living, going to church, staying out of theatres . . .'

'That was Mam, never Dad, and you know it.'

'Just tell me one thing.' He picked up the bottle of beer the maid had placed next to his plate and poured it into his glass with an unsteady hand. 'What do your precious, respectable husband and in-laws think about our father living in sin with the mother of his bastard?' He laid an emphasis on the last word that made her flinch.

'Andrew knows about Phyllis, he likes her. Dad and Phyllis often visit with Brian, just as the rest of the family do.'

'But not Mam?'

'After she walked out she didn't want anything to do with any of us. She didn't even answer my letters.'

'She turned up at your son's funeral.'

'To tell me that Edmund's death was God's retribution for my sins. Haydn, what's the matter with you? I never expected you, of all people, to react like this.'

'Like what, Beth?' He drank his beer. 'Can't you see that I'm overjoyed at the thought of sharing my home with a bastard and a . . . what do we call her?'

'Try Phyllis. Look, if that's the way you feel you don't have to live at home. You can stay here. We have more than enough room.'

'And miss the opportunity of living in the bosom of my father's new-found family. Oh no, not for worlds.'

'Haydn . . .'

'Don't worry, I'll be polite. You won't be able to fault a word I say. Just one thing.' He jabbed his fork in the air. 'I won't answer for what I'll do to anyone in the family or outside who dares criticise the way I live. If I choose to sleep with every girl in the Revue and the town, and get drunk twice a night, I'll regard it as entirely my own business.'

Exhausted and defeated, Bethan stared at her plate. It was difficult enough trying to engineer the fairy-tale happy ending for herself and Andrew without bringing her entire family into the scenario. Haydn and her father would have to work out their problems just as she and Andrew were trying to do. She'd done all she could – for now.

Chapter Two

Clutching a spare workhouse dress that had been turned inside out and fashioned into a bundle with string, Jane stood before the first of the two gates that led out of the workhouse precincts into Courthouse Street – and the town. Heart palpitating, she dug her fingernails into her palms in an effort to calm herself.

'Remember what I told you,' Eira Williams whispered as she waited with her. 'Keep your head down, try not to get noticed, and don't let any man, even if he says he's the Prince of Wales, into your knickers.'

'That's a bit difficult,' Jane replied, 'when you consider I'm not wearing any.'

The gatehouse keeper unlocked the gates. 'They're in the waiting room.' He gestured to a door on their left. Eira knocked before opening it. The woman was sitting, her bulk covered by acres of black, greasy skirt, the man standing impatiently at her side.

'You took your time,' the woman complained.

Jane hung her head and said nothing.

'Is she a mute?'

'No,' Eira replied for Jane.

'I'd like to hear it from her.'

'No I'm not . . . ' Jane hesitated, unsure whether to address the couple as 'sir' and 'ma'am' as she did the workhouse staff.

'Ma'am and sir will do when you have to speak to us,' the woman advised. 'And be sure you speak only when you're spoken to, and then respectfully.'

'Yes, ma'am.'

'I hope you realise what an opportunity we're giving you. It's not everyone who'll take in workhouse dregs. Well come on then, if you're coming. We're not used to wasting time, and neither will you be once we get you working.'

Clutching her bundle, Jane hobbled over the cobbled entrance, out of the first gate and past the Master's house. She looked back as the grey stone buildings disappeared from view. She'd scrubbed her last inch of workhouse ground. No matter what lay ahead, it had to be better than what she was leaving behind.

The pennies rocked against her empty stomach as she followed her new employers to the lodgegate. A swift nod of the head and she was outside. On the street. The first time in over two years she had actually stood on a street.

'I said no time to waste girl,' the woman reminded harshly. The couple turned right and Jane trailed clumsily in their wake. They walked past the Union offices and the Court House, both faced in the same dour granite as the workhouse, past Jubilee Hall where she had watched the Salvation Army feed the children of the un-employed through the windows of the female ward, down a short, steep flight of narrow stone steps and into High Street. She stretched out her hand, gripping the windowsill of a shop, steeling herself against the sudden onslaught on her senses. There were people everywhere, more than she could remember seeing in one place before. And the shops! She stared through the window into the one beside her, its atmosphere thick, buzzing with flies, its shelves loaded with trays of bread and wilting vegetables. A woman with a child in her arms was standing before the counter, watching as the shopkeeper unscrewed a jar of brighty coloured lollipops.

'Girl!'

She wrenched her ankle painfully. It was impossible to walk quickly in clogs. A marvellous smell of coffee, mingled with baking meats, pastry and hot chocolate, wafted appetisingly towards her. She saw a café, read the sign above the door, RONCONI'S TEMPERANCE BAR. One day she'd have enough money to eat in a place like that. Anything she wanted. One of those meat pies from the glass case on the counter, and an enormous ice cream piped into a tall silver horn exactly like the illustration in the window. Remembering her new employers' injunction to hurry, she turned, just in time to see their padded rumps waddle into the gloom beneath the railway bridge at the foot of the hill. She followed, passing white-tiled walls blackened by layers of soot and coal dust at the higher levels, but rubbed to a cleaner grey-white where queues of passengers leaned as they waited for their buses. The short tunnel opened on to the Tumble. On the left was station yard.

One of the unmarrieds who'd scrubbed a corridor alongside her had told her about station yard. How a girl with a 'bit about her' could make as much as two bob a time for what most of the unmarrieds, had given away for free. And how the station yard girls sometimes 'packed in' as many as ten men a night if they could find them. A pound for a night's work! It had seemed like unimaginable riches. But then the story had been tempered by the tale of one station yard girl who'd ended up in the workhouse. She hadn't thought to save a penny when she'd been earning her pound a night, and when her condition had prevented her from working, she'd been forced to throw herself and her baby on the mercy of the parish guardians.

Jane looked around the station car park for evidence of girls with 'a bit about them'. There were none that she could see. A row of old men sucking empty pipes sat on the low grey and red brick wall that separated the yard from the hustle and bustle of the crossroads. A few families were dashing up the stone steps that led to the platforms and the trains. Disappointed that there were no painted ladies on show, she clutched the string that bound her spare dress and crossed the road, careful to keep her employers within sight.

There'd been more people on the Graig hill than there were in town. But then it was Sunday. She knew from what someone in the workhouse had said that market days were Wednesday and Saturday. She'd never seen the market, but she'd heard about it. Children in the orphanage who'd been there had talked about stalls groaning with all kinds of toys and sweets. Perhaps she'd be sent to do the shopping there. Maybe she'd even be paid enough to buy a few things for herself. Books – she loved books – clothes, because she needed them, and a few sweets. Her mouth watered at the thought as she trailed behind her benefactors, an insignificant rowboat bobbing in the wash of two fully rigged yachts. Straining her neck to the right and left she tried to take in all that the shops and cafés had to offer. To her, Pontypridd was a strange and exotic place. She'd only walked through it a few times in her life. Once to attend a special Chrismas Day showing of films in the White Palace put on for needy children, courtesy of the manager; once to attend Harvest Thanksgiving service in St Catherine's Church when the Maesycoed orphans had been relegated to the back two rows of pews, and twice on outings to Pontypridd Park. She looked around for the entrance to the park. It had been a magical place. With green lawns, flowers, a playground . . .

'Look where you're going!' a young woman shouted as she accidentally walked into a pram.

'I didn't think they let them out of the workhouse to mingle with decent people.' The woman's companion looked Jane up and down as if she had no right to be on a public street.

Upset, Jane stepped out of their path into a doorway. Her eyes widened at the poster in front of her.

> *All this week, straight from their triumphant success in the West End, Alice Delysia, Queen of Comedy in her latest success A PAIR OF TROUSERS.*

'Girl, keep up. If you don't, I'll be sending you back, sharpish!'

'Sorry, ma'am.' She wasn't, not in the least. Thirty seconds in the doorway of the New Theatre had been enough to make her forget the disagreeable encounter with the two women and evoke her most treasured memory. The night the orphans from Church village had been taken to the Town Hall Theatre to see a circus. Four years on she could still recite the sequenece of acts off by heart. Gyto the juggling clown, Pooples the performing dog, the flying . . .

'I have to call in a café. We're out of bread,' the woman announced.

'I thought you were going to send the girl.'

'How could I when she knew we intended to take her back? She would have run off with the money.'

They walked on past the New Inn and the deserted entrance to Market Square.

'Girl!'

Tearing herself away from Gwilym Evans's window display of ladies' summer fashions, Jane caught up with them at the other end of Market Square. A little further on she saw a café set behind an ornate fountain; to the right were two massive doors, one sporting a poster headed TOWN HALL. Jane stared at the lettering. So that's where she'd seen the circus? The woman disappeared into the café, the man inched towards her. Afraid he'd touch her, she walked into the café and stood behind his wife.

'Mrs Bletchett, how are you today?' A dark young man with a foreign accent leaned over the counter.

'Fair to middling. I'll have four large loaves if you can spare them.'

'Business must be good,' he said cheerfully as he heaped the loaves in front of her.

'Full house, thanks to the pits reopening and people flocking in from all over the country looking for work.'

'Anything else?' The man, taller and better-looking than any of the porters in the Graig, winked at Jane as he flashed a wicked, insincere smile at Mrs Bletchett. Jane lowered her eyes. She'd seen and heard enough reactions and comments as they'd walked through the town to know that her workhouse dress stuck out like a sore thumb. Still, now she was in work she'd earn money.

More to add to the shilling and elevenpence concealed beneath her dress. She'd be able to buy herself something pretty like the blue cotton the woman who'd shouted at her had worn.

She turned to avoid the man's eye. On the back of the café door was a poster advertising a revue in the Town Hall: *All London Girls*.

She studied the sketch of three striking blondes wearing nothing but beautifully arranged curls and ostrich feather fans that concealed what her housemother in the Homes would have called 'the naughty bits'. Jane was wondering just how London girls differed from Welsh ones when she saw another notice. Small, handwritten, it was pinned below the poster.

VACANCY. USHERETTE/CONFECTIONERY
SALES ASSISTANT. APPLY ASSISTANT
MANAGER, TOWN HALL, 10.00 A.M. MONDAY.
PROMPT.

Monday – tomorrow – there was a chance of getting a job in a theatre; the same theatre she'd sat and watched the circus in.

A woman wearing a hat trimmed with blue feathers strolled past the open doorway arm in arm with a younger woman dressed in the uniform of a waitress.

'I can't see any decent girl crossing the threshold of the Town Hall again, let alone applying for *that* vacancy,' she snorted in a loud voice. 'Not with the type of show the Council has allowed the management to bring into the town. I don't know what they think they're doing, turning Pontypridd into Sodom and Gomorrah.'

It was then Jane noticed the small print below the word REVUE.

Al nudes straight from London stage success. Compere, and singer, Pontypridd's own Haydn Powell. Fresh from a stormingly successful spring season in Torquay.

Nudes – naked girls on stage? Jane continued to stare at the poster in bewilderment.

'That's the bread bought.' The brown paper and string carrier bag was dumped in Jane's arms. 'And you can stop gawping when you like,' Mrs Bletchett admonished when she saw what Jane was looking at. 'In my experience girls like you have enough ideas along those lines, without getting any more from the theatre.'

Red faced, Jane whirled around. The handsome counter hand caught her eye, gave her a smile and another wink. She tossed her head high in the air, for once forgetting her cropped, pauper-style short-back-and-sides haircut. She'd had a few dealings with boys in the school in Church Village. Enough to know that they expected only one thing from 'Homes' girls. She had no illusions about her looks. Even without the drab grey dress, austere workhouse haircut and clogs, she was plain by any standard. Mousy hair, brown eyes, thin face, fat lips, and a figure like a broom handle. But then boys were never particular about the appearance of girls they thought they could take liberties with.

Now she was finally out, she intended to stay out of the workhouse, and the unmarrieds ward. But she knew if she was going to succeed in her intentions she'd have to keep one step ahead of everyone. The workhouse guardians, the Master, her new employers – and especially boys like that counter hand.

'That's a pretty shawl.'

'Haydn gave it to me.' Bethan folded the square of blue and green crêpe de Chine, and left her chair. 'Would you like tea?'

'I asked the girl to bring it in. You have help in the house, remember?' Andrew pressed her gently back into her seat.

'How did Haydn get on with the family?' she asked, her mouth dry with apprehension.

'Fine. I told them you were resting, and they all send their love.' He pulled a newspaper out of his briefcase and settled into the chair opposite hers. He looked up, the paper unopened on his lap. A frown creased his forehead as he noted the dark shadows beneath her eyes. She hadn't been able to take proper care of herself during her last pregnancy, but he was determined that it would be different this time. 'I don't know what you said to

Haydn, but he certainly seems to be trying with Phyllis and Brian.'

'In what way?'

'He asked me to run him down High Street so he could buy presents for them. He brought something back for everyone else, but of course not knowing about Phyllis and Brian he'd left them out. And I'll say this much for him, he's not stingy with whatever he's earning. He bought the big toy lorry out of Edwards's window for Brian and a large box of chocolates from the café for Phyllis.'

'Then he won Brian over?'

'I didn't stay long, but you know Haydn. He can charm the birds off the trees when he wants to.'

'Or the knickers off a showgirl.'

'Mrs John!' He lifted his eyebrows in amusement.

'He warned me that he won't tolerate any interference in his private life.'

'Nor should he. He's a grown man. It's time big sister left him to get on with it.'

'I suppose you're right.'

'You know I am. Come on, let's go.'

'Where?'

'Upstairs. I've got some reading to catch up on and you need a rest.'

'Andrew it's the middle of the day. What will Annie think?'

'She'll think we're resting before going out tonight.'

'We're not going out tonight.'

'We are now. I've booked dinner in the New Inn. Everything's arranged. You don't have to do anything except look beautiful, which you always do very well. Trevor and Laura are picking up William, Eddie and Diana in their car. We're taking your father, Phyllis and Haydn in ours. Mrs Ronconi is having Brian for the night and Charlie and Alma are meeting us there.'

'When did you arrange all this?'

'When I took Haydn into High Street.'

'Can we afford it?'

'Have to welcome the star home. And as he'll be working every night next week, tonight seems to be the logical choice.'

'That was kind of you, but you don't have to keep trying quite so hard with my family. They'll come round in their own good time.'

'For purely selfish reasons, like your peace of mind, I'd prefer "their own good time" to be sooner rather than later.' He left his chair, and held out his hands. She took them, and he helped her to her feet.

'I love you, Mrs John.' He kissed her on the lips.

'I love you too, Doctor John.'

'Now we've cleared that up, let's forget Haydn for five minutes and go to bed.'

'Here's where you sleep. It's clean. I made sure the last girl left it as she found it.'

Panting from the exertion of climbing three flights of stairs, Mrs Bletchett opened the door to the small attic bedroom. It was undeniably clean. Clean and bare except for a rickety wooden chair and a metal-framed bed. The mattress was stuffed with horsehair; Jane knew because brown fibres oozed from the side seams. A pair of threadbare sheets and a single thin, grey blanket lay folded on top. The floor had been scrubbed almost white, the boards dried and bleached by successive applications of washing soda and water. Jane could smell the soda: a dry, astringent odour that caught the back of her throat and reminded her of the workhouse.

'I'll expect you to wash the sheets when you wash the lodgers' bedding. There's a chair for your spare dress.'

Jane obediently laid her bundle on the seat. At the head of the bed was a small uncurtained window. She glanced through it. She was higher than she'd thought. Below her stretched an undulating sea of slate roofs and smoking chimney pots.

'Now you've seen where you'll sleep, you can start earning your keep.'

The lodging house was vast. Larger than it looked from the outside, and it had appeared daunting then. Crushed to learn she was the only 'help', Jane followed her new mistress down warrens of corridors into dormitories that reeked of male sweat, soiled clothes and stale air. Washrooms and toilets flooded with pools of foul-smelling water were situated at the end of every passage, and everything she was shown looked as though it hadn't been given a thorough cleaning in years.

The ground floor was little better. An ill-ventilated, smoky kitchen, filled to capacity by an enormous table and dresser that might have been made for the ogre in Jack and the Beanstalk, opened into a dingy bar furnished with round tables and rickety chairs. A counter was set at one end, barrels of beer and cider ranged behind it, the gleaming china handles of the pumps polished – no doubt by the previous skivvy.

'You served beer?' Mr Bletchett demanded.

Jane shook her head.

'I've yet to meet a workhouse girl who's good for anything besides scrubbing floors,' his wife sneered. 'Well, we've no time to teach you how to pull a pint now. Into that kitchen and peel all the potatoes in the basket. You have peeled potatoes before?'

'Yes ma'am.'

'Then what are you waiting for?'

'You're the last person I expected to see here.'

'Why's that, Eddie Powell? Think I'm not good enough for the New Inn?' Jenny Griffiths flirted provocatively.

'Of course not,' he apologised, anxious not to upset her. She certainly looked different to the everyday Jenny who served behind the counter in her father's shop. Her long, blonde hair had been crisply waved and styled into a bun at the nape of her neck, and she was wearing a shiny blue dress that showed the creamy skin on her neck and arms to fine advantage. He found himself wishing they were alone.

'You here to celebrate your Haydn's homecoming?'

Eddie's hopes of making any headway with her were dashed as they glanced over to where his brother was holding court at the head of the table that Andrew John had booked. The look in Jenny's eye told him everything he would have been happier not to know. She had been Haydn's girl before she had been briefly – very briefly – his. And she couldn't have made it any plainer that she still carried a torch for Haydn if she had screamed it from the band's microphone.

Oblivious to everyone who wasn't sitting at his table, Haydn's laughter echoed around the room, cutting Eddie to the quick. Although Eddie would sooner have died than admit it to anyone, he loved his brother. But standing next to Jenny Griffiths he wished Haydn a million miles away, or at least back in London.

'Do you want to talk to him?' he enquired tersely. 'I could take you over if you like.'

Jenny looked at the others seated at Haydn's table. The Johns, Andrew and Bethan, Dr Trevor Lewis and his wife Laura, Eddie's father Evan, Phyllis Harry, Diana, William, Charlie and his wife Alma – there were too many people. She wanted to meet Haydn Powell again, more than she wanted anything else in life, but not now, not like this. She shook her head. 'I don't want to break in on a family party.' When she saw Haydn again she intended there to be only the two of them, so she could tell him all the things she'd dreamed of and stored in her memory through the long winter months that had frozen her emotions as well as her body. 'I'm here with my mother and my aunt and uncle,' she explained. 'It's my aunt's birthday. Why don't you come and meet them? Then, after we've eaten, if you want to and the band's playing, I'll go to the ballroom with you.'

'For the last waltz?'

She found it difficult to look at anyone except Haydn. Her heart was pounding so erratically it was a wonder Eddie couldn't hear it. Six months of absence hadn't diminished her feelings for Haydn in the slightest. One look had been enough for her to know that she still loved him, and would always love him. But after that last awful row she also knew he wouldn't come to her. She'd have to be the one to make the first move. And what better way than on his brother's arm? Jealousy just might be the way to accomplish what loving endearments couldn't.

'Tell you what, Eddie,' she touched his arm gently, her breath

34

blowing warm as she whispered in his ear. 'As you asked nicely I'll give you all the waltzes. Including the last.'

Eddie glowed with pleasure as he walked her to her table before returning to his own. Haydn might be the big success on stage, with a whole revue of gorgeous showgirls waiting in the wings, but he could still show big brother a thing or two when it came to picking the cream of the Pontypridd girls.

Jane's Sunday afternoon was a marathon of drudgery. In between peeling potatoes and scraping and boiling tripe for a supper that was served to the lodgers in the upstairs dining room, necessitating several trips up and down stairs with heavy trays, she cleared up messes of spilt beer in the bar, washed glasses, boiled dishcloths and cleaned out the stove chimney to prevent any more soot falling into the tripe.

Going into the bar was the worst. It soon became evident that the men knew she wasn't wearing underclothes. She turned more than once to catch one of them lifting the back hem of her skirt with the poker from the bar-room fire. Temper rising, she emptied a bucket of slop water she'd used to mop beer dregs over one persistent lecher, earning herself a tongue lashing from Mrs Bletchett with the promise of more to come.

At midnight she was still on her feet washing glasses in the kitchen. Mrs Bletchett's final order to her husband before retiring for the night had been to make sure that 'the girl' cleaned both the bar and the kitchen before going to bed. Although Jane heard her she didn't dare set foot in the bar. Mr Bletchett was still there, talking to the man who'd lifted her skirt.

She felt spent and weary enough to cry. Exhausted and ravenously hungry, she bitterly regretted not taking Eira Williams's advice. Life in the workhouse had been grim, but not as grim as this. In the institutions she had been able to cling to a routine of sorts. Regular mealtimes with food of indifferent quality and varying quantity, but nevertheless food. And although she had served both tea and supper to the lodgers, there had been no mention of her eating anything; nor had there been any leftovers for her to scavenge.

At one o'clock when she could find nothing more to do in the kitchen she steeled herself and pushed open the connecting door to the bar. Mr Bletchett was sitting alone counting the night's takings into a leather bag.

'I've finished cleaning the kitchen. Can I leave the bar until morning, sir?'

'You've banked the fire down?'

'Yes, sir.'

'The potatoes are done for tomorrow's dinner?'

'Yes, sir.'

'And the table laid upstairs for the lodgers' breakfast?'

Jane nodded wearily.

'Then I suppose you can go. But mind you're up early to square this room before my wife sees it. You can take up that stub of candle. Light it in the kitchen. Mind you blow it out as soon as you get into bed. We'll stand no waste in this house.'

Jane took the saucer which held a pool of melted wax and a thread of blackened wick. Uneasy as she was in her employer's company, some demon made her press her diminishing luck. 'In the workhouse I was told I'd be paid something above my board and keep. When will I get it?'

He dropped the coins he was counting and stared at her.

'I was just wondering,' she ventured hesitantly.

'Wonder no more, you'll get a shilling a week after your board and keep, and that's what your washing will come to.'

'Washing?'

'The sheets on your bed, and your dress. I don't know what you're used to, girl, but in this house we expect you to wash yourself and your clothes.'

'Then there'll be no wages?'

'There'll be a shilling a week, which will cover your washing. Now upstairs with you. The lodgers on early shift will expect their breakfast on the table at five, and this room will have to be cleaned and the fire and stove lit before that. You'll need to be up, dressed and in the kitchen by four to get everything done on time.'

Jane took a home-made newspaper roll taper from the jar on the mantelpiece. She lit the stub of candle and ascended the stairs, burning with indignation, determined to leave the first minute she could.

The back staircase had doors that opened out on every one of the four floors, but the stairs from the third to the attic floor were half the width of the others. When Mrs Bletchett had taken her up them earlier, she had looked at the narrow margin between her employer's hips and the wall, amusing herself with thoughts of Mrs Bletchett getting stuck half-way, just here, where the staircase bent back on itself.

A floorboard creaked overhead and she froze, waiting for the sound to be repeated. After a full minute she breathed out. She'd spent her whole life sleeping in dormitories and was nervous of being alone, that was all. And the dosshouse was old. Old houses creaked. She had read that somewhere; probably in one of the Dickens volumes in the homes. There'd been no books, or time for reading in the workhouse. And she only had to look at the doors and rotting window-frames of this place to see that it was bound to give rise to odd noises.

Gripping the candle firmly she climbed the last few steps. The first thing she saw as her head rose level with the floor was the light. A candle, fatter and more efficient than hers, illuminated a pair of feet next to her bed: men's feet, encased in muddy working boots and tartan socks. Caked mud had fallen out of the treads, and lay in great dirty clumps on the scrubbed floorboards.

'You're taking your time to climb those stairs, Missy.' It was the great brute of a man she'd tipped water over earlier.

Shrinking back against the wall, she held the saucer with its stub of candle in front of her like a shield. 'Get out of here this minute or I'll scream the house down,' she hissed.

'You do, and I'll tell everyone you invited me up here to earn yourself a shilling.' He walked out of her room. Standing on the top step, he reached down and grabbed her wrist between the thumb and forefinger of his right hand. She took a step backwards and fell. He released his hold as she clattered down the stairs, still struggling to keep a grip on the candle that scuttered out before she reached the third-floor landing.

Cursing, he followed. She sensed him standing over her in the blackness, his breath panting in ragged, uneven gasps. When no sound came from the rest of the house he thrust the bolt across the inside of the door, sealing them off from the corridor that led to the dormitories.

'Back up those stairs.'

'No.' She took another step downwards.

He grabbed at her dress. Holding her close, he squeezed her small breasts painfully through the covering of thick flannel. 'You don't, and I'll start shouting you're not giving me value for money. There's over a hundred and twenty men living in this house. How do you fancy servicing all of them?' His rancid beer-and tripe-laden breath filled the claustrophic atmosphere.

'I'm going.' Quicker than him, she stepped over the shattered saucer and lumps of hot wax and darted back up the stairs. Running into her room she sat on the bed, fear crawling over her skin as she clutched the bundle of pennies hidden beneath her dress as though it was a talisman.

'We'll have this off for a start.' He lumbered towards her and tugged at the hem of her dress.

'Not until you pay me.' She clamped the dress to her knees with her fists, and swung her legs over the bed away from him.

'You already on the game?' She recognised disappointment and anger in his voice. He'd obviously hoped to find a sweet little workhouse virgin. Like the last one?

'What did you expect?' She forced herself to look him in the eye. 'I may have been born in the workhouse and trained for nothing better than skivvying, but that doesn't mean I'm not ambitious.' She held out her hand. 'Half-crown.'

'Half a bloody crown!'

'The patients in the clinic were glad to pay me. They thought I was worth every penny.'

'What clinic?'

'The VD clinic. There's no other clinic that I know of in the Graig.'

38

Chapter Three

Jane sat on her bed for a long time after the man had gone cursing and kicking down the stairs. She'd broken her one cardinal rule: she'd made an enemy. In the institutions she'd worked hard to keep her feelings under control, be nice to people, get on with everyone, even when it actually, physically hurt to wear a smile on her face and keep a pleasant tone in her voice.

She recalled every foul, filthy name the man had flung at her. He was the first. If she stayed there would be others. And they might not be so easily fooled or, even worse, they might be diseased themselves. She had to get out before he said something to the other lodgers or the Bletchetts. But where could she go?

She tried to remember the prices in the shop windows in town. How much would one and elevenpence buy? Would it be enough for a dress, and food and lodging until – until when? Of course – she clutched desperately at the straw of hope. There was the job in the Town Hall. If, as the woman in the feathered hat had said, no decent girl would want it, then perhaps, just perhaps, she stood a chance.

She looked across at the bundle on the chair. Her sole possession, and she didn't even own that. Workhouse dresses had to be returned, or paid for if they were kept. And who would willingly wear a workhouse dress if they had the choice? Judging by the stares she'd attracted walking through the town behind the Bletchetts, no one would employ a woman wearing one. If she was going to apply for the job she had to get out and find another dress – now, this minute, before someone woke and stopped her. But first, she looked down at her dirt-streaked hands and arms, she had to wash. Her head swam with an intoxicating mixture of exhaustion and panic. So many things to do. And the only way to tackle them was one at a time.

Creeping down the stairs, she bolted herself into a washroom on the first floor. There was a bath, but the soap in the dish was hard, cracked and yellow. It would give out no more lather than the ones in the workhouse. She stripped off and ran herself a four-inch bath. Although she'd only run the tap marked hot, the water was freezing. Well she'd had cold baths before, and at the height of winter. It would help her stay awake. She sat in the bath and picked up the scrubbing brush. Her arms and legs were soon pink, the water grey. Her hair wasn't so easy: as the soap softened it stuck in thick waxy strands to her cropped head, and rinsing didn't help. She looked around. The only towel hung grey, filthy and limp on a wooden rail. Her dress was cleaner. Nothing else for it.

She dried herself as best she could with the non-absorbent flannel, untied the string and put on her second dress. Lacking even a comb for her hair, she stared downhearted at her reflection in the brown spotted mirror. The yellow gaslight had turned her complexion sallow. She looked thin and sickly. Picking up a matted strand of hair she held it away from her face. No one would take her on, even to scrub floors, looking like this. Her one and eleven-pence would have to stretch to cover a hat. She bundled her damp dress into the string. She'd return both dresses later – after she'd bought herself the outfit she needed.

Everything was about to change for the better. She'd soon have decent clothes, a new job and somewhere good to live. Her life was about to begin. All she had to do was believe it enough to make it happen.

Carrying her clogs and using her hands and feet to feel her way in the darkness, Jane stole barefoot down the back staircase into the kitchen. The gas lamp had been left burning low. Mindful of Mr Bletchett's comments on waste, she peeped around the corner to make sure that the room was empty before venturing inside. The door that led to the street was locked. Setting her dress and clogs on the flagstones she slid back the bolts, jumping uneasily at the rasping sound of metal scraping over metal. Finally she turned the knob, picked up her belongings and stepped outside.

The air was cool: fresh and clean after the fetid beer, cooking and sweat odours of the dosshouse. Street lamps burned, casting amber spotlights on to grey pavements and black roads. She hesitated and looked around in an attempt to get her bearings. Whichever way she turned terraces of houses stretched, long and winding into the distance. And on the horizon even more houses loomed, up – down – left – right – absolutely nothing in any direction struck her as familiar from her arrival. There was no indication as to which road led back into town. She studied the rooftops, hoping to see the spire of St Catherine's church. She knew it was only one street away from Taff Street, but it eluded her.

A sense of urgency, or minutes ticking past, drove her to action. If she remained any longer she'd risk being seen and forced back into the dosshouse. Trusting to instinct, she turned right and walked on in her bare feet, still carrying her clogs lest their clatter betray her presence.

She covered a mile before she realised she was moving away from the town. When she had followed the Bletchetts they had walked the distance between the café and the dosshouse in minutes. Pale haloes of light were already forming and growing in intensity above the rooftops. She didn't dare risk returning along the same street. There was no way of telling what time it was. She might already be missed. The Bletchetts could have alerted the constables. They could be out, now, combing the streets for her, wanting to return her to the workhouse or, even worse, the dosshouse. Either way she'd miss the interview.

She tried to cheer herself by recalling every detail of the uniform the usherettes had worn in the Town Hall when they'd shown her and the other orphans to their seats. A plain black dress. Smart and elegant. A white cap and apron, and torches slung at their belts. Tomorrow that would be her. And she'd find somewhere to live. A nice room in a warm house, with furniture like the pieces in the *Anne of Green Gables* picture she'd seen at the Christmas showing in the White Palace: a padded chair with arms and cushions, and a soft bed and plump pillows covered by a brightly coloured patchwork quilt. And when she had her wages she'd be able to buy a glass vase for flowers similar to the one that had stood on the windowsill of the Master's house. A table with a pretty cloth edged with lace . . .

She halted abruptly as reality intruded into her daydream. The darkness had melted, the sky was light grey and a bridge stretched in front of her spanning a river that flowed far below street level. She ran to the centre and looked over the parapet. Upriver there were trees and a row of houses that disappeared into a band of dense woodland. Downriver, terraces of imposing villas wound high above the steep banks that followed the flow of water. If she crossed the bridge and walked downriver, sooner or later she had to reach the town. Even if the road was longer, she would run less risk of discovery than returning the way she'd come.

Dropping the clogs to the ground she slid her dirty feet into them and crossed the bridge. For the first time she noticed bird-song in the air and a hint of warmth in the cold morning light. A magnificent house with mullioned windows and beautiful gardens stood high on a rise in front of her. She gazed at it, trying to imagine what it would be like to live within its walls. When the curtain moved in an upstairs room she began to run. One day she intended to find out about that kind of life, but she'd never get the chance if she wasted time fantasising now.

'She's gone.'

'Don't be stupid woman, where would she go?'

'I don't know,' Mrs Bletchett replied, furious at being called stupid on top of being faced with making and serving the lodgers' breakfasts herself.

'You haven't looked properly. You never do.' He sat up in the bed and scratched his armpits.

'I've been everywhere. The kitchen, the dining room, the bar the attic . . .'

'The bathrooms?'

'I've knocked on all the doors. There's lodgers in every one.'

'Get me a cup of tea then I'll – '

'Don't you cup of tea me! There's no time for that this morning. You get out of that bed and see that the lodgers' breakfasts are put on the table before they start holding back their money. Then you walk up the Graig Hill, report the slut missing and pick out a replacement.'

'I'll bring back the one you wanted,' he grunted, in an attempt to mollify her.

'You and your skinny ones. I saw through her from the start. Whore and slut. Just like the last one you chose, and the one you insisted on giving house room to before that.'

'None of them are our problem any more. Not even this one.' He left the bed and pulled his trousers on over his long johns. 'When she's picked up the guardians will see she's taken back to the workhouse.'

'And she stays there. Do you understand me? I'll see her rot in hell before I allow her over this doorstep again.'

Jane saw the old bridge and her step quickened. She was on the right road. The old stone footbridge that arched alongside the flat, serviceable modern bridge that connected the town to Merthyr Road was the one landmark in Pontypridd everyone recognised. She even knew the story of how it had been built by William Edwards nearly two hundred years before. He'd watched his first attempt wash away in a flood, his second collapse on the bed of the river, and, undaunted by failure, he'd designed and built a third that still stood for all to see. Her Standard One teacher had told the class that William Edwards's courage had spawned the saying 'Three tries a Welshman' and that all of them should follow the builder's example and refuse to be disheartened by life, no matter what problems it presented.

As she drew closer to the steps that rose to the summit of the arch she changed direction. On impulse she ran up the bridge. If one man could build this, then *she* could get a job. It was simply a matter of perseverance and effort, just like the teacher had said.

Jane walked quickly down Taff Street, sticking to the shadows of the shuttered shops. A clock chimed. She stopped and listened, but it couldn't have been the hour because there was only one peal. A tantalising smell of roasting meat wafted in the air, teasing her taste buds and knotting her empty stomach into tight, hungry spasms. She clutched her handkerchief until the edges of the coins bit into her palm. A penny or two spent on food wouldn't make that much difference, and she couldn't very well go to an interview starving. What if she fainted?

A sign over a shop alongside the fountain proclaimed CHARLIE'S COOKED MEATS. It was the only one in the row with a light burning in its windows. She crept closer. it was definitely the source of the mouthwatering smell. The window was steamed up, but through the mist she could make out the counter, and behind it trays of food. Hunger overcoming wariness, she lingered for only a few seconds then pushed open the door, jumping nervously as the bell above it shrilled loudly.

'Good morning.' A young man stood behind the counter. Skilfully wielding a fish slice, he whisked steaming hot pasties into china display trays at bewildering speed. 'You're an early bird.'

'I couldn't sleep.'

'You after something? Most of our meats are still cooking and won't be ready for slicing for another hour.'

'How much are those?' She pointed at the pasties.

'Well, seeing as how you're our first customer of the day . . . ' Used to serving the ladies of the town, Eddie Powell didn't even think about what he was saying any more, let alone consider the effect his banter might have on a workhouse girl. ' . . . I can let them go for two shillings a dozen. But if you want just one, it'll be twopence halfpenny'

'Twopence halfpenny. But if I took a dozen they'd be two pence each,' she protested indignantly.

'Everything comes cheaper by the dozen.'

'Sixpence on a dozen pasties is downright criminal.'

'All right, tell you what I'll do,' he gave her the benefit of his most dazzling smile. 'I'll give you six for a shilling.'

Jane was hungry enough to eat six, but there was no way she was going to part with more than half of her life savings. She was also beginning to worry about the cost of an outfit. If one pasty cost twopence halfpenny, what was a second-hand dress going to set her back? And that was without a hat, shoes, stockings and underclothes.

'I only want one.'

'To eat now?'

She nodded.

'Well why didn't you say so? You can have this one.' He scooped one from the end of the tray on to a paper bag, and handed it to her.

Her mouth was already watering, but she held back to ask, 'How much?'

'It's misshapen,' he lied, glad that Charlie who owned the shop was down the slaughterhouse, and Charlie's wife Alma was upstairs seeing to her mother who'd managed to catch bronchitis at the first sign of spring. 'We wouldn't be able to sell that one. The crimping on the edge is all crooked.'

'Are you sure?'

'It would go in the bin.'

She halved it with her first bite.

'You working round here then?' he asked, setting the fish slice to work again.

She shook her head, her mouth too full to talk. She swallowed the last mouthful and ran her tongue around her teeth in search of crumbs. 'I hope to, though. I'm going to apply for a job in the Town Hall this morning.'

'The usherette's position?' He emptied one tray and turned to another. She was ambitious, he'd give her that much. But in those clogs and that grey flannel dress she didn't stand a chance.

'I know what you're thinking.' She set about the other half of the pasty.

'Do you now?'

'You think no one will take me on looking the way I do. Well I've money.' She lifted the handkerchief containing her precious pennies close to her flat chest. 'Enough to buy a dress, shoes and a hat before I apply for the position. When I'm all dressed up I'll look different. Then they'll give it to me. You'll see.'

'Don't mind me asking, but how much have you got?'

'What do you want to know for?' she asked, suspiciously grasping the handkerchief even tighter.

'My brother used to work in the second-hand clothes trade. His old boss might be able to organise you a good deal.'

'You're not pulling my leg?'

'Why would I do that?'

'Why would you want to help me?' This boy was a lot handsomer than the man who had tried to put his hand under her skirt and climb into her bed last night, but the one thing she had learned from the women in the workhouse was that sooner or later payment was demanded for every favour a man offered a woman.

'If you don't mind me saying so, because you look as though you could do with some.'

She thought hard for a moment before replying. He was good-looking enough to have any girl he wanted without resorting to tricks. And he'd said he knew someone who ran a second-hand clothes stall . . .

'One and elevenpence.'

'That's not enough to buy a dress.'

'But it has to be. I need that job.'

'There'll be other jobs. Why don't you go back to wherever it is you're working now?' he suggested tactfully. 'Save your wages. In a few weeks you'll have enough to buy yourself a dress, then you can – '

'There are no wages.'

'Wherever you work, they have to pay you something. It's the law.'

'My keep and a shilling, and they take that off me for my washing.'

46

'Look – what's your name?'

'Just tell me where the second-hand clothes shops are.'

'Don't you even know your way around Pontypridd? There are no shops. Just stalls. In the old Town Hall.'

'Is that where the theatre is?'

'No, it's the other end of the block in Market Square.'

'I'll find it.'

'Wait . . . ' The door closed and she was gone. Eddie continued arranging the food display. Idiot girl. Just how long did she think she was going to last in that get-up before a constable picked her up and took her back to the workhouse, or wherever it was she'd run away from? Well there was nothing he could do to help her. He had his own life to lead, and he wasn't even doing that very well. Not when he'd failed to get Jenny to agree to go to the pictures with him during the last waltz.

Jane crossed the road by the fountain. The light had grown strong enough to read the price tickets on the goods displayed in the shops. She lingered in front of Leslie's Stores consoling herself with the thought that a boy wouldn't know much about the price of women's clothes. A dummy dressed in a spring suit of navy and white dominated the central display; it was the kind of outfit the ladies of the parish wore to attend Workhouse guardian meetings. She read the ticket and blanched. Two pounds fifteen shillings!

The dummy was standing in a sea of elegantly draped underclothes: 'Petticoat and knicker sets, 3/11. Vests 1/11. Bust shapers 2/11.' She didn't even have enough for underclothes. She walked around the window into the porchway, reading the prices pinned on the hats, the stockings, the shoes. She could afford to buy a cheap-quality vest for a shilling and a pair of knickers for tenpence halfpenny, that was it. But then, this was a shop. That boy had told her about the second-hand clothes market. Things had to be cheaper there.

She set off up Taff Street, only just remembering to turn into Market Square. A clock chimed out again, and this time it carried on chiming. Seven strokes. She had no idea when the shops opened. One or two of the cafés and food shops, like the cooked-meat shop, had unlocked their doors, but the clothes shops were still shut. The first market entrance she came to was shuttered. She went to the end of the block where a man was unfastening the steel grids at the entrance to an arcade. Alongside it was a side-street, cobbled like the square, and half-way along she spied another doorway and a light shining out on to the narrow strip of pavement. She'd found her market. A man was standing behind the stall in front of the entrance lifting clean, ironed shirts from a flat cardboard box and hanging them on a rail at the back of his stall. The counter itself was bare.

'Want something?' he demanded gruffly when he noticed her standing at his stall.

'An outfit.' She opened her handkerchief to show him she had money. The pennies were still wet, green and slimy with copper mould.

'What kind of an outfit?'

'I'm applying for a job. As an usherette.'

'Plain black dress then.' He registered the coins but not the amount.

'And shoes, and stockings, and underclothes, and – ' she patted her hair, still sticky with gobs of yellow soap – 'a hat.'

'That little lot isn't going to come cheap. Let me see what I've got.' Taking a key from a chain on his belt he unlocked an immense chest in the centre of the stall. He delved into its depths, re-emerging moments later with three black dresses. He stood back and eyed her for a moment. 'This is the smallest I've got in at the moment.'

It was cotton. Short sleeved black, and plain, it was also drab and shapeless. She'd always imagined her first non-uniform dress would be something special, but she could hardly complain when it was serviceable and what she'd asked for.

'How much is it, please?'

'Half a crown.'

'I've only got one and elevenpence.'

'I'd be robbing myself if I let that quality go for less.'

48

'I really need that job. Would you give me what I want for a down payment of one and elevenpence if I promise to pay the rest when I've got the job?'

'And if you don't get it?'

'Couldn't you do with some help here?' She glanced around the stalls. All the others had helpers.

'I thought workhouse girls were only allowed to take live-in work.'

'I'm not a workhouse girl.'

'You just like the clothes?'

'I'm trying to change them.'

'If you're not in the workhouse, where do you live?'

She could hardly say Bletchetts' because only men lived in the dosshouse. She couldn't say nowhere, or he wouldn't advance her the clothes. 'The Graig.' She named the one area of Pontypridd she did know a little bit about.

'What part?'

'Graig Avenue.' There had been a woman called Phyllis in the Homes who'd left to go and live in Graig Avenue. Eira Williams had told her Phyllis's story after Phyllis had been rescued from the Homes by a man who loved her. It had been very romantic. Phyllis had run out on her lover with her baby, thinking he didn't want her, but he'd come to the workhouse to look for her, telling the matron that he wanted to employ Phyllis as a domestic.

She'd got to know Phyllis really well in a short time. They'd had adjoining beds in the dormitory. She'd been nice. Older than her, more like what she imagined an aunt would be than a friend, but really nice. She was sure Phyllis wouldn't mind her using her name or address in an emergency like this.

'Who you staying with in the Avenue then?'

'Phyllis, Phyllis Harry.'

The old man's attitude changed at once. 'Well, why didn't you say so, girl? Keep your money, take what you want, and I'll add it up. You work for me on my busy days, that's Wednesday, Friday and Saturday. After you've worked off your outfit I'll pay you half a crown a full day.'

49

'You mean it?' All she could think of was that she'd better learn the value of money, and fast. No wonder the boy in the shop had given her a funny look when she said she had one and eleven-pence.

'I'll be after Phyllis for the money, mind, if you don't turn up first thing tomorrow morning. And it'll be long hours – six until nine at night.'

'But that'll interfere with my job as an usherette.'

'I took on a boy once who worked in the Town Hall. The only matinée day is Saturday. You can still work the other two if I let you off early, and give you half-day on Saturday. But then your wages will drop to one and threepence on Saturday and two bob on week days.'

'It's a deal, sir.'

'You can call me, Mr Horton.' He pointed at a sign at the back of the stall that read WILF HORTON, BEST FOR PRICES AND QUALITY. 'Shoes, dress, stockings, hat, underwear . . . anything else?'

She smiled as she shook her head. There'd been no point in her worrying. None at all. She'd make that interview; all she had to do now was get the job.

'I can make you bacon and eggs, Haydn,' Phyllis offered. It was all very well Evan telling her to treat the boy as she did the rest of the family, but Haydn wasn't like the rest of the family any more. He'd been gone for months when she'd moved in. She wasn't used to him or his ways, and he'd changed, becoming a lot more worldly wise and sophisticated than either Eddie or William. He didn't dress, or even speak, like them any more. If it hadn't been for Andrew's introduction she would never have recognised the bespoke-suited, handsome, confident young man as the ragged Haydn who'd grown up across the road from her, and run errands for every shop on the Graig.

'Nothing too heavy, thanks. Toast will do.'

'Are you sure?' she asked doubtfully as he walked through from the washhouse in his vest and trousers with his shaving kit in his hand and a towel slung around his neck.

'I'm sure.' He smiled at Brian who was playing on the hearth-rug with the truck he'd given him. 'Hi-ya, nipper.'

'Hi-ya,' Brian answered, less inhibited than his mother.

'What time will you be back tonight?' Phyllis pushed a slice of bread on to a toasting fork and opened the stove.

'Not until after the last show, about eleven or half-past.'

'What sort of meal would you like then?'

'None, thanks.'

'Haydn, you have to eat.'

'Between rehearsals for the Variety in the day and Revue performances in the night the best thing you can do is forget about me for the next two weeks.' He left the door to the passage open as he walked into the front room that had been Charlie's. He'd agreed with this father that working the irregular hours the theatre dictated, it made more sense for him to move downstairs into Charlie's old room than back into the bedroom he'd shared since babyhood with Eddie. But as he'd watched his cousin William walk up the stairs with Eddie last night he couldn't help feeling a twinge of jealousy, and something more. A sense that his absence from the family had relegated him to the position of outsider. That he was now more lodger than eldest son. He slipped on his shirt, picked up his collar and returned to the kitchen.

'You'll be ill if you don't eat.' Phyllis laid the first piece of toast on a plate, buttered it and handed it to him, then poured out his tea. 'Milk and sugar?'

'I'll put it in, thank you. And I do eat. Variety people eat after and between houses ... shows,' he corrected reading the bemused expression on her face. 'We send out for food all the time.'

Phyllis pushed the prongs into a second piece of bread and began to toast it. Polite, and distant. She couldn't fault Haydn's behaviour towards her, only his lack of warmth. She slipped the finished toast on to his plate.

'I'll butter it,' he interrupted as she reached for the butter dish.

'Would you like another piece?'

'No thank you. I'll be rehearsing all day and that's best done on a light stomach.'

'You're sure about tonight?'

'As I said, we'll either send out, or go out after the show. Eat before and you risk throwing up on stage.'

'Haydn . . .'

'I have to go.' He pushed the last piece of toast into his mouth and picked up his collar from the back of the chair. 'See you.'

As she sat down to finish the last cup of tea in the pot before clearing up, Phyllis realised he hadn't once addressed her by name. Neither the 'Miss Harry' he used to call her, nor the more familiar 'Phyllis' that the rest of the family now used.

Wilf Horton chose Jane's outfit for her. She only hoped he knew what he was doing, because she certainly didn't know enough about clothes to contradict him. The whole outfit came to twelve and sixpence, seven shortened days' work before she'd be able to pay him off, but she wasn't worried. Once she got the job in the Town Hall as well as this one, she'd have money coming out of her ears. Taking the parcel and promising to be at the stall at six prompt the next morning, she looked around for somewhere to change.

'Toilets by the fountain,' Wilf suggested. 'You can have a wash and brush-up there for twopence, and if you don't mind me saying so you look as though you need it.'

She walked back out into Market Square. A pedlar was standing outside the entrance, a tray of combs, brushes and matches around his neck.

'Twopence,' he said when he saw her looking at the combs.

She handed the money over and returned to the fountain. Walking down the steep flight of steps that led to the Ladies she paid the old woman who sat at a table in the entrance her twopence, and waited while the woman went into a cubicle, wiped a seat with a damp cloth and dried it with a towel. Closing the door and the seat, Jane set the parcel down on it, stripped off her dress and put on her new clothes. The bloomers were pink, long and fleecy lined with elastic legs that ended just above the knee. The tops of the stockings were covered by the bloomer legs and fastened by plain black elastic garters. White cotton vest and petticoat – Wilf had told her she could dispense with a bust shaper – black dress, and the shoes. Low heeled with a bar. She turned her foot first one way, then the other, admiring her ankles in them. Elegant. They were really elegant. Although Mr Horton had warned her they were only oiled cloth and wouldn't last long, it didn't matter. They were far lighter than the rough wooden clogs.

Picking up her two workhouse dresses and the clogs, she made a bundle of them. She would ask the woman if she could leave them here. She had done with them. From now on this was the way she intended to look. The new Jane Jones: market-stall assistant and usherette, someone to be reckoned with. Not a workhouse skivvy and a nobody. Taking the black felt beret Mr Horton had thought 'suitable' for her, Jane left the cubicle.

'Well that's an improvement I must say,' the plump, motherly woman beamed, wrinkling the skin on her face until it resembled a winter apple that had been kept too long in storage. 'Off somewhere special, love?'

'An interview.'

'Well, one look at you dolled up to the nines like that, and the job will be yours.' She went back to her knitting as Jane washed at the sink. As Jane dried her face on the roller towel she caught sight of herself in the mirror. Her hair was appalling. Like a balding, battered old doll's, it stuck up in dry, rigid tufts. She took the comb from her dress pocket and tried to tug it through the mess without much success.

'You'll have no hair left if you carry on like that,' the woman warned. 'Always from the bottom up when it's tangled like that, that's what my old mother always used to say. "Daisy, you start at the bottom and work up." ' She took the comb from Jane and tried to run it through the last half-inch of hair. 'You've something stuck in this.'

'Soap. I tried to wash it.'

'When's this interview of yours?'

'Ten o'clock.'

Daisy glanced at the clock on the tiled wall behind her. 'Why, we've all the time in the world to sort it out. Tell you what, how about I rinse the soap out for you, comb it and then we'll try the hat on.'

'How much?' Jane asked warily.

'Bless you,' the woman smiled. 'No charge. Monday mornings are always slow. It'll be a good way of passing the time. Come on, sit on the chair over here. I'll run a sinkful of water and get a jug.'

No one had ever taken such pains with Jane's hair before, but no matter how much effort Daisy put into rinsing, dampening, combing, teasing and parting, it persisted in sticking out, short and plain in what was very obviously a workhouse cut.

'We could give you a fringe, I suppose.' Daisy held up a piece at the front and stared doubtfully at it. 'It wouldn't mean cutting much more than has already been taken off, and it might look better in the long run. But then again it might not. Good job you've got that tam. If I were you I'd wear it all the time until your hair grows long enough to wave.'

'I intend to.'

'Well, shall I cut it, or not?'

Jane looked at her reflection in the mirror, and nodded. Nothing could make it look worse than it already was. Daisy pulled a short-bladed pair of scissors out of her pocket. Combing the front of Jane's hair forward, she separated a thin layer from the rest and cut straight across. The ends she cut fell limply over Jane's forehead, shortening the length of her thin face.

'Just as I thought, young lady: the right hairstyle and you're a really pretty girl.'

'You think so?' Jane treasured the first compliment she'd ever received.

Daisy looked down at the shining eyes and smiling lips. 'I think so.' At that moment with that smile, it was almost true.

Chapter Four

Jane climbed the steps to street level just as St Catherine's church clock chimed nine o'clock. She paused on the top step, her new clothes feeling surprisingly strange and light against her skin. A smartly dressed middle-aged woman walked towards her. She glanced at Jane before adjusting her hat to the fashionable side angle then descended the steps to the Ladies. Jane felt ridiculously pleased with herself. For the first time since she had left the workhouse someone had passed by after only a cursory look. She was anonymous, no longer set apart by her clothes, just one of a crowd. She felt like dancing and singing in the street.

She stepped down from the fountain. Having an hour to spare before the interview she strolled leisurely up Taff Street towards Market Square. A young boy tipped his cap as his path crossed hers. She quickened her step but had to fight the urge to turn back and thank him. He'd seen her as a girl. Perhaps even as Daisy had said, a pretty one.

She lingered in front of shop windows, enthralled by the new and fascinating clothes, shoes, handbags, iridescent bottles of scent, green eau-de-Cologne, clear lavender water – the scent Daisy had splashed behind her ears 'for luck' after her transformation – and luscious, tiny, blue bottles of Evening in Paris. She made a promise to herself that the moment she had worked off her debt to Mr Horton and had some money in her pocket she would buy a new bottle for Daisy. But first she had to get that job.

Three girls were already stationed in front of the locked stage door entrance to the Town Hall when she arrived. Furious with herself for taking time out to window-shop, and with the girls for being ahead of her, she moved up behind them. The first in line was dressed in a low-waisted, rose pink suit of soft, clinging material that showed off the kind of curved, rounded figure Jane imagined she possessed in her daydreams. The girl was also blonde, with curls that could have graced a cocoa advertisement. Jane tried not to look at the others, lest her confidence be dented even more. Folding her hands, she automatically adopted the institution stance that had been drilled into her since babyhood, stared at her feet, and prepared to wait.

Two girls, one brunette, one blonde, wearing fox furs, lavishly trimmed hats, jangling, glittering rings and bracelets, and make-up thicker than a firegrate's coat of blacklead, bestowed condescending looks on the queue as they skipped past and banged on the steel door.

'Coming! coming!' an irritable voice boomed from inside. Bolts scraped back and the door creaked open to reveal a wide, steep flight of red-painted steps. The girls ran up them, their short skirts swirling high, revealing shapely ankles, silk-clad calves and brief flashes of naked white thighs. An overly sweet, flowery perfume trailed in their wake, overpowering the final vestiges of Jane's lavender water.

'I'm here about the job.' The girl at the front of the queue jumped smartly through the open door.

'By the look of them so are the dozen behind you, Miss,' the doorman grunted. 'Manager'll see you when he's good and ready. Not before.' Standing his ground, he forced her back and slammed the door in her face. The two girls in front of Jane conceded the advance they'd made, creating room for the first girl to rejoin the line. Losing her balance, Jane accidentally trod on a foot behind her. Turning to apologise, her spirits plummeted at the sight of eight more hopefuls.

'They were Revue girls,' the girl in pink nodded knowledgeably to those around her. 'They're rehearsing for tonight.'

'How do you know?' Jane asked eagerly, hoping to pick up crumbs of knowledge that might impress the manager.

'I'm walking out with one of the stagehands,' the girl responded, in a tone that said the job was already hers. 'He told me what kind of person they're looking for. It's not just standing around selling programmes and showing people to their seats, you know. All the usherettes are expected to take a tray out in the intervals.'

'A tray?'

'Of ice cream and sweets,' the girl said patronisingly as though Jane were a backward infant. 'And then of course there's the dancers and the performers to look after. The management likes to employ people who can make themselves useful when the occasion arises. Help them dress, make up, mend costumes . . .'

Costumes! The one thing Jane could do was sew. From the day she'd been old enough to hold a needle she'd had mending baskets thrust upon her.

' . . . they also like to employ people with an interest in the theatre. People who know how to present themselves.' She lowered her Vaselined lashes, and Jane saw smudges of bright blue powder on her eyelids. Her confidence took another dive. Who was going to offer an untrained, naive girl like her a position, over the head of a sophisticate who knew about make-up and dressed, looked and talked the way this girl did?

'Hello ladies, and good luck to all of you.'

Wide-eyed, Jane stared at the most handsome man she'd seen off a picture poster. Tall, slim, with deep blue eyes and hair the colour of gorse blossom, he flashed a smile that every girl in the queue instantly took as intensely personal. Straightening the red cravat he'd tucked inside the open collar of his shirt, he thrust his hands into his pockets and waited for the doorman to respond to his knock. The door opened a good deal quicker than it had done for the girls.

Jane caught a snatch of conversation as he entered.

'How's the rheumatism, Arthur?'

'Better now the fine weather's almost here, thank you . . . '

The door slammed before she heard his name. She strained her ears and looked around in the hope that someone would mention him. To her dismay she saw the line had grown even longer, snaking out of sight around the corner into Market Square.

'That was Haydn Powell,' the girl with the eye make-up and rose-pink suit announced to the queue in general. 'He's singing and compering the Revue, and the week after next he's opening in the Summer Variety.'

'He's so handsome,' her companion murmured dreamily.

'My young man says he's a – ' the girl hushed her voice but not so low that Jane couldn't hear the whisper – 'a ram.'

This time Jane needed no explanation. The workhouse separated men and women into opposite blocks, in segregated yards. They even ate on different sides of the dining room, across a divide of nurse-patrolled gangway. But women, especially the unmarrieds, gossiped every opportunity they got. She knew exactly what a ram was.

'It's nothing for Haydn Powell to have half a dozen girls on the go at once, and some of them, well they're showgirls. And as my mam says, most of them are no better than what you see in station yard after dark, if you get my meaning.'

'That's why my mam didn't want me going after this job,' the first girl interrupted. 'My father was all for it, said it was better than domestic, which is all I've been offered, but my mam told my dad that all Variety women are tarts.'

'Tarts?' The tallest of a group of six dancers echoed indignantly from behind the queue. 'Tarts!' she repeated menacingly, looking down from her superior height. Her lurid crimson hair and green eye make-up reminded Jane of an illustration of the witch in 'Hansel and Gretel'.

'I didn't mean . . . ' the girl squirmed in embarrassment.

'Leave it off, Rusty,' one of the other dancers said as the door opened.

'Don't worry, sunshine,' Rusty couldn't resist a parting gibe, 'no one will ever mistake you for a tart. The arse end of a cow maybe, but never a tart.'

An awkward silence settled over the queue, but not for long. Prompt on the strike of ten the door opened and the elderly doorman waved them through. For the second time in her life Jane entered the Town Hall theatre. She climbed the steps quickly, careful to safeguard her precious place in the line. At the top of the stairs the box-office kiosk was shuttered behind dome-shaped glass. Like the Pied Piper, the doorman led the crocodile of applicants past it and down a corridor. On the left Jane noticed an alcove that had been turned into a sweet stall. She had no time to do much more than register jars of barley twists and boiled sweets, before they turned right into another corridor. From somewhere up ahead came the sound of muffled giggles and shrieks of laughter.

'The dressing rooms,' the girl in pink muttered.

'Wait here,' the doorman commanded as they reached the end of the corridor. He marched ahead and knocked a door. It opened and he disappeared, leaving behind a heightened air of tension and expectancy. Jane checked the queue; she'd held on to fourth place, but only just. The girls behind her were pushing and jostling in an attempt to move further up the line.

A youngish, prematurely balding man in shirt-sleeves and braces opened the door and stared at the crowd of girls. He straightened his tie and withdrew. He re-emerged with a resigned look on his face, a sheaf of pencils, a notepad clipped to a board and a pile of papers in his arms.

'Follow me.'

He led, the girls trooped after him. He pushed a door, and there it was, shimmering in all its crimson gilt glory. Rooted to the spot, Jane could only stand and stare. The lights were set low in the auditorium, the stage was uncurtained and brilliantly lit, illuminating blue boiler-suited stagehands who were heaving on ropes and giant hooks, fastening them to enormous slices of scenery stacked in the wings.

'All of you, front row.'

Remembering why she was there, Jane rejoined the line only to find she had lost her precious place. She eventually sat, sixth girl from the right-hand end of the row.

'I'm the assistant manager, Mr Evans. Before we go any further, I'll tell you exactly what being an usherette in the Town Hall means, and what will be expected of the successful applicant. If any of you don't like what you hear, the door is behind you. Close it on the way out. I'm a busy man, and I've no time to waste on anyone who thinks that a theatre is all glamour. The successful applicant must be prepared to work, and work hard. Those of you who wish to be considered for an interview after I've spoken will have to fill in these forms.'

'Sir.' Jane dared to raise her hand.

He glared at her, annoyed at being interrupted, but used to being ordered around by workhouse staff she didn't flinch. Rising from her seat she spoke steadily and directly.

'How soon do you want someone to start?'

'Next week.'

Next week! The words tolled in her mind like a funeral bell. With no money and no lodgings, she had to start now. Tonight!

'The hours are long. Monday to Friday, four in the afternoon until eleven at night, sometimes later – the staff are only allowed to leave when their work is finished, and the theatre ready to open the next day. On a Saturday when there's a matiné as well as two evening shows we work from one until eleven. If things go well the usherettes sometimes manage a break on a Saturday between the matinée and the five o'clock show, but only when all the preparation has been completed for the doors to reopen. There are five usherettes here, including the new appointment. Their duties include showing patrons to their seats, selling programmes and taking a tray out in the intervals. They also make up their own confectionery trays, and check the money from their sales. Any small discrepancies will be deducted from wages. A large one will lose the girl her job. All usherettes are responsible for keeping the confectionery areas clean, including the trays and the ice-cream storage machines. They assist the stagehands and callboy to pick up litter from the auditorium after, and between performances.

Lips pursed in disapproval the girl in pink lifted her hand. 'Surely usherettes aren't expected to clean?'

'We have cleaners, but their job is to dust and sweep out the theatre and scrub the washrooms. As I said, it's the usherettes' responsibility to keep the confectionery areas clean and pick up litter from the auditorium.' Joe Evans frowned. Apart from the girl in pink he'd already marked as a madam to be avoided, he could barely tell the others apart. They were all fresh faced, keen and eager to please, and there had to be at least forty of them sitting in front of him. Even if he rushed the interviews and gave them only ten minutes each, it would still take him more than six hours to produce a short list of five or six for the manager. He shuddered at the prospect, but bowed to the inevitable. He'd have to whittle the numbers down with the aid of the forms, and the sooner he started the sooner the whole business would be finished.

'Remember what I said: if you don't like what I've told you, there's the door.' He pointed to the back. The girl in pink tossed her head and left, her heels clattering in the silence. Another hand went up.

'Do we get the same night off every week?'

'Yes. Sunday when the theatre's closed.'

'No other?'

'Not if you want to keep the job.'

'And the wages?' The speaker was older than the majority of applicants. A brassy blonde who looked as though she knew all there was to know about life.

'Twelve and six a week to start, negotiable after the trial period ends.

'That's slave labour rates.'

'At the risk of repeating myself, there's the door if you don't like it. Plain black dresses . . . ' He looked along the row, pausing when he came to Jane and the only other girl dressed in black ' . . . to be worn at all times. You'll be supplied with two sets of aprons and hats, which you'll be expected to wash, starch and iron. From the minute you go on duty until the minute you finish clearing up after the last performance you'll be on your feet. If you're nervous about walking home late at night, this isn't the job for you. The manager gives preference to girls who live within easy distance of the theatre so they can get in, even if the trams and buses are on stop because of flooding or snow. Right, you have ten minutes to fill out these forms.' He held up a sheaf of papers. 'If you're still interested, hand them to me on your way out.'

Jane put up her hand again. 'What about the interview, sir?'

'We'll get in touch with those we want to see again.'

'But . . .' In touch! All she could think of was her lack of address. She could hardly write 'Female Ward, Workhouse, Graig', any more than she could 'The most sheltered shop doorway in town.' ' . . . I thought we'd know today.'

'Today?' he sneered. 'I've more important things on my plate to see to today than appointing an usherette. A new show is opening tonight.'

She took the form and pencil he handed her and bent her head. Name – that was easy enough, so was age, but when it came to address she bit down hard on the pencil. Graig Avenue? She'd told the lie once today; it had to be Graig Avenue, she had no other option. Taking the form she walked over to the orchestra pit to use the wooden divide to press on. She wrote, 'care of Miss Phyllis Harry, Graig Avenue, Graig, Pontypridd'. Education – she wrote down the name of her schools and the date of her labour certificate; she'd come close to the top of her class but Homes children were always taken out of school at fourteen. The parish couldn't be expected to foot the bill for grammar school uniforms, not even for those who won scholarships. Previous jobs – she toyed briefly with the idea of inventing something, then remembered that stories could, and in a place like this, would probably be checked out. There was no point in writing out her life the way she would like it to have been, but she couldn't risk putting down the truth. If the workhouse staff had been alerted to her absence, and the assistant manager contacted them, they'd track her down in five minutes and return her to the dosshouse or the ward. And after only an hour of wearing ordinary clothes she couldn't bear the thought of returning to either.

She chewed the end of the pencil to a soggy pulp while she deliberated. The only real option was a slightly revised version of the truth. Cleaning – and mindful of the comment about mending costumes – sewing work in homes. 'Homes' could mean many things. She didn't have to say 'Children's Homes' or 'Central Homes'. They might even take them to be private. But the sentence she'd written didn't fill one-tenth of the space they'd allowed for 'previous jobs'.

She glanced slyly over the shoulder of a girl standing next to her to see what she'd written. 'Shop work, serving customers, taking money' – she'd be doing all of that as an usherette, but no one had ever as much as shown her a penny in any of the homes she'd lived in, let alone allowed her to touch one. She licked the end of her pencil thoughtfully and looked around. None of these girls could want or need this job as much as her. Keeping her head low so no one could see what she was putting down, she began to write. A cacophony of sound blasted into the auditorium, causing the few girls who still lingered to jump.

'Five minutes to start up!' Norman Ashe shouted to the orchestra as he swept majestically through a side door. 'Boy,' he snapped his fingers at the youngest stagehand and shouted to him in a voice designed to carry over the loudest music, 'run go the dressing rooms. Tell them I'm ready to rehearse the opening scene, though heaven only knows how we're going to manage with the flats dangling all over the stage like this. It's absolute bloody chaos.'

'All forms to be handed to me,' Joe Evans cried anxiously. Theatrical people were notoriously temperamental, and the manager wouldn't thank him for upsetting the director of a show on opening night. 'We'll let the successful applicants know who they are as soon as we've made a decision. All forms to me, thank you. All forms . . .'

Jane hung back, wanting to be the last to leave, and hopefully make an impression. She handed over her form, but too embarrassed to return the mutilated pencil she slipped it in the centre of the pile he'd laid on a seat.

'Could you give me an idea of when I'm likely to hear, Mr Evans?'

'When I've had time to sift through this lot.'

'You must have some idea,' she pressed boldly. 'The girl you've got now must be leaving.'

'Not until next week.'

When he'd mentioned 'a week' earlier she hadn't wanted to believe him. Now she did. A week – a whole week! Without knowing for certain one way or the other. A week with debts that needed paying off, no money, no food, no lodgings and nowhere to go.

'If you give me the job, I'd work for nothing the first week so I could learn the ropes.'

'Would you now?' He shuffled the papers together.

'Well it stands to reason, doesn't it? Someone new taking over from someone experienced is bound to make a lot of mistakes. Now if I came in, properly dressed of course, and stood next to the girl I'd be replacing for a few days, I'd soon pick everything up. The take-over would be a lot smoother than if you threw someone in at the deep end. It would be better for the theatre and better for me. I wouldn't get shouted at, and you'd have no reason to shout.'

'Used to being shouted at, are you?'

'Yes.' She took a deep breath and plunged in at the deep end. 'Working for the Master of the workhouse wasn't easy.'

'What did you do in the workhouse?' he peered at her warily.

'It's all in there.' She pointed to her form on top of the pile he was holding. 'Cleaned the Master's house, and he was ever so particular. Everything, even the garden paths had to be just so. Spick and span without a hint of dirt.'

'You were an inmate?'

'Only for a short while after my parents died. I was put there because I was orphaned, but a family friend took me out as soon as she discovered where I was.'

'Where do you live now?'

'Graig Avenue with my friend. You might know her. Phyllis Harry?' She gambled on the name meaning something to him as it had done to Wilf Horton.

He shook his head. Jane breathed a little easier. She'd taken a risk that had paid off. Wilf Horton must have known that Phyllis had a son although she wasn't married. He'd been all right about it, but some men weren't. She'd seen what the unmarrieds had to put up with from one or two of the porters. Stupid really, when all most of them wanted to do was put a hand up a girl's skirt.

'So, I'll get in touch with you there if you're lucky enough to be offered an interview.'

Although she knew she was being dismissed, Jane remained in front of the door, hoping, even at this late stage, that she could somehow talk the assistant manager into giving her the job; she'd rather run the risk of losing everything than live with an uncertainty that meant picking up her workhouse dresses and clogs from Daisy, and haggling with Wilf Horton to take one and sevenpence and his clothes back in lieu of a few hours' hire.

'I've dreamed of working in a theatre like this, all my life,' she said as the musicians struck the opening bars of the overture.

'Because you want to see the shows.'

'No, sir. I know I'd be far too busy working to look at what's happening on stage. But then, when the seats are being checked before shows, and we're selling confectionery,' the word fell awkwardly from her tongue. It had taken her five minutes to connect the word with sweets, 'I might get to hear one of the songs, or see a costume. I love sewing.'

'Do you now?'

Jane realised she'd hit a chord, and pushed the small advantage for all it was worth. 'They save all the fine mending for me at home because I can do such small neat stitches.'

'Where did you say you've been between coming out of the Homes and here?'

'My friend's house. She was really a friend of my family, that's why she took me in. She's very kind, but she's not well off and I can't just live off her. I have to pay my own way. I really need this job . . .'

'So you keep telling me.' He opened the door that led out into the corridor; she dogged his heels.

'And as I said, sir, sewing, cleaning, serving people, it's all second nature to me. And as for getting on with awkward customers, well there's never been anyone I couldn't calm down after a few minutes.'

'Probably because you send them to sleep with your endless chatter.'

'I do know how to be quiet when I have to, sir. I would never say a word during a performance. Not even if I was showing late-comers to their seats.'

'I believe you.' He looked pointedly at his watch. 'Now if you'll excuse me.'

'Sir,' she looked up at him, wide eyed and smiling, emulating Deanna Durbin on the film posters. But all Mr Evans saw was a pushy, scrawny kid in a dress four sizes too large for her – her friend's? – cheap oilcloth shoes, and a large beret that flopped un-flatteringly around a head that seemed to be blessed with very little hair, judging by the wisps on the forehead. 'You will think about what I said, won't you? About working for nothing and starting tonight?'

'Evans!' a voice bellowed from the side corridor.

'Goodbye, Miss.' He turned his back.

'My name is Jane, Jane Jones,' she called after him, but he'd already gone. A sound filled the air, louder and sweeter than any-thing she'd heard in a long time. Unable to resist its lure, she pushed open the door and crept back into the auditorium.

The stagehands had shifted an entire scene into place, trans-forming the white-bricked stage into a moonlit garden filled with blue irises, blue daffodils, full-blown blue roses and clouds of blue and silver fruit blossom. It didn't occur to Jane that it was im-possible for all those flowers to be that colour, or bloom together in any one season. Transported into the instant, make-believe illusionary world of blossoms and music, it was enough to simply breathe and feel.

A swing decorated with leaves and flowers floated gently down from overhead. Sitting on it, smiling, gorgeous and alluring, was one of the girls who'd entered the theatre while she'd been queuing. Her curls had been fluffed out and were now the same shade of blue as the scenery. Her perfect, bow-shaped mouth gleamed in the artificial moonlight, her silver-painted eyelids highlighting eyes a darker blue than the garden. Dressed in a very short silver skirt and sleeveless blouse, she looked the perfect partner for Haydn Powell, who stood in silvered shirt-sleeves and black trousers waiting to catch her.

'From the top, maestro?' he shouted into the orchestra pit.

'When the others see fit to join us,' Norman Ashe snapped peevishly from the front row. He clapped his hands. Half a dozen girls dressed in the same outfit as the girl on the swing crowded on stage and arranged themselves in elegant but wooden poses amongst the painted foliage.

'Opening bars, then over to you Haydn.'

The music played. An expectant hush descended, then there was only Haydn's voice, sweet and pure as it rose to the rafters.

'Tonight just let me look at you . . . Don't talk . . . Don't break the spell . . .'

Jane caught her breath. Inching towards the last row she fumbled her way into a seat. The first verse ended. Haydn held out his hand, the girl on the swing remained rigid, unmoving. He danced a few steps to the next girl and launched into the second verse. The background dissolved into unrelieved blackness as Jane absorbed every gesture he made, every note he sang as he danced gracefully from girl to motionless girl. His shoes gleamed like polished black ice, his eyes glittered, twin sapphires under the lights. It was only a moment, an instant in time, but it lasted long enough for Jane to fall hopelessly, completely and irrevocably in love. With the magical, exquisite moonlit garden. With the electrifying atmosphere . . . and with Haydn Powell.

'Miss Jones.'

She jumped to her feet. The seat banged noisily behind her.

'Stop . .. Stop!' Norman yelled furiously. 'We'll continue *only* when the management cease their noisy partying in the back stalls.' He cast a diabolic eye at the assistant manager.

'I'm sorry,' Jane apologised, speaking so fast she stumbled over her words. ' . . . I know I shouldn't have stayed but – ' This was worse, far worse, than the time she'd been caught stealing currants from the pantry in the Children's Homes. 'But . . . ' she stammered, desperately searching for an excuse that would stand up to scrutiny.

'This way,' Mr Evans commanded, 'before you disturb them even more than you already have.' She followed him out into the corridor. A man stood there, stiff, imposing in an evening suit, starched collar and black bow tie. Jane had never seen a man in evening dress before. She stared curiously until the stern look in his eye caused her to remember her manners and lower her head respectfully.

'You told Mr Evans you'd be prepared to start tonight?'

'Yes, sir.'

'One of our usherettes has let us down. Said she was going to work until the end of the week, now she can't. You know what kind of show we are running here at present?'

'Yes, sir.'

'What kind?' he barked intimidatingly.

'A Revue, sir. The posters said nudes.'

'Your mam doesn't mind?'

'I'm an orphan, sir.'

'Living with?'

'Friends,' Mr Evans supplied hastily.

'Right, one week's trial. See to it, Mr Evans.'

'Yes, sir.'

'Twelve and six a week to start,' he bellowed, as if Jane was about to argue the matter. 'If you prove satisfactory, you'll be kept on.'

'Thank you, sir.' Jane looked up at him in bewilderment. 'Does that mean I have the job, sir?'

'What do you think I've been talking about, girl?' He glowered at her, wondering if he'd hired a simpleton.

'Starting tonight,' Mr Evans supplied helpfully.

'I'll be earning tonight?'

'You'll have to work a week in hand. First wage packet will come a week next Friday.'

She swallowed hard: she'd just have to find some way of borrowing money against her wages. It wouldn't be hard now she had a job. After all, she'd done it with the clothes.

'My cap and apron, sir?'

'You'll have them when you come on shift at four. Anything else?'

'Just one thing,' her brown eyes sparkled triumphantly as the enormity of her achievement finally sank in. 'Thank you very much, sir.' She turned to the assistant manager. 'And you, Mr Evans, sir. I won't let you down.'

'If you do, you'll be out of that door quicker than you came through it,' Joe Evans assured her sourly. 'Make sure you're here at four, on the dot.'

As she walked away, head up, treading on air, she didn't see Joe Evans take out his pocket handkerchief and mop his brow. When the usherette who'd already given notice had sent a note round to say that her mother wouldn't countenance her working even one night in a den of iniquity frequented by lecherous men whose only interest was in peering at naked female flesh, it had been the final disaster in a disastrous morning. If the girl thought she was lucky so be it. He wasn't going to disillusion her by telling her that they would have been prepared to take on a two-headed octopus five minutes ago. Even so, he hoped he wouldn't be within earshot if the manager ever found out that he'd taken on an ex-workhouse girl.

As Jane emerged into the clear, fresh air of Market Square, it was as much as she could do to stop herself from skipping down the street. She'd done it! She'd actually done it! All she had to do now was find herself a place to stay where they wouldn't press her for her lodging money for two weeks. Twelve and six a week.

Riches! She'd soon have savings. Enough to buy clothes, food, everything she needed to keep herself.

She turned left and ran out of the square to the fountain.

'I've got the job,' she shouted as she hurtled down the steps to Daisy. 'I got it!'

Daisy beamed. 'Knew you would. Now, you'll be wanting these.' She handed Jane her dresses and clogs. 'Don't forget to take them back and tell them what to do with them, love.'

Jane folded the clogs inside the dresses. 'I couldn't have done it without your help.'

'Girl like you? Course you could have.' Daisy picked up her mop and bucket. 'Just watch the people you'll be meeting in that theatre, that's all. Especially the men. Don't go lifting your skirts, leastways, not until you get a wedding ring on your finger.'

Chapter Five

'Can you tell me where Graig Avenue is, please?'

The old man removed his cap, scratched his head and eyed Jane suspiciously. 'You're not from the Graig?'

'No,' Jane replied, wishing she'd asked someone else for directions.

'Thought not. I've lived on the Graig all my life. Born and bred there.'

'Then you know Graig Avenue?'

'Oh ay.'

'It's up the hill, Miss.' The man sitting next to him on station yard wall pointed under the railway bridge. 'Stick to the main road out of High Street into Llantrisant Road. Carry on past the turn to Factory Lane, past the Morning Star on the right, the Graig Hotel on the left, turn left at the Vicarage and that's Graig Avenue.'

Hoping he was right, Jane began her walk. The hill was steep and peppered with groups of children. Scruffy, barefoot boys, clustering around the High Street shops in the hope of picking up a paying errand. Girls playing with whipping tops and skipping ropes in the middle of the dusty road. She smiled as they stared curiously at her. Clearly not many strangers ventured up the

Graig. She hesitated at the turning to Courthouse Street. Looking down at her bundle she walked up to the workhouse lodge. At the gate she dropped her parcel, rang the bell and ran away. Heart pounding, she kept on running, expecting a shout to echo behind her at any moment.

When none came, she slowed her pace, feeling clean and free. It was as though she'd put a lot more than the uniform behind her. She carried on, her step lightening despite the steepness of the hill. By the time she reached the vicarage she began to wonder if it had a summit. There was a dairy on the opposite corner ending a terrace of houses that were larger and grander than the ones lower down the hill. At the sight of these houses she began to panic. What if the man who had taken Phyllis out of the workhouse wouldn't let her stay and share Phyllis's bed? What if she had to make her one and sixpence last two weeks? Would the assistant manager let her sleep in the theatre?

A rag and bone cart creaked, groaned and rattled around the corner, drawn by an enormous, snorting piebald horse.

'Mister!' Jane shouted. The middle-aged man driving it pulled on the reins. Dark and well set up, Jane noticed, and there wasn't an ounce of fat on his body – unlike some of the guardians who inspected the workhouse.

'I'm looking for Phyllis, Phyllis Harry.'

'Why?'

'Because she's a friend of mine.'

'From where?'

She looked around. There was no one else in sight. 'That's her and my business.'

'This way.' She followed the cart up a short rise to a second terrace further up the street. The man halted, secured the reins, leapt from the seat and slipped a nosebag over the horse's mouth. The animal slumped in harness and chomped noisily. 'This is where Phyllis lives.'

A short flight of steps and sloping path led to the front door where a key protruded from the lock. Jane had to stretch up to reach a highly polished brass knocker.

'Come in.'

Not believing the summons was meant for her she knocked again.

'If Phyllis is your friend, you should know her voice.' The rag and bone man was standing behind her. Pulling the cap from his head he opened the door. 'Phyllis, there's someone here who says they know you,' he called out as he hung his cap on one of the hooks screwed into the wall behind the door. 'Come on then,' he ordered, turning to Jane.

She followed him into a small hallway with a passage leading off. A private house was a strange, alien environment, one she'd never set foot in before. The first thing she noticed was the smell. Warm, cosy and inviting. A delicious soup and bread smell mixed together with floor polish, beeswax and soda, which for once didn't seem harsh and antiseptic.

The man was waiting for her, holding the door open at the end of the dark passage. She preceded him into a back kitchen fitted with an enormous black stove that belched out heat. She looked around: the room was furnished with heavy, dark wood pieces, and the only light came from a small side window that overlooked a walled-in yard, but the room wasn't gloomy. It glowed, bright with multicoloured fabrics. Red and blue crocheted cushion covers on the easy chairs that stood either side of the range, a summery, yellow and green check cloth thrown over the table, jewel-bright patchwork of curtains framing the window. The dresser was loaded with gleaming blue and white china, the black range glistened like freshly hewn coal, its brasswork rail and knobs shone dull gold, and standing in front of it, a small boy playing at her feet, was Phyllis. She looked expectantly towards the doorway, the ladle she'd been using to stir the soup in her hand.

'Jane, what on earth are you doing here?'

'You do know her, then.' The man hung his muffler and jacket on the back of a chair before going into the washhouse. Jane heard water running as he washed his hands.

'My, but you look smart.' Phyllis stood back to admire her.

'You must be doing well. Sit down. Take your hat off. Have some soup with us. Who took you out of the workhouse? What are you doing now? Come on, pull that chair out, that's it.' Phyllis bustled over to the dresser and lifted down another bowl. Opening a drawer, she took out a spoon and laid it on the table. 'Evan,' she smiled at the man as he returned, 'this is Jane. We met in the workhouse.'

'Pleased to meet you.' He held out his hand and Jane took it, struggling to match the firmness of his handshake.

'Well, woman, you going to dish up that soup or we going to wait all day?'

'Sorry, Evan.' Phyllis took his bowl and filled it. Jane's was next. Lifting her son from the floor, she filled his and finally her own. 'I don't know what I'm thinking of. I've cut the bread and I haven't even put it on the table.' She reached for the breadboard on the dresser. 'Doesn't Jane look smart, Evan? But then I expect everyone does after workhouse clothes. Jane was really kind to me when I was in the workhouse. We used to scrub the kitchen yard together .. .'

'Looks to me as though the pair of you are best off out of it,' he interrupted brusquely. Both women fell silent. Jane because she wasn't at all sure of the relationship between Evan and Phyllis, and Phyllis because she'd mentioned the workhouse, one of the few topics Evan refused to discuss because it reminded him of his failure to look after her and Brian when they'd been evicted from their lodgings. Phyllis could never understand why he was so sensitive about it, as he'd been in prison and in no position to help them at the time.

'When did you leave?' Evan asked Jane, feeling the need to break the silence.

'Yesterday.'

'And you've come to see me today? How kind.'

'It's not really.' Jane looked from Phyllis to Evan and decided that this was one occasion when only the truth would do. She began hesitantly and ended up pouring out everything. The Bletchetts taking her out of the workhouse, the way they'd treated her. The man in her room. Her trade with Wilf Horton, the job in the Town Hall, the white lies she'd told to get it, and the use she'd made of Phyllis's name.

'How old are you?' Evan asked when she finished.

'Eighteen,' she countered defensively.

'I don't know what the workhouse guardians would say to an under-age girl working in the Town Hall with the show they've got running there for the next two weeks.'

'They'd rather she was working in a dosshouse wearing no knickers with a man's hand up her skirt.' The ignominy of not being allowed underclothes still mortified Phyllis every time she thought about it.

'I'm just trying to see things the way they would, love. You know as well as I do that the situation in this house is far from ideal, from the parish point of view.'

'Love?' Was Phyllis married now? Jane dropped her spoon into her untasted soup. 'Could I use your toilet, please?' she asked, sensing that Evan wanted to speak to Phyllis alone.

'In the yard.' Phyllis indicated the washhouse door. Jane stepped outside and breathed in a great gulp of bracing mountain air.

She'd schemed, planned and, if not entirely told lies, coloured the truth in an effort to make a life for herself outside of the institutions. And now, when that life was almost within reach, the shadow of the workhouse walls still stretched over her, grey and forbidding. Perhaps she ought to go out and break a window, steal something, hit a policeman. If she was put in gaol she'd be given a finite date to mark the end of her sentence. And afterwards, if she was lucky, they might allow her to walk free. The way things were, she felt as though she'd never escape the clutches of the parish guardians.

'She needs help Evan.'

'I'm not disputing that. But we're not the right ones to give it to her. You know as well as I do how the authorities will see the situation. A couple living in sin . . .'

'She was in the workhouse, Evan. You've no idea what that's like for a woman.'

'I know only too well what prison's like for a man. Please, love, don't cry.' He felt in his shirt pocket, found a handkerchief and handed it to her. He couldn't stand to see her in tears, and she knew it.

'She was kind to me when I needed kindness. She has no family, nowhere else to go, no one else to turn to. You're lucky. You've always had your family.'

'Kids to support.'

'Not any more. You've given them independence and the will to succeed. All that girl is trying to do is stand on her own two feet like Diana and Bethan. She's spent her whole life in institutions. She told me she was born in the workhouse, shunted to Maesycoed Homes when she was three, Church Village Homes when she was eleven. No one's ever loved her or cared a fig what happened to her. And she's already found work so it's not as if she's going to be a burden on us.'

'You heard her, same as me. The Bletchetts took her out. They signed for her to work in their dosshouse. They're responsible for what happens to her.'

'And if she returns to them she'll end up back in the workhouse in a couple of months, abandoned and pregnant like the last two they took out.' Phyllis's tears gave way to anger.

'Look, love, she's taken a job in the Town Hall at a time when no decent woman will cross the threshold – '

'In case they come face to face with one of the nudes *your* Haydn goes on stage with twice nightly.'

'Haydn's a man.'

'And that makes it right? What are you saying, Evan? That it's fine for a young man to sing on stage surrounded by naked women, but it's not all right for a young girl desperate enough to take on any job, to earn her living showing people to their seats and selling ice creams in the same theatre in case she catches a glimpse of what the men in this town are queuing up to see? You among them,' she added warmly. 'I saw Haydn slip Will four tickets. You and Charlie might have women warming your beds every

76

night but you're still not above a bit of titillation when the opportunity's put your way.'

'If you don't want me to go to the show, I won't.'

'That's not the point, Evan Powell, and you know it.'

'The point is we're not in a position to take her in,' he explained patiently. 'Not when we're living together without a wedding ring in sight, and she's about to start work in a theatre that every preacher has banned his congregation from setting foot in. You know as well as I do what people in this town are going to say.'

'Better than you, it seems,' Phyllis's voice rose precariously. 'And I'd have thought that after some of the things this family has been through in the last couple of years, you wouldn't give a damn what anyone says about you, or any other Powell.'

'It's not just us. There's Diana to consider, and the girl herself.'

'Diana's got a lot more common sense than you when it comes to something like this. And as for Jane, if she's found the courage to take a job in the Town Hall now, when the Revue's playing, I hardly think she's going to worry about a few gossips.'

'I don't think she has a clue what she's got herself into. If she's found and charged with being a recalcitrant pauper, she could end up in prison . . .'

'All the more reason for us to take her in before she is found. Couldn't we say that she's my cousin from Church Village?' Phyllis wheedled. 'Let her stay, just until she gets her first week's wages? Please?'

'And if the workhouse finds out?'

'How will they? They're looking for a girl in a workhouse dress and clogs. Not an usherette. I hardly recognised her myself when she walked in. And you heard her, she told the man who hired her that we took her out of the workhouse.'

'And if the Town Hall checks?'

'They won't. Not now they've taken her on. From what she said they're only too glad to have someone who's prepared to work at short notice.'

'Phyllis . . .'

'Please, Evan. It's not that long ago I was in her shoes, wearing a workhouse dress with no one to turn to. I doubt she's got a penny in her pocket now, but with two jobs lined up she'll soon be able to pay her way, and with Charlie gone, we could do with the money.'

'We're managing fine with what I bring in and the three boys and Diana paying their way.'

'Haydn will be leaving when the Summer Variety ends.'

'And we'll survive, just like we did after Charlie left.'

'Extra always comes in handy.'

'I'll not argue with that, but even if I did say yes, where's the girl going to sleep? With Haydn downstairs, all the bedrooms full and Brian in the box room, there's no room.'

'The old cot Bethan used is big enough for Brian. He can come in with us for a week or two, and Jane can have the box room.'

Evan fell silent. Money and a place for Jane to sleep were minor considerations. Although the rag and bone round had never done as well as he would have liked, with his nephew and niece's lodging money and his son Eddie in steady work they managed; not as well as some, but better than most. Haydn returning home had been an unexpected bonus. For the first time since the pits had closed he could look forward to setting a little aside against emergencies. Another lodger wouldn't make much difference to the household, but another scandal would. He couldn't bear the thought of people gossiping and prying into his private life just as he and Phyllis were quietly, and happily settled. But there was no denying the girl needed help.

'Please, Evan?'

'Until her wages come in. Not a day longer.'

'Bless you, I knew you wouldn't let me down.' Phyllis hugged him before opening the washhouse door. 'Jane, is seven and six a week for full board and lodge all right?'

The box room was seven foot by five. A single bed was pushed beneath the window. Alongside it, a chest of drawers with a jug and bowl on top did double service as a washstand, leaving an area only just large enough to stand, or stretch out your legs if you sat on the bed. The curtains and bedcover were of a faded green cotton which hadn't even been pretty when new. But to Jane the room was the most beautiful she'd seen. The first that was hers, and hers alone.

'There's no wardrobe, not even room for one,' Phyllis apologised, stripping the bed and replacing the embroidered linen cloth set below the jug and bowl with a fresh one. 'But the drawers in the chest are deep enough to take most things, and if you've anything that needs hanging up, I'm sure Diana won't mind making room for it in her wardrobe. Her room is across the landing, the boys are next door, and Evan and I are in the middle,' she added, making certain Jane understood exactly how things stood.

'I feel awful turfing your little boy out of his room like this,' Jane apologised as Phyllis picked up Brian's teddy bear.

'He won't mind, leastways not for a week or two until you get your first wage packet. Now, I'll move Brian's things across to our room.'

'Please don't bother. All I've got is what I'm wearing.'

'But you're going to need clothes to change.'

'I'll get them. Just as soon as I've made some money.'

'Until then, you're going to have to let me lend you what you need.'

'I couldn't. You've done enough for me already.'

'For a start, young lady, you're going to need a towel, and a flannel.' Phyllis walked across the landing to the bedroom she shared with Evan and pulled out the bottom drawer of a tallboy. Jane, unsure whether to follow or not, hovered outside the door, staring in fascination at the largest bed she'd ever seen. 'And a brush and a comb,' Phyllis continued.

'I bought this from a pedlar outside the market.' Jane pulled the comb from her pocket.

Phyllis glanced at the cheap bakelite comb. She'd owned one like it. If it lasted a week Jane would be lucky.

'Let me see, soap, a nailbrush,' Phyllis removed the items from the drawer that Evan's wife had always kept well stocked with stores she never dipped into. 'And underclothes and a nightgown. Did they give you one in the workhouse?'

Jane shook her head, ashamed because she needed so many things.

'Here,' Phyllis took a floor-length white cambric, lace-trimmed gown from tissue paper.

'Oh no. I couldn't wear this. It's far too grand.'

'Take it.' Phyllis thrust it at her. 'It belonged to a very good friend of mine who kept it for best. She was over eighty when she died, and her "best" never came. I think she'd rather like the idea of you wearing it now.'

'I don't know what to say.'

'Try thank-you. It's generally enough for most people.' Phyllis held out her arms and hugged Jane. Jane shrank from her touch. Being embraced was a new and bewildering experience. 'Now if you're going to be in the Town Hall at four o'clock, it's time we warmed that soup up you didn't touch at dinner time so you can go off on a full stomach.'

'Haydn, I can't dance another step or sing another note.' Babs Bradley, the pretty, curly-haired blonde, who'd landed the choice leading lady role in the Variety, made a face as she slumped on the floor of the rehearsal room.

'Then we'll have no show to open a week Monday.' Haydn was warn out and impatient from the morning's rehearsals. 'Come on, Babs, act like a trouper.' He gripped her hands and pulled her to her feet.

'We're not going to get anywhere if you persist in playing the Prime Donna, Babs.' 'Chuckles' Byrne complained. The show's producer had been given his nickname because he'd never been known to smile, much less laugh. 'Take five, everyone.'

'Thank God.' Babs miraculously perked up. 'I need an ice cream.'

'If you ask me she needs a good kick up the arse.' Max Monty, the show's comedian muttered to Chuckles. 'If it was Haydn who was playing up, I could understand it. After all, the poor sod's been rehearsing revue all morning.'

'The way she's carrying on, anyone would think Babs was the bloody star of this show.'

80

'As opposed to you, Helen?' Chuckles suggested drily, turning to the tall, dark girl who stood behind him.

'You said it, Chuckles, not me.'

'Well, star or not, as you're here you can run through the Avenue routine with Haydn and Max.'

Haydn managed to summon up more energy as Helen walked into the centre of the room. Dressed in a skirt cut higher and a bodice even lower than those of Babs, she exuded sex. And with her make-up-free face and open smile, it was a cleaner, healthier sex than the titivating, astringently perfumed eroticism that the girls of the Revue radiated. Max joined them, carrying three canes. He tossed one to Haydn, the other to Helen.

Chuckles nodded to the pianist, who hit the opening notes. He chanted, 'One, two, three, go.'

'We would drive up the avenue . . . ' Chuckles beat time to the music then screamed, 'Stop!' Trained by endless fraught rehearsals, all three froze. 'Max, you're the shortest, you go in front. Helen, you next. Haydn, bring up the rear. That's it, and again . . . one two three . . .'

'Chuckles is a bloody slave-driver,' Babs said as she came back with her ice cream. Eating it one-handed, she took off her shoes and rubbed her feet. 'Him with his, "one more time, one more time". I'll have no feet or voice left by the time this show actually opens.'

'Then Helen had better rehearse lead, and you second fiddle,' Mousie Summers, the 'head' chorus girl sniped.

'I suppose you'd prefer it if I was out altogether, so you could be promoted to second fiddle?' Used to giving as good as she got, Babs mimicked Mousie's bitchy tone perfectly.

'Well, if you're giving up . . .'

'One dusting of talcum powder and I'll be back on form. Don't worry your pretty head about me, Mousie.'

'That one's a cow,' Harriet, the youngest of the chorus girls declared as Babs left in search of a drink.

'Aren't we all when we set our sights on a higher rung in this bloody business,' Freda the oldest and most cynical of the girls observed.

'Full chorus for Avenue!' Chuckles yelled, carried away by the momentum of the music.

'That's us.' Mousie stubbed out the cigarette she'd lit up in defiance of the No Smoking signs, beneath the toe of her tap shoe. Freda clamped her hands on Mousie's waist, Harriet did the same, and as the piano belted out the refrain they shuffled behind Haydn, Helen and Max, three in a snake of twenty toe-tapping, singing girls, all of them desperately trying to look as though they hadn't a care in the world.

'No! No! No! Call yourself chorus girls!' Chuckles stamped his foot so hard he hurt his ankle. Hopping and swearing, he took his anger out on the hapless dancers.

'Haydn, Max, Helen take a break. You deserve better than this row of dancing bears at your back. Now . . .'

Glad to be out of the spotlight for five minutes, Haydn slipped out through the door and made his way across the theatre to the bar. He glanced up at the clock. Three o'clock. Half an hour left of Variety rehearsals, if he was lucky, none involving him, then an hour and a half's break before the curtain went up on the first of the two Revue performances. Another eight hours before he could walk home, and he was on his knees now. It wasn't as if he didn't know what rehearsing was like. Why, oh why had he agreed to open in the Variety?'

Money! the little nagging voice at the back of his head sang out. It had been barely six months since he'd left home. He'd sent half his wages to his mother until his father had written and told him to stop because they no longer needed it. After that he'd been able to keep himself in style, or at least what he considered style, and he'd still managed to save over a hundred pounds, which he'd stowed safely away in a Post Office account book. And between getting nine pounds ten shillings a week for playing in the Revue – above rates because few Welsh singers were prepared to be associated with nude revue on their home territory – plus five pounds rehearsal fee for the Variety until it opened, when he would be cut to a flat seven pounds a week, he was well on the way to making it a great deal more. Life was good. So good in fact, it was worth putting up with Babs' tantrums and his own aching feet.

'Beer, Haydn?' Joe Evans asked as he walked into the deserted bar.

'Those words are magic to my ears.'

'Seeing as how doubling up on work has put you in desperate need, this one's on the house.' Joe walked behind the cream and gilt bar, lifted a bottle from a crate and poured the beer into a glass. It frothed over the top and down the sides.

'You might be a first-rate assistant manager, but you'll never make barman.'

'That's just as well, seeing as how I've no intention of tending bar.'

Haydn climbed on to a stool, stretched his legs and picked up the glass.

'You'd better make it up with the lady.'

Haydn looked blankly at Joe.

'None of your innocent looks. This is Joe who knew you when you were a callboy, remember. The whole theatre understands exactly why Babs is being difficult. I heard her shouting at you earlier for making sheep's eyes at Helen.'

'I barely know either girl.'

'That's not what I heard. You and Babs made quite an impression in the Brighton pantomime. And not only on stage, from what I've been told.'

'By who?'

'The same little bird who told me you've made a great deal more than just sheep's eyes at Rusty from the Revue.'

'Busy bird.'

'Haydn,' Joe shook his head as he bent over the bar account book. 'Take the word of a happily married man . . .'

'There's no such thing.'

'You're looking at it. Why don't you stop playing around, settle down and join us?'

'You suggesting I should marry Babs?'

'No, and not Rusty from the Revue either.'

'Her husband might object if I tried.'

'All the more reason to stop playing around and settle down with a nice, normal girl. We've a monopoly on them in Ponty.'

'Introduce me to one who'll go out with a boy who does what I do for a living, and I'll think about it.'

'Is that a challenge?'

Haydn sipped his beer and thought about Jenny. 'No it's not. Perhaps I'm not fit company for showgirls let alone decent girls any more, Joe. Have you thought of that?'

By the time Haydn left the bar, Chuckles had called halt to rehearsals for the day. He and Norman were in the auditorium talking to the manager. Haydn glanced at his wristwatch. He had three-quarters of an hour to himself before Billy and the girls from the Revue came in. Joe was right about one thing: he ought to apologise to Babs. After all, he'd be rehearsing with her for the next two weeks, and working with her for six weeks after that. If she took her anger with him out on everyone else as she had done this afternoon, the situation would soon become intolerable for the whole cast.

He walked around the back of the stage and down the corridor that led to the dressing rooms. There were only four. He'd managed to commandeer one for himself because he had to store not only his half-finished costumes for the Variety, but also his costumes for the Revue. He put his hand on the door handle, and hesitated. Babs and Helen had been given the daytime use of Rusty's room, next door to his. She might still be there . . . He took another step and knocked.

'Yes?' The voice was thick with tears. He wished he hadn't bothered, but he could hardly turn back now.

'Babs, it's Haydn.'

'So?'

'Come on, open up. I can't talk to you through a plank of wood.'

'It's open.'

He stepped inside, negotiating his way around the usual litter of greasepaint, costumes, odd shoes and dancing slippers. 'Where's Helen?'

'She went early. She's meeting a friend for tea. A *gentleman* friend.'

'Can I sit down?' He picked up the only other chair in the room, swung it towards him and sat on it the wrong way round, leaning his hands on the back.

'Why should I let you after you spent the entire afternoon flirting with Helen?'

'Babs, Babs, can't you tell the difference between rehearsing and real life?' He reached out and ran his fingertips over her bare arm.

'That wasn't rehearsing, Haydn Powell, and you know it. You were trying to get into her knickers, and she, tart that she is, was lapping it up. If it had been anyone else I wouldn't have given a damn. But Helen! You know I have to share a dressing room with her. And where does that leave me? Well I'll tell you, looking a right bloody fool.'

'I was trying to get to know her. We have to work together. I want her to become a pal, like Max.'

'I've never seen you kiss Max when you thought no one was looking.'

'That's because I don't have to kiss Max on stage, thank God. We were practising, that's all. Come on Babs, I don't have to tell you how hard it is to kiss someone for the first time in front of a man like Chuckles. He'll shout that I'm puckering my lips all wrong, or kissing too fast, or too slow, or not in step, or so badly I must be a fairy.'

She smiled in spite of herself.

'That's better.' He left his chair and locked his arms around her waist, but she wasn't prepared to be placated. Not yet.

'The trouble is you're a flirt. I don't know where I am with you. After Brighton you said you'd write, count the moments until we could be together again. I never got a single letter.'

'I sent them.'

'Did you?' She gazed at him sceptically.

'You're here with me now, that's what's important.' He aimed a kiss at her lips, but she turned her head and he found himself kissing the back of her neck. Undeterred he slid his hands round to her small, pointed breasts.

'How about I send out for sandwiches, cream cakes and tea,' he murmured in her ear as he teased her nipples through the thin fabric.

'You think I can be bought that cheap?'

'I'd suggest dinner, but I have to work tonight.'

'With nudes.' She wrenched herself from his embrace.

'You know I'd prefer to be with you. How about Sunday? Lunch at the New Inn. It's not the Ritz, but it's the best place this town has to offer.'

'And afterwards?'

'Never mind afterwards, how about before? We could go for a walk in the country. Work up an appetite. I know a few secluded beauty spots.'

'I bet you do.'

'You're irresistible when you're angry.' He moved towards her, pinning her into the corner next to the make-up mirror.

'Haydn . . .'

As his lips closed over hers, he reached out and turned the key in the lock. Her skirt was short and very full. Once he'd unfastened the button at the waist it fell around her ankles. He lifted her into his arms. Still kissing her, he opened one eye and looked around. A purple velvet cloak trimmed with rabbit fur dyed to imitate ermine was draped over a peg on the back of the door. Without relinquishing his hold, he lifted it down and dropped it to the floor.

'Haydn, it will get filthy.'

'I'll brush it afterwards.'

'But . . .'

'Nothing's too good for my lady,' he teased with mocking gravity, lowering her on to the bed he'd made. Leaning on his elbow next to her, he slid his hand beneath the skimpy silver top.

'Naughty,' she smiled as his fingers encountered bare skin.

'Beats me how you don't freeze to death on stage.' He lifted the hem and pulled it over her head.

'I do freeze to death.' She arched her back and thrust out her breasts.' But I have no choice, my costumes aren't exactly built to accommodate woolly vests.'

'So I see.' He slid his hand into her silver cloth knickers.

'Don't.'

'Why not? We've plenty of time, and,' he smiled as his hand slid deep between her thighs, 'it's not as though you don't want it every bit as much as I do.'

'The door . . .'

'Is locked.'

'The others . . .'

'Are gone.'

'What if someone hears us?'

'If the noise you make is true to form they'll think I'm a very lucky man,' he murmured as he pulled off his shirt and moved on top of her.

Chapter Six

Jenny Griffiths meandered restlessly from the end wall of the shop where she was dusting shelves in a half-hearted fashion, to the window and back. Logic told her that Haydn Powell wasn't likely to call in, not after she'd thrown herself at Eddie in the New Inn last night, but logic didn't stop her from hoping otherwise. She glanced at the clock for the sixth time in less than a minute. The hands were fixed obstinately at four o'clock. The first show in the Town Hall started at five. If Haydn had gone home to eat before the performance he would have had to start back by now. She knew he'd gone out early that morning because she'd seen him pass by on the opposite side of the road. But he hadn't turned his head in the direction of the shop. Not once, although she'd clenched both fists and willed him to do so with all her might.

The door clanged open and she started nervously.

'Jenny,' Eddie Powell greeted her.

'You gave me quite a turn. I didn't see you coming.'

'I came up Factory Lane. I've been delivering over in Maesy-coed.'

'Charlie's got a butcher's round?'

'You know Charlie, any chance of making a bob or two and

he's there. I only hope he makes enough to buy a van to replace the bicycle before next winter.'

She moved in front of the till, glad the counter was between them. Eddie unsettled her and it wasn't simply his dark, brooding good looks, or even the passion she nurtured for his brother. She didn't love Eddie, not in the same way she loved Haydn, but neither had she forgotten the night she had lost her senses and succumbed to his physical, almost brutal lovemaking. Every time she remembered it, like now, it brought floods of colour to her cheeks, and the shameful urge to repeat the experience.

'Packet of Woodbines and a box of matches.' He pushed a two-shilling piece across the counter.

Thursday, the day before pay day and Eddie had two shillings in his pocket. But then times had changed from the days when Haydn and his sister Bethan had been the only breadwinners in the Powell family. She put the cigarettes on the counter and took his money. 'I enjoyed last night,' she ventured, hoping he'd say something about Haydn. Any news, even second-hand from Eddie, was preferable to no news about Haydn at all.

'Like to do it again some time?'

'In the New Inn?'

'Why not?'

'It's expensive.'

'Not that bad,' he said airily. 'I can afford to take you.'

'I'm not sure.'

'What about Saturday?'

She turned her back on him as she counted his change out of the till. Why not go out with Eddie? It wasn't as if she could go out in the evenings with Haydn. Even if he'd wanted to take her he wouldn't be free. And Eddie would be able to tell her what Haydn was doing. She'd find out if there was another girl . . . She gripped the till hard with both hands, not wanting to consider the possibility.

'Well?'

She turned to see Eddie staring expectantly at her. 'Do I book tickets for the next supper dance, or not?'

'I'd rather to go a show.'

'The one that's opening tonight in the Town Hall?' he teased suggestively.

She glanced outside before answering, to make sure no one was likely to walk in on them. 'My mother would have a fit if she thought I even knew what kind of a show is running there at the moment.'

'Our Haydn said it's not all it's cracked up to be. Most of the girls have something on underneath the fans and flowers. None of them – well none of them have nothing on at all,' he divulged, trying to conceal his embarrassment at discussing nudes with a decent girl like Jenny Griffiths.

'I'd like to see your Haydn on stage.' She almost choked on Haydn's name, but Eddie didn't appear to notice.

'I'll get tickets for his opening night in Variety,' Eddie offered, expecting her to wriggle out of giving him a straight yes or no, just as she'd done with the supper dance.

'I'd like that.'

Taken aback, he stared blindly at her outstretched hand and the change in it.

'Then I'll get tickets for a week Monday, shall I?'

'That would be nice.'

'First or second performance?'

'Second, I'm never sure what time I can get away from here. It will finish before half-past ten though, won't it? My mother won't let me stay out any later than eleven on a week night. I keep telling her that I'll be twenty-one next month, but you know what mothers are like.' She could have bitten off her tongue. Before the words were out of her mouth she remembered that Eddie's mother had walked out when his father had been jailed.

'It finishes at ten. I'll have you back by half-past.'

'I'll make a supper for us. Do you like ham sandwiches?'

'Yes.' As he took his change from her he decided to drop the subject of Saturday's supper dance. She'd agreed – actually agreed to go out with him in two weeks' time. A smile played at the corners of his mouth as he walked up on the hill. It would have died on his lips if he'd known her reason for accepting his invitation.

'The tickets are marked with letters and numbers. The letter tells you which row to direct the patron to, the number gives you the seat. Here's a copy of the seat plan. Memorise it. There's nothing the manager hates more than an usherette clogging up the auditorium by misdirecting the audience. And here's your programmes. One pound's worth of change in this bag.' Joe Evans offloaded a leather money bag, belt and a pile of programmes on to Jane. 'Usually the programmes are sixpence each. These are specials just for this Revue, they're two and six. Mind you get the money right and no one lifts the odd programme from the top of your pile, or it will cost you the half a crown. And be careful to fold the top of the leather pouch over at the end of every sale. As I warned you this morning, all discrepancies will be deducted from your wages. You have fifty programmes, we'll expect either the money for fifty or the unsold programmes.'

'Yes, sir.'

'As the customers come through that door you offer them a programme and pass them on to Ann,' he pointed to a hard-faced older woman who was standing in the aisle. 'For this first night only she'll take them into the auditorium. Tomorrow, after you've memorised the plan, you'll be doing both.'

'Yes, sir.'

'You'll show everyone to their seats then stand at the back for the first quarter of an hour ready to direct any latecomers. Afterwards you go upstairs to the bar, Ann will show you where it is. You'll make up your confectionery tray for the interval there, but I want you out before the bell rings and they start serving drinks. That's the barman's job. Am I making myself clear?'

'Yes, sir.'

Joe Evans stood back and looked Jane over critically. Her dress was pressed, her apron tied in a neat bow. She'd come in wearing a decent coat – it belonged to Phyllis, who'd overridden all of Jane's protests and insisted that she borrow it. Phyllis had also styled Jane's hair as best she could, combing it into a straight back and sides boys' cut. Anything but attractive, its one saving grace was that it looked neat, both under the hat Jane had coaxed from

Wilf Horton and the starched usherette's uniform cap that Ann had helped to fix on her head.

'Your shoes could do with a bit more polish,' Joe Evans commented, feeling the need to make at least one criticism.

'They're oilcloth,' she murmured apologetically.

'Then they won't stand any wear. Buy a pair of leather ones as soon as you get paid, and see that you polish them every night.'

'Yes, sir.'

He looked into the auditorium. The lights were on full strength. Avril, the oldest and most experienced of the usherettes, had taken position at the first door the stall customers would come to. He had placed Jane at the second, which was never as busy, and with Ann waiting in front of her to show customers to their seats he hoped she'd manage, although he was only too aware that he was throwing her in at the deep end. Myrtle and Myra were upstairs, Mrs Brown was behind the sweet stall, Mrs Arkwright in the ticket booth. The callboy was backstage, the artistes in their dressing rooms and the manager loose on the prowl. He stepped into the corridor. 'Open the doors!' he shouted down to Arthur, the doorman.

A torrent of men who'd queued to buy their tickets the day they'd gone on sale thundered up the stairs and past the box-office. Ragged lines formed in front of Avril and Jane. Soon both were fumbling in their bags, feeling for the sixpenny pieces and shillings that had to be given in change for two florins. As the queues grew longer and more impatient, Jane began to wonder what was in the thin booklets that made them worth a day's pay.

Conscious of the assistant manager's eye on her, she struggled to remain calm, even when the men crowded around her. Keeping the customer's money in one hand, she doled out the change with the other, a trick she had learned from watching her house-mother run the fête stalls on the orphanage's open days, and one that stood her in good stead when a man insisted he had given her two florins when he had only given her a florin and a shilling. Ann moved closer when she heard his voice rise in protest, but the manager was there before her.

'What's going on here?' he demanded, eyeing Jane.

'This girl short-changed me,' the man shouted indignantly. 'I gave her a couple of two-shilling pieces and all she gave me was sixpence change.'

'I've been trying to tell you that this is what you gave me.' Jane opened her left hand and displayed a two-shilling piece and a shilling.

'She's right,' Ann asserted. 'I've been watching her and I noticed her putting every customer's money in her left hand and holding on to it. I wondered what she was up to until I saw she dropped it in the bag after the customer checked his change.'

The manager nodded sagely, wondering why he hadn't thought of implementing such a simple measure. There were half a dozen arguments over short-changing every week. If not with the usherettes then in the box-office, the bar or the confectionery booth.

'I must have made a mistake.'

The manager gave the man a stern look as Ann took his ticket. He stood back from the crowd and watched Jane. She didn't seem to be flustered by his presence any more than she'd appeared bothered by Ann's admission that she'd been watching the way she handled money. In fact she completely ignored him, and he found that in itself peculiar. Usually the staff fumbled and faltered when he drew near.

Jane carried on selling programmes and counting money, grateful that her Standard Four teacher had drummed addition and subtraction of money sums into her until she'd seen pound, shilling and pence signs in her dreams. The teacher had cut out cardboard coins to enable them to see the shape, and once she had even laid out coins on her desk and allowed the class to go up, two at a time, to touch and hold them, so they'd recognise them, if and when the time came. So Jane found herself handling money with increasing confidence, barely conscious of the manager's presence. It was no worse than the cooks who'd watched her like hawks on the few occasions she'd been allowed to help out in the kitchens of the homes.

The manager had to replenish all the usherettes' programmes

twice over. Jane was half-way down the third stack when the lights dimmed and the orchestra struck its first tentative notes. She moved towards the door in response to a signal from Ann who walked beside her. Avril was stationed in front of the other door. Two youngsters who'd delayed their entrance until the last possible moment charged in behind them. All that could be seen of their faces between their turned-up collars and pulled-down caps were the tips of their noses.

'Let's hope their fathers won't be sitting alongside them,' Ann whispered. The music accelerated in speed and volume. The curtains twitched, the excitement of the audience escalated. The red satin drapes parted, allowing smoke to billow out into the auditorium.

Powdery grey clouds wafted from the blue, twilight scene Jane had lost herself in that morning. Blue-skinned ladies with the scantiest of blue floral garlands and ostrich feather fans draped strategically around their thighs stood on pedestals set among the painted flora. Jane's mouth opened, but no sound came out, which was just as well because the orchestra fell unexpectedly silent. When it struck up again the swing descended from overhead, only this time the occupant wasn't even wearing the saucy cover of shorts and skimpy top. Haydn, his black suit and bow tie contrasting soberly with his blue face, shirt and hair, stepped out from behind the trees and sang the opening bars of 'Just let me look at you', all the while gazing at the girl who sat, muscles tensed, immobile on the swing. Jane knew she must be the girl she'd seen Haydn rehearsing with in the morning, but with her hair swept up beneath an enormous feather, and her face, neck and breasts covered with a coating of shimmering silver, she looked more statue than living, breathing girl. She'd crossed one leg elegantly over the other, shielding the area of her body every man in the auditorium was straining to look at.

The first verse ended, Haydn danced from the swing to the girls poised among the painted trees. He moved from one to another, looking up at them, moving his hands as close to their bodies as it was possible to get without actually touching them, and once Jane could have sworn he'd winked at the girl on the swing.

Ann tugged at the sleeve of Jane's dress, pulling her out into the corridor.

'Do they do that every night?' Jane asked when they were outside.

'Twice nightly and three times on Saturday. Myrtle, Myra and Avril threatened to walk out when they found out what kind of show the management had booked. Myself, I couldn't give a monkey what happens on stage as long as I get my wages at the end of the week. But the manager got worried and offered us all a shilling extra in our pay packets for every week the Revue runs. And for that, it can run six months as far as I'm concerned.'

'How much do you earn?'

'More than a raw recruit who's new to the work,' Ann answered shrewdly.

'But those girls, they're stark naked they're – '

'They're earning six pounds a week.'

'Six pounds!' Jane's eyes grew to enormous proportions in her pale, thin face.

'Makes you think doesn't it? If I looked like one of them without my clothes on, I might be tempted. Beats the hell out of working here for fifteen and six a week.'

The slip went unnoticed by Ann, but not by Jane. She filed the information away at the back of her mind for future reference.

The manager checked Jane's takings, counting twice over the number of unsold programmes. The money was spot on. After slipping the coins into a cloth bag which he locked away in his office safe, he decided to return the leather pouch to her and risk sending her out with a tray in the interval. Nine customers out of ten went to the girls in the front, even when the girl at the back had no one queuing in front of her. He decided to put Jane at the back and watch her to see if the programme selling had been a fluke, or if she really was quick on the uptake.

The usherettes went in half-way through the last song before the interval, when the auditorium was still plunged in darkness. Glad that she wasn't expected to walk the full length of the aisle with the unaccustomed load around her neck, Jane stood at the back and faced the stage. The blue lighting had been exchanged for something remarkably akin to summer sunlight. To her amazement she saw that the trees weren't blue at all, but dark green, the flowers around their trunks varying shades of pink, blue, yellow and crimson. The imposing redhead who'd flung insults at the queue of would-be usherettes was standing centre stage, dressed in what would have been a stunning, long flowing satin gown if it'd had a bodice sewn in to cover her bare breasts. Haydn was offering her a bunch of rigid artificial white carnations and singing 'I kiss your hand Madam'. In the background a chorus of girls dressed in top hat, tails and shorts instead of trousers, danced a ballet which made inspired use of the white canes they carried.

The audience's attention was fixed on the redhead; Jane's on Haydn. She wondered which of the girls she was in love with, then decided it couldn't possibly be any of them. Someone who looked as good and honest as him would want a decent girl, not one who displayed herself to any man able to afford an admission ticket.

The music ended, the curtains closed and the lights went up. A patient orderly queue formed in front of her.

'An ice cream, love, to cool my mate down. He needs it.'

'My staff are not here to take comments like that.' Jane looked up: Mr Evans was standing over her.

'Cornet or wafer?' she asked abruptly, feeling the need to impress him with the way she coped with awkward customers.

'Cornet please, Miss,' came the subdued reply.

Picking up a thick round of ice cream, she tore off the paper strip that encircled it and pushed it into a short, squat cornet. Fortunately, Ann who faced her had been asked for a cornet almost before the curtain had gone down, so she'd had an opportuntiy to see how they were assembled. She carried on serving, painstakingly, steadily, always polite, if a little slow. The assistant manager noted and approved. Speed was something that came with practice. The queue dwindled, the lights dimmed, the orchestra played. Jane waited until Ann moved alongside her and followed her out through the door.

'Money in the office first.' Ann dumped her empty tray on the confectionery stall. 'We'll be back to check those in a minute, Lil,' she said to the woman behind the counter. The woman nodded as she carried on counting out change into a boy's hand.

'Any chance of a couple of ice creams, sweetheart?'

Jane froze. Haydn Powell, the blond Adonis from the stage, was peering around the corner that led to the dressing rooms, his face painted garishly like the girls. Blue eyelids, red lips, pale pink and ivory skin, rosy cheeks. The femininity it symbolised strangely disquieting.

'How many you treating, Haydn?' Ann asked familiarly.

'You, if you want one.'

'Not tonight, thanks.'

'In that case it will just be the two.'

'Beside yourself?'

'Myself included.'

'If you don't get them in the next two minutes, Haydn, we'll be eating the bloody things on stage.'

'Language,' Ann reproved primly.

'Sorry.' Dressed in a scarlet satin robe, Rusty walked up behind Haydn and rested her arm on his shoulder.

'Cornets or wafers?' Ann asked.

'Cornets, we daren't risk any dribbles,' Haydn laughed. 'Not with the costume Rusty'll be wearing.'

Ann nodded to Jane. 'You serve them and I'll start counting the money.' She turned the corner that led to the office. Money bag banging against her hip, Jane went to her tray on the counter, lifted out two cornets and rammed two ice-cream slices into them. They were alredy melting, thick and sticky at the edges. Hurrying back she held them out.

'That'll be fourpence.'

Haydn took them and gave her a sixpence. 'Rusty, I've got your ice cream.'

Jane rummaged in her bag for two pennies. When she looked up to give Haydn his change, her cheeks burnt crimson. Rusty was standing inside Haydn's dressing room. She'd dropped the robe, and was wearing nothing underneath, nothing at all.

'Your change,' Jane snapped as Haydn bit into his ice cream and snaked his free hand around Rusty's waist.

'Keep it.'

'I don't take charity,' she countered acidly, turning her back as Rusty burst out laughing.

'And what have you done to her, dear boy? Whatever it was, it must have been quick, considering we only moved into the theatre this morning.'

The callboy ran down the corridor. 'Three-minute call for Mr Powell. Three-minute call for Mr Haydn Powell.'

His noise drowned out any reply Haydn might have made. Still seething, as much from her own prudish reaction as from Rusty's exhibitionism, Jane unfastened the bag from her waist. She went into the office where Ann was piling money on a side table in view of the manager, emptied out her own coins, and proceeded to count, bag and label them.

'You seem to be coping with the workload, Jane,' the manager said when she'd finished. 'But there's the unsold goods on your tray still to be checked. Afterwards you can help wash the glasses in the bar, and set up everything except the ice creams on your tray ready for the second house interval. When the finale begins, go back into the auditorium to help see this audience out, check for litter and anything left behind, then if there's any time free before the next show starts, take a break. The girls usually manage a cuppa.'

'Thank you, sir.' Jane tried to sound enthusiastic. But she stifled a yawn as she pushed the last few coins into her bag and wrote the amount it contained on the label. It seemed a very long time since she'd been in a bed.

'At last, feet up time.' Ann sank down on a stool in front of the barman who was polishing glasses. 'Any chance of an orange juice, Des?'

'For you darling, anything.' He adjusted his bow tie and addressed the other usherettes. 'Orange juice all round?'

'How much will it be?' Jane asked.

'On the house, love,' Ann answered. 'We don't get given much in this job, but the manager recognises that even horses need to be watered between hauls.'

'Wish he'd realise they need feeding too.' Avril dragged herself up on the stool next to Ann's.

'That'll be the day.' Ann took her glass from Des. 'Ooh, it's nice and cold.'

'Kept the water in the ice chest. Nothing too good for my girls.'

Jane sat beside Ann, watching, listening, taking everything in, without contributing to the conversation. Everyone seemed nice and friendly, but she had learned at an early age that appearances could be deceptive.

'Any chance of a tray of orange juices?' The blonde who'd descended on the swing peered around the door.

'How many?'

'All the girls and two extra; we're treating Haydn and the comic.'

'Lucky fellows. I'll bring it round for you when I've poured them.'

'Thanks.' Flashing a toothy, theatrical smile she backed away.

'I'll take them if you like,' Jane offered.

'Volunteering for anything's not a good idea in a job like this, not when you'll be back on your feet in ten minutes.' Des opened the chest and lifted out a pitcher of iced water.

'I don't mind, really.'

'In that case who am I to look a gift horse in the mouth?'

'Don't take any lip from those prima donnas,' Ann warned as Jane lifted the heavy tray from the counter.

The distance between the bar and the dressing rooms seemed to have doubled since Jane had last walked it. Holding the tray out at arm's length so as not to spill a drop, she finally made it to the dressing-room corridor. Not wanting to witness a repeat of Rusty's exhibitionism she called out, 'Drinks.'

'You darling.' The girl who had ordered them came out of her dressing room. 'Come and get it!' she shouted.

'Get mine for me will you, Mandy, I have to mend the run in this bloody body stocking, and I'm useless at sewing.'

'I'll do it for you,' Jane called out.

'Did I hear that right?' A dark girl ran out of the dressing room wearing a pair of spangled shorts, and sequined stars stuck over her nipples. She was carrying what looked like a giant stocking.

'I'll mend it,' Jane repeated, 'for a price.'

'You take in sewing?' two of the other girls asked in unison.

'Yes.'

'You absolute godsend.' Mandy dumped her empty glass back on the tray. 'Last tour, the wardrobe mistress did all our mending, personal as well as costume, but Norman said a wardrobe mistress was unnecessary on this tour. Old skinflint.'

'How much would you charge for this?' The girl in the spangled shorts waved the stocking in front of Jane.

'Twopence halfpenny,' Jane answered, eyeing the run.

'Done.' The girl bundled the stocking together.

'What about straightforward holes in the toes and heel?' Mandy asked.

'Penny each.'

'A torn seam?'

'Depends on the length, penny if it's short, twopence if it's long.'

'Can you do this by tomorrow?'

The body stocking had a needle stuck in it, and was wrapped around a spool of thread. If she was given those along with the mending, that would take care of all the stockings. Anything else and she'd have to borrow thread from Phyllis, as well as scissors, but it was a way of keeping herself until her wages came in. There was electric light in her room, and she was used to coping with very little sleep. The workhouse ward had always been bedlam with people crying out at all hours.

'You'll have it back before first house tomorrow,' Jane promised.

'Right, that's me sold.' The girl thrust the needle, thread and body stocking at her. 'Name's Judy.'

'Here's a petticoat.'

'A bust shaper.'

'I can't take them now. Why don't you pin slips on everything, with your name and what you want doing, and I'll pick the lot up after the show, then when I've finished I'll write my price on the slip and you'll know what you owe me.'

'You won't forget to pick them up, though, will you?' Judy pleaded. 'If I don't have this body stocking tomorrow, I'll have to wear a dirty one or give the punters more of an eyeful than the Lord Chamberlain allows.'

'And I need this blouse,' Mandy insisted. 'It's silk, Bought it in the best shop in Lewisham, there's no point in even looking for something remotely like it in a backwater like this.'

'I won't forget,' Jane promised solemnly. She looked down at the tray. Three glasses of orange juice still stood untouched. Mandy followed her glance.'

'Billy!' she yelled. 'We've bought you a drink, though why we bother when you can't get off your behind to fetch it is beyond me.'

'I'm busy,' Came the muffled reply from behind a closed door.

'He takes more money off that orchestra every week than they earn,' Judy said sharply. Opening the door to his dressing room she handed in the orange juice. 'Won enough to stand me a supper after the show yet, Billy?'

'And the rest of the girls as well,' the German orchestra leader answered in his guttural tones.

Jane filed the knowledge away. Apart from the occasional game of Snap and Happy Families in the orphanage she'd never played cards, but if it was a way of making money it might be as well to learn. That's if she could manage it cheaply.

Judy took the last two glasses and placed them on the floor outside the dressing room Jane already recognised as Haydn's.

'They'll knock them over when they come out,' Mandy warned.

'When those two emerge, they're going to need cooling down,' Judy retorted flatly.

By the time the space between the last rows of seats had been checked for abandoned gloves, scarfs and handkerchiefs, and the final sweet wrappings and crumbs of cornet had been picked up from the floor, Jane could have lain down in the aisle, and slept. There had been no need for her to negotiate lodgings at seven and six a week. She would have been better off wangling a key to the theatre. Everything she needed was here: toilets in the dressing rooms, a sink and drinking water in the bar, a carpeted floor to lie on . . .

'You walking our way, Jane?' Ann untied her apron. Her cap was in her hands, the hairpins that had clipped it in place bunched together at the end of the starched strip of cotton.

'I live on the Graig.'

'I live in Hopkinstown, Avril here lives in Mill Street and Myrtle and Myra in Pwllgwaun.'

'Sheppard Street,' Myra explained. 'It's handy because we can all walk home together, but it's not your way at all.'

'Know anyone who lives on the Graig?' Ann asked Myra.

'Only our prima don, or should I say Don Juan.'

'If you're at all worried about walking home by yourself, I could ask him for you,' Ann suggested. 'Underneath all that make-up Haydn's quite human, or he was when he was a callboy.'

'Haydn was a callboy here?'

'Until just before last Christmas. We all thought a lot of him.'

'But that was last year,' Avril interrupted. 'He's changed. And if you want my opinion I think Jane would be a lot safer walking up the Graig hill without him escorting her.'

'I'm not worried about walking home by myself,' Jane lied. Last night had instilled terror enough in her for a lifetime. But perhaps tonight would be different. She wasn't wearing workhouse clothes, and with lodgings to go to she wouldn't be walking in dread of hearing a constable's footsteps at every turn.

'Well we can go as far as Mill Street with you,' Ann consoled her.

'I've just got to get my coat.'

'See you tomorrow, Mr Evans, Des,' Ann called out to the under-manager and barman.

'Night, girls.'

Jane went along to the dressing rooms. The mending was waiting for her at the end of the passage. She could hear loud conversation interspersed with laughter, and Haydn and Billy's voices rising in unison, as they sang a rousing comic song about knickers and knockers – whatever they might be. She picked up the brown paper bag. One of the girls, probably Judy, had scrawled MENDING FOR THE USHERETTE across the outside in lipstick. Taking Phyllis's coat from the peg at the back of the confectionery kiosk she followed the others along the corridor and down the stairs. A crowd of men had gathered at the stage door.

'Now boys, remember what I said. No annoying the ladies,' Arthur bellowed above their noise.

Head high, Jane carried on walking behind Avril, Ann, Myrtle and Myra. As she drew closer to the crowd she saw that one or two of them were holding bunches of flowers.

'It's only the usherettes.'

The voice might have been announcing a deeply mourned loss.

'Could have told you that, Gwilym.' His mate nudged him in the ribs as Jane faltered, debating whether to push her way through the crowd or walk around the perimeter as the others had done. That young one's got a figure like a broomstick. No tits worth speaking of.'

'Here, you, move on,' the doorman shouted angrily. 'I'll have none of that language here. These here are ladies.'

'We can see that by the look of them, Grandpa,' An anonymous voice cried.

'Move on before I call the police.' The doorman's fury heightened with his colour.

'Jane,' Ann called sharply.

Jane ran past a row of shining black cars and taxis parked in Market Square until she caught up with them.

'Take no notice of them, love. You'll soon get used to it. The rest of us have.' Avril pulled a triangular paper bag out of her pocket. 'Peppermint?'

Jane shook her head. Accepting sweets meant that sooner or later she'd have to buy some to share around and she intended to save as much as she could.

'What you got there?' Ann asked, looking at the bag.

'Mending. Some of the girls wanted sewing done.'

'And you offered to do it?'

'They're paying me.'

'I hope you set your prices at the same hourly rate you earn in the theatre. There's no fun in working for nothing.'

'I'll make a profit.'

'Just see that you do. Though why you have to mend and sew for the likes of them is beyond me,' Avril commented acidly. 'Seems to me it's always the decent women in this world who get the worst deals.'

'At least we're respectable. And able to hold our heads up in any company.'

'I'll tell you now, Myra,' Ann asserted forcefully. 'For six pounds a week I'd think long and hard about giving up my respectability. My old man expected a sight more from me than just a peep show, and even when the pits were open and he was in steady work, the most housekeeping I ever got out of him was fifteen bob a week, and that was to keep me, him and the kids. After his accident it was all down to me. Work all night in the Town Hall, and all day cooking, cleaning, washing, sewing, and looking after him, and for what? He never took me on a bus trip let alone out in a fancy car like the ones that were waiting for those girls.'

'Those cars in Market Square?' Jane asked. 'They were waiting for the Revue girls?'

'You didn't think they were waiting for Billy or Haydn, did you?'

'There's one or two men I know who wouldn't say no to a night out with Haydn.'

'Go on,' Myra gasped. 'Haydn's not like that.'

'I never said he was. But some men are.'

'Those girls got it made,' Ann harped on. 'Silks and satins, best food, men sniffing around ready to shower them with flowers, jewellery, posh restaurants, trips out.'

'Come on, Ann, you know as well as I do, you'd rather die than show what you've got to the world,' Avril said in an attempt to end the conversation.

'Nowadays there's no one who'd pay to look, more's the pity, so I can't prove it to you one way or the other.' Ann patted her grey hair into place. 'But tell you what,' she pointed at Jane, 'if I was her age, I'd make the most of it and forget all about chapel morality. You can't eat respectability and one of those Revue nudes told me before the show started that she's got over two hundred pounds saved, and she's only been touring for a year. She reckons she can live on under a pound a week. And the minute she's got five hundred she's getting out and buying herself a nice little business. A dress or hat shop, with a girl to help out. Now doesn't that sound better than having to work the hours we do . . .'

Jane never heard the reply, as they'd reached Mill Street. She parted company with the others and began the long trek up the Graig hill, her mind awash with money-making ideas, but none as attractive as earning six pounds a week plus bunches of flowers, free dinners, outings and jewellery.

Chapter Seven

'I kept a supper warm for you.' Phyllis was alone in the kitchen when Jane walked in.

'You didn't have to. The last thing I want is to create extra work after you've gone to the trouble of taking me in.'

'Seven and six a week includes breakfast and a hot meal.'

'But I had soup earlier.'

'First day, double rations. Tell me how did it go?'

'It went fine.' Jane took off Phyllis's coat and hung it on the back of the chair before going into the washhouse.

'It must be tiring, though?'

'Nowhere near as tiring as scrubbing out the workhouse every day. Do you remember that time we stole dripping from the kitchens to put on our knees because they were so sore?'

'And the time you pinched a whole loaf of bread from the nurses' kitchen, hid it under your skirt and shared it out after lights out.'

'Your . . . ' Jane hesitated, not quite knowing how to refer to the man of the house.

'My Evan,' Phyllis supplied to save both of them further embarrassment.

'He's right. We are better off out of it. That's if I manage to stay out.'

'This is only your first day. Everything, including the job, is bound to get easier as you get used to it, and if you want my advice – ' Phyllis lifted a dinner of mince, and cabbage and potato hash off a pan of boiling water and set it on a cork mat in front of Jane – 'you'll go to bed as soon as you've eaten this. You look washed out. Not that it's surprising, considering you didn't get any sleep last night. And another thing: I think as soon as you've worked off what you owe Wilf Horton you should drop the market, otherwise it will all get a bit much, and you'll end up doing neither job properly.'

'You know how hard we had to work in the workhouse. I'll manage.'

'It was different in the workhouse.' Phyllis took the teapot from the warming rack on the range and poured out two cups. 'If we didn't work long hours we'd have gone without food, but life is different on the outside. Especially for a pretty young girl like you.'

'Pretty?' Jane laughed.

'You are,' Phyllis assured her seriously. 'When your hair starts to grow, and you get some decent food into you and fill out a little . . .'

'Fill out – enough to work in Revue?'

'Is that what you want to do?' Phyllis was shocked at the notion of any girl actually wanting to work in Revue.

'Did you know they get six pounds a week?'

'No I didn't, but money isn't everything.'

'If we'd had money we'd never have had to go into the workhouse. And if I succeed in staying out, it'll be money, not clean living, that will keep me on the right side of the walls.'

'That's as may be, but do you think for one moment that those girls are happy with what they're doing?'

'As sandboys. You should have seen the cars queuing up in Market Square after the show to take them home. And the men waiting with bunches of flowers and boxes of chocolates. Ann – she's one of the usherettes – said they get given all kinds of presents: chocolates, lace handkerchiefs, even jewellery.'

'At the end of the day they're just things. You can't hold them up against what really matters.'

'And you should see the clothes they wear. Silks, satins, lace, furs and – '

'And to pay for them they take their clothes off twice a night in front of hundreds of men.'

'Not all their clothes.' Jane blew on a forkful of piping hot mash. 'Just their top bits.'

'Oh, Jane,' Phyllis began to laugh.

'Have I said something funny?'

'Not really. It's just that you've got a lot to learn, about life, money and men. Have you thought about what you want to do, not now, but . . .'

'When I grow up?' Jane joked. 'Make a lot of money. Buy a house, and – ' she remembered what Ann had said about one of the Revue girls – ' a business that will keep me out of the workhouse for good.'

'Not marriage and children?'

'And be mauled around by a sweaty man every night? No thank you.'

'Some women like being mauled, provided the mauling is done by the right man.'

'Not this one.'

'You've had a couple of bad experiences, that's all. One day you'll meet someone.'

'If I have to, I hope he's a millionaire.'

'You never know, you might be lucky. But in my experience millionaires are pretty thin on the ground in Ponty.' Phyllis re-filled both their cups. 'I'm sorry you had to work so late, otherwise you might have met everyone else. Eddie is still out.'

'Eddie?'

'I told you about the family earlier. Eddie's Evan's son, he and Evan's nephew, William, share the bedroom next to yours. They both work for a butcher, but Eddie is training to be a boxer. That's where they both are tonight. At a match.'

'In the workhouse you told me you had no one. Now all of a sudden you have this huge family.'

'Not that huge. Just Evan and the three – four now Evan's eldest son has returned – boys, and Diana. I find it odd myself. I never thought Evan and I would live together this way.'

'I'll try to remember who's who.'

'You've had an awful lot to remember for one day. Tuesday is a busy day for them. Eddie has to open the shop early so they can cook meat enough for both Tuesday and Wednesday's market day, and William has to be at the slaughterhouse by four to cut meat for Charlie's stall, so you probably won't see them at breakfast. Diana, she's Evan's niece, she tried to wait up for you, but she just couldn't keep her eyes open. You'll meet her tomorrow.'

'That'll be nice.' Jane leaned back in her chair. She felt warm, and comfortable. The hash was good, and very welcome after a long shift with just one glass of orange juice to sustain her. She wondered if she'd ever feel flush enough to be as free with money as Mandy who'd bought three Fry's chocolate bars between houses.

'Did you see any of the show?'

'I saw a few minutes of the first act and a couple of minutes of the last act before the break.'

'And?' Phyllis continued, feeling she knew Jane well enough to press for gossip.

'As I said earlier there were a lot of girls standing on stage with no clothes on top. They hid their bottom bits with fans and things, but most of them were wearing knickers of one sort or another. Except one. When I saw her on stage she was wearing a pair of tiny knickers, but backstage she was nude all right.'

'Nude?' Phyllis repeated as though she couldn't believe her ears.

'Not a stitch.'

'I don't know how they can do it.'

'Six pounds a week,' Jane reminded her.

'I wouldn't do it for fifty.'

'I would if I had the offer.'

'You can't be serious?'

'If someone showed me the banknotes you'd soon see how

serious I was. Honestly, the girls wear so much make-up on stage you'd never recognise them off. Most of them look quite ordinary in their street clothes. Just a bit more made up and dressed than most. There's a couple of men on stage too, a comic, Billy and a singer, Haydn.'

Totally unaware that Haydn was Evan's son, Jane prattled on, and Phyllis let her. After his distant politeness that morning, she was curious to discover exactly what had transformed the old Haydn into the detached, well-mannered man who'd breakfasted with her. His easy going charm and good looks had always been there for all to see, even when he'd worn rags. But since his return she sensed that Haydn the professional singer wasn't the same person as Haydn the market and callboy. A hint of cynicism and lack of sincerity, a hardening of attitude and compassion – it was nothing she could put her finger on; just an underlying coolness she felt, more than observed. The smiles were still as frequent, the banter as humorous, but the smiles were too easily dropped, and genial bouts of talkativeness, even with Evan, had ended in silences which in his younger brother Eddie would have been construed as moodiness.

'This Haydn, he's incredibly handsome and he's got an eye for the ladies,' Jane chattered on, unaware of Phyllis's heightened attention. 'You know that nude I told you about, she was with him. In his dressing room. When I brought them ice creams during the break she was standing next to him.'

'Alone with him, with no clothes on?'

'They locked themselves into his dressing room between houses – shows. The other girls bought orange juices and I took them to the dressing rooms. They left two glasses outside Haydn's door, said he and the girl he was with would need cooling down when they came out. He's got quite a reputation. Avril – she's another usherette – well, she said I'd be safer walking up the Graig hill by myself than with him – he lodges somewhere around here. And there's rumours that he's got more than one girl on the go.'

'On the go?'

'Come on Phyllis, you've been in the workhouse. You know what I mean.'

The front door closed. Footsteps echoed down the passage and halted outside the door. It opened, and Haydn stood there, his blond hair covered by an expensive trilby, a camel-hair overcoat draped over his shoulders. 'I thought I heard voices. You didn't have to wait up for me, Phyllis.'

'I waited up for our new lodger.'

He looked into the room and saw Jane sitting at the table. A crooked smile played at the corners of his mouth as he removed his coat. 'Well, hello again. That was good ice cream you brought us earlier, even if it was mushy around the edges.'

His greeting dashed Phyllis's fragile hopes that Jane had exaggerated the story simply to entertain.

'So where did you two meet?' Haydn had demolished his plate of hash in record time and was now sitting in his father's easy chair smoking a gold-banded cigarette and watching Jane.

'She's the daughter of a friend, from Church Village,' Phyllis told him, deciding that with Haydn working in the Town Hall it would be safer to perpetuate the myth Jane had created when she'd applied for the job.

'And when I was offered the usherette's job today with an immediate start, Phyllis very kindly said I could stay here.'

'Jane's in the box room.'

'Where've you put Brian?'

'In with us. It's only for a couple of weeks until Jane gets her first wage packet.'

Jane picked up Haydn's plate as well as her own.

'I'll do those along with the breakfast dishes in the morning,' Phyllis intervened.

'Then if you're sure there's nothing I can do, I'll go to bed.'

'I told you when you came in, you should have gone right away. What time would you like to be called in the morning?'

'Early. I promised Wilf Horton I'd be there before six.'

'You work for Wilf Horton?' Haydn asked.

'Only since this morning.'

'Holding down two jobs, particularly two that start opposite ends of the day, isn't going to be easy.'

'I know. That's why I'm off to bed now.'

'I'll call you at five,' Phyllis promised.

'Thank you.'

'Just be sure you don't make enough noise to wake me,' Haydn warned. 'I don't have to be in rehearsals until nine and I've no intention of getting up until at least eight o'clock.'

'Just one more favour, Phyllis. I have some mending to do, so please could I borrow your work basket?'

'Help yourself.' Phyllis picked up a work box and handed it to her.

'Can I take it up and bring it down in the morning?'

'Of course.'

The last Jane saw of Haydn as she closed the kitchen door was his head resting on the back of the chair, his long legs and stockinged feet stretched out towards the fender. She knew there wasn't a chorus girl in the theatre who wouldn't have given her eye teeth to lodge under the same roof as him. But for the first time that day she was looking forward to having enough money in her pocket to live elsewhere. She picked up the mending she had hidden under the coats in the hall. Climbing the stairs quietly she closed her bedroom door, switched on her light, sat on the end of her bed, and set to work.

Her light was still on when Eddie and William came in at one in the morning. Eddie had been boxing, William drinking, and the after-fight party had gone for a long time. Eddie saw the lamp burning and went to bed wondering if the new lodger was afraid of the dark.

'You're prepared to graft, I'll give you that much.' Wilf Horton looked past Jane to the people wandering between the stalls. The steady flow of the morning had slowed to a dinner-time trickle. Women had made their way home to cut bread and scrape for those of their children who didn't have free school milk and meals. 'If you want to go to dinner now, that will be all right by me. Just be sure you're back within the half-hour.'

'I don't mind staying, Mr Horton.'

'No point in both of us manning the stall when the market's half empty.'

Jane picked up Phyllis's coat. The bag of mending was beneath it. There was no point in taking it, but she carried it with her all the same. It represented one shilling and twopence of work. Put together with her savings it would increase her wealth to two shillings and ninepence. She debated whether that gave her enough security to splash out on a pasty, but decided against it. The one and twopence wasn't in her hand, not yet. When it was, that would be the time to buy pasties. Until then she'd survive on the salt fish breakfast Phyllis had given her. And tonight there'd be another hot meal waiting after work.

She left the clothes market, turned the corner into Market Square, which was empty as the outdoor market only set up on Wednesday and Saturday, and headed towards Woolworth's. Half an hour was long enough to walk over the bridge into the park. The sun was shining, and the weather warm enough for her not to bother with the coat which she carried on her arm. Flowers would be blooming, and for the first time in her life she'd be able to stand and admire them without anyone shouting it was time to move on. She crossed the road, glancing back at the polished windows and columned, grand façade of the New Inn.

'Jane! I didn't expect to see you in town. I thought you'd be sitting at home sewing.' Mandy was with Judy, both of them dressed in sober dark blue suits and white blouses that were buttoned to the neck, but if they'd sought to project a Sunday School teacher image it was somewhat tarnished by the thick make-up and profusion of glittering jewellery they both wore.

'Your mending's done.' Jane held up the bag.

'*Done!*' Judy shrieked in a theatrically loud voice for the benefit of a passing bank clerk. 'You little darling. Can I see?'

'Not here, Judy. Let's go into the New Inn,' Mandy suggested.

'Good idea, we'll order coffee.'

'And sandwiches,' Mandy added. 'I'm starving.'

'I don't want anything,' Jane demurred.

'Nonsense, you'll have coffee with us. Our treat.' Mandy took hold of her arm and dragged her across the road.

'But I can't stay long, I have to get back. I'm helping out on a market stall.'

'What time does your break end?'

'A quarter to two.' Jane gave herself five minutes to spare.

'In that case you've all the time in the world,' Judy insisted.

Judy couldn't wait for the coffee to come before laying her hands on the parcel. Ripping off the paper she examined her body stocking while Mandy ordered for all three of them.

'But this is perfect!' she exclaimed as she tried and failed to find where the ladder had been.

'I picked up the stitches with a crochet hook and secured them at the seam. It shouldn't go again.'

'You sweetheart. And just look at this blouse.' Judy handed Mandy the silk blouse. 'No one would ever guess that it had been torn. Where did you learn to sew like this?'

'My aunt,' Jane lied, grateful for the exacting demands of a tyrannical housemother, who'd insisted on all the girls in her care becoming proficient in both fancy and plain stitching.

'How much do we owe you?' Judy asked as the waiter returned with a silver tray loaded with coffee and hot-water pots, sugar bowls, milk jugs, plates, spoons and knives and a separate tray of daintily arranged triangular cucumber sandwiches.

'One and twopence,' Jane answered, her mouth watering at the sight of the sandwiches.

'Here, I'll pay you now, and get it off the girls later.' Mandy dug into her purse and handed Jane four halfpennies and a shilling. 'How do you like your coffee?'

'I haven't time.'

'Of course you have.' Mandy poured coffee into three porcelain cups and handed one to Jane together with the sandwiches.

'I'm not hungry,' Jane protested stubbornly.

'You'd be doing Judy a favour,' Mandy giggled. 'After what she's just been told.' She glanced over her shoulder to make sure there was no one close enough to overhear. 'A few more ounces of fat on you, young lady, and your price will drop.'

'Mandy, you promised you wouldn't say anything,' Judy remonstrated.

'It's only Jane. And she's practically one of us.'

'You're not in the least bit fat,' Jane said quickly, wondering if they'd been in station yard. What did they mean by price?

'I know what you're thinking,' Mandy gurgled, laughing at the expression on Jane's face, 'but it's not like that. We've been in a photographer's studio. He's going to pay us for the privilege of taking our pictures. In our stage costumes,' she said archly, with a lift of her finely plucked eyebrows.

Jane bit into a sandwich, too disconcerted to comment on their costumes, or rather lack of them.

'It's good work when you can get it,' Mandy continued, blithely oblivious to Jane's embarrassment. 'Ten pounds for one afternoon beats the hell out of six pounds for a full week in a cold draughty theatre.'

'Ten pounds!' Jane's jaw fell open.

'And from a provincial photographer. Mind you, he'll probably make a hundred from the negatives,' Judy said philosophically.

'And all you have to do is pose in . . .'

'In a little less than our stage costumes,' Mandy whispered. 'He's going to take quite a few of the girls. He's looking for a couple of new ones too. He asked if we knew any young girls, really young ones. Apparently there's quite a demand. I don't know how old you are but with a little help you could pass for twelve or thirteen . . .'

'I'm eighteen.'

'There's no need to sound offended. I believe you. He just said girls who look young. If you're short of a few bob why don't you try it?'

'Me?'

'Why not? I know you're a bit on the thin side, but then young girls usually are.' Mandy pushed back her chair and surveyed Jane analytically. 'Even though you're skinny, you've got nice legs by the look of your ankles. Your hair – well you'll need a wig, but we've plenty of those in props and costume you can borrow. Bit of make-up, especially rouge and shadow to plump out your cheeks. A couple of plasters to push up those small tits of yours, you'd probably look all right. What do you think, Judy?'

'I think with a bit of coaching, may be you're right.'

'I have to go.' Jane rose quickly from the table, sending her cup flying across the carpet with the edge of Phyllis's coat.

'We're going back for another session next week. Why don't you come with us? There'll be nothing lost if he doesn't want you. And a tenner's not to be sneezed at,' Mandy added tactfully, knowing Jane was paid a fraction of the Revue girls' wages. 'It'll keep you in cologne and stockings for a year if nothing else. Think about it.'

'I will,' Jane said automatically as she walked towards the front door. Ten pounds! What an opening balance for the Post Office account she'd dreamed of owning. Security. Real security. No one would be able to return her to the workhouse once she had that kind of money. It was lodging money for half a year, and you'd have to have something really wrong with you if you couldn't find work in six months of trying.

Feet sinking into thick carpet, head swimming with intoxicating images of pound notes, and surreal impressions of the gold and gilt ornaments and mirrors of the first hotel she'd ever been into, Jane made her way back to the market.

'I like punctuality in a girl,' Wilf said as she lifted the flap and walked behind the stall. 'Now let's see how good a salesgirl you are. That's Mrs Jones from Top Road on her way over. The insurance money from her mother's burial policy is burning a hole in her pocket. You sell her a going-out outfit as well as a mourning suit and I'll knock the price of the hat you're wearing, off what you owe me.'

Jane was tired but happy as she left the stall at ten minutes to four for the Town Hall. Mrs Jones from Top Road had been easy to persuade. She'd not only sold her the mourning clothes but two 'chapel' suits and a summer dress. A little flattery about colour suiting complexion here, a few words about quality there. Nothing too drastic, or different from the methods she'd employed in the Children's Homes to avoid a row or a slap.

'You're looking pretty tonight, ma'am. Such lovely colour in your cheeks.' She hadn't always had to lie either. A couple of glasses of sherry in the evening was all that was needed to turn most of staff's noses as red as Rudolf's.

'Well, have you decided?'

Mandy and Judy stood behind her.

'Yes,' she said boldly. After all, hadn't she told Phyllis last night that she'd play in Revue if she could for six pounds a week? Ten pounds for an afternoon seemed far more, for far less effort and embarrassment.

'Tell you what,' Mandy whispered. 'Saturday. Between the matinée and the first show, come to our dressing room. We'll see what we can do to tranform you into a star turn.'

'And in the meantime eat as much as you can,' Judy advised. 'Especially cream, milk and butter. It puts inches on where men like to see them.'

Eddie walked slowly up the Graig hill. Not because he was tired. Anything but. Charlie was a good man to work for, easygoing as long as the work was done and the shop and kitchens kept spotless. And although the job involved a lot of physical work, humping, carrying, loading and unloading, it wasn't taxing, not to him. Besides days in the shop were generally shorter than those in the market. Cooked meats spoiled easily, and Charlie preferred to understock, which inevitably meant closing when the last slices and scraps were sold out of the door. Poor William was still working, setting up the Market stall for the morning, but Eddie didn't feel too sorry for his cousin. Next week it would be his turn to work late.

He had a whole evening free and enough energy left to go down the gym and fight half a dozen sparring matches, but for once boxing wasn't on his mind. Jenny was. Charlie'd paid him a small bonus for picking up three new customers on the meat round, and this week he'd promised to put his, and his cousin Will's wages up from seventeen and six to a pound a week. Eddie knew William: his pay rise would be swallowed up in the tills of the town's pubs. But he was determined his wouldn't.

After work he'd changed out of his working clothes in Charlie and Alma's small bathroom above the shop. Polished his shoes with his handkerchief, slicked his hair back with a 'borrowed' fingerful of Charlie's hair pomade and bought a sixpenny box of chocolates from the sweet shop next to the New Theatre which was run by Diana's boss Wyn Rees. He couldn't stand Wyn, and was usually the first to apply the name of 'queer' to the man. But then, when it came to sweet shops, Wyn's was the only one he could think of where his purchase would pass without comment. If he'd stopped off in the High Street shop run by Diana, he'd face an inquisition, and later, after Diana had imparted the knowledge to the entire family, endless teasing from Will. Ronconi's café wouldn't be any better; all the boys who couldn't afford a pint, and most of the girls from the Graig, congregated there after work on a week night.

He stopped opposite Griffiths' shop on the corner of Factory Lane and looked through the window. It had been much easier in the winter, when the lamps were lit, to see who was serving. Deciding it wouldn't do any harm to go in, even if he found Harry Griffiths behind the counter, he walked across the road.

The shop was teeming with urchins, all with requests for last-minute tea items to be added to their mother's tab. Jenny was rushed off her feet, slicing the thinnest possible slivers of brawn, cutting pieces of cheese that could be more accurately called slice than wedge, fishing pickled onions out of an enormous jar and slipping them into cones of greaseproof paper. He hung back, pushing a child behind him to the front of the queue, while apparently studying the arrangement of cigars and matches laid out on the top shelf.

'Tell your mam, that's all we have,' Jenny said to a small girl as she tucked a bundle of newspaper-wrapped cabbage under her arm. 'It's a small one, but she can have it for twopence. Don't forget to tell her the price now.'

'I won't. It's twopence, Jenny. Ta.' She bounced out, her string-tied pigtails jerking comically behind her as she skipped past the shop window.

'Eddie?' Jenny's enormous blue eyes finally looked at him and his knees turned to jelly.

'Five Woodbines and a box of matches, please.' He pushed a shilling across the counter. She reached up to the top shelf. Lost in admiration for her slim waist and the full curve of her breasts beneath the pinafore she was wearing, he forgot to pull out the box of chocolates he'd hidden beneath his jacket until she faced him again.

'That'll be . . .'

'I bought them for you.'

'For me, how kind.'

'I had a stroke of luck today. A pay rise. I hoped, well . . . ' the Eddie who didn't think twice about facing any opponent in the ring, shuffled awkwardly from one foot to the other. ' . . . I hoped you might come out with me to celebrate. I know we're too late for the pictures, or the musical that's on in the New Theatre, but we could go for a walk, or to one of the cafés.'

Jenny looked up at the clock. 'Second house in the Town Hall doesn't start until eight o'clock.'

If it had been one of the boys who'd suggested the outing Eddie'd have taken him up on the offer like a shot, although he'd already sat through the opening night on the free tickets Haydn had dispensed. But despite the daring reference he'd made to the show in the shop yesterday, he had no intention of sitting through it again with any girl, especially Jenny.

'You know what's playing there?'

'Course I do, we talked about it yesterday.'

'Only men go there. No decent girl would want to go near the place.'

'I would. But tell you what, to spare your blushes I'll borrow my dad's suit and cap. He won't miss them. Come on Eddie,' she wheedled. 'I'll turn myself into a passable boy and it would be fun.'

'We wouldn't be back until after eleven,' he said, remembering the lecture she'd given him about not being allowed out late.

'It wouldn't matter, not tonight. My mother's visiting my aunt; she's ill, so my mother's staying over. My father's taking over the shop, but he's always in the Morning Star by half-past nine and never out of there before two in the morning. I'll tell him that you're taking me out. He'll trust me to be in before time, but he won't check. I can get his suit and cap now and leave them in the storeroom. I always go in and out that way. I'll change on my way out, hide my dress, and meet you outside the back door, at – shall we say half-past seven. We can walk down Albert Road rather than High Street, it's quieter, and by the time we come out of the theatre it will be dark, so even if we run into someone we know, they won't recognise me.'

'I don't know . . .'

'Oh come on, Eddie. Please.'

'What if someone recognises you inside the Town Hall?'

'Who, the vicar? He can hardly tell anyone he was there himself, can he? Besides, you know full well everyone will be too busy looking at the floor, terrified of being seen there by someone who knows them, to notice me.'

Eddie knew she was right. There wasn't a man in Pontypridd who would freely admit to his family that he'd been to the show, but that didn't alter the fact that yesterday's houses had both been packed and the show was three-quarters pre-booked for the run. A record for the Town Hall. And if Haydn was to be believed, the Saturday afternoon matinée was usually a 'special' for church and chapel ministers, council members and the crache of whatever town they were playing in.

'Will you take me?' she demanded, 'because if you won't, I'll find someone who will.'

The threat decided him. 'All right,' he conceded reluctantly.

'You'll pick me up then? In three-quarters of an hour, at the back entrance. I'll be waiting behind the storeroom door. Call out so I'll know it's you.'

'I'll whistle.'

He opened the shop door; the bell clanged overhead.

'Oh, and Eddie?'

He turned, wondering what was coming next.

'Thanks for the chocolates,' she smiled.

Chapter Eight

'Two please.'

'We've only got back circle left.' Mrs Arkwright who manned the ticket booth squinted through the glass, sizing up Eddie's companion. Jenny had purloined the smallest of her father's suits. It had been his wedding suit, and was hopelessly outdated even by Pontypridd standards where one suit frequently had to last a man a lifetime. Neither did it fit very well. With the belt hooked on a new hole she'd made, the trousers still hung ridiculously loose and would have fallen down around her ankles if it hadn't been for the braces that pulled the waist half-way up her chest. The jacket was ludicrously wide shouldered on her slender frame, and the cap she'd pulled down over the nape of her neck to conceal the bump of her long hair, and low at the front to cover her eyes, only succeeded in making her look bizarre and shifty.

'Your friend there?'

'My cousin,' Eddie explained.

'Whoever he is. Aren't his clothes a bit big for him.'

'You know how it is in the old Town Hall, you buy the best you can get for your money. Particularly if you're a bloke.'

'Suppose you're right.' Mrs Arkwright continued to eye Jenny suspiciously as she took Eddie's money. 'How old is he?'

'Twenty-one. Same as me.'

'And I'm sweet sixteen.' She didn't say any more for a moment, then, just as Eddie was ready to take Jenny by the hand and run, she handed him his change and the tickets. 'Go on, off with the pair of you, but close your friend's eyes when it gets naughty. Next!'

Without thinking, Eddie took Jenny's hand and led her up the stairs to the circle. A piercing wolf whistle followed by the cry 'Watch out, queers about!' stopped him in his tracks.

Jenny pulled her hand out of his. 'You might be my cousin but you're not my keeper,' she complained in an astoundingly deep voice.

He continued to walk alongside her in silence. An usherette offered Eddie a programme. He shook his head, hoping she wasn't the one Phyllis had taken in as a lodger and he hadn't as yet met. This one looked older than the young girl Phyllis had described. With any luck, the lodger would be working safely out of his and Jenny's way, downstairs. They were shown to their seats. They weren't good: the top right-hand corner of the last row offered limited vision of the right-hand side of the stage, but on the plus side he and Jenny weren't likely to attract any more attention.

'At least we can put our seats up and sit on the edge without anyone behind us complaining,' Jenny whispered.

'Ssh!' He glanced around to see if anyone was watching them, hoping that none of the boys from the gym had seen him holding Jenny's hand as they'd walked up the stairs. He knew exactly how much stick queers like Wyn Rees got, and he could well do without it.

'I'll walk you home tonight, Jane. Wait for me by the kiosk if I'm late.'

'Thank you, but there's no need,' Jane replied stiffly as she dumped her half-empty tray on the sweet counter.

'No trouble at all seeing as how I'm going that way anyhow, besides, I don't think any girl should walk up the Graig hill alone at that hour. You never know who's about.'

'I managed perfectly well last night.'

'Last night I didn't know you were going my way, and it would be foolish of us not to take the opportunity to get to know one another, since we're living under the same roof.' While Jane was searching for an excuse, he ended the conversation: 'Here then, as soon as you're through?'

'Now that's what I call quick work, Jane,' Ann congratulated her as Haydn returned to the dressing-room corridor. 'Tell me what it is you've got, and where I can get some of the same. I'd give three years of my life to have Haydn Powell walk me home. One night would be all I'd need to create enough passion-filled memories to warm my old age. God only knows I was too damned scared of the minister and the deacons to do anything when I was young that's worth looking back on now.'

'It's not like that at all,' Jane remonstrated, wishing she hadn't allowed Haydn to bulldoze her. 'I lodge in his father's house, that's all.'

'You lodge in Haydn Powell's house?' Avril's eyes gleamed as she unclipped her money bag from her belt. 'Now I know who to go to when I want to hear the latest gossip.'

'I hardly see him. He gets up after I leave the house.'

'But I bet you eat supper together. No one I know outside of theatre people eat at the funny hours we do.'

'Was everyone else in bed when he came in? Did you have him all to yourself? What *did* you talk about? Come on, Jane tell Auntie Avril and Auntie Ann all.'

'His . . .' Jane hesitated for a moment, wondering how to describe Phyllis. 'His stepmother was with us,' she said finally.

'Bad luck.'

'Good luck, I call it.' Avril opened the office door and tipped the contents of her leather bag on to the desk. 'Otherwise Jane might have been in dire danger of becoming one more nick on Haydn Powell's pole of conquests. And I can't see any girl with a brain in her head wishing that on herself.'

Squirming with embarrassment, Eddie sank lower and lower in his seat, looking neither left nor right, rarely at the stage and never at Jenny. She, on the other hand, sat perched on the edge of her seat, her eyes focused on the static nudes. She studied their curves, comparing them to what she saw reflected in her dressing-table mirror when she undressed for bed. She tried to read the expression in Haydn's eyes, listen to the inflection he put into the lyrics as he serenaded each girl in turn. He seemed so sophisticated, so debonair, and so very different from the Pontypridd Haydn she had gone out with. She no longer knew him well enough to draw any conclusions from his stage performance, other than it was totally and utterly professional and – to her eyes and ears – mesmerising.

There were so many questions she would have liked to ask Haydn. Was he going out with one of the girls on stage? Had he fallen in love since he'd left Pontypridd – seriously enough to talk about marriage, the way he had once done with her? Had he forgotten her and what they'd meant to one another? Was he still angry because she'd allowed Eddie to take her home after they'd had that final, bitter, stupid quarrel? And above all, the one obsessive preoccupation that haunted her day and night dreams, was there a chance – any chance at all – that he might take her back? Would he ever walk into the shop again with that old, loving smile on his lips, the smile he'd kept just for her, only eight short months ago?

Eddie bought Jenny an orange juice and ice cream in the interval. A small pang of guilt beset her as he handed them over. A six-penny box of chocolates and now these, as well as the tickets. He was spending a fortune on her. She'd try to make a point of making it up to him with a ham supper – but just a supper, nothing else. While she waited for the lights to dim and the orchestra to start playing again, she stole a glance at him. He was very good-looking, there was no denying it, but to her eyes he could never be as good-looking as Haydn. How could he, with a nose pushed slightly out of shape as the result of too many sparring matches? There was also a dark bruise high on his cheekbone that had nothing to do with the shadows in the darkened theatre. She'd noticed it in the shop.

Boxing, always boxing, that was Eddie; all the old, retired

fighters who bought their tobacco in her father's shop prophesied a real future for Eddie Powell. The next Jimmy Wilde they called him. She remembered Peg-Leg Dean's words:

'I knew the minute I saw him in that booth, he'd go all the way to the top. Mark my words, he'll be hanging a Lonsdale belt on his wall. You'll see if I'm not right. He'll have everything money can buy, just like my brother did. The cars, the best hotels, the best food, women queuing up to do a bit more than just shake his hand, the best of everything.'

Eddie, as dark as Haydn was fair. Quieter, more sullen, but, as she'd found out in a single fleeting moment of passionate ecstasy that had led to bitter feelings of guilt, remorse and misery, a savage and unrestrained lover in private. Eddie – her Eddie. If she wanted him, and couldn't get Haydn, he could be hers.

The thought lingered, worming away like a maggot in an apple. Of course she was going to get Haydn back, but it wouldn't hurt to hold Eddie in reserve. Someone she could turn to as a last resort. That way if she couldn't have Haydn as a husband, she could have him as the next best thing, a brother-in-law. Then he'd never be able to get away from her, not completely. After all, a man could leave a wife, but someone like Haydn would never leave a brother – and if that brother was besotted with a beloved wife . . .

'You haven't said a word to me for the last two hours.'

'You want me to say something?'

'Thank you for coming out with me, Jenny. It was a lovely evening. I enjoyed it.'

'I didn't,' he contradicted her sullenly, preoccupied by the wolf whistles that had followed them when he had caught hold of her hand.

'Well I had a good time. So thank you very much, Eddie.' She looked at his face, dark and angry in the lamplight.

They'd walked up the Graig hill side by side, both of them keeping their hands in their trouser pockets, a foot of empty space between them that Eddie had been careful to maintain. Every time she'd tried to narrow the gap he had moved away, even when it meant he had to walk in the gutter.

They reached the corner of Llantrisant Road and Factory Lane.

'Home,' she murmured.

'And before eleven.'

'We could have gone for a cup of tea.'

'With you looking like that?'

'I didn't realise you were ashamed of being seen with me,' She mocked. She crossed the road and he followed, still careful to maintain his distance. She put her hand on the latch. Eddie looked around. The hill was deserted.

'I made some sandwiches. You coming in to eat them?'

'Just for a minute.'

She disappeared through the high door set in the eight-foot wall. After one more quick check to reassure himself that no one was watching, he followed, closing the yard door behind him.

Jenny faced him, her back against the storeroom door, the cap pulled from her head, her long plait hanging over her shoulder.

'Now that I'm not a boy any more, you could kiss me.' He'd earned a kiss, but this time she was determined to keep control, and make sure it *was* just one kiss.

Eddie need no second bidding, with the images of the girls he'd seen on stage fresh in his mind. Setting his hands on her shoulders he pressed his body against hers. She crashed backwards, hitting her spine painfully on the knob of the door. Her cry was smothered as his mouth closed over hers. He seemed to be drawing breath from her body. She fought an onset of giddiness that threatened to engulf her senses, but everything – the yard, the star-strewn night sky, Eddie – faded. A cat screeched in the street behind them. She registered the noise, and as she did so she realised that Eddie had unfastened the buttons on her jacket and was plundering her body with his hands. Weak and lightheaded, she wrapped her arms around his neck and clung to him, immobilising his caresses with the weight of her body.

'I remember being here once before,' he mumbled hoarsely.

'So do I, and it's not going to end the same way. You can eat your sandwich and go.' She reached behind her and opened the stockroom door. They tumbled into the small, stuffy room that smelled of dust and stale vegetables. He pushed her down on to the sacks of swedes, potatoes and turnips.

'No,' she thrust him away, trying to conjure an image of Haydn to mind. She was using Eddie to get to Haydn. That was all. Using him ... 'I'm not that kind of girl,' she pronounced vehemently as he drew close to her again.'

'What kind of girl?' He bent over her.

'The kind I was once before, when you turned my head.'

'Jenny,' he nuzzled the nape of her neck. 'I like you. You know I do.'

'We have to take things more slowly.'

'Why?'

'Because ...' she tried to think, but his lovemaking had destroyed her capability for coherent reasoning. She almost blurted out that she needed time to make Haydn fall in love with her all over again, before another, more trite phrase came to mind: 'Because I think we should get to know each other better before we repeat what happened last time.'

'You enjoyed it as much as I did.'

'The one thing a girl wants from a boy is respect. You're treating me like you would a girl you picked up in station yard.'

'What do you know about station yard?'

'I've got eyes in my head like everyone else.'

'As long as you haven't worked there,' he baited.

'Eddie Powell, I've told you I'm not that kind of a girl. I never was until I met you.'

'I know,' he answered in a gentler tone. He kissed her again, tenderly and less urgently than before, then moved away. When she opened her eyes, the latch was closed. He had gone. Locking both the door that led into the yard and the door into the shop she turned on the light and retrieved her dress from behind a box of tinned sardines. Hoping her father hadn't missed his suit, shirt or tie, she took off the jacket. Shivering, she looked down. If Eddie Powell had been there, boxer or no boxer, she would have punched him. Every button on the front of the shirt and trousers had been unfastened. Her breasts were bare, the restraining band of crêpe bandage she had wound around them pulled down to her waist, and he'd succeeded in doing all of it without her feeling a thing. What was it about Eddie Powell? She didn't love him. Yet every time she allowed him near her, she was no more capable of resisting his lovemaking than she would have been Haydn's.

'Want chips?'

'No.'

'I'll pay.'

'It's still no. Phyllis will have a meal ready, and if we stuff ourselves with chips we won't be able to eat it.'

'Yes we will. I'm hungry enough to eat an ox, and I bet you are too. These hours are real killers when it come to eating. Come on, truth now, when was your last meal?'

'Dinner time.' She tried not to think of the cucumber sandwiches. She'd only allowed herself one: it had been tiny and a *very* long time ago.

'Come on, a couple of pennyworth of chips,' Haydn coaxed. 'Can't you smell them?'

She could. She'd never eaten chips from a fish shop, but she'd often joined the other children from the orphanage when they'd pressed their noses against the window of the fish and chip shop in Church Village. The smell had always warmed her and never failed to make her mouth water. Just the thought of piping hot chips liberally sprinkled with salt and vinegar, the way she'd seen, decided the matter.

'All right. But only if you let me pay for yours next week.'

'You strapped for cash? But of course, how stupid of me, you must be. Working a week in hand is a real killer, isn't it?'

'Yes,' she agreed shortly.

'And I don't suppose your people could give you much to tide you over?'

'Nothing.'

'So that's why Phyllis took you in.'

'It's not charity. I'll pay back every penny before I move on.'

'Hey.' He held up his hands as though he were warding off blows. 'Did I say you wouldn't?'

'No, but I can see what you're thinking. It's all too easy for people to assume that a girl on her own is out for everything she can get.'

'Sounds like you've been listening to Ponty people talking about the girls in the show.' He turned the corner and walked down Leyshon Street towards Fred's fish and chip shop. 'Two threepennyworth of chips, please, Fred!' he shouted as he walked through the door.

'Only just caught me, Haydn. I was ready to close up.' Fred picked up an iron shovel and pushed it into the warm cabinet of cooked chips. 'Working hard?' Fred winked suggestively, not seeing Jane behind Haydn.

'You know how it is. Nose to the grindstone. Nothing but singing, champagne, beautiful girls and the high life.'

'If you ever want to unload your work troubles, remember your old mates.'

'I'll bear that in mind but for the moment I'll struggle on.'

'Salt and vinegar?' Fred held up a giant battered tin salt cellar.

'Jane?' Haydn looked down at the girl. She really was preposterously small, more like a child than a grown woman.

'Please.'

'Sorry if I said anything to offend you, Miss,' Fred apologised. 'I didn't realise Haydn had a young lady with him.'

'This is Jane, our new lodger,' Haydn introduced her, hoping to scotch any rumours of romance before they started. He was prepared to cope with the odd raised eyebrow over his relationship with Rusty, or Babs, but not the small-town gossip that would ensue if he was suspected of courting a 'decent' girl.'

'Pleased to me you, Jane.'

Jane shook Fred's hand before taking the chips he handed her, and leaving the shop.'

'Best chips in the country.' Haydn blew on his fingers after trying to pick one up. 'I know, I've tried all the others.'

'It must be fun touring the country.'

'You think so? Different digs, different town every week. No one close to talk to . . .'

'Except the twenty-odd people in the show.'

'Even they change. One whiff of a better engagement in the offing, and all you see is the dust at their heels.'

'Is that what you would do?'

'I'm doing it. Leaving the Revue at the end of next week for Summer Variety. It's a simple case of self-preservation. The Revue only has two more weeks to run in the provinces before being disbanded, and the Variety's booked in the Town Hall for a season.'

'And if something better than the Summer Variety comes up?'

'I'll be gone the minute they can replace me.' He looked across at her. She'd only eaten one or two of her chips, while there was nothing but hard crumbs left in his paper. He screwed it into a ball, and lifting the lid of a dustbin pushed it in. 'One word about these to Phyllis, or one mouthful of the meal she's cooked left on your plate and I'll brain you.'

'I'm not a tattle-tell.'

'You're not?'

They were under the lamp that burned outside the Graig Hotel. Something in the tone of his voice made her look up. She was glad she did. The expression on his face made her remember the story she'd told Phyllis about Haydn and Rusty last night, before he'd walked into the kitchen and she'd realised he was Evan's son.

'So that's why you wanted to walk me home!' she retorted angrily, suspicion clearing her mind. 'To ask me not to carry any more theatre gossip back to your family.'

'It might help to make my stay in Pontypridd run a little more smoothly.'

She wrapped her chips in the newspaper that Fred had left open so she could dip into them as she walked. 'I suppose Phyllis said something to you about cavorting with naked girls in your dressing room.'

'She mentioned that she hoped I knew what I was doing, so I

guessed that you'd told her about Rusty. There's no point in you upsetting the family over nothing.'

'Nothing! And I suppose that kiss you gave Mandy tonight when you came off stage and she was waiting in the wings, was nothing either?'

'Theatre people kiss and hug each other all the time, it doesn't mean a thing. And even if it did, what are you getting so worked up about? What I do is my affair and none of yours.'

'I never said it was. I didn't even know you were related to Evan when I told Phyllis about you and Rusty last night. If I had, I wouldn't have said a word. And I'll tell you something else for nothing, Haydn Powell. I'm not a gossip. And the last thing I want is to be associated with you, lest I get mistaken for one of your . . . your . . . ' she remembered reading *The Arabian Nights* and found the word she was searching for. ' . . . concubines. And if you thought you could buy me off with a walk home and a few pennyworth of chips, you have another thing coming. Keep your damned chips.' She dumped them in his hands. 'And in future I'll walk myself home.' Striding ahead, she stepped into a puddle of water.

Haydn watched her go, shaking his head and cursing Phyllis for bringing a girl into the house who worked in the Town Hall and had a mouth he couldn't control.

'Here's everyone's mending.' Jane handed the parcel to Mandy, hoping she would do the same as she had done the rest of the week and pay the whole bill, the other girls as well as her own. Today's was half a crown. Once the rest of the chorus girls had seen the neat stitching on Mandy's blouse they had queued up to hand over their own chemises, petticoats and fine lingerie.

'Thanks, you're a gem.' Mandy opened her bag and took out her purse. Reading the label, she handed over two shillings and sixpence. 'You haven't forgotten about coming to the dressing room after the matinée, have you?'

'No,' Jane assured her, trying to keep her mind on the ten pounds she might earn, and not the prospect of taking her clothes off in front of a male photographer.

'I hate bloody matinées!' Judy complained as, cigarette in mouth, she left the dressing room in search of a light. 'Locked up here all day with no one to talk to except Billy. Nothing to do except listen to Haydn and Rusty banging away through the wall. Nothing decent to eat except chocolate bars and cold sandwiches . . .'

'There's a shop down the road that sells hot pasties. I could get you one after the first show,' Jane offered.

'Now, that's an idea. I'll give you the money.'

'I'll get it with this,' Jane held up the money Mandy had just given her. 'You can pay me when I bring it.'

'Bring one for me too,' Mandy asked. 'And I bet the others will want some too.'

'I'll come back afterwards to see how many you want.' Slipping the money into her pocket Jane went to the manager's office, sealed it into an envelope and put it in his safe lest it get mixed up with her tray money.

'We're going to be bored rigid this afternoon,' Avril grumbled. 'No one will risk being seen by their neighbours coming to a show like this in broad daylight.'

'The men of Pontypridd might give us a wide berth,' Ann agreed, 'but those who live further afield won't. We'll be inundated with boys from the top end of the valleys, and Abercynon and Aberdare. The trains will be fuller today than they are for a rugby match.'

Ann's prediction proved correct. As soon as the doors opened, the by now familiar masculine horde surged up the stairs. 'Quick,' Ann sniggered as one man glanced over his shoulder, 'before you're seen by a scandalmonger who'll tell the wife.'

Jane had no time to think about the transformation Mandy and Judy were going to effect on her between the shows. The interval had to be extended by ten minutes for all the usherettes to refill their trays, an unheard-of phenomenon in a matinée. At the end of the performance the hall resounded with claps, cheers, wolf whistles and demands for encores, but Haydn wasn't egotistical enough to think the audience wanted to see or hear any more from him. He retired gracefully after the final curtain, leaving the girls alone on stage to stand through two more curtain calls.

The increase in ice-cream and sweet sales brought a corresponding swell in rubbish. Jane filled a sack entirely by herself before she was finally able to take her break.

'An hour before we're on duty again,' Avril sighed wearily, pushing a cigarette into her mouth as she sank down on a bar stool. 'Mine's an orange juice, Des.'

'I'll have mine later please, Des, I promised to get the girls hot pasties from Charlie's meat shop.'

'That sounds a good idea, Jane, get me one too.' Avril pulled her purse from her pocket.

'And me,' Ann and Des chimed together.

Jane ran down to the manager's office to get her half-crown.

'We want twenty,' Mandy called out as Jane tried to force her way to the dressing rooms through the milling crowd of half-dressed girls.

'I haven't enough money for that many.'

'How much are they each.'

'Twopence halfpenny,' Jane said, forgetting the discount the boy had offered her for bulk.

'Here's ten bob, we'll square up when you come back.'

Even the air in Saturday's crowded Market Square felt clean and invigorating after the stuffy confines of the Town Hall. Jane suddenly realised just how little time she'd spent outside since she'd left the workhouse. There, she'd seemed to spend every waking minute when she wasn't eating, scrubbing down the outside steps, and yards. And because she'd worked through the height of the winter, the skin on her hands and face had become red and roughened, and her feet plastered with chilblains. Now, in warm summer, she spent her days cooped up in the artificial darkness of the Town Hall. She looked up at the clear blue sky. Whoever was organising her life should try to do better.

Pushing her way through the crowds, she shivered in her thin, short-sleeved dress. Although the air was warm, it was colder than the moist, steamy atmosphere of the theatre. Next week, if the sewing kept coming in, she resolved to ask Wilf Horton to look out for a coat for her. She hadn't taken Phyllis's today, because Phyllis needed it to go shopping.

There was a long queue in Charlie's shop. The good-looking dark boy who'd given her the misshapen pasty was serving alongside an attractive auburn-haired woman. By giving up her place to an old woman, she managed to be served by him again.

'Twenty-three pasties please.'

'You must have liked the last one.'

'I did, thanks.'

'And it looks as though you're doing better than you were?'

'I can't complain.'

The auburn-haired woman looked at him. He picked up a pair of tongs and began to pile warm pasties into brown paper bags.

'Twenty-three pasties will cost you four shillings and three pence halfpenny. Twenty four, four shillings. Cheaper by the dozen, remember.'

'In that case I'll have two dozen, please.' She did some more mental arithmetic. Twopence each when bought in dozens, two pence halfpenny when bought singly. She'd made sixpence on the first dozen, threepence halfpenny on the eleven and had a free one thrown in for herself into the bargain. It might be worth trying to make the pasty trip a regular run. It was certainly a quicker and easier way of making money than sewing.

The boy bagged the last of the pasties and handed them to her. 'Careful now, they're hot,' he warned as he took the ten-shilling note.

'I'll be careful.' She waited for her change.

'You working round here then?'

'Not too far away.'

'Eddie, there's customers waiting,' his fellow assistant reprimanded.

'Two slices of pickled tongue, cut extra thin mind,' A woman wearing a hat with a glass-eyed bird balanced precariously on the crown, ordered brusquely, clearly none too pleased at being kept waiting while Eddie flirted.

'Right, soon as we finish these,' Mandy held up her pasty, 'we'll see what we can do with you.'

'I will be able to get the make-up off afterwards, won't I?' Jane asked, looking from Mandy's glossy, luridly painted face to Judy's.

'Of course.' Judy held up a jar of cold cream. 'All we have to do is plaster this over you.'

'I'll just take these pasties to the girls in the bar.'

Jane dashed into the corridor, straight into Haydn who was demonstrating a complicated dance step to Billy and four adoring chorus girls.

'Look it's easy. So easy, you don't need any formal dance training to follow it.' He sidestepped past Billy and the girls and took Jane's arm, sweeping her in front of him down the corridor.

'Let me go,' she hissed between clenched teeth, trying to hold on to the pasties and keep them from getting crushed at the same time.

'One thing you should know about me, I get upset when people don't like me,' he whispered into her ear.

'I couldn't give a damn.'

'Language! Struggle any more and people will think there is something going on between us. That's it,' he shouted in a louder voice for the benefit of the watching girls. 'One two three, one two three . . .'

'If I drop these pasties you're going to have to pay for them.'

'Take them off her, Billy, there's a good man while we show you how it's done.'

Billy grabbed the bag and Haydn locked his fingers firmly into Jane's. With Haydn gripping her hands and the girls cutting off her retreat, Jane had no choice but to go along with him.

'Right, look down,' he ordered, holding her out stiffly at arm's length, 'watch my feet and do everything I do. And a *one* and *two*,' Haydn's taps echoed on the floor of the corridor, Jane's soft-soled shuffle following one step behind.

'You know, that girl's definitely got something,' Billy commented thoughtfully, as Jane finally capitulated and began to copy Haydn's steps.

'She's certainly quicker and lighter on her feet than you, Billy,' Mandy laughed.

'Probably because she's got something more than sawdust between her ears,' Rusty commented nastily, frowning at the attention Haydn was paying to the usherette.

'Right foot forward, hands up, half-turn to the right, and another half-turn and another . . . That's it.' Haydn relinquished his grip on Jane's hands. 'And . . .'

'And now I've got to take these pasties to the bar.' Jane retrieved her bag from Billy, and dashed through the cordon of girls.

'Give the kid her due, she's actually got talent,' Billy said admiringly.

'But not stage presence,' Rusty declared flatly. 'She's too short and skinny, and that's before you look at her face.'

Haydn said nothing; he was too busy watching Jane's legs as she ran along the corridor away from him.

Chapter Nine

'You going out tonight, love?' Harry Griffiths asked his daughter as he dragged two boxes of tins into the shop ready to restock the shelves that had been emptied by Friday's wages and dole money.

'Not tonight, Dad. I was out last Tuesday, remember, and I've promised to go down the café tomorrow with the girls.'

'In that case you won't mind watching the shop for me?'

'Of course not. You off somewhere special?'

'Just picking your mother up from your Aunt Edna's. If I go over to Trallwn early I thought I might call in the Queen's.'

'For a game of cards?'

'I haven't had one in months.'

'I wouldn't mind if you did.'

'Don't you dare go saying anything to your mother.'

'As if I would,' she protested indignantly.

'I know you wouldn't say anything intentionally, love, but I also know what your mother can be like when she's ferreting around after my doings.' He ripped open the top of a box, took out a couple of tins and pushed them on to the shelf. 'Who did you go out with on Tuesday?'

'Diana Powell,' she lied.

'Then you must have been back early. I saw her passing the

windows of the Morning Star on Tuesday night ~~before~~ ten o'clock.'

'It was somewhere around then when I came home.'

He looked hard at her. 'Sure you've got the right Powell there?'

'There's nothing going on between me and any of the Powells, Dad.'

'Look, love, I'm not angry, just concerned. I know how upset you were when Haydn went away. I half expected him to turn up on the doorstep when he came back, I suppose I sort of hoped he would. You seemed happy enough together before you had that row.'

'I suppose we were,' she conceded.

'I know, it's none of my business.' He pushed the last of the tins from the box on to the shelf and punched the box flat. 'I'm just trying to tell you that if you need someone to talk to, I'm here. That's all, and if you need money for a new dress or anything else . . .'

'Now you're talking, Dad.' Of course! Why hadn't she thought of that? Haydn spent all his working time in the company of glamorous girls. Girls who travelled the country, and made enough money to patronise good shops like Gwilym Evans, and even expensive department stores like Howell's in Cardiff. She'd had hardly anything new in the last six months. 'There's a dress in the Co-op I've been fancying.'

'How much is it?'

She held her breath, hoping he was prepared to dig deep into his pockets. 'One pound seventeen and six.'

'Well seeing as how you're minding the shop for me tonight, here's five pounds.' He pulled a large white note out of his wallet. 'Call it an early birthday present. Go and spend it on some nice things for yourself.'

'Dad, you sure?' She took the note and untied her overall, giving him no time to reconsider.

'Just mind you're back here before five o'clock.' He smiled fondly at her as she went to the door. 'I'd like ten minutes to change before I go out.'

'I'll be here.'

She ran up the stairs, pulled her large felt tam on her head and picked up her short coat, checking the clock as she went out through the front door. She had two hours. Time enough to buy a new dress, some cologne, a little make-up – not too much or she'd end up looking cheap, like the chorus girls who occasionally called into Ronconi's for tea and cakes between shows at the New Theatre. Then after she'd bought everything, all she had to do was dress up and waylay Haydn as he walked home. It would be simple to inveigle him into the shop on some pretext or other. When they were alone she'd tell him she still loved him. It wouldn't be that difficult, not when she remembered all that they'd had to say to one another before last Christmas. And if Eddie had already boasted to his brother about his night out with her, she'd tell Haydn the truth. That she'd only gone out with Eddie twice in her life: the first time to hurt him after their argument and the second because it was the only way she could think of seeing him on stage.

'Hello, Jenny.'

'Hello, Mr Richards.' She caught sight of her reflection in the large mirror that flanked the porch of Richards' barber's shop. She didn't compare too badly with what she'd seen of the girls in the Revue, and once Haydn saw her in a new outfit, her hair freshly washed and waved, and smelling of the best scent she could find, he wouldn't be able to resist her. But first she had to buy the clothes and watch the hill. Sooner or later Haydn had to walk up it. It was simply a matter of time, patience – and waiting for the right moment.

'We'll lend you one of the long wigs from the costume department.' Mandy brushed bright green powder on to Jane's eyelids with the largest, bushiest paintbrush Jane had ever seen. 'I realised your hair was short, but I had no idea it was this short. Good job you have an usherette's band to hide it under. What on earth possessed you to cut it like this? There isn't even enough left to take an iron waver.'

'I burnt it, trying out a home perm.' Jane repeated a tale of woe she'd overheard one nurse tell another in the workhouse.

'Take a tip from me.' Mandy dropped the brush on top of a mess of squashed sweets and spilt powder on her shelf, and proceeded to attack Jane's eyebrows with tweezers. 'Never, never, touch a home permanent. If you can't afford to pay a good, and I mean a good, hairdresser to do your hair, then leave well alone. Tie it back, put it up, or cover it with a headscarf until you can beg, borrow or steal the money. What do you think?' She looked at Judy who'd been watching her efforts.

'More rouge, and lipstick?'

Mandy stood back. 'You're right.'

'Can't I see yet?' Jane pleaded. Mandy had turned the chair away from the only mirror in the room, so Jane couldn't watch what was being done to her.

'Absolutely not until I finish. Do me a favour, Judy, fetch one of the Lady Godiva wigs.'

'Black or blonde?'

'Blonde, oh please, blonde,' Jane begged.

'Blonde would be disastrous with your colouring,' Mandy declared decisively. 'You need blue or grey eyes and a fair skin to get away with blonde hair. Dark lashes, brows and eyes like yours are a sure-fire giveaway to the dyed blonde.'

Judy slipped on a wrap and left the dressing room. She was back a few minutes later with a waist-length black wig.

'And we don't even have to pin your hair back to go underneath it.' Mandy pulled it down over Jane's head.

'It's tight,' Jane complained.

'You have to suffer to be beautiful.'

'I'd have to do a lot more suffering to achieve that.'

'Turn around.'

Jane left the chair. She turned and stared at her reflection in disbelief. Her skin had the smooth, artificial, highly coloured porcelain quality of a mask. And the hair transformed her. It cascaded to her waist, soft, shimmering strands of fine silk that caught the electric light and reflected its glow, lightening her face, lending it an ethereal, translucent quality.

'We have to call the other girls in to see this.' Mandy put her hand on the doorknob.

'No,' Jane protested.

'Come on, sweetie, I'm proud of my handiwork. I want to show it off.'

'Someone might be around. The manager or one of the other usherettes.'

'She's right, Mandy, management might not like it.'

'Management might not, but I know someone who will. We called in the photographer's today to tell him you're coming. You haven't changed your mind?'

Jane hesitated.

'Ten pounds, remember,' Judy reminded.

'I said I'd go with you.'

'Right,' Judy pulled a cigarette from a packet in her skirt pocket and lit it with a small silver lighter. 'It's fixed for next Tuesday, two o'clock.'

'Where will I meet you?' Jane asked nervously.

'His place will probably be best. It's the photographic studio on top of the furniture shop. You know it?'

Jane shook her head.

'Why don't we meet in the New Inn again?' Mandy suggested, remembering her own first time in front of the camera. 'We could have coffee and sandwiches there, like we did the other day.'

'That would be nice,' Jane agreed in a small voice, despising herself for allowing Mandy to see just how uneasy she was.

'Don't worry, it's going to go fine. Just close your eyes and think of the money.' Judy patted her arm encouragingly.

'If we're going to send the usherette and not the glamour puss out on duty it's time to turn the princess back into Cinders and wipe this lot off your face.' Mandy picked up a wet sponge, the jar of cold cream and set to work.

'You sure you know what you're doing, introducing that girl to Merv?' Mandy asked after Jane had gone.

'You heard Merv, two pounds for every usable new girl we introduce him to, and four for a local within easy distance who'd be prepared to work for him again.'

'But Jane's such an innocent. An absolute baby.'

'An innocent baby who's greedy for money, just like the rest of us. Come on, Mandy, have you been in this business so long you don't remember what it was like to work forty-eight hours a week for ten bob? The girl's ambitious, and if she's got what it takes, she'd have found her own way in sooner or later. All we've done is give her a head start. And if the worst comes to the worst and Merv turns her down, there's no harm done.'

'Isn't there?'

'For pity's sake, the man's after photographs, not some of the other.'

'But both you and I know what photographs can lead to.'

'Only what you want them to lead to.'

'Sometimes I think all you care about is money and that bloody shop you want to open.'

'Too royal. I'm not getting any younger, and we all know what happens when the wrinkles come out and the firm bits start to sag. Make money while the men are smiling, that's my motto. And they don't smile at us for long in this business. Rusty told me London's coming next week to see the show.'

'They got new girls they want in?' Mandy asked anxiously. Judy and Rusty were the oldest in the Revue, but it wasn't always the oldest who were laid off. She'd put on a pound or two recently. She'd hoped no one had noticed, but what if Norman had, and he'd wired London?

'Who knows? All I know is last time they came up, Ginger was in and Alice was out on her ear.' Judy threw the dog end of her cigarette into the bin. Three years! If she could only last three more years, she'd have enough to buy not only a shop outright, but one in a good area of London with a flat above it. And then, God help anyone who tried to tell her that sinful employment leads to tragedy, as her vicar cousin had done the time she'd worn a fur coat into his church.

'I changed extra quick so I wouldn't keep you waiting.'

'And I told you last Tuesday that I wouldn't walk home with you again.'

'But I knew you didn't mean it.'

'I most certainly did.' Jane turned her back on Haydn as she removed her usherette's cap and pulled on her tam.

'I thought our dance changed everything.'

'It changed nothing.'

'My, but you can be hard-hearted towards a fellow when you want to be.'

'I don't like people who fool around and make fun of others.'

'Well if that's the way you want to play it, why didn't you say so?' He fell to his knees and laid his hand theatrically over his heart, much to the amusement of three passing chorus girls, who couldn't resist knocking on Rusty's door to get her out to witness the spectacle. She was just in time to hear Haydn declaiming in his best Shakespearean voice, 'I promise faithfully to be most serious, walk beside you without taking advantage . . . and . . .' he gazed at Jane with round, pathetic eyes 'most definitely not buy you any chips.'

'I'd still rather walk home alone.' Jane turned on her heel and followed the other usherettes out of the door, leaving Haydn to run after her.

Jenny had bought not one but two new dresses. She was wearing one now, a thin red crêpe, that was dressy enough to go out in, but not too dressy, she hoped, to wear in the shop without exciting comment from the customers or her mother. She should have closed and locked the front door hours ago. Her father wouldn't be pleased if he knew she'd stayed open this late, especially on a Saturday when there were likely to be drunks around. She looked up at the clock. Half-past ten. The people who'd been to the pictures had already walked up the hill. She could lock up now and keep a lookout, but when she saw Haydn she wanted their meeting to appear accidental, not contrived. She'd spent all evening planning it. She'd step outside, look up and down the street as though she were checking to see if there were any last-minute customers. He would see her, stop and say hello and then … then … then what? She could hardly invite him in straight away or blurt out that she loved him in the street. No of course not – he'd say more than 'hello.' He'd ask her how she'd been. She'd answer, 'Lonely.' Or would that be too obvious? Perhaps she should play hard to get. But what if that put him off, when she wanted him so much?

She looked across the road. The small grocer's had closed hours ago. Then she heard a laugh she'd recognise anywhere. Haydn was standing beneath the lamp in front of the shop, talking to a couple of boys from Leyshon Street. Standing next to him was the small, slight figure of a girl. A tiny, mousy girl wearing a plain black dress, without a single ornament. She wasn't even wearing a coat, although the night was cool enough for all the boys, including Haydn, to be wearing theirs. Jenny craned her neck trying to make out features that were half hidden below an enormous beret. But all she could see was a wide-lipped mouth and the tip of a nose. Whoever she was, she certainly wasn't any Powell Jenny knew of, and none of the Graig girls she could think of were quite that short.

One of the boys staggered slightly. He must have come from either the Graig or the Morning Star. Haydn moved protectively closer to the girl and put his hand on her elbow. She shrugged it off. Did that mean they'd quarrelled? Or weren't they going out together, after all? Well, even if she couldn't see Haydn alone, she could still make sure that he saw her. Patting her hair to make sure the waves she'd created were still in place, she left the counter and opened the door. The clang resounded across the road. She looked up and down the hill, but Haydn didn't turn her way, although he must have heard the shop bell. The other boys were looking at her, but not him. Trembling from a peculiar mix of emotions including anger, resentment and a sudden fear that it might be even more difficult than she'd thought to get Haydn back, she leaned through the open door and turned the sign from OPEN to CLOSED.

'You're working late tonight, Jenny.'

Glan Richards, a porter in the workhouse who lived next door to the Powells, had joined the group. Before she had a chance to answer him, the girl who was with Haydn took one look at Glan and ran off up the road. Jenny thought it strange, particularly when Haydn called after her and she kept on running.

'Thought you might want a packet of cigarettes, Glan,' she shouted, still hoping Haydn would turn and acknowledge her. He didn't. Instead he followed the girl. A dry, burning sensation choked her throat as she slammed the door and thrust the bolts home. Tomorrow! Haydn would be in Ronconi's with everyone else. He had to be. After all, where else could he go in Pontypridd on a Sunday evening?

The bells on St Catherine's church were called the faithful to morning service when Haydn turned up on the doorstep of Babs Bradley's digs. She'd been looking out for him for half an hour although she would sooner have forgone the outing than admitted it.

'Where we going, then?' she asked, keeping him waiting as she pinned on her hat and pulled on her gloves.

'The park?' Haydn suggested. 'We have an exceptionally good park here in Pontypridd.'

'Really?'

'Don't let the slag heaps fool you. There's some beautiful countryside around here. When you're in a more amenable mood I'll show you a lake where you can swim.'

'What's to say that I'll ever be in a more amenable mood with you than I am now?'

'No girl can resist my charm for long.'

'Really?'

'Really.' Irked by her theatrical airs and graces, he mimicked her cockney accent. 'But then, even if by some miracle you were in a loving and adoring mood, today wouldn't be a good day to go. Every child on the Graig congregates around Shoni's pond on a Sunday afternoon at this time of year to catch young frogs and baby minnows.'

She wrinkled her nose as she closed the door behind them. 'What do they do with them?'

'Fry them in dripping.'

'You're teasing me.'

'Would I do that?'

'Yes.'

'On my word of honour,' he said with a straight face as they walked along Broadway towards Taff Street and the park.

'You're pulling my leg.'

'If you come to the theatre early next Wednesday, I'll take you to the food market before we start rehearsing. Show you our laver bread. It's black and sticky, and made from the most delicious seaweed. Goes down a treat fried with bacon and cockles.'

'Now I know you're lying.'

'I'm trying to give you a lesson in Welsh delicacies, woman. And if there's a better topping for bacon, cockles and laver bread than fried leggy tadpoles, I haven't found it.'

Taking her arm he led her down the side of Woolworth's, past the Park Cinema and over the bridge into the park.

'This is lovely. All this greenery, you'd never guess we were in the middle of town.'

'What did I tell you?'

They turned right, past a covered seating area and flowerbeds, brilliant with roses and geraniums, past a lido and through a children's playground.

'You used to play here when you were little?'

'When I wasn't kidnapping little girls and having my evil way with them. Come on, I'll show you some of my secret places.'

'I want to go over to that wall. Look, there's someone walking down behind it.'

'Oh that. That's nothing.'

'It has to be something.'

'Just a sunken garden.'

'Oh do let's look. Do . . .'

She clattered off, tottering on her ridiculously high heels and leaving him no other option but to follow. When he caught up with her she was standing on a crazy-paved stone platform which had steps leading down either side. It looked over a heart-shaped sunken garden set with raised flowerbeds that bloomed in dazzling blazes of colour several feet below ground level. Benches were set in recesses built into the walls at intervals, most of them occupied by middle-aged women dressed in black.

'Why are they sitting there?' Babs demanded in a shrill voice.

'This park is a Memorial Park to the dead of the last war,' he said flatly hoping to shame her into leaving.

'The war to end all wars?'

'So they said until the newspapers started telling us that another's going to start any day now.'

'Three of my dad's brothers never came back from France,' she spoke in the strained, reverential tone her father had always adopted when talking of his dead kin and comrades.

'Neither did my father's brother or half the young men from Ponty. This park was bought and planted with money raised by public subscription. Just about everyone gave something.'

'And this garden?'

'Is somewhere where people can sit in silence and mourn the ones who never came home, not even in a coffin.'

He left, wishing he'd never brought Babs to the park, or at least that he'd walked off in the opposite direction when she'd spotted the sunken garden. She looked as inappropriate in that sacred spot, with her bright red suit, blue blouse, painted face and nails, as a tart in a convent.

'You cross with me?' she asked breathlessly when she finally caught up with him.

'No. Over there, as you can see, are the tennis courts where the sons and daughters of the idle crache play, but if we go down here to the left, we end up in a wild, wooded area that leads down to the river. Not many people walk this way.'

'Is that why you want to walk here? Because you're ashamed to be seen with me?'

'Hardly, when I've booked a table in the New Inn for lunch. You can't get any more public in this town than that. It's just that after half a season spent apart I thought we should take time to get to know one another again. Preferably in private.'

She'd made him angry. She looked and acted like she didn't have a brain in her head, but she exuded a blatant, arousing sexuality he found irresistible after a week of sleeping alone. One brief session with her, and others with Rusty in his dressing room between shows, were no substitute for the shared bed and sex on tap he'd enjoyed with Babs in Brighton, and Rusty in Finchley.

'Supposing I don't want to get to know you again?' she goaded him.

'Oh, but you do.' He kissed her lips.

'Now you've got lipstick all over you. Here.' She dabbed ineffectually at his mouth with a scrap of lace.

'What say you, we retreat into those bushes and put some more on.'

'Haydn, you're always so . . .'

'Wonderful?' He fought his way through the undergrowth and gained access to the secluded copse he'd had his eye on.

'No . . . so like nothing ever matters to you. Especially me.'

He took off his mackintosh, and spread it on the ground. 'I assure you, madam, after a good time, you're the most important thing in the world to me.' He picked a daisy and solemnly presented it to her.

'Really?'

He was finding it hard to keep up the jocular style he habitually adopted in the theatre, after looking down on the sunken garden. He should never have led her anywhere near the place. It had been special to him since the day his father had taken him there and explained why it had been built, and how it was the only grave his Auntie Megan had for her husband. And that whenever any of the grown-ups in the family wanted to mourn his brother William, that was where they went.

'Ooh, you looked quite nasty then. What were you thinking about?'

'You,' he lied, suppressing his mood. 'Come here woman.'

'Why, so you can have your wicked way with me?' She batted

her eyelashes. He was left with the uncomfortable feeling that they were playing out the leading roles in a Victorian melodrama. He was growing tired of women who never stopped acting, on and off stage. For an instant, a brief instant, he almost walked away, then he noticed the swell of her breasts beneath her thin jacket, and the fullness of her legs, clearly outlined beneath her tight skirt. Grabbing her hand he pulled her down beside him.

'Ow!' she shrieked rubbing her bottom.

'I'll give you a lot more to complain about in a minute.' Pushing her down on the ground he kissed her firmly, and thoroughly.

'Is this the sort of rehearsing you've been doing with Helen?'

'Who's Helen?'

'You know.'

'Not when I'm with you.'

'Haydn, when are we going to eat?'

'When we've worked up an appetite.' He slid his hand up her skirt.

'Just be careful you don't tear the lace on my knickers when you pull them off. They're my best ones.'

Sunday was William and Eddie's lie-in day, the one day a week they didn't have to get up, and generally didn't until dinner was on the table. Diana usually rose earlier, not as early as she did during the week, but soon enough to prepare the vegetables for Phyllis, who liked to adhere to the strict Welsh tradition of a good Sunday dinner.

Jane was up before Diana. She'd brought back another pile of mending from the Town Hall, and intended to do it in daylight. Surprised to find herself the only person up, she settled herself comfortably in Evan's easy chair and set to work.

'Hello, Jane,' Diana said as she walked into the kitchen. 'Funny to think you've been living here a week and we've hardly said more to each other than "pass the butter" at breakfast.'

'Sorry,' Jane apologised, 'early mornings have never been my strong point.'

'Mine neither. You're busy,' Diana commented looking at the mountain of mending.

'You can sit here if you like,' Jane offered, jumping to her feet, embarrassed because she'd taken the best seat in the room, next to the range and in front of the window.

'No thanks. I'm just about to clean the vegetables.'

'I can do that.'

'I think you'd better get on with your mending. Looks like there's enough there to keep you going all week.'

'It's for the girls in the Town Hall.'

'I trust they're paying you.'

'They are. I hope to make enough to buy a change of clothes.'

'Judging by the pile you've got there, you should have enough to buy a whole new wardrobe.'

'I took Phyllis's mending basket, too.' Jane snapped a thread with her teeth before tossing a stocking on to the repaired pile.

'You charging Phyllis too?'

'Of course not. It's just a small thank-you for letting me stay here until I've worked my week in hand.'

'Phyllis will be pleased.' Diana hadn't quite made up her mind about Jane yet. She'd gleaned a little of her history from Phyllis and her Uncle Evan, but not a great deal. Just that Jane Jones had lived in Church Village and got herself a job in the Town Hall, in itself a rather daring thing to do when a Revue was playing there. Jane invariably came home after she was in bed, left on market days before she was up, and on the other days came down so late there'd been little time to exchange anything other than the barest of pleasantries. But even so, Diana had noticed that there were a few things about Jane that didn't quite ring true. Her lack of clothes for a start. Diana knew she occasionally borrowed Phyllis's coat because she didn't have one of her own. She seemed to have arrived on the doorstep with only the clothes she stood up in. And when Diana had checked the box room one night in a search for Brian's lost teddy, she couldn't help but observe that it was clean, neat, and completely barren. No photographs, no ribbons, no stockings, not even a hairbrush on the chest of drawers, and when she'd looked further, even the nightdress folded beneath the pillow had turned out to be one Phyllis had inherited from her landlady. Diana had never come across a girl before who owned nothing at all. Even the poorest of the skivvies in the Royal Infirmary in Cardiff, where she had once worked, had owned a change of clothes.

'If you've any mending, I'll do it for you if you're quite sure I can't help with the vegetables,' Jane offered.

'I couldn't let you do that.'

'It's no trouble, not now I've everything to hand.'

'Tell you what, I'll give you my mending, and in return I'll cook breakfast for both of us.'

'That sounds good. I'm a terrible cook.'

'I thought that was the one skill every mother tried to instill in her daughter,' Diana probed. 'My mother used to get me to repeat my disasters over and over again. The lodgers and my brother had to put up with some pretty indigestible meals before I finally got it right.'

'I never got that far,' Jane said uncomfortably, mindful of Phyllis's fears that her origins might come out.

'Right, breakfast it is. Porridge do you?'

'Yes, please.'

'What are you going to do today?' Diana asked as she fetched oatmeal from the pantry, tipped it into a pan, added water and salt and stirred it.

'I hadn't thought. Perhaps, if Phyllis lends me some clothes, my washing.'

'Washing?' Diana laughed. 'The neighbours regard this house as ungodly enough without you hanging out on a washing Sunday.'

'Ungodly?'

'I take it you've no intention of going to chapel? If you had you'd be there by now.'

'I'm church,' Jane answered without thinking. She'd been in St John's church once to be confirmed by the Bishop. It had been a special ceremony for workhouse inmates, just as occasionally they held special christenings for abandoned babies and converts. Otherwise the vicar held services in the dining room of the

Homes. 'Out of sight and out of mind' applied to workhouse in-mates even where Christians and church were concerned.

'Well, are you going to church then?'

'No,' Jane replied hastily.

'Can't say I blame you on a day like this. So what you going to do?'

'The mending.'

'That's not going to take you all day. Look, the boys and I will probably go for a walk down the park, or over Shoni's after dinner and we always end up in Ronconi's . . .'

'Ronconi's?'

'The café on the Tumble. You don't know much about Ponty, do you?'

Jane shook her head.

'Well, it's about time you learned.

'I don't know.' It was bad enough making the trips she had to. Even with the added protection of her black dress and hat pulled low over her head, she was terrified of meeting someone from the workhouse, like the porter she'd seen the other night. If he'd recognised her and said something she wouldn't be sitting here, but scrubbing out yards again.

'Look, if you're bothered about clothes,' Diana said, suddenly sorry for the girl, 'why don't you borrow one of my summer dresses? I have two, and one of them matches your hat a treat. Then you can wash your clothes and we'll hang them in the wash-house out of sight of Mrs Richards next door. If we leave the window open they should dry by tomorrow. Come on, we work all week, we're entitled to a little fun.'

Jane thought for a moment. It wasn't money that was holding her back. Thanks to the mending she could easily afford the couple of pence a cup of tea would cost in a café. It was simply fear of who she'd meet there. 'What do you do, and who do you see in the café?'

'We do absolutely nothing. That's the whole point of having a day off. We drink tea. Talk. The Ronconi girls, Tina and Gina, always get the latest Hollywood magazines so everyone takes a look at those. The boys play cards . . .'

'Cards! The comic in the Revue is always winning money from cards.'

'Then he's lucky. You're more likely to lose money than make it.'

'But if you know what you're doing . . . '

'My brother William thinks he's an expert on cards, but I've yet to see the day he comes out on top from the card table. Right, the porridge is done.' Diana lifted down two bowl from the dresser. 'Porridge for you too, darling?' She opened the door for Brian who was hammering on the panels with his small fists as he couldn't quite reach the knob.

'Yes.' He put his finger in this mouth and stared at Jane.

'Yes what?' Diana asked.

'Please and thank you.' Dragging his teddy by the ear he climbed on to one of the chairs and sat at the table.

'I see you dressed yourself this morning?' Diana took his bowl and filled it at the range. As he began to eat she deftly undid and refastened his shirt, matching buttons to corresponding holes. Jane watched, feeling a pang of something she couldn't quite quantify. Diana was only doing what she herself had done often enough for the babies in the Homes. But although she could re-member doing it for others she had no recollection of anyone ever doing it for her.

She supposed that at one time or another someone must have. It would be marvellous if she could remember just one person – someone, anyone – she'd had a relationship with that had lasted more than a few weeks. Someone like Diana who'd dressed and fed her, lifted her on to chairs when she'd been too small to climb on them herself. Someone she could visit and discuss her prob-lems with. Someone she could love the way Brian would come to love Phyllis and Diana. If there had been someone she wouldn't be here, a paying lodger in a stranger's house, living in fear of being dragged back to the workhouse – or Bletchetts' – at any moment.

Chapter Ten

'Well, that's whipped up my appetite nicely, Haydn Powell,' Babs cackled, attracting the attention of two black-garbed elderly spinsters who'd been walking along a path a few feet away from the copse. They stared disapprovingly as Babs and Haydn emerged from the bushes, their frowns escalating into 'tuts' as Babs dusted off the seat of Haydn's trousers. Babs attempted to stare them out, and when that didn't succeed in shifting them, she stuck out her tongue. If he'd been in any town other than Pontypridd, Haydn would have joined in and laughed the incident off along with Babs. As it was, he only hoped the women didn't know him, his mother or his father. But it was a forlorn hope with the posters plastered with his and Babs' photographs pasted all over town to advertise the Summer Variety.

As they walked through the park towards Taff Street, he cast his mind back to last autumn when he'd spent his days working on Wilf Horton's stall, and his evenings as callboy, drudge and general dogsbody in the Town Hall; a position even lower down the theatrical social scale than usherette. He'd never managed to organise a free evening to take Jenny out, but even if he had, there'd never been any spare money to pay for one. And then, worse of all, he'd quarrelled with her. Before he'd left home he'd reached bleak, rock bottom. And yet here he was, two seasons later with everything – or almost everything – he had ever dreamed of.

He was on stage making a living as a singer – not quite up to West End standards, but a good living, way beyond anything he could have aspired to if he'd remained in Pontypridd. And if the impresarios and critics were to believed, the world was poised, waiting for him to take it by storm. National success was around the next corner. And although he might not have a regular sweetheart – he glanced at Babs; by no stretch of the imagination could he apply that word to her – that was his choice. He had all the women he could handle and more throwing themselves at him, not because of his looks and talent, but because the ratio of girls to men on variety tours favoured men, which meant that he'd often found himself with five and sometimes as many as ten willing and able paramours to choose from. As his father would have said, 'He was in God's pocket.' So why had he felt so damned miserable ever since he'd come home?

'More coffee?'

'I couldn't eat another thing.' Babs lifted the damask napkin from her lap with an exaggerated flourish and blotted her lips, imprinting a vivid red mouth on the glossy, starched surface.

'Really?' Haydn arched his eyebrows as she tossed it over the crumbs of chocolate cake that littered her plate.

'Really,' she laughed.

'Then I'll walk you home.'

'Must you?' She opened her enormous handbag and pulled out a powder compact and lipstick. Screwing her mouth into a bow, she coated it liberally with Red Passion. 'Do you know what I'd like to do? Spend this afternoon the way I used to spend Sunday afternoons when I was a kid.'

'Making mud pies?' he enquired sardonically.

'No,' she countered touchily. 'My sister and I would help our mum clear the table and wash the dishes . . .'

'I'll ask if you can help out in the kitchen, shall I?'

'If you'd let me finish, I was going to say, then we'd all go to bed with a book.'

'The same bed?'

'Of course not. My sister and I in our bed, my mum in hers. But then I can't say whether she took a book, or not. You see my dad would be there, waiting for her between the sheets.'

'Then it's a fair bet she didn't do much reading.'

'Well, I did.'

'What were your favourites?'

'Fairy tales, especially "Cinderella" and "Sleeping Beauty". That's why I prefer working in Christmas panto to Summer Variety.'

'Perhaps we ought to get Norman to put in a couple of panto sketches so you can play Cinderella.' He signalled to the waiter.

'To Helen's Prince Charming? No thanks.'

'Forget Prince Charming. I'll play Buttons. Cinders does get to kiss Buttons.'

'I'd much rather kiss you off, than on stage,' she remarked loudly as the waiter arrived. Haydn extracted a pound note from his wallet, tucked it into the bill and replaced it on the salver.

'You're not really going to walk me back to those awful lodgings, are you?'

'Really.' He rose to his feet.

'But why . . .'

'Because my family want to see something of me. Next week between day rehearsals and twice-nightly performances of Revue, not to mention matinées, I won't have a minute to see anyone.'

'I've a good idea,' she enthused as the waiter returned with the change and their coats. 'Why don't I go home with you? You could introduce me to your family and – ' she was interrupted mid-sentence by the waiter helping her on with her coat.

'Absolutely not.' Picking up his change minus a tip, he took her arm and frogmarched her out of the hotel.

'Why?' she asked as they crossed Mill Street.

'I told you. Because I have a family who would like to see something of me. They weren't very happy with me eating out today, as it is. Sunday dinner is quite a tradition in Wales.'

'I think you won't take me home because you're ashamed of me.'

'I won't take you home because if I did, you wouldn't get a minute's peace. My cousin and brother would be panting after you, my little brother would want you to sing him nursery rhymes. My girl cousin and the lodger would pump you mercilessly about make-up and clothes and my father would ask if we've fixed a date.'

'I could cope with that.'

'I couldn't.'

He looked down at her as they crossed the street where the road narrowed in front of the New Theatre. The bright sunlight highlighted her lurid red lips and the blue greasepaint she'd smeared across her eyelids, making them shine like new paint. He knew his father would be horrified at the thought of any son of his courting a girl like Babs. Not because of the way she looked, but because of the way she thought: nothing beyond the latest fashion in dresses, the latest vogue in make-up, in eating out, in entertainment.

'If I don't see you this afternoon, when will I see you?'

'Tomorrow's rehearsals.'

'But what about tonight? It's Sunday. You know how much I hate Sunday nights in a strange town.'

'Don't we all, but it goes with the territory. Just one more small price that has to be paid for stardom.'

'If you say so,' she replied, momentarily mollified by his use of the word 'stardom'.

'Who's in digs with you?' He knew, but it was still a ten-minute walk to her lodgings.

'Helen, Gill and Christine.'

'Digs good?'

'All right, I suppose, although I'm used to better. The landlady's a Welsh dragon, but as Christine said, at least it's clean.'

'Christine would say that.'

'If you ask me, I'd give up cleanliness any time for a bit of fun, even if it did come coated in dirt.' She dug him hard in the ribs and cackled again. He gritted his teeth, smiled hollowly, and quickened his pace.

'No breakfast for those who don't get up until dinner time, and that includes you, Eddie Powell.' Diana hit her cousin with a tea towel as he attempted to step past her into the pantry to get at the cake and biscuit tins.

'Come on, Di.'

'Come on nothing. You can wait until dinner's on the table, and while we're on the subject, you and William had better turn up with shirts on your back for once. Have you met the new lady lodger?' Diana nodded to the corner, where Jane sat, still busy with her mending.

Eddie looked at her. 'No pasties today?'

Jane dropped her needle in surprise.

'I didn't know . . .'

'Neither did I.' He walked across the room, pulling his braces up over his vest. 'I'm Eddie, the handsomest man in this house.'

'You hope,' William burst through the door. 'Diana, where's my clean shirt?'

'In the wardrobe where it should be. Have you met Jane?'

'No. So you're Phyllis's friend?'

Jane tucked her needle into her mending and rose from her chair to shake William's hand.

'Looks like you came to live here just in time. They obviously didn't believe in feeding people where you've come from.'

'Well that's not surprising . . .'

'I really did enjoy those pasties, what do you put in them?' Jane broke in hurriedly, terrified Eddie was on the verge of saying something about her workhouse clothes.

'Mostly dog meat,' William answered.

'Are you serious?' Jane didn't think about what she was saying, all she knew was she had to keep talking, and not allow Eddie to get a word in edgeways until she'd had a chance to speak to him privately. Then, somehow she'd have to convince him that he couldn't mention her and the workhouse in the same breath, for Phyllis and Evan's sake as much as her own.

'Excuse my brother, he's an idiot with a weird sense of humour.' Diana turned towards William, fists raised.

'This I got to watch, might pick up some pointers from Diana.' Eddie threw himself into the chair opposite Jane.

'Come on then, sis.' William put up his fists and bounced around the few square feet that wasn't covered by furniture.

'Now, what does Charlie put in his pastries?' Diana asked.

'Best meat ... Talking of which,' William dodged past her towards the stove, 'what have you done with that round of beef I brought back last night?'

'Cooked it, what did you expect me to do?'

'Burn it like you usually do.' William opened the stove and lifted the lid from the pot.

'Where's Evan and Phyllis?' Eddie asked.

'Taken Brian and the dog over Shoni's for a walk to work up an appetite for dinner.' Diana punched her brother's arm as he picked up a basting ladle.

Uncertain whether the argument between brother and sister was serious, Jane was glad when Eddie left his seat and went into the washhouse. Waiting until the other two were engrossed in yet another sharp exchange of words, she followed him into the yard, where he was cleaning his boots.

'Please, don't say anything to anyone about the clothes I was wearing when you first saw me?'

'You ashamed of them?'

'Wouldn't anyone be?'

'That depends on what they were in the workhouse for.'

'Ssh,' she looked over her shoulder to check if Diana or William had followed them outside. 'It's not just me, it's Phyllis and Evan. They know all about me, I thought it only fair to tell them everything before they took me in, but if either of them knew that someone had seen me walking around the town in that uniform . . .'

'What's the matter? You run away, or something?'

The voices were suddenly stilled in the kitchen. Disturbed by the silence, Jane crept to the window. Diana was alone. William had obviously gone in search of the elusive shirt.

'Well, did you?' he repeated.

'If I did, Phyllis and Evan know about it.'

'You actually escaped from that place.' He let out a long low whistle. 'What did you do? Climb the walls?'

'Not exactly. Someone took me out and I ran away from them.'

'Who took you out?'

'Phyllis asked me not to talk about it.'

He pushed the brush he'd been using to apply the polish back into a battered wooden box, and pulled out a larger, buffing brush. 'That seems a bit dull to me, considering I know half the story already.'

'If I tell you, will you promise not to tell anyone else?'

'I'm not likely to do that when it could get my own father into trouble with the law. He's had enough of that already.'

'I was working as a skivvy in a dosshouse over in Trallwn.'

'Bletchetts?'

She nodded.

'No wonder you scarpered. Now that's one woman who really does buy dog meat. Rumour has it she feeds it to her husband as well as the lodgers. Tell me, what did she feed you on?'

'Nothing. But then I wasn't there very long.'

'You know,' he looked at her with a new respect, 'you haven't done half bad for yourself, all things considered. You're a damned sight better off now than you were last Monday morning when you were standing in town with nothing to your name except a workhouse dress and one and elevenpence.'

'I couldn't have done anything without Mr Horton's, and your parents' help.'

'Phyllis is not my mother.'

'I'm sorry, I didn't mean anything by that. It's just that I knew Phyllis before I knew anyone else here. She was my first real friend. That may not sound much to you, I'm sure you know lots of people, but where I've come from, people aren't always nice to one another. Phyllis was. She knew one of the nurses and used to get a bit extra now and again. Fruit even sometimes, and she always shared it with me although I didn't have anything to share with her in return. And now, well, seeing her with your father, I can't help thinking how right they look together.'

Eddie stopped brushing his shoes and considered what she'd said. Jane was right. His father and Phyllis were a couple. A middle-aged, happy couple. They were always smiling at one another. And looking back he couldn't remember a single happy, secret smile that his father had shared with his mother. When they'd been together they had looked like misery and martyrdom personified. But right or not, there was still one question that needed answering.

'How come you ended up in the workhouse in the first place?' He lacked the courage to ask outright if she'd been an 'unmarried' like Phyllis.

'I was born there. When I was sixteen I had to leave the Children's Homes. When they couldn't find a job for me I was sent back.'

'That must have been rotten.'

'Once you got used to the routine, it wasn't so bad. Not as good as living here, of course, but nowhere near as bad as the dosshouse'

'That I can believe.'

'So you won't tell anyone where I've come from?'

'Your secret's safe with me.'

'Thanks, Eddie. I'm really grateful.'

'On one condition.' He wasn't always sensitive to the situation of others, but something in her story had touched a chord. It was nothing she'd said, more what she'd left unsaid. He'd heard enough about the workhouse to know the people of the Graig didn't fear it without good cause. 'That you come out with us this afternoon. Diana's coming, and we generally have a good time. Seems to me you could do with one of those.'

'Diana's already asked me.'

'And?'

'And I was a bit worried about bumping into someone who might know me.'

'Like me'

'Like someone who works in the Central Homes.'

'Don't worry. Most of the staff there see no further than the uniform. No will recognise you when you're with us.'

'You're sure?'

'Sure.'

She returned to the kitchen. Diana was pouring batter into a Yorkshire pudding tin and William was sitting hunched at the table still dressed in his vest, his nose buried in the *News of the World*. She sat in Evan's chair and resumed her mending. She'd long since finished the pile she'd brought from the theatre and was half-way through Phyllis's basket.

'That's my shirt!' William shouted, pouncing on the garment Jane was inspecting. He held it up in disgust. 'I can't wear this. It's not even ironed, and it's my Sunday shirt.'

'There's a button missing on the cuff,' Jane said. 'If you like I'll mend it, and iron it when I iron the rest of these things.'

'You little sweetheart.'

'Call me that and I'm not likely to do it.'

'Prickly, aren't we?'

'Only when big clumsy boys are around,' Diana interrupted. 'Now both of you, out of here,' she pushed her brother from the front of the stove into Eddie who'd emerged from the washhouse. 'I've a dinner to cook and you're underfoot.'

A traditional Sunday dinner eaten with a family was a new experience for Jane. Nothing could have been more different from institution eating than sitting around the big kitchen table with the Powells. The room was warm, steamy and full of cooking smells. The conversation, loud, raucous and humorous, was deafening after the stern silence of workhouse meals, where the only sounds had been an occasional 'Stop talking there' shouted by duty staff above the tinny clang of cutlery scraping on plates.

'Jane will think we're savages,' Evan observed after a particularly loud outburst of laughter. He lifted Brian from his high chair on to his lap, and presented him with a stick of Yorkshire pudding soaked in gravy.

'He's going to get you into a mess, Evan,' Phyllis warned.

'Doesn't matter,' Evan beamed benignly, gratified by Phyllis's disclosure that Jane had already presented her with seven shillings and sixpence for her week's lodgings, and better still that she had come by the money honestly, doing mending for the chorus girls. It wasn't so much the money that concerned him, but that Phyllis's good opinion of Jane had been endorsed. The small things, such as window cleaning and scrubbing down the back yard that Jane had done to help Phyllis had already proved her industrious. It was good to know that she was trustworthy as well. He knew just how upset Phyllis would have been if Jane had hadn't deserved the confidence put in her.

He sat back and watched Diana check on an enormous treacle pudding in the oven. Brian caught a glimpse of it and jumped up and down on his lap.

'Finish your meat and potatoes first,' Phyllis ordered.

Evan smiled indulgently at his small son, as he soaked another piece of Yorkshire pudding in gravy for him. Diana was a first-class cook, and by taking over the Sunday dinner she'd freed Phyllis's Sundays, not only for her, but also himself. He'd begun to enjoy his day off as he hadn't done since he was a child. Early morning walks, followed by a good dinner, 'afters' and tea; then a half-hour rest sitting next to the stove with his pipe and newspaper before walking down the Graig hill with Phyllis and Brian to have Sunday tea with William and Eddie's boss, Charlie and his wife Alma. Ever since Charlie had left to marry Alma and set up home in the flat above the shop the two families had taken it in turns to visit one another for Sunday tea. And supper would be eaten in his daughter Bethan's house. Soon there'd be a grand-child. Life was looking up for the first time since the pits had closed and the depression had begun to bite.

'Do you think Jane could wash out her dress and hang it in the washhouse to dry?' Diana asked Phyllis. 'She only has the one, and although Mrs Richards would have a fit if she saw it on the line on a Sunday I thought it might dry in the washhouse with the window open.'

'It might, but it would do better in here over the airing rack.'

'I never thought of that.'

'Put it in the washhouse first, Jane. Then when everyone goes out I'll move it in here.'

'Thank you.'

'If I lend her my green dress, she can wear that until tomorrow morning. You don't have to be in work until the afternoon do you, Jane?'

'Not tomorrow, no.'

'Well, that's settled.' Diana collected together her own and Jane's plates, but the boys were still jealously guarding theirs, soaking up the last vestiges of gravy with great slabs of bread that William had cut in the pantry, much to Diana's disgust.

'I'll help Jane wash out her clothes after we've done the dishes, but first you'd better come up to my room and see what you can borrow, Jane.'

'You going out?' Evan asked.

'With us,' Diana answered. 'You wouldn't believe how little Jane knows about Ponty.'

'Enjoy yourself, love, but be careful who you talk to.' There was a note of caution in Phyllis's voice.

'Come on, Phyllis,' William ribbed. 'Who could she possibly run into in Ponty who'd wish her harm?'

'You for one, Will,' Eddie winked at Jane. 'He fancies himself as a ladykiller. But don't worry, Phyllis. I'll take care of her for you.'

Haydn didn't walk home after he left Babs at the door of her digs. Instead, he retraced his steps into the centre of town. The weather was glorious, not just sunny, but for the first time that year, really warm as well. Even the grey stone that clad the railway embankment sparkled in the bright light. And the sun dancing on the gleaming windows of Ronconi's café practically blinded him as he passed.

'You're a stranger.' Tony Ronconi was standing in the doorway looking out for potential customers. 'Too good for our company now you're a big star.'

'You know better than that. I'll be in this evening, same as when I lived here.'

'A man can't pay his rent on promises.'

Haydn threw back his head and laughed. 'You sound just like Ronnie used to, when he was running this place.'

'I'm beginning to find out why he was always so bad tempered.'

'Heard from him lately?'

'Not since Laura and Trevor came back from Italy'

'Maud writes.'

'I know. Diana shows us her letters, but I don't recognise the man, or should I say paragon of virtue, she married as brother Ronnie.'

'That's what love does to you.'

'So they say,' Tony murmured sceptically.

Haydn carried on walking, nodding to people he knew, but careful not to get involved in any more time-wasting conversations. When he reached the fountain he cut up Penuel Lane on to Gelliwastad Road, through Gelliwastad Grove, past the library and on to Tyfica Road. He'd always admired the houses in this part of town. The streets were wider than on the Graig and lined with mature trees. The semis they shaded were broad built and solid, with steep steps leading up to stained-glass doors and porches. He walked the length of the road checking numbers. When he found the one he wanted, he looked around before mounting the steps. Ignoring the highly polished brass bell he knocked softly with his knuckles on the glass.

'I've been waiting for you for hours.'

'I got held up. Family dinner, you know what it's like.'

'Not any more.' Rusty opened the door wide enough for him to slip into a dark-panelled hall. 'Let me take your jacket.'

'Where's your landlady?' The house seemed unusually silent, even for a Sunday.

'She's not my landlady. Just a friend of my sister's. They went to school together, and,' she smiled wickedly as she undid the top three buttons of her blouse, 'she's out, won't be back until late. Her husband insists on a weekly visit to his parents' farm. It's somewhere with a totally unpronounceable name.'

'Like Ynysybwl?'

'Like Ynysybwl,' she agreed softly, taking his hand and leading him up the stairs.

The park was packed with people dressed in their summer Sunday best. Light cotton flower print dresses, and straw hats for the girls and ladies, white shirts and flannels for those of the men who were in work and could afford them. Dark trousers and collarless shirts for those who couldn't. It was as crowded as town on market day, and whether it was the throng of people, the brilliant green of the manicured grass, the display of radiant blooms in the flowerbeds, or simply the fresh air, birds soaring overhead and the company, Jane felt suddenly and inexplicably happy. The prospect of an afternoon's holiday beckoned enticing and exciting in front of her. She had a shilling in her pocket (she'd put aside the rest of her money against the day when she would open her bankbook) and she had Diana to talk to, who'd turned out to be every bit as nice as Phyllis.

The others were constantly turning around and urging her to keep up. She didn't meant to lag, it was simply that there was so much to see and linger over. Clouds of violets bloomed in the shady spots at the bases of tall beeches and elms, and in the cultivated flowerbeds roses, pansies and lilies were opening their buds and raising their multicoloured heads. She had only been in the park twice before, both times when she had lived in Maesycoed Homes. They had been marched directly to the playground after church in a crocodile so hedged about with housemothers there had been no opportunity to admire anything. Then they had been allowed to run around for precisely ten minutes before being herded together again for the return journey.

A young man eyed her up and down, tipped his hat and ventured a 'Hello'. She didn't think he'd been in the workhouse, but even now, in the park, dressed in Diana's clothes, she still felt vulnerable despite Eddie's assurances that no one would recognise her.

She walked away, half expecting the man to call her back. When he didn't she began to wonder if it could be as Daisy and Phyllis had suggested. Was it possible that she was pretty? She certainly felt it in Diana's dress. It was a light flowery green on a background of white. Diana had declared that her tam had been too heavy for it, and insisted that she borrow a straw hat. Diana had also managed to wave the front of her hair before tucking the rest of her shorn crop beneath the brim. The effect had been dazzling when Jane had viewed herself in the mirror. Not as dramatic as the change Mandy and Judy had effected, but certainly more ladylike.

She ran on, leaving the boy behind and caught up with Diana who was talking to Jenny Griffiths. Eddie had insisted on calling for her as they had walked down the hill. She was very pretty, blonde and delicate looking, a perfect foil for Diana's dark exotic beauty.

Jenny eyed Eddie as they reached a row of benches overlooking the tennis courts, where members of the tennis club, dressed expensively in tennis whites, were playing.

'I'm absolutely whacked. I refuse to move another step until you buy me an ice cream, Eddie,' she proclaimed as she perched daintily on the handkerchief she'd spread out on a seat.

'Ice creams all round?' Eddie looked at William, Diana, Jane and the two Ronconi girls, Tina and Gina who'd joined them as they'd walked past the café, much to their brothers' annoyance.

'Yes, please.' Diana linked arms with Gina and Tina and walked to the next seat where they sat in a huddle and began to giggle.

'I'll get the ice creams if you like, Eddie,' Will offered.

'I'll come with you,' Jane volunteered. Lacking the confidence to join Diana and the Ronconi girls, she was far too embarrassed to join Jenny and Eddie. From the adoring looks Eddie was sending Jenny's way it was easy to see which way the wind was blowing there.

'You coming?' William asked impatiently. Jane had been waiting for him to collect money from everyone, but he was already striding down the path towards the open-air swimming pool.

'How do you like living in Pontypridd after Church Village?'

'I like it well enough,' Jane replied guardedly.

'It's not a bad place to live,' he declared with the world-weary air of a middle-aged man. He was unsure how to treat Jane. If she hadn't been living in the same house as him, he would have tried flirting with her – out of Tina Ronconi's earshot. For as long as he could remember he had nurtured a passion for Tina, that had extended to two kisses at the back of the Catholic Hall after a dance, but their embryonic relationship was one that her brothers and father had so far successfully thwarted at every turn.

'You work for the same butcher as Eddie?' Jane asked, steering the conversation on to safer lines.

'I do, but I spend most of my time on the market or in the slaughterhouse. Eddie's got the cushier option in the shop.'

'I think he'd disagree with you.'

'Probably, but that doesn't mean I'm wrong. But what about you? How's the Town Hall going?'

'Fine.'

'Haydn always used to moan that it was hard work. He hated picking up litter after the shows. He was always complaining about the chewing gum sticking to his fingers.'

'I've done a lot worse than scrape chewing gum off floors.'

'Like what?'

'Scrub outside steps and yards.'

'There must be a lot of those on a farm.' He walked up a short path that led to a low-built café. The windows opposite the door looked out over the swimming pool. Clear blue water bubbled and boiled with rubber-capped heads, and the occasional foot of those who dared to do underwater handstands.

'It's always like this on a warm Sunday,' William said, following her glance. 'Look, you can't squeeze a pin between the people sunbathing at the top end. It's a regular suntrap below those walls. An hour there can be as good as an afternoon in Porthcawl.'

'Porthcawl?'

'The seaside. Don't tell me you've never been there?'

She shook her head.

'You prefer Barry Island?'

'I've never been there either.'

'We'll have to do something about that.' He pushed a green

wicker table and chair aside and walked to the counter. 'How many are we?'

Used to doling out ice creams in the Town Hall, Jane said 'Seven' without hesitation.

'Seven ice-cream cornets, please, Dai?' He picked out a shilling and two pennies from the change in his pocket.

'You've got a nice day for it, Will.'

'Nice day for what?'

'Courting, by the look of you'

'Me? I thought you knew me better than that.'

'I know you, all right. You Powells are all alike. Haydn was down here this morning with a very nice bit of blonde skirt on his arm. Wouldn't have minded giving that one an airing myself. Don't suppose you know who she is?'

'Haydn's too afraid of losing his girls to introduce them to me.'

'Judging by the way she was hanging on to his arm I think there was more danger of him straying, than her. And talking of straying,' Dai smiled at Jane as he pushed an ice cream into the last cornet, 'aren't you going to introduce me to your friend?'

'No.' William took the cornets from him. 'She's a sweet, innocent country girl, and as she's temporarily in my charge I intend to see she stays that way.'

'She won't if she remains in your company.'

'Better my company than that of a lecherous old man like you.' William divided the cornets between Jane and himself and led the way out.

'Haydn is your cousin and Eddie's brother, isn't he?' Jane asked, not quite sure if she'd sorted out the Powell family connections correctly.

'He is.'

'You and Eddie look more like brothers than Eddie and Haydn. Eddie is so dark, and Haydn is so fair.'

'Their mother's fair, and you've seen Uncle Evan. I've never really thought about it before, but I suppose it is odd. You haven't met their sister, have you?'

Jane shook her head as she licked a cornet that was melting over her hand.

'Bethan's dark like Eddie.'

'She doesn't live at home?'

'Married crache, a doctor no less, but she calls in, not quite so often now she's expecting at the end of the summer. There's a younger sister too. Maud, she's blonde like Haydn. She married and moved to Italy.'

'Lucky girl.'

'You wouldn't say that if you knew her husband, Ronnie. He's Tina and Gina's brother. He used to run the café like a Tartar. Made people pay in blood if they didn't settle their bills on time,' he hissed in a theatrical voice.

'You want to go on stage like Haydn?'

'Me? Not on your nellie. I'm happy where I am. Besides, I haven't Haydn's voice. That's the only edge he has over me, of course. When it comes to looks, I am, without doubt, the best looking of all the Powells. If silent pictures were still being made I'd be a star.'

Jane laughed, a rare sound that made Diana look up.

'What's dear brother said that's so amusing?'

'He's just told me he's the best-looking man in the family.'

'After me,' Eddie contradicted.

'Lots of girls in Pontypridd would disagree with both of you,' Tina said provocatively. 'Haydn looks very handsome on the posters advertising the Summer Variety.'

'His picture's been touched up by an artist. Any fool can see that.'

'It's just like him,' Tina maintained.

'It doesn't matter whether it's been touched up or not, cousin Haydn is unavailable as far as the ladies of Pontypridd are concerned.' William sat as close to Tina as he could get. Stretching out his long legs he started to lick his cornet from the bottom up.

'What do you mean?' Jenny asked sharply.

'Dai just told me he saw Haydn parading around the park this morning with a very tasty blonde.'

'So that's what he calls rehearsing.' Eddie leaned forward so his cornet wouldn't dribble on his shirt.

'I didn't know Haydn was going out with a showgirl.' Jenny failed to keep her voice steady. Hoping no one had noticed, she busied herself by wrapping a handkerchief around her cornet.

'He isn't,' William answered blithely, oblivious to the suspicious look Eddie was sending Jenny's way. 'Not *a* showgirl. Last I heard he had at least two or three on the go.'

'William!' Diana reprimanded.

'What's the matter'

'Ladies present.'

'Where?'

'If you're going to be like that, I'm going to walk to the bandstand. One of the cadets told me a military band's playing there today, from Cardiff. Coming girls?'

Only Gina left her seat.

'Can I come?' Jane asked, as William sidled closer to Tina.

'Of course,' Diana held out her hand. 'Right, let's see who can get the most, how-do-you-dos from the soldiers. Winner gets free tea from the losers back in Ronconi's.'

Jane smiled, happy even at the thought of losing. She was beginning to find out just how much difference friendship and family could make to life.

Chapter Eleven

'Haydn! Time to move.' Rusty dug the comatose figure in the ribs.

'What's the time?' he mumbled sleepily.

'Six o'clock. You promised to buy me evening dinner.'

'Did I?' His eyes remained closed as he dug his head deeper into the pillows.

'Bathroom's next door. I'll get us a drink.'

'Tea?' he opened one eye.

'Whisky if you prefer. I bought a bottle for the house, they won't miss a couple of glasses.'

'Just a small one.' He watched as she slipped a red silk dressing gown over her magnificent body. He followed the sounds she made walking down the stairs, heard her opening a cupboard door. Time to move! Swinging his legs out of the bed he slumped forward and buried his face in his hands. He felt as though he was suffering from a mammoth hangover although he hadn't had more than a couple of beers in days. His head was fuzzy and every muscle ached like toothache, probably the result of too many vigorous rehearsals, too much sex, and too much concentration – the inevitable result of telling different stories to different women, and trying to remember just who he'd told what to.

Picking up his clothes, he staggered into the bathroom. The bath was enormous: a massive, white-enamelled, cast-iron affair. There would have been room in it for him, Rusty and Babs if he could have persuaded both of them to join him. On impulse he put the plug in and ran the cold tap. The dip didn't do a great deal for his aches and pains but it certainly woke him up. All he had to suffer now was Rusty's moans throughout dinner about the precariousness of her position as the Revue's leading lady, then he could go home, to bed or even better to see his father. He hadn't done much in the way of real talking to anyone since he'd been home – or for that matter since he'd been on stage. And then what? Sleep, more rehearsals tomorrow, followed by another two performances of Revue. What was the matter with him? He had a budding career, more sex than he could handle, and yet he still couldn't shake off this emotion-numbing sense of depression that was slowly paralysing his senses.

'You work in the Town Hall?' Tina sat next to Jane at one of the tables in the front room of Ronconi's café. Of choice Jane would have played cards with the boys to see if she could add to her savings, but both the boys and Diana had made it plain that it wasn't done for any girl to sit in the back.

'Only since Monday.'

'Have you seen the Revue?'

'A couple of numbers.'

'I don't know how your Haydn can do it,' Tina continued in a low voice to Diana. 'Walk around all those naked girls, and sing while they're –'

'How do you know what he's doing, Tina?' Jenny interrupted as she carried a cup of cocoa over from the counter.

'Tony and Angelo went on Friday night. They told Papa they were going to an Italian club meeting, but Glan Richards saw them and told me where they'd been, so I threatened to tell Papa what they'd been up to unless they told me everything.'

'Everything?' Diana echoed suggestively.

'I couldn't get a lot out of them. Tony said the girls were stark naked, although Angelo complained that between the feathers and the lighting he couldn't see all that much.'

'Tina!'

'I'm only repeating what Angelo said.'

'The lighting is dim,' Jane agreed. 'And most of the girls do wear something, even if it's only a body stocking and a couple of sequined stars.'

'Then you have seen the Revue?'

'As I said, only bits of it. The opening numbers when we show people to their seats and wait for stragglers, and the last number before the interval when we go out with our trays.'

'I don't know how you can sell ice cream in front of something like that,' Jenny asserted primly, uncertain just where Jane fitted into the Powell household, but wanting to make it clear that the nature of her job put her on a par with the nudes.

'I needed a job, it gave me an immediate start.'

'I bet you see a lot of Haydn,' Tina giggled.

'Haydn doesn't strip off,' Diana stated forcefully.

'But those girls do,' Tina nudged Gina. 'Imagine standing on stage naked as the day you're born. How can they do it, even with a few bits and bobs covering . . . well, covering . . . you know what I mean.'

'Six pounds a week.'

'Six pounds? You sure, Jane?'

'I'm sure. Some of them get more. The head girl, for instance.'

'What's a head girl?'

'The one in charge of the chorus, she gets an extra two pounds a week, and Mandy, she sits on a swing that's hauled up high, close to the ceiling. She gets an extra ten bob a week danger money; and Rusty, the female lead. She gets a lot more.'

'I couldn't do it,' Tina declared. 'Not for a hundred pounds.'

Jane didn't answer. From the way Tina had been back and forth to the counter helping herself to hot chocolate and chewing gum she guessed that the girl had never gone short of anything in her life. The first lesson she was learning on the outside was that it was easy to express moral outrage when you hadn't tasted parish charity.

'Time I went.'

'It's not ten yet, Jenny.'

'I promised my father I'd open the shop for the early-shift miners tomorrow.' She reached for her coat and stood in the open archway that divided the front and back rooms of the café As she'd hoped, Eddie saw her. Five minutes later he was escorting her through the door.

'Something going on between Jenny and your Eddie, Diana?' Gina asked.

'Nothing I know about.'

'Wasn't she sweet on Haydn at one time?'

'Haydn and Jenny Griffiths?'

'They were as good as engaged,' Tina informed Jane knowledgeably. 'No one's really sure what happened between them, but they stopped talking to one another before Haydn went away. Now it seems if she can't have one brother, she'll settle for the other.'

'Jenny . . .'

'One kiss, Eddie Powell, that's your lot.'

'Just five minutes.' His hands gripped her waist.

'No.' Jenny pushed him aside and opened the storeroom door creating a gap just wide enough for her to slip through. She closed it in his face.

'Jenny,' he whispered from the yard.

'Go away, Eddie.'

'You'll see me tomorrow?'

'You know where to find me.'

Leaning with her back against the door she heard the outside gate open and close. Wrapping her arms around her shoulders she tried to stop herself from shaking. She'd succeeded. She'd sent Eddie home and for the first time that day she was free to think of Haydn.

Was it serious between him and the blonde he'd been seen with in the park? Or was the blonde an acquaintance from the show? A girl he was using to make her jealous? Of course. She sat down abruptly, lightheaded with relief. That had to be it. He was deliberately flirting with the showgirls, flaunting them around town, knowing only too well that everyone he met would be delighted to give her the news about his latest sweetheart. They hadn't progressed very far since the days when their quarrels had been confined to the school yard. But even then, despite the childish games of one-upmanship, she had known that deep down Haydn had really cared for her. Just as she knew he cared for her now, even though she had allowed his brother to make love to her. It would have been better, far better for both of them, if she had gone to him as soon as she'd heard he was home. A whole week wasted because she hadn't the sense or the courage to tell him the truth: that she loved him, and would always love him.

Feeling the chill of the floor she rose to her feet and went into the shop. The street outside the window was deserted. A thin line of light shone beneath the door that led to their living quarters. Her mother was home and in bed, but not her father. The lamp was always left on until he returned from the pub. The fact that it was a Sunday made no difference. The landlord of the Morning Star unlocked his back door for selected regulars. Her father wouldn't return until the early hours of the morning. And who could blame him, when her mother wouldn't even allow him into her bedroom, let alone her bed.

When she and Haydn were married, she'd never banish him to another bedroom. She'd sleep with him all night, every night of their lives. Making love . . . she closed her fists tightly, trying to forget that Eddie had been her first lover, consoling herself with the thought that it wasn't the first, but the last who was important. And it wasn't as if nothing had ever happened between her and Haydn. He'd been the first man to unfasten the buttons on her blouse, the first to touch her breasts – to kiss her. But then after hob-nobbing with nude Revue girls she couldn't expect him to be satisfied with half-measures like those again. She'd have to be prepared to allow him to do what he wanted. Give him everything she had to give – she trembled at the thought of the nights they'd share for the rest of their lives. Then she'd show everyone – especially her mother – that a marriage could have a fairy-tale ending, 'happily ever after'.

She pictured Haydn as he'd been on stage, his fair hair shining beneath the spotlight, suave and handsome in his dinner jacket and bow tie. A man to weave dreams around like Clark Gable, Robert Taylor or Leslie Howard. Remote, sophisticated and unattainable while performing, yet hers. The Haydn she had grown up with and come to love more than anyone else in the world. She had been stupid to allow him to leave Pontypridd without making an effort to clear up that last quarrel. Perhaps she should have stayed in the café and waited for him tonight? Tony'd said he'd promised to call in. But then staying on in the café would have meant remaining with the girls, listening to their speculations about Haydn and various showgirls. Besides, although he'd told Tony he was going to call in, he might have been held up – but where? Eddie and William didn't even know where he was spending the day. Eddie had mentioned something about rehearsing, but did the Town Hall rehearse on a Sunday? Jane hadn't known, but then Jane was so mousy no one was likely to confide anything of any importance to her.

Mousy and small – her heart contracted as she recollected the slight, insignificant figure who'd stood next to Haydn on the hill the other night. Haydn worked in the Town Hall and so did Jane. Why had it taken her so long to put two and two together? Jane! As suspicion hardened into certainty it hurt more than the knowledge that Haydn had been seen around town with a blonde. Everyone knew showgirls were flighty, that no man took them seriously. But Jane! How could he go around with such an insignificant nobody – so thin and downright plain – after courting her?

Perhaps he'd walked Jane home because they lived in the same house? She had a vision of him singing on stage, gazing at the blonde as she descended on the swing. She'd had a stunning face and figure, and for all her immobility she'd stared at Haydn with adoring eyes. Had it been acting, or simply a trick of the light? Either way, no man, Haydn included, would look twice at girl like Jane while he was surrounded by a glamorous chorus.

Trying to put all thoughts of rivals firmly out of mind, she continued to gaze out of the window. Unless Haydn walked up the steps in Graig Street and along Leyshon Street he had to pass this way. And he couldn't be much longer. Hardly anything was open on a Sunday night, although he could be visiting one of the chorus girls in her room. Did landladies allow that? A vivid image of Haydn, dressed in evening clothes kissing a naked girl, came to mind. If she didn't stop tormenting herself, she'd drive herself mad.

She leaned against the counter and began to wait, her eyes focused on the blackened street, seeing flickers of movement on the fringes of every pool of lamplight. Straining her senses to their utmost, she tensed her muscles and remained motionless. A man walked out of the Morning Star; pulling his cap down low he walked past the shop and turned the corner into Factory Lane. Old Mrs Evans opened the door at the side of the small shop opposite and put out her cat for the night. Footsteps echoed up the hill. Heart pounding, Jenny looked, and looked again.

A tall, slim figure walked purposefully upwards, long, light-coloured coat draped over one shoulder, a trilby on his head. She tried to decipher the features but the face was in shadow. There wasn't time to do any more. Another minute and he'd be alongside the shop, then past it. What if she went outside, called out and it wasn't Haydn? And what if it was? She could wait weeks for another opportunity like this.

Running around the counter she tripped over a sack of carrots and broke a fingernail in her eagerness to wrench open the door. The bolt stuck. Manipulating it from side to side, she finally succeeded in wresting it open just as the man drew alongside the shop across the road.

'Haydn?' she murmured softly, uncertainly.

He slowed his steps. 'Jenny.' He tipped his hat and would have walked on, but she crossed the road and blocked his path.

'I haven't seen you since you've been back.'

'I haven't had time to see anyone. I practically live in the theatre.'

'So I've heard. Diana and Eddie told me.' She could have kicked herself, she hadn't intended to mention Eddie's name.

'Well if you'll excuse me . . .'

'Couldn't we talk, just for a minute. It's important.'

'I have to get home. Everyone except me has to be up early for work tomorrow. I don't like disturbing them by walking in late.'

'Just a few minutes.' She hated having to beg. This wasn't the way she'd intended their reconciliatory conversation to go. 'I was just making cocoa . . .'

'I couldn't eat or drink another thing today.'

'Just a few minutes.'

He hesitated. Footsteps rang out higher up the hill. If he stood here arguing with her he risked attracting attention he could well do without.

'Five minutes,' he agreed reluctantly, following her across the road and into the shop.

'Cocoa and cheese sandwiches all round?' Diana offered as she walked into the house with Jane, Eddie and William.

'I could make them.'

'You mend, I cook, remember.'

'Sandwiches and cocoa isn't cooking.'

'It is in the boys' eyes. They can't even manage that much.'

'That's the last pot of tea I make you, sis,' William sniped.

Phyllis and Evan were sitting in the kitchen either side of the fire, Phyllis busy knitting the better parts of a worn sweater into a smaller one for Brian, Evan engrossed in a library book.

'You have a good time?' Phyllis asked.

'Terrible,' William complained. 'Eddie won twopence off me at cards, and as if that wasn't enough, Glan Richards burnt a hole in my jacket with his cigarette.' He held up the offending garment.

'It's on the seam,' Jane remarked, 'and it's not too bad. A couple of threads pulled out of an inside hem and sewn over the worst, and no one will notice it.'

'I'll put it in the mending basket so dear sister can spend the next twelve months ignoring it.'

'If you give it to me now, I'll do it.'

'See and take notice,' William addressed Diana. 'This woman

actually wants to take care of me. I think I'll adopt her; she makes a better sister than you.'

'I've got first claim on Jane,' Phyllis smiled. 'Anyone who can empty the mending basket when I take a walk is an honorary member of my family.'

'I like sewing, really,' Jane protested, unused to compliments, even when they were given in William's jocular fashion. She took Phyllis's work box and lifted it next to the chair she'd pulled out from under the table.

'Keep up the good work, young lady, and we won't be willing to let you go when you get your wages,' Evan murmured half seriously from behind *Ten Days that Shook the World*.

'Here we are: cheese, bread and cocoa. William, when you've finished telling everyone what a dreadful sister I am, fill the kettle. Eddie, get a jar of pickles out of the pantry, I couldn't carry everything.'

'You should go into the army, sis,' William said, picking up the kettle. 'I hear they're looking for sergeant-majors.'

'Tony Ronconi reckons they're looking for soldiers because war's coming in the next week or so.'

'They've been saying that all year,' William scoffed. 'If you ask me it's just something for politicians to shout and the papers to write about.'

'Not this time,' Evan cautioned. 'It's coming, and it's not far off.'

'Will it be like the last one?' The death of the father she'd never known, and her mother's grief at his loss, had cast the only shadow over Diana's childhood.

'If this fellow Hitler keeps trying to take over all the countries around Germany, I can't see what else the Allies can do except dig themselves in around his borders.'

'Build a sort of Allied Hindenburg line?'

'Something like that.'

'Then we'll all have to go and fight. How do you fancy your brother in uniform, Di?'

'I don't,' she snapped. 'I think you'd look an utter fool.'

It was then that Evan wondered if Diana knew that her father had died in an offensive on the Hindenburg line.

'Well now I'm here, what's so important you have to stop me in the street?'

Jenny had led Haydn through the shop into the storeroom. She had hoped the surroundings would evoke memories of the nights they had spent here when they'd lacked the money to go out. Sitting, and later lying on the sacks and boxes, wrapped in each other's arms, making plans for a future they had intended to live out together.

'I just wanted to see you, to ask how you've been keeping.'

'As you can see.' He held out his arms and revolved slowly in front of her.

'Haydn, it was my fault that it went wrong between us. I had to tell you to your face how sorry I am.'

He breathed a sigh of relief. Was that really all she wanted to say? Sorry? He'd been dreading a scene: at best a raking over of the circumstances that had led to their argument, at worst angry, emotional recriminations. 'It's water long gone under the bridge, Jenny. I don't think about it any more, and I hope you don't.'

'I can't help thinking about it. In fact I think of nothing else. Haydn, I should never have let Eddie do what he did . . .'

'Jenny, don't you understand? I don't want to know. The truth of the matter is, I don't care. Not any more.'

'But I hurt you.'

'I got over it.' He turned to leave.

'Haydn!' Terrified of losing him, she threw all caution to the wind. Flinging her arms around his neck she kissed his lips, and as she did so she moved her body close to his, caressing his thighs with her own, thrusting her breasts against his chest, running her fingers through the hair at the nape of his neck. She summoned and utilised every trick, every artifice she had seen portrayed on the cinema screen, as well as the erotic responses Eddie's rough, abrasive style of lovemaking had taught her.

'No!' Haydn grabbed her hands. Disentangling them from the

back of his neck he pushed her away. 'No, Jenny, it won't work, not any more.'

'Haydn . . .'

'Goodbye, Jenny.' He walked purposefully towards the door that led into the shop and opened it.

'Haydn, what is it? Is it another girl? I know you've been seen around town with a blonde. Please, I don't mind being one of a crowd,' she begged, casting off her final remnants of self-respect. All she could think of was that if she inveigled him into remaining with her this once, he would stay with her for ever. One more kiss, that's all it would take. He had always wanted to sleep with her. One more kiss: she would give him everything he could possibly want in a woman, show him how much she loved him. And after that he wouldn't be able to leave her – not ever again.

'It's no use, Jenny. I've changed.' He stressed the final word, wanting to make her realise that he'd made his decision, and it was irrevocable.

'So have I Haydn. But there's one part of me that will never change. I still love you. I will always love you.' Unbuttoning her dress she stepped back away from him. He heard the swish of fabric as her clothes settled at her feet. He turned and looked at her. After the professional poses of the showgirls, her nakedness made little impression. She looked gauche, clumsy. He suddenly found it strange to think that he'd been angry with her. There had been nights when he'd lain awake, dreaming of a situation like this – what he'd do and say if he ever had the upper hand. He'd been obsessed with revenge, with hurting her every bit as much as she had hurt him. Then he would have given every penny of his wages to see her wretched and heartbroken just as he'd been, night after lonely night when he had first gone to Brighton, too wounded and too wrapped up in his own misery to even try to make friends among the cast of the pantomime he'd played in. But now, when he was actually faced with her baring herself, pleading for forgiveness, all he wanted was to put as much distance between her and himself as possible. He laid his hand on the doorknob and turned it, only to find she'd rammed the bolt home.

'If you walk out on me now, I'll marry Eddie.' She stepped out of the storeroom towards him, not caring that her nudity could be seen by anyone who looked in through the window. 'I'll marry him, Haydn,' she threatened. 'And I'll marry him loving you.'

He stared contemptuously at her. 'Eddie deserves better. And if you go near him again after tonight, you'll have me to reckon with.'

'There's nothing you can do to me that you haven't already. Eddie loves me. You couldn't stop him from marrying me.'

'The last thing he'll have on his mind is marriage after I've told him about this little episode.'

'And who do you think he'll believe? You, or me when I cry on his shoulder and tell him how you came around tonight and tried to force yourself on me? How you wouldn't take no for an answer when I refused to sleep with you. Perhaps I should get some witnesses down here right now. Show them just how brutal you can be.' She picked up the knife her father used to cut the cooked meats and held it poised above her arm. He knocked it out of her hand. It fell with a clatter on to the flagstoned floor.

'You really don't give a damn about anyone other than yourself, do you, Jenny?'

'I love you,' she cried out passionately. 'I'd do anything for you. You have to believe me.' She clawed at his arms, raising bloody welts on his wrists. 'Anything at all.'

'Even make a mockery of my brother's life.' He heaved the bolt back on the door, and strode out without a backward glance.

'You all right Haydn?'

'Fine.' Haydn sat in the easy chair opposite his father's. 'Everyone in bed?'

'Yes. Sure you're all right? You look just like you used to when you were a boy and had a fight.'

'I told you, I'm fine.'

'That's a good suit,' Evan tactfully changed the subject. 'Good quality cloth. Made to measure, by the look of it.'

'It is. I had it made in Brighton.'

'Going up in the world.' Evan was proud that his son was doing so well. He only hoped Haydn would hang on to his position at the top of the provincial bills. He didn't know much about Variety except that the acts that topped the bill one year in Pontypridd sometimes returned half-way down the next, that's if they returned at all. 'Thought I'd wait up and share a cuppa with you.' He left his chair and poured two teas out of the pot he'd kept warm on the stove. 'I don't think we've exchanged more than half a dozen words since you've come home.'

'I'm sorry about that. I feel as though I'm living in the theatre. Comes of rehearsing for the Summer Variety all day and performing in the Revue all night, but it will ease up at the end of next week when the Revue moves on.'

'Done much of this Revue work, have you?' Evan's face was impassive as he puffed on his pipe, but Haydn knew his father.

'When the pantomime ended in Brighton it was a question of taking whatever I could get to see me through the quiet time until Summer Variety started. I worked in a concert party in Torquay for a while, then I did six weeks around the outskirts of London with this show, before going into Variety. When both tours were extended to cover Wales and I was offered roles and contracts in both, I thought, why not? It's hard work, but good money.'

'I don't doubt it. Double wages?'

'Rehearsal wages are less than performing wages, but I'm not complaining. You getting any stick from the neighbours about the show?' he asked bluntly, wondering if that was what his father had been building up to.'

Evan smiled as he tapped his pipe against the iron door of the stove to loosen the ashes. 'The women I meet are generally too embarrassed to mention it, and the men ask if I can get them free tickets.'

'As long as you're not upset by it.'

'Why should I be? It's your life. You're doing what you want with it, aren't you?'

'Yes and no. I want to be a singer. Revue isn't exactly my idea of a perfect engagement, but at least it's getting my name known.'

'Aye, it is that.'

'I know Mam would have a fit.'

'Well as she's not around we won't bring her into it.'

'Have you seen her?'

'Not since Bethan's baby was buried. But don't let the disagreement between your mother and me stop you from going up the Rhondda. Our differences aren't yours.'

'She never was very keen on me going on stage, and if she knows what kind of a show I'm in she'll show me the door. Always providing she lets me over the doorstep in the first place. If she doesn't know, I'd sooner drink a pint of Taff water than tell her.'

'Don't be too hard on her, Haydn. When all's said and done, she's still your mother.'

It was an odd sentiment for his father to express after the loveless married life he had led for over twenty years. And he had obviously thought little enough of Elizabeth to 'carry on' with Phyllis during that time. Brian was testimony to that. Two years old, and Phyllis had only moved in since his mother had moved out, last winter. 'Do Eddie and Bethan visit Mam?'

'You'll have to ask them that. If they do, they haven't mentioned it to me. But it's you, not your mother, who concerns me. You are all right aren't you, son?'

Haydn would have liked to tell him about Jenny and her threat to marry Eddie, but he didn't know where to begin. Whichever way he phrased it, the story would sound like sour grapes: as if he regretted losing Jenny, and was jealous of Eddie's success with her. 'All right enough. What about everyone else?'

'I'm happy with Phyllis.' Phyllis hadn't said anything to him about Haydn's coolness towards her, but then she hadn't had to. Evan was especially sensitive when it came to Phyllis. 'There was a time not that long ago, when your mother and I were still together and you were all growing up and moving away, when I thought I'd never be content, let alone happy again. I don't mind telling you, boy, I made a pig's ear out of what should have been the best years of my life. Trying to please your mother when I knew deep down that nothing I could ever do would satisfy her. Hitting policemen out of sheer frustration and ending up in gaol. But then, no experience is ever all bad. It was those couple of months behind bars that gave me time to think what I was doing with my life. Somewhere within those walls I found the courage to live openly with the woman I love.'

'You going to divorce Mam?'

'She'll never wash our dirty linen in public by divorcing me; and as I'm the guilty party, that puts me in the dock with nothing to shout about. Elizabeth was a good wife and mother in her way, and I can't hurt her any more than I already have by demanding she divorces me. But I would like to marry Phyllis for both her own and the boy's sake. I worry that if anything ever happens to me . . .'

'You don't have to worry about that, Dad, I'll see Phyllis and Brian all right.'

'Bethan and Eddie have said the same thing, and seeing as how the house is in my name and I've left it in equal shares between all my children, including Brian, I was hoping you wouldn't put Phyllis out on the street. But for all that, it's good to know that none of you bear a grudge against me, Phyllis or Brian.'

'Why would we?'

'Because I brought another woman into the house to take your mother's place. Not to mention a half-brother, and a bastard to boot.'

Haydn shifted forward in his chair, drawing it closer to his father.

'It wasn't just a fling between me and Phyllis, I want you to know that. We were engaged to be married when I was about Eddie's age.'

'You and Phyllis?'

'Your grandmother adored her. Phyllis was lodging with Rhiannon Pugh across the road even then. Her own people had died. She practically lived with us. Two months before the date we'd set for the wedding, her and Mam Powell were spending every spare minute sewing her bottom drawer, my brother William and I were decorating the front room, the room you're sleeping in now, as a room Phyllis and I could live in, and then we quarrelled. The stupid thing is I can't remember what it was about. Phyllis says it was over a lino pattern. That doesn't sound right to me but as I really can't remember I have to take her word for it. Then right in the middle of it all I went out to drown my sorrows, got drunk before going to a chapel social and ended up with your mother. Before I knew where I was, we were married.'

'You thought you'd fallen out of love with Phyllis?'

'I loved her all right. And I married your mother knowing I loved her. I think your mother knew it too. That's probably why it went wrong between us from the outset. She didn't stand much chance with me, not really. It wasn't fair on her.'

'If you knew you loved Phyllis, then surely it would have been better to have left Mam, and risked a breach of promise action.'

'It would have, but I wasn't in a position to leave her. You see, by then Bethan was on the way.'

Haydn suddenly saw Evan, not as his father, but as a man. Someone who had once been as young as he was now. And just like he'd been after Jenny's defection to Eddie, bitter and angry. Angry enough to have made a mistake that had affected more lives than his own, even into a second generation. For the first time he was able to put many of the events and attitudes that had puzzled him during childhood into context. The cold, bitter silences that had characterised the relationship between his mother and Mam Powell, the warm loving woman who had been his father's mother. Silences he'd never understood. Just as he'd never understood why his mother had to make so many offensive, cutting remarks that she knew would hurt. Had that bitterness been rooted in the knowledge that her husband had never loved her? Would never have married her if she hadn't been pregnant? How different would his own and his brother's and sisters' lives have been if his mother had been loved? And if his father had married Phyllis, he wouldn't even be here.

'My mistakes cost others dear. Phyllis didn't deserve to be stoned out of chapel when she was carrying Brian, and have her name dragged through the mud and end up in the workhouse just because she bore my bastard. And I had no right to go near your mother. She was earmarked for one of her own kind – a minister or a teacher who had an interest in lay preaching. But because I couldn't hold my beer and let my senses rule my head, I made two women and myself wretched, and blighted a lot of years.'

'But it's all right now, Dad.' Haydn tendered the platitude in an attempt to alleviate the pain his father obviously still shouldered.

'After a fashion. Phyllis has no wedding ring on her finger. Her name, not mine, is on Brian's birth certificate, and your mother feels she can't hold her head up even in the Rhondda because of the shame I've brought on her and her family.'

Any thoughts Haydn might have had of telling his father about Jenny and Eddie dissipated as Evan lad his cold pipe on the mantelpiece and rose stiffly to his feet. 'Well I'm for bed. You going?'

'After I've smoked a cigarette. And thanks, Dad.'

'For what? Piling my misery on to you?'

'For telling me the truth.'

'Don't sit up too long.'

'I won't.'

When the floorboards overheard stopped creaking and Evan finally joined Phyllis in bed, Haydn realised that his father might have been more astute than he'd given him credit for. He could have told him his history any time, yet he had chosen this night. Why? Was it because rumours of his affairs with showgirls were already circulating around Pontypridd? Had Jane said something more to Phyllis? He thought about the idea and dismissed it. After the row over the chips, Jane wouldn't have said anything about him, especially to Evan or Phyllis.

No, if Evan had heard anything it must have come from another source. But then, he hadn't even tried to be discreet. Any one of the waiters in the New Inn would know that he'd wined and dined two different girls there today. And if Jane had seen him kissing Mandy in the wings from the stalls, anyone else in the auditorium could have done the same. And knowing now how his father felt about his own disastrous marriage, had Evan chosen this moment to speak out because he was afraid his son was about to repeat history by playing around with girls he didn't care for?

Haydn took a packet of cigarettes from his pocket and removed one. He lit it and stared blindly at the old, familiar prints on the wall opposite. His father had hit the nail on the head. The problem was he didn't care for Rusty, Babs, Mandy, Helen or any of the other girls he'd had brief flings and affairs with since leaving home. He'd once cared – no, loved Jenny, but tonight she'd driven the last coffin nail into that relationship. Not just because of what she'd said, but because he'd changed. More than he would have believed possible in eight short months.

By returning to Pontypridd, walking familiar streets and meeting old friends he'd been given the opportunity to look at himself through other people's eyes: like Tony's 'Too proud to associate with us now' or Fred's 'hard life on stage'.

And he hadn't helped matters. He cringed as he heard himself say, 'Nothing, but singing, champagne, beautiful girls, and the high life.' What had Jane thought of him?

Suddenly, Jane's opinion of him was very important. He didn't know why. Perhaps because she was the only girl he'd talked to recently apart from Diana and Jenny who wasn't on stage, and who he hadn't slept with.

He'd been a fool. Using the excuse of pain at Jenny's defection to Eddie, pain, he'd discovered that evening which no longer existed, as an excuse to rush headlong down the selfsame road of destruction that his father had travelled before him. And as his father had found out, accidents happened. Any one of the girls he'd slept with in the last months could be carrying his child. Rusty, Babs, even Mandy who'd beckoned him into the rehearsal room between shows in the last town. The thought of being tied to any one of them for life made his blood run cold. He had a sudden vision of spending each and every day with a woman he didn't love, running a typical theatrical retirement business. A pub, or boarding house. Watching Babs's prettiness turn to blowsiness as she put on weight and let herself go.

He resolved to get a grip on his life. Start being honest with the girls, and himself. Making the resolution eased his conscience . . . a little. But his biggest problem still remained. Jenny – and more important still, his brother's happiness.

Chapter Twelve

'Your pasty, Haydn.' Jane knocked at his dressing-room door, which for once he'd actually left open between houses.

'Thanks.' He stretched out his hand from behind the *South Wales Echo*.

'Haydn?'

He recognised the tone. It was one a woman adopted when she wanted something. 'Yes,' he replied warily.

'You said the other day that I picked that dance step up quickly.'

'The one I was demonstrating to Billy out in the corridor?'

'I was wondering if there's any chance of you teaching me more?'

'Why?'

'Because I'd like to learn.'

'You're too short for a chorus girl, you do know that?'

Jane didn't. Used to being one of the shortest, if not the shortest, in any group of girls, she'd assumed it was simply coincidence that all the chorus girls were taller than her. But, well versed in the art of concealing disappointment, she answered, 'Of course.'

'Then why do you want to learn?'

'It might come in useful.'

'For what?' He lowered his newspaper and looked at her with

narrowed eyes. 'You're not thinking of going on stage by any chance?'

'What if I am?'

'Because at your height you've got to have something more than dancing to offer. Can you sing?'

'I've never tried.'

'If you could sing, you would have found out by now. Weren't you in the school or chapel choir?'

'I'm church.'

'They have choirs too.'

'Only for boys.'

'Look, I really haven't the time or the inclination to play teacher to a . . .' The paper slid from his hands and fell to the floor. 'This isn't about lessons at all, is it? It's about Mandy.'

'Mandy?' she echoed in bewilderment.

'You're thinking of carrying tales back to the family about what Mandy and I did in the wings?'

'No,' she protested.

'I saw you talking to Rusty earlier . . .'

'About her mending. I told you the other night, I'm not interested in your carryings-on. What you do is your business.'

'And it will stay that way if I teach you how to dance?'

'If you think I'd blackmail you into giving me lessons, you don't know me, Haydn Powell.'

'No? I've met some scheming shrews in my time, but you take the biscuit with your sweet innocent airs and graces. I suppose you even have the time and place for the lessons all worked out?'

'Forget I mentioned them.'

'Oh no, you don't get off the hook that easily. You want a lesson. I'll give you one, right now.' He gripped her wrist between his thumb and forefinger.

'Let me go. You're hurting me.'

'You think this is pain. Wait until we start, madam. Pain is when your feet bleed. Come on, let's go.'

'Where?' There was a strange expression on his face that made her blood run cold.

'You've finished your work, run your errands and the doors won't open for the next house for another twenty minutes. We can practise on stage.'

'And if I want to rest?'

'You? The great Jane who can work the market, the theatre and sit up all night sewing. You don't know the meaning of the word.'

'Haydn . . .' Rusty barged in without knocking, her silk dressing gown floating elegantly around her tall slim figure, revealing far more than it concealed. It was obvious why she'd come, but a suspicious look hardened her face as she turned from Jane to Haydn. 'Am I interrupting something?'

'Dancing lessons,' Haydn said abruptly, pushing Jane past Rusty and out through the door.

'Dancing lessons?'

'Dancing lessons,' he repeated, realising he'd just found the perfect excuse to keep all maneating women at bay.

As two o'clock on Tuesday afternoon approached Jane grew more and more agitated. She tried to take Judy's advice and think only about the money. Ten pounds meant security. But every time she allowed her imagination free rein, she trembled at what she was about to do. And then there was Phyllis – Phyllis who'd been shocked when she had talked about the money that could be made working in Revue. How much more shocked would she be if she knew what Jane was contemplating now? As she came to the workhouse walls she slowed her steps. Was it her imagination or could she hear the sister's voice ordering the female paupers into line?

Phyllis was her first and best friend, but she and Evan had made it clear from the outset that she could only stay in Graig Avenue until she had her first wage packet, and although she'd assumed that wages meant unimaginable riches before she'd left the workhouse, she knew better now. Wages meant keeping a job, on never being ill, or unemployed. Ten pounds in the bank would mean staying on the outside even if the worst happened. She hurried on, looking ahead, not back, but her breathing didn't steady until she stood below the clock outside the jeweller's at the junction of Mill and Taff Street. The hands pointed to twenty-five minutes past one. Mandy and Judy had told her to meet them at half-past, and the last thing she wanted was to walk into the New Inn early, and risk facing the waiters alone.

She idled five minutes away window shopping, studying trays of wedding and engagement rings, and next to them eternity rings. She knew about rings because the nurses in the workhouse had talked about them, the unmarried ones, that is; all the married ones discussed was ways of making ends meet.

She gazed at glittering arrays of brightly polished gold engagement rings set with tiny diamond chips. Some had two, some three, but the ones she liked best had just one central stone set in the middle of the band. She wondered if any man would ever buy her a ring like that. The housemother in Church Village had warned her to forget marriage and concentrate on getting a domestic position with a good family, because no decent mother or father would allow their son to ally himself with an orphan: there was no saying what kind of tainted blood might flow in her veins.

She thought of the boys she'd met since she had run away from Bletchetts'. Boys like Eddie who looked with adoring eyes at Jenny Griffiths; and who could blame him, giving Jenny's milk white complexion and golden hair. And William, despite his friendly manner and humorous pleasantries, kept his flirting for Tina Ronconi. Neither of the boys had ever attempted to kiss her, or put a hand on her knee as some of the boys in the orphanage had done. Not that she'd wanted them to, but it would have been nice if they'd made allowance for the fact that she was a girl, as opposed to treating her as though she were part of the furniture. It merely endorsed what the housemother had said: being an orphan meant she had no right to expect romance. She would have to learn to be grateful for the blessing she did have. A room of her own in a temporary home with Phyllis. And even Phyllis was an unmarried who had no ring. Just a bastard by someone else's husband, a man who couldn't even marry her. Was that the most she could expect for herself? If it was she'd settle for it, and happily. It was preferable to accepting that no man would ever look at her the way Eddie looked at Jenny, or kiss her the way Haydn had kissed Mandy when he'd thought no one was looking. She wanted something to look forward to, even if it was only as fleeting as the affairs Haydn had with the showgirls. What was it Ann had said? 'Memories to warm old age'. Something to hold on to: the knowledge that a man had cared for her, if only for one night.

Perhaps that ten pounds could buy her even more than security. In freeing a portion of her wages for pretty clothes and perfume, it might go some way towards buying her a boyfriend, one who didn't care too much about where she'd come from.

The clock pinged as the large hand reached the half-hour. Taking a deep breath, she steeled herself and crossed the road. Walking up the short flight of stone steps, she pushed open the etched glass-panelled mahogany door and stepped on to the thick carpet of the foyer. She stood there, mesmerised by her reflection in the gilt-edged mirrors. She never thought the day would come when she'd be surrounded by glittering chandeliers, wood panelling, a sumptuous staircase and silk wallpaper. Overwhelmed by the opulent atmosphere, and the curious stares, clothes, hats and scent of the women walking into lunch, she failed to notice the uniformed porter approaching her.

'Can I help you, madam?' He laid an emphasis on 'madam' that turned the word into an insult.

'I'm meeting friends,,' she stammered uncertainly.

'The dining room is that way, madam.'

'I know, thank you.' She held her head high as she walked away. But for all her show of self-possession she couldn't help feeling that the porter knew she didn't belong here. She wondered if the ten pounds would really stop her from feeling inferior to everyone else.

It was then she decided that the money took precedence over her loyalty to Phyllis, and her modesty. Savings would provide her with the buffer she needed against illness, or unemployment, and perhaps even lend her the confidence to face people like that porter and look them in the eye.

'We've ordered salad sandwiches again.' Mandy greeted her as she walked through the double doors into the smaller of the two dining rooms. 'And a pot of coffee for three. Is that all right with you?'

Jane murmured assent as she sat down. She put her hand into her pocket and fingered the knotted handkerchief that still did service as a purse. 'Isn't it my turn to pay?'

'Mine,' Judy said, 'yours next time.'

'And then you'll have your ten pounds.'

'Nervous?' Judy poured coffee into the cups set out on the table.

'A bit.'

'Only a bit?' Mandy giggled. The sound attracted disapproving glares from two matrons at an adjacent table. 'I went doolally tap the first time I posed in the altogether.'

'Did you, really?' Jane demanded earnestly. 'You're not just saying that to make me feel better?'

'Good Lord, no. I was gibbering, a complete idiot. The photographer had the patience of an angel. If he hadn't, I'd be back in Bermondsey now, working as a skivvy in a dosshouse or a pub.'

That was a little too close for comfort for Jane.

'Most Revue girls start by posing for photographers.' Judy divided the sandwiches between their plates.

'Is that how you got started?'

'I think I saw the inside of every studio in London before I got a break in Revue. But it's not easy to make a decent living, or an indecent one come to that, out of snapshots. A couple of afternoons' work here, a couple of nights there. Money coming in dribs and drabs, nothing regular. All the while hoping that someone who matters will see your pictures and offer you a contract with a weekly wage. I was almost at the point of giving up when Adrian, he's the one who produced this Revue . . .'

'I thought Norman Ashe was the producer,' Jane interrupted.

'Only for this tour. He works for Adrian just like the rest of us. Adrian's the real driving force. He devises and opens revues in London. If they take off, he organises the money for a provincial tour, and in the meantime starts off another Revue in another London suburb. That way he always has at least two, and sometimes more shows running simultaneously. He's a good man for a showgirl to know.'

'I thought the Revue made its money at the box-office.'

'Darling, you're a complete innocent. It costs hundreds, if not thousands of pounds to put a show like the one we're in, on the road. There's the wages for a start, then the train tickets, the scenery to be constructed, painted and lugged around, the costumes, and Lord only knows they cost the earth. The fans alone cost over ten pounds each.'

'Ten pounds!'

'Real ostrich feathers, and a lot of them. They never come cheap, and the cloaks, spirit gum and sequined stars, they may not be big, but they are expensive, and there's Haydn's and Billy's suits. Not to mention the wages bill for rehearsals as well as the show. Not just ours, but the orchestra's, and Norman's as well. Then there's all the fees that have to be paid for the use of the music, and the cost of making all the bookings in the theatres, costs that have to be met no matter whether anything's made in ticket receipts, or not.'

'I've never heard of a revue that lost money, or an impresario who's gone broke,' Mandy said picking up a sandwich.

'Not a Revue,' Judy agreed, 'but there have been shows that have bombed.'

'All too often.'

'Well anyway, as I was saying, Adrian saw some pictures I'd had taken in a studio in Southwark, or perhaps it was Brixton. Where doesn't matter, only the pictures, they were being sold in packets of twelve for a pound like they are, and –'

'Twelve for a pound!'

'The photographer's got to make his money somehow, sunshine. He's not going to pay ten pounds just for the pleasure of looking at what we've got. He can see that for a darned sight less in any Revue.'

'But twelve for a pound. He could make . . .'

'Hundreds,' Mandy mumbled through a full mouth. 'Most of them do. Here,' she pulled an envelope out of her bag. 'Look at these, only for heaven's sake keep them under the tablecloth. The old hag behind us has already turned purple listening in on our conversation. We don't want her choking to death.'

Jane opened the envelope and the white folder inside it. After the Revue she thought nothing could shock her. She was wrong. Seeing Mandy posed in front of a dark grey backdrop which accentuated every curve and contour of her pale, naked body was somehow far more shocking than seeing her standing among the smoke, fans, feathers and coloured lighting on stage.

'I keep those because I think they show my assets to their best advantage.'

Jane flicked through them, conscious of her burning cheeks as she tried to concentrate on the props, the strings of beads, feathers, and wisps of gossamer scarves that drew attention to, rather than concealed what Mandy so disarmingly called her 'assets'.

'So, we make an easy tenner for an hour, or at the most two's work, which can't be bad by anyone's standard.' Judy finished her sandwiches and poured out more coffee. 'The photographer's happy, although he's had to foot the bill for our fee, the studio, film and developing, because he knows he's going to make his profit by selling the photographs . . .'

'To theatre people?'

'Don't be a goose. To anyone who wants to buy them.'

'Like who?'

'Well, he can hardly put them up on the wall of the local bookshop. Most of them are sold around pubs.'

'For anyone to buy?' Jane was alarmed at the thought of Eddie, William, Evan and especially Haydn seeing hers.

'I wouldn't think many people in Pontypridd have a pound to spare so the chances are this lot will end up in Cardiff. Come on, finish your coffee, if we don't make a move we're going to be late.'

'I was expecting you to call in yesterday.'

'Charlie kept me busy all day, then I had to train in the evening. Didn't get home until two. Exhibition fight tomorrow in the Palais de Danse,' Eddie explained, his spirits soaring. Jenny was behaving as though she was already his girlfriend.

'I saw your Haydn.'

'That's more than anyone in the family's done since he's been home.'

Jenny leaned on the counter as an energy-sapping tide of relief swept through her veins. She'd been terrified that Eddie had stayed away because Haydn had told him about Sunday night. As Eddie obviously had no idea what had happened between her and his brother, she still had a chance to carry out her threat. She smiled at him. 'If there's a big fight tomorrow, I suppose you're training tonight?'

'I can take a couple of hours off to take you somewhere,' he offered, his pulse racing at the thought.

'If you come here straight from work, we could go for a walk. I'll make us something to eat, then you can go directly to the gym afterwards, that way you don't have to go home for tea.' All she could think of was that the closer she kept Eddie to her, the less time he'd have to spend with his brother.

'If you're sure about the tea.' Joey Rees, his trainer, would play hell if he didn't get to the gym at all the night before a fight. But if he ran up the hill after finishing in the shop he could be with Jenny by half-past six; if he'd stayed until half-past nine that would give them three hours together, and him a couple of hours' sparring practice before Joey left the gym. The old man rarely went home much before midnight.

'I'm sure.'

He felt as though he were drowning in her limpid blue eyes. 'In that case, the sooner I make the rest of my deliveries the sooner I'll be through for the day.' He went outside and pulled his butcher's bicycle away from the wall beneath the window. She left the counter, and followed him to the door. 'Then you didn't call in the shop for anything in particular?'

'Only to see you,' he admitted sheepishly.

'In that case, you'd better have this to be going on with until tonight.' She bent forward and kissed him full on the lips, much to the horror of her mother, who chose that moment to walk down the stairs and into the shop.

Jane's heart beat more and more erratically as she climbed the steep flight of narrow stairs. Mandy ran confidently ahead as though she hadn't a care in the world, and Judy brought up the rear, effectively sealing off her escape should she change her mind, making Jane feel like a prisoner flanked by two guards.

At the top of the stairs facing them was a door bearing a dog-eared, handwritten cardboard plaque that announced 'Studio' in rickety letters. Mandy pushed it open without knocking. Not quite knowing what to expect, Jane found herself in a large, rather grubby room, with two doors leading off, one marked w.c. the other DARKROOM. A tattered papered screen stood in the corner, shawls and dressing gowns draped in multicoloured confusion over the top.

'Yoo-hoo, Merv!' Mandy shouted. 'It's us.'

'Nice and early like good girls should be,' Merv beamed as they trooped in, one after the other. He was short, fat, round, looked young, but could have been any age between twenty-five and forty-five, and had a high-pitched, squeaky voice. Jane wasn't at all sure what an exotic photographer should look like, but if she'd been asked to describe one she wouldn't have come up with Merv. He waddled from behind his camera to kiss first Mandy, then Judy on the cheek. 'And this is?' He looked Jane up and down, and any warm feelings she might have felt towards him dissipated as she sensed him mentally undressing her.

'You did say you wanted someone new?' Judy explained.

'Someone – yes ducky, but this one hasn't got very much on the top storey, has she?'

'I thought you wanted someone young.'

'Of course,' he slapped himself lightly on the forehead with the heel of his hand. 'For the older man who likes young girls. But she is *really* young, isn't she?'

'I'm eighteen,' Jane asserted.

'And I suppose you think that's old enough to be kissed, and know your own mind?' He walked around Jane assessing and appraising every inch of her diminutive figure. 'I can see it now: young and waiflike. Just right for the market I had in mind. You're a clever girl.' He tweaked Judy's cheek. 'She might do. Her figure's right, but her hair. Oh ducky, the hair.' He pulled off Jane's beret and tugged at the cropped strands that much to Jane's despair hadn't grown an inch in the nine days since she'd left the workhouse.

'There's no need to worry about her hair, we've brought a wig.'

'A long one that can be put in plaits for the schoolgirl look?'

'Or left loose. She looks good with a layer of make-up. We practised last Saturday. And just wait until you see her legs. They're long, slim, and perfect . . .'

Jane cringed in embarrassment. She felt like a bargain offer that Judy was trying to offload on to a reluctant customer. What was she doing in this room with this ghastly man? What *would* Phyllis say if she could see her now?

'You girlies get ready. I'll do you first, Mandy, then you, Judy. That way one of you can get her make-up on while I take the other's pictures. Then I'll give her a trial. But I'm warning you now,' he looked Jane in the eye for the first time since she'd entered the room, 'if I don't like what I see, there'll be no payment. If I do, it'll be ten pounds, same as the other two.'

'Don't worry Merv, you'll like what you see.' Judy ran her fingers lightly along the check worsted that was stretched tighter than a second skin across his buttocks. 'I promise you, you'll love her.'

'So,' Babs wiggled her fingers inside Haydn's collar. 'When am I going to meet your family?'

'Not this week,' Haydn growled, very aware of Helen's eyes focused on him as they stood in the wings waiting for Chuckles to call them.

'But you promised,' Babs whined. 'You said . . .'

'I didn't promise you could meet my family.' Leaving the chest he was sitting on, he paced closer to the stage. Shame seared, hot and suffocating in his throat. Despite the pouts and dramatics, he knew Babs was genuinely hurt, and it was his fault. Babs was what she was. Honest, if nothing else that he admired. He'd made use of her, or rather her body, and now, because of the talk he'd had with his father he could only see her through Evan's eyes. And he didn't like what he saw. The tawdry looks that might have aspired to prettiness if they hadn't been submerged beneath layers of greasepaint both on and off stage. The transparently shallow emotions and conversational lines born in a scriptwriter's mind, not any original thought.

What was he doing? To himself, to Babs – to Rusty, Mandy and all the other girls he'd courted for a night, occasionally a few weeks but never longer. What was he trying to prove by making love to every attractive woman who crossed his path? That he could have any female he wanted?

Could he still be subconsciously trying to hurt Jenny? Had there been anything left between them before last night? If there had, she was certainly out of his life now. Only there was Eddie. Hot-headed, irresponsible, reckless Eddie. His temper had been getting him into trouble since their cradle days. Always had to go at everything bull at a gate, even courting. But Jenny had been right about one thing: Eddie would be putty in the hands of a woman who gave him what he wanted. And after last night, he didn't doubt that Jenny would do just that.

He pictured Eddie and Jenny making love as he had done so many times in Brighton. Did he still love her? How could he, when he had been only too happy to climb into bed with so many other woman? Perhaps that was the trouble. So many women, who'd been only to happy to strip and indulge in sexual athletics with him, and amongst all of them, not one he'd wanted to talk to afterwards, as he'd once talked to Jenny. Jenny – everything always came back to Jenny . . .

'Haydn!' Chuckles was leaning on the edge of the orchestra pit shouting up at him. 'When you've woken up, perhaps you'd care to join us?'

'Sorry, miles away,' Haydn apologised, walking on to centre stage.

'Rehearsing all day and doing two shows a night doesn't make for a lively boy,' Chuckles conceded. The lad did look tired, but then he was the one who wanted to make it in the toughest profession in the world. He should start taking better care of himself. Sleep at nights instead of rolling about with chorus girls.

'Right, opening number from the top. Babs stage left, Helen stage right.'

The orchestra struck, Haydn counted the beat – one – two – three – one – two – three – and sang the opening refrain. Babs and Helen joined in the chorus, dancing in from the wings. Babs was smiling like a trouper through the tears on her cheeks because she'd pushed her luck too often with Chuckles, and daren't risk another shouting match. Haydn held out his arms, they took them. The three of them together, high-stepping, kicking and singing.

He had a vision of himself the way Pontypridd would see him now: centre stage with fine clothes on his back, money in his pocket, beautiful girls hanging on to his arms. If only they knew the sordid truth behind the illusion of glitter and glamour. Wine, women, song and the high life of variety were nothing like they were cracked up to be.

'There, that's it.'

'You sure this covers . . .'

'It covers everything that needs to be covered. Jane, stop fussing, an inch higher and Merv won't be able to sell a single photograph.' Judy stood back and surveyed the triangle of flesh-coloured silk she'd stuck over Jane's pubic hairs with spirit gum. She knew exactly how uncomfortable it was and, unlike Jane, how much hell it would be to pull off afterwards.

'Merv's right,' she mused, staring disapprovingly at Jane's small breasts. 'You haven't got much on the top storey. You'll have to use whatever you're holding to push up what little you do possess. But then, I've seen worse come out reasonably well in black and white.' She picked up the wig. Holding it on her arm she swept Jane's short fringe aside and pulled it on over her head. 'Wonderful, Lady Godiva personified. Touch more lipstick –' she dabbed another glossy application on to the bright red bow she had made of Jane's mouth. 'Bit more shading on your cheeks to highlight your cheekbones. I do envy you your arms and legs. They're so thin; mine are beginning to turn flabby. I know they are, so don't try telling me otherwise. A couple more years and I'm going to be out on my arse. But then a couple more years and hopefully I won't have to worry where my next crust is coming from.'

'When you've stopped gabbling in there, Judy I've got photographs to take.'

'Coming, Merv. Here,' she pushed Jane out from behind the screens ahead of her. 'Let's show him the swan we've made from the ugly duckling, shall we?'

Jane stumbled out into the studio. By holding her fan in front of her she succeeded in covering her breasts and all trace of the scrap of cloth glued between her thighs.

'Mm, not bad. Not bad at all,' Merv circled her again. 'Good legs, good arms, good bum. Stand over there, and stop shaking if you can, ducky, or you'll be nothing but a blur on the prints.'

'Come on, love.' Mandy, who was wearing the briefest of G strings, took Jane's hands and guided her on to a raised dais set in front of a plain blue backcloth. Jane stood there trembling uncontrollably while Merv studied her for what seemed like for ever.

'Schoolgirl,' he announced.

'Plaits,' Judy groaned.

'And hockey stick, and school shirt and tie. They're in the chest in the changing room. Get them for me would you, ducky?' he asked Judy. 'And while you're rummaging I'll set up a Lady Godiva back shot. Turn your back to me – what's your name again?'

'Jane,' Mandy supplied helpfully.

'Think I'd remember plain Jane, wouldn't you? Look over your shoulder and stare at the camera. Leave the fan out of it,' he shouted in exasperation as Jane draped the ostrich feathers behind her to hide her exposed buttocks. 'Take it off her, will you, Mandy. Turn your head again. Sweep her hair over her left shoulder, it's hiding her back and that's what the customers will

203

want to see. That's it, *hold it*, and smile.' There was a click and a whirr, then another and another, and another. 'Smile, for pity's sake, smile. And again, and again. Good. No! Move her head on to the other shoulder, Mandy. You're still way too stiff and awkward, plain Jane.'

'Look at that lens as though it's the best-looking boy you've ever seen and he's in love with you. Imagine him down on one knee proposing,' Mandy hissed in her ear. 'That's what I do, and it hasn't failed to work for me yet.'

Jane gazed at the lens and imagined Haydn. Not tired and grumpy as she'd seen him when he'd emerged from his room that morning badly in need of a shave, but handsome, carefree, debonair, as he was every night when he danced in the enchanted moonlit garden. She pictured him standing alongside her, singing to her the way he did to Rusty and Mandy.

'Absolutely perfect! Spot on! You little love. Couldn't be better. Hold it, *hold it*!' More clicks and whirrs, clicks and whirrs. 'And while you're in the mood, ducky, let's try the other shoulder again.'

'All right, Merv,' Judy grinned when he finally called a halt to the proceedings to change the films in his cameras.

'She may not have much jutting out upstairs, but I'll grant you she's not bad for a beginner. You did say she hadn't done this before?' he glanced over to where Mandy was plaiting Jane's wig.

'Virgin fresh,' Judy confirmed drily.

'And she's not with the show?'

'Would you believe, an usherette?'

'If she lives right here in Ponty, I might be able to put more work her way.'

'And what about us?'

'You'll get your cut.'

'Four not two?'

'If she agrees to do more than this one session.' He clapped his hands loudly. 'Ready for front shots now, ducky. Mandy, show her how to stand, and where to put her legs and the hook of that hockey stick. Hold the shirt together. Under, not over your tits, they need pushing up, not covering up.'

Judy took Jane's hand and manoeuvred it into the position Merv wanted, carefully arranging the hockey stick so it concealed the scrap of cloth welded between her thighs. 'Breathe in and push your chest out,' she ordered. 'That's it, as far as it will go. All right Merv?'

'Get her a fraction sideways, there isn't much of a curve, but taken at the right angle it might do.'

With orders being flung at her from all directions, Jane had no time to worry about her nakedness. Between remembering to hold her breath, her position, her smile, and imagining the camera lens as Haydn's eyes, the whole experience passed so quickly she was surprised when Merv shouted it was over.

'As soon as I develop them, I'll give you a set.' He unhooked the camera from its stand and carried it into the darkroom.

'When will they be ready?' Judy asked, walking towards the screen that closed off the corner Merv had grandly referred to as the 'dressing room'.

'Tomorrow morning soon enough for you?'

'I'll pick them up.'

'You'll get your money then.'

Jane looked at the other two. She'd been expecting her money straight away.

'Standard practice, love,' Judy reassured. 'If something goes wrong with the film, or the pictures are duds, the photographer's entitled to another session.'

'Don't worry, nothing's likely to go wrong with these.' Merv read the crestfallen expression on Jane's face. 'Here, as it's your first time, take a fiver on account.'

'Thank you.' Clutching the shirt to her chest Jane tried to pass him.

'You'll be available again. Perhaps next week?'

'I don't know,' she answered doubtfully looking from Judy to Mandy

'Up to you, love, we'll be gone by then,' Judy said.

'Without Mandy and Judy I'd have no one to do the make-up, or the hair.'

'No need to worry about that, ducky. I'd get someone in to help.'

'I'll think about it.' Now that it was finally over, all she wanted to do was get behind the screens and dress.

'Hold on to the top of the screen and clench your teeth,' Judy ordered as she followed her. 'And try not to scream while I pull this triangle off you.'

Merv was sitting, talking to Mandy when Judy and a red-faced Jane finally emerged from behind the screens. He noted Jane's simple, black work dress, so very different from Judy and Mandy's elaborate 'walking-out costumes'. The girl looked as though she was on her uppers, and in his experience it was the poor ones who were generally the hungriest for work, and incidentally made the most profit for him.

'Mandy tells me you're not with the Revue, you're an usherette.'

'That's right.'

'Look, I meant what I said earlier about putting more work your way. As you live in Pontypridd, on the job as it were, I could make you quite a wealthy girl.'

'Would you want me often?' Jane ventured, tempted by the money, but disinclined to repeat the experience without Judy and Mandy's support.

'Depends on the reception the portfolio I took today gets. My customers are always on the lookout for something new, and at the moment you're new. Then there's always the camera club. That pays more, of course . . .'

'No,' Mandy broke in forcefully. 'No camera club. What kind of a girl do you take Jane for?'

'The kind who wants to make money.' Merv shrugged his shoulders. 'But if I've offended, sorry I suggested it.'

'What's a camera club?' Jane asked as they left the studio.

'A lot of dirty old men who pay Merv to use his studio. In return for their money they get the use of a camera without a film in it and a model. Generally a girl who's desperate or naive enough to work completely in the nude.'

'And with one girl and anything up to twelve or more men in one room I give you one guess as to what can happen to the girl.'

'If you do decide to work for Merv again, then make sure you lay down the rules,' Mandy advised her seriously. 'Only him in the studio, no one else. And you're safe enough with him, he's as queer as they come. Insist on a locked door, check the rooms to make sure no one is hiding, and always, always . . .'

'Take a girlfriend, if not two or three with you. Preferably big, heavy ones.'

'Has anything ever happened to you?'

'No, because we're too bloody careful, but it has to some of the other girls. It's a way of making a living, love, but let's face it, it is slightly tacky.'

'Speak for yourself,' Mandy retorted.

'I was, actually,' Judy answered, regretting the greed that had led her to manoeuvre Jane into a position where she could be used and abused by Merv, and with the Revue moving on, no one to turn to for help after next Sunday. 'Look all I'm saying is if you take your clothes off again, just be sure you don't do it where a man will be able to take advantage of you. Promise me you'll remember that much of my advice even if you forget the rest?'

'I promise.'

'And if you can, come into the New Inn lunchtime tomorrow and I'll give you your money, and your photographs.'

'What are you going to do with the ten pounds, Jane?' Mandy asked. 'Buy a new wardrobe?'

'Save it,' Jane answered decisively. 'I'm going to open a Post Office account.'

'Wise girl. My mother used to tell me that a Post Office account was a girl's best friend. The type of relationship you could always fall back on provided you put enough into it.'

'I'll tell you something for nothing,' Judy said caustically. 'It's the only one that will never let you down.'

Chapter Thirteen

'You look as though you're in a dream, love. Everything all right?' Harry Griffiths asked his daughter as she stood in front of the shop window, dressed in one of her new frocks and her mother's 'best' embroidered apron.

'On top of the world.'

'Seen Haydn yet?' he ventured apprehensively, wary of stepping into an emotional minefield.

'It's over between us, Dad.'

'You sure?'

'Absolutely certain.' She gave him a bright, insincere smile, as Eddie walked into the shop dressed for an outing in a light grey sports coat, well pressed, dark grey trousers, clean white shirt and lurid red and blue tie.

'Hello, Mr Griffiths, hello Jenny.' He pushed a shilling across the counter. 'Packet of Woodbines, please.'

'You look smart, Eddie. Off to a match?'

'Not exactly, Mr Griffiths.'

'Charlie must be doing well if he can afford to pay you enough to dress like that.'

'So well he bought a van today.'

'Times must be getting better.'

'For everyone since they've reopened the Maritime.'

'Your dad going back on shift there?'

'I don't know, Mr Griffiths. If he is, he hasn't said anything to me about it.'

Harry was suddenly aware of Jenny hovering at his elbow. As he reached down the packet of cigarettes he glanced from her to Eddie. 'I'd better get those sacks of potatoes in from the yard before they get damp. Will you give Eddie his change, love?'

'You won't be long will you, Dad? I was just about to go out.'

'Two minutes.' Harry closed the storeroom door behind him.

Eddie didn't notice Jenny's new dress. Only that she looked prettier than usual. He couldn't help wondering if she'd made the effort for him. 'Where we going for our walk then? Town?'

'How about Shoni's? It'll be light for a while yet, and it's warm enough to sit outside.'

Shoni's was the only place on the Graig where the trees grew thick enough for a courting couple to find a spot that wasn't overlooked.

'Suits me,' he mumbled, running his tongue over his lips.

'I've packed a picnic tea.'

'I could eat something.'

'I've yet to meet a man who couldn't. Just give me a couple of minutes to get my hat and I'll be with you.'

The storeroom door opened.

'I'll wait outside,' he called to her, hoping to avoid exchanging more small talk with her father. He backed out into old Mrs Evans, almost knocking her over.'

'Sorry Mrs Evans,' he tipped his cap apologetically.

'That's the trouble with young people today,' she muttered darkly from between toothless gums. 'Always barging around, never considering anyone except yourselves.'

'Really sorry . . .'

'Can I help you, Mrs Evans?' Jenny stepped in, enabling Eddie to escape.

'Two ounces of sugar, on the slate.'

'So that's the way the land lies,' Harry Griffiths observed as Mrs Evans left the shop, only to continue lecturing Eddie on the pavement.

'What way?' Jenny opened the door that led to their private quarters and lifted her hat and jacket from the stand.

'Don't play innocent with me, it doesn't wash, young lady. Has Eddie taken over where Haydn left off?'

'How could he, when I haven't been out with Haydn in over eight months?'

'All right, I'll put it another way. How long has this been going on between you and Eddie?'

'Nothing's "going on" as you put it. Eddie took me to the theatre the other night.'

'And?'

'And I enjoyed myself, so I thought I'd repay him with a picnic. I made some sandwiches earlier with the shop's ham and roast pork. I hope you don't mind.' She picked up a bulging shopping bag she'd stashed under the coats.

'I don't care what you take from the shop, as long as it's in moderation, you know that. But I'm warning you now, watch what you do with Eddie Powell. Behave yourself and see that he behaves. You know what I'm talking about?'

'Dad, we're going on a *picnic*.'

'And Eddie's Haydn's younger brother. Just don't go doing anything silly like trying to get back at Haydn through Eddie. Blood's thicker than water. And when push comes to shove, the Powells have always been a close-knit clan, and Eddie – well, he's a nice enough lad, or at least I've always thought so, unlike some around here. Good boxer too, with a great future if Joey Rees is to be believed, but he has a quick temper.'

'And what's that supposed to mean?'

'I'd hate to see it turned on you, or his brother. I know you, Jenny; if you cause an argument between those two boys and either of them gets hurt, you won't be able to live with yourself.'

'Dad.' She left the hall, leaned over the counter and kissed his grizzled cheek. 'You're worrying about nothing. I promise you, nothing's going to happen between Haydn and Eddie, or between Eddie and me. We're just friends, that's all.'

'As long as it stays that way.'

'And what other way is there? Expect me when you see me.'

'It had better be early. Your mother's home and it's a week night,' he called as the shop bell clanged behind her.

'Ready, Jane.'

'For what?' She eyed Haydn suspiciously as she stood in front of the confectionery kiosk. 'Three Fry's Five Boy bars, and a bag of dolly mixtures please, Mrs Brown.'

'Sweet tooth?'

'Buying them for the girls.'

'They can buy their own, you know.'

'I don't mind running errands for them.'

'Because they pay you?'

'Only to do their mending.'

'Not to mention the pennies you make on the pasties you buy by the dozen in Charlie's.'

'I'm trying to make a living. One day I hope to earn as much as you.'

'*Touché.*' He watched as Lil Brown handed her the sweets and her change. 'You were the one who wanted dancing lessons and as I've half an hour to spare, I thought we'd fit another one in.'

'Now?'

'Right now.'

'But what about Rusty?'

'What about Rusty?'

'Won't she mind?'

'What if she does?'

'I know why you're giving me the lessons. But you've got it all wrong. I haven't said a word to her. I wouldn't, not to anyone . . .'

'I know you wouldn't,' he broke in irritably. 'Now do you want this bloody dancing lesson or not?'

Her legs were still aching from the last one, but she hesitated for only a moment. Opportunities had to be grabbed before they were snatched away. Haydn might be willing now, but it was anyone's guess as to what mood he'd be in tomorrow, with her –

or Rusty. 'I'll be with you just as soon as I've taken these sweets to the girls.'

Haydn insisted on going on to the stage. The garden set had been erected by the stagehands less than five minutes after the final curtain had fallen on the first performance, and it was the one area of the theatre that could be guaranteed to be deserted between houses. Most of the cast were in their dressing rooms, eating, smoking, quarrelling or playing cards. The theatre staff were in the bar and would remain there until the doors opened again. And the manager, Joe Evans and Norman Ashe were ensconced in the office, talking business with a brandy bottle at their elbow.

Jane followed Haydn out from the wings. Even with the curtains closed she found the surroundings bizarre, the floats lending a maze-like, nightmarish quality. Close up, the trees and flowers were just so many clumsy brushstrokes on canvas. They bore little resemblance to the luxuriant foliage of the magical garden that had enchanted her from the auditorium. An entrancing, glittering wonderland that, like Alice, she'd assumed she was doomed to catch tantalising glimpses of from afar, and never enter. It might have been better for her if she never had, she decided as she surveyed the scuffed wooden floor and worn fringes on the silk curtains. That way she could have clung to her fantasies.

Haydn walked confidently towards centre stage, the taps on his shoes ringing out over the boards, making their own music; her soft shoes, already showing sad signs of wear, shuffled uncertainly behind.

'Stand here,' he ordered brusquely like a sergeant-major on parade. 'Here. Facing me.' He stood with his back to the curtain. 'Watch every move I make, and copy it.'

He lifted his right leg; she followed suit. He brought it down sharply, crashing the toe tap on the staging. It rang out, killing the soft thud of her thin-soled shoe. He repeated the movement using the other leg; switching from one leg to the other he escalated the pace. Watching his every move intently Jane struggled to keep step with the tempo he set, determined to give him no cause for complaint.

'I was right, you do have a little talent,' he acknowledged after ten minutes of arduous foot gymnastics.

'Then it's worth me persevering?'

'That depends on what you intend to do with what you've learned. You have something in mind?'

She looked at her feet. She hadn't needed Mandy and Judy to tell her that she hadn't much going for her. Thin, skinny, with hair and features like a scruffy kid, and an undernourished kid at that. How could she even begin to tell Haydn, six feet two in his stockinged feet, well built, with the figure and face of an Adonis, and talent to match, that she wanted to go on stage? She'd never even attempted to dance a step until he'd swept her along the dressing-room corridor, and apart from hymns in school assemblies and church, she'd never sung a song through from beginning to end.

'You have nothing in mind?'

'Not at the moment.'

'No aspirations to be a chorus girl?'

When she didn't answer, some devil provoked him into goading her. 'Because if you have, you'll never make it. As I said, quite apart from looks, you haven't the height. There isn't a girl in Revue or Variety who's under five foot three or above five foot five. You might occasionally find the odd show with a taller chorus, but I've yet to hear of an impresario who hires midgets under five foot.'

'I might have some more growing to do.' She drew herself up to her full height.

'I doubt it. How old are you anyway? Sixteen, seventeen?'

'Eighteen.'

'You look about twelve.' He was aware that he was damaging more than her pride, yet was unable to stop; in some peculiar way, needling her eased his own frustration.

'Well then, perhaps I should forget about the chorus and become the British Shirley Temple.'

There was such a fierce, angry expression on her face he burst out laughing. 'There may be something in that. I could buy you a frilly frock and knickers and teach you to sing "The Good Ship Lollipop". Then when my star goes into decline you can keep me.'

'Jane?' Ann's voice echoed down the aisles.

'I have to go.'

'If you wait behind after the show I'll give you another half-hour lesson.'

'You don't have to. Really. You misunderstood –'

'For pity' sake, woman, stop apologising. I believe you.'

'Then why do you want to carry on?'

'Because it gives me something to do between houses other than cavorting with nudes in my dressing room.'

'I would never have told Phyllis that if I'd known you were Evan's son.'

'Isn't that bloody typical of a woman? First you ask me for dancing lessons, then, just as you show signs of a little – only a very little, mark you – talent, you start apologising and finding excuses as to why I shouldn't give them to you.'

'You were the one who said there was no point in my learning how to dance.'

'I merely asked what you intended to do, once you'd learned.'

'That's my business.'

'Do you, or don't you, intend to stay on at the end of the show tonight?' he demanded in exasperation.

'Yes!'

'In that case I'll see you in the rehearsal room as soon as I've changed out of costume. There's mirrors there that will show you *precisely* where you're going wrong.'

'The bluebells are still out.' Eddie pointed to a light dusting of colour brightening the green and brown shadows beneath an elm tree.

'Those aren't bluebells, silly, they're violets.'

'Same difference.'

'Most certainly not.' Jenny smiled to take the sting from her contradiction. 'Violets are smaller and sweeter.'

'Eat them, do you?'

She laughed at his poor joke then stretched out her arms to the warm evening air. 'It's good to get out like this. I feel as though the winter has lasted for ever. And it seems a million years since Christmas.'

'It always does once it's over. You're looking nice.'

Jenny smoothed the skirt of the blue dress she was wearing, the second of the two she had bought with the unexpected windfall from her father. 'Thank you.' She reached for his hand. It wouldn't have been much of a compliment coming from anyone other than Eddie, but she knew him well enough to realise it was the nearest he'd get to poetry.

'Where do you want to stop?'

Shoni's pond lay in front of them, its dark, tree-fringed expanse shimmering with the sparkling crimson and gold beams of the slowly dying sun. Willow boughs bent low, fingering the surface, sending ripples over the undulating surface to break against the bank. The flat rock known to all the Graig children as the diving rock lay on their right, half lost in undergrowth that would be trodden flat before school reopened for the autumn term. On the left bank a narrow meandering path led deeper into the valley, past secret copses and groves where lovers had held trysts since houses had been built on the Graig.

'How about we walk a little further?'

'If we go much further we'll be walking back in the dark.'

'Five minutes,' she pleaded.

He picked up the shopping bag and shouldered it again. It was heavy. He'd asked her what was in it, but she'd refused to tell him. Ten silent minutes later she was still leading the way, following the bed of the stream deeper into the woods.

'That's it, absolutely it.' He left the path and walked into a clearing. Jenny studied their position, trying to recall, from her outings with Haydn last year, where they were in relation to a sheltered, thickly wooded spot that couldn't be overlooked from either the path or the hill above.

'Here.' She ran a little way ahead on the opposite side to where he was standing. 'There's more wood violets. I can pick a posy for my room.'

'Bloody women and their flowers.' Eddie cursed under his breath as he followed. 'Jenny? Jenny?' He looked around. It was as though she had stepped off the face of the earth.

'Here.'

He heard her voice, but still couldn't see her. Two close-growing bushes parted, and her tousled blonde head emerged wreathed in leaves.

'There's a lovely sheltered hollow here. There's a blanket in the bottom of the bag. If we lay it down we'll be as snug as two birds in a nest.'

'No wonder the bag's so heavy.' He pushed his way through the bushes and dumped it at her feet. She opened it and took out not one, but two rugs. Spreading them side by side, she sat on one.

'There's room for two here.'

'Then why did you make me carry two rugs?'

'In case the ground was damp.'

'It hasn't rained in days.' He sat next to her. Resting his arms on his knees he unbuttoned his shirt pocket and pulled out the packet of Woodbines he had bought from her father, and a box of matches. He smoked while she busied herself with the rest of the contents of the bag. Extracting a tablecloth she laid it alongside the rug. On it she arranged a tin box of sandwiches, a shop-bought apple pie on a tin plate, a bottle of Thomas's orangeade, and two packets of biscuits, one plain, one chocolate.

'Your father got anything left to sell in the shop?'

'One or two things. The sandwiches are ham and mustard this side, cheese and pickle the other, and roast pork in the middle. Go on, try one.'

Helping himself, he began to eat. 'This isn't so bad. At least the midges don't seem to be out looking for human blood, and it's warm enough to sit without freezing your –'

'Thank you, Eddie.'

'Thank you what?'

'I know what you were going to say.'

'No you don't.' He took another sandwich and demolished it in two bites. The bread was cut thin, the butter spread thick, and he couldn't fault the quality of the meat. It was Charlie's best. 'I was going to say your posterior,' he grinned.

'If you were, it would have been the first time.'

'You accusing me of being crude?'

'Yes.' She poured out two enamel beakers of orangeade.

'You're probably right.' He took a beaker and held it up. 'Nice glass.'

'My father got them free for buying in Beecham pills.' She took a sandwich and curled up close to him, her head on her hand, her face inches away from his.

'It's dark in here, but the light will soon begin to fade outside too. We'd better not stay too long,' he warned, thinking about the fight tomorrow, and the temper Joey Rees would soon be nursing because he hadn't showed up for training.

'We could wait until the moon and stars come out to guide us back.'

'You thinking of setting up home here?' He took the last sandwich from the box, oblivious to the fact that he'd eaten nine to her one.

'Not home, but it's cosy enough for one night.'

'Your father might have something to say about that.'

'What? I'm a grown woman, I know my own mind.'

'Do you, now?'

'Yes,' she affirmed, hoping she wouldn't have to spell her intentions out. It would be less obvious if he took the lead. 'Can I cut you a slice of apple pie?'

'My mouth is still full of sandwich.'

'I was just wondering if you had the pie or something else in mind for afters?'

He tried to read the expression on her face. It was difficult to see her features in the green and gold twilight of the copse. 'The other night, you said you wanted no more funny business. That

217

we should "get to know one another better" before we went any further.'

'The other night we were in the storeroom. My father walks in that way from the Morning Star.'

'And I thought it was me you were backing away from. Why didn't you say something?'

'Because I wanted to wait until we were completely alone, with no danger of anyone disturbing us.' She picked up the tablecloth by the corners and moved it to the head of the blanket they were lying on. Stretching out on her back, she rested her head in the crook of her elbow. Lifting her other arm she caught the hem of her skirt, raising it half-way up her thigh, exposing her stocking top. She gazed into his eyes, seeing her own reflection mirrored in their depths. 'Like now, for instance.'

Eddie stared at her. She shuddered as though she'd been hit by a jet of cold water. If he'd told her at that moment that he had the power to see past the coquetry and teasing to the scheming and subterfuge that had induced her to arrange this picnic, she would have believed him.

Unable to bear his look a moment longer, she closed her eyes. A vivid image of Haydn intruded into her mind. Once again she heard the bitter, angry words they had flung at one another. What was she doing? In love with one brother and about to make love to another? She'd made the same mistake once before and paid dearly for it. Now she was compounding the whole disastrous mess.

Eddie rolled on top of her and closed his lips over hers. His tongue, warm, probing, darted between her teeth; his hands set to work on the buttons of her dress.

'Eddie I . . .' the feeble protest died as he bent his head to her throat.

'I like your idea of a picnic place.' He lifted her with one hand, pushing her dress down over her shoulders with the other.

She shivered, the cool air raising goose pimples on her skin as he tore off her underclothes. When she was naked, he straightened his arms, rose above her and looked at her. She waited, willing him to say he loved her, but he remained silent as he stripped off his own clothes.

'The other blanket is behind you.' She regretted the words almost before they were out of her mouth. Eddie was no fool. He would realise she'd planned this from the outset. Trying to rectify matters, she slipped her hand between his thighs.

'That's man's work.' Pushing her legs apart with his knee he drove relentlessly into her, paying no heed as she uttered a cry of pain. Making no allowances for her feelings or her needs, he made love to her the only way he knew how. Savagely, ruthlessly, fondling her breasts and thighs with rough embraces that bruised her delicate skin. His was a wild, uncaring act that had more in common with blows than caresses, born in primitive barbarism and driven by an appetite knew nothing of foreplay or finesse.

She arched her body, and dug her fingernails into his back, tearing his skin, wanting him to stop. But as the blood flowed, warm and sticky beneath her hands, it roused him all the more. Pain dissolved, first into excitement than into a pleasure bordering on anguish as she finally countered his brutality with a fierceness born of her own sudden, unexpected and overpowering lust.

'Jenny . . . Oh Jenny!' They were the only words he spoke as his passion peaked and died, but she treasured them. He had called her by name: that had to mean something. He'd realised he was with her, not some other girl he'd picked up. A few weeks of this and he'd be pleading with her to marry him. She'd see to it that he would.

'Watch carefully. This is where you're going wrong.' Haydn executed three small steps. 'Don't you see, all my movements are downwards, all of yours upwards.'

'Is that so bad?' Jane queried, weariness making her peevish. When she'd asked Haydn to teach her to dance she had no idea he'd take her request so seriously or devote so much time to it. She had a bag of mending which had to be done tonight as she'd have to be up first thing in the morning to be on Wilf Horton's stall by six.

'In tap all the movements are downwards, in ballet upwards. I'm trying to teach you tap,' Haydn retorted testily.

'Can't we carry on tomorrow?'

He looked into the full-length rehearsal mirror. They were standing side by side, her small, slight figure alongside his, her face white, pinched with exhaustion and strain. He glanced at his wristwatch. It was half-past eleven.

'Sorry,' he apologised, realising that in his eagerness to avoid Rusty and Mandy he'd lost all track of time. 'I had no idea it was so late.'

'It's just that I have to be up early tomorrow. Market day.' She walked across the room and picked up a carrier bag.

'But you're still doing the girls' mending.'

'I told you, I have to make a living.'

'Until you get a stage booking?'

'I'm an optimist, but not that much of one.'

He followed her out of the room, switching off the lights as they walked along the corridor. 'We'll leave by the stage door.' He fumbled in his pockets for the key.

'Have you had a lot of singing and dancing lessons?' she asked as they walked down the stone steps and out of the building.

'None.'

'But you're brilliant. All the girls say so.'

'When I went to Brighton last Christmas to do pantomime, I had two left feet. This time last year I was working here as a call-boy, and when they gave me a chance to go on stage I knocked everyone over. Just like a skittle ball.'

'You're pulling my leg.'

'I most certainly am not.'

'Then how come you're on stage now?'

'A week or so before my disastrous début, the lead comic of a show took the entire cast and Town Hall hands out for a drink.' He locked the door and tested it with his weight before walking on. 'I tagged along and someone persuaded me to sing. A rather wonderful head girl remembered my voice and wrote a couple of weeks later offering me a booking in Brighton. It was my first break, but it was my voice, not my feet, that got it. If she'd seen me dancing she wouldn't have picked up her pen.'

'But you can dance now.'

'Only because the choreographer in Brighton was a martinet who drilled me until I mastered the routines. Afterwards I got the girls to show me a few steps in between shows and rehearsals. I've never had a proper lesson.'

'What about singing lessons?'

'School and chapel choir, that's all.'

'I'd give anything to be able to sing like you, or Rusty.'

'Do you know that you can't?'

'No one's ever told me I can.'

'But you must have been in the school choir?'

'I was never able to stay behind for practice.'

They walked through Market Square, past the brightly lit windows of Rivelin's, through the deserted Tumble, under the railway bridge and up the Graig hill.

'What do your parents say about your ambition to go on stage?' Every righteous, God-fearing chapel woman Haydn knew in Pontypridd would move heaven and earth to keep her daughter away from the evil influences of the theatre.

'I'm an orphan.'

'I thought Phyllis said you'd lived on a farm in Church Village?'

'I did,' she said hastily, caught in a trap of her and Phyllis's making. 'But the people there took me from the orphanage.'

'You've no idea who your parents are?'

'I never knew them.'

He fell silent. Her admission explained some of the things that had puzzled him. Her lack of clothes, her quick readiness to do whatever people asked of her – for a price. Her eagerness to please, which he had never felt was entirely sincere, and the inner reserve he had never quite broken through.

'So they were right.'

'Who was right?'

'My housemother. I had dozens of them, but when I was fourteen one came into the home who was nicer than the rest. She used to allow us older girls to sit up with her and do the mending after the little ones had been put to bed. She told us,' she glanced defiantly at Haydn from under her hat, 'that people would never think we were as good as them, because none of us knew where we came from, or what kind of blood was flowing in our veins. That it could be bad blood, criminal's blood, even a murderer's.'

'And you believed her?'

'It's true, isn't it? You haven't said a word to me since I told you I'm an orphan'

'It wouldn't make a shred of difference to me if you were King Kong's daughter.'

'Yes it would. You know who your mother and father are. You have a brother and sisters, uncles and aunts. You know exactly who they are, and what they've done. The only thing I know about my mother is that she was unmarried, and registered in the workhouse three months before I was born as May Jones. When I was six weeks old she was found a job as a domestic outside the workhouse, but she ran away the first night she was there, and disappeared. Not that I blame her after . . .' she fell silent, remembering Phyllis's counsel.

'After what?'

'After seeing the way people look down on workhouse girls, especially unmarried mothers.'

'Were you in the workhouse with Phyllis?' he asked shrewdly. 'Is that where you met her?'

'It's none of your business where I met Phyllis.'

'Were you?' He gripped her arm.

'What I am, and where I've come from is no concern of yours.'

'If you've been lying to my family . . .'

'Your father and Phyllis know the truth. And as its their house I'm living in, they're the only ones who need to.' She tried to pull away from him, but he tightened his grasp.

'You're an unmarried mother, aren't you?'

'No!'

'Then why won't you tell me the truth?'

'Because it's none of your concern.' She finally managed to wriggle out of his hold and ran on ahead. He followed at a slower pace, resolving to ask his father just what he thought he was doing, taking in a workhouse girl with a past she felt she needed to lie about.

Chapter Fourteen

Haydn glanced up at the windows before climbing the steps that led to the front door. The only light burning was the one in the centre of the three bedroom windows – the box room. What Jane did with her free time was no concern of his, yet an irrational anger boiled up in him as he visualised her sitting up in the tiny room until heaven only knew what hour, forgoing rest and weakening her eyes just to do the chorus girls' mending. Despite her evasiveness and his suspicions, he couldn't help feeling that she was worth ten of them, yet she was the one earning a pittance while they made enough to buy whatever they wanted – including her time.

He turned the key and stole inside. Jane might not be sleeping, but the rest of the house probably was. A thin line of light shone beneath the kitchen door at the end of the passage. He hung his coat and hat in the hall before opening the door. The room was deserted. Two saucepans of water were on the warming rack on the stove, topped by plates covered by saucepan lids. He lifted one. Phyllis had left dinners for Jane and him – mashed potatoes, sausages, cabbage and onion gravy. His stomach, still knotted after the strenuous dancing lesson, heaved at the sight of the food. He looked around. There was no sign that Jane had been in the room, but he could hardly go upstairs, knock on her door and plead with her to come down and eat, not without risking waking the entire household.

He shouldn't have pressed her so hard. Before he'd asked her about the workhouse, he'd felt as though she was beginning to trust him. He hadn't realised until now how much that meant. In the competitive theatrical world, trust and friendship were luxuries in short supply. He regretted the impulse that had driven him to question Jane about her past – but then what if he hadn't? The secret she was trying so desperately to conceal could conceivably surface at any time, causing heaven only knew what damage, not only to her, but possibly to his father and the rest of the family – even Phyllis and Brian. No matter what he thought, his father had made it plain last night that they were now as much part of the family as he was. Probably more so, since he no longer lived at home. He had to find out what it was that Jane was hiding, warn his father. . . .

The front door opened and closed. Hobnailed boots grated over the flagstones of the passage, as Eddie tramped towards the kitchen door, totally oblivious to the din he was making.

'Big brother still up?' Eddie went to the range and lifted the lids on the pans. 'Supper, and you're not eating it. Where's Jane?'

'Gone to bed, I think.'

Haydn's uncertainty warranted a second glance from Eddie. 'You think? Didn't you walk up the hill with her?'

'I started to, but I wasn't walking quick enough for her.'

Eddie sat in his father's chair and unlaced his boots. 'Don't tell me there's actually one girl in Ponty who hasn't been smitten by the great Haydn Powell.'

'I wouldn't have Jane as a gift. Far too spiky for my liking.'

'I suppose she is, but then that's hardly surprising, considering . . . ' Eddie fell silent, remembering his promise.

'Considering what?'

'Considering she's living among strangers and just started a new job,' he finished unconvincingly.

'Pull the other one, Eddie. Aren't I a member of this family

225

any more? I live here, but no one thinks to tell me what's going on. I go away for eight months and all of a sudden I don't matter any more. Bloody hell, sometimes I think I'd know more about the people living in this house if I was the lodger.'

'You are the lodger.'

'Thank you very much.'

'What's the problem, big brother? Aren't we giving you the star treatment you're used to? Well if you don't like it, all you have to do is find a house where the inmates are impressed by the posters plastered all over town. God only knows there's enough of them hitting the eye at every turn.'

'What's that supposed to mean?'

'It means we all know you're a big man. You're famous, you have money to burn, and you've made it quite obvious you don't need any of us, so why do you insist on hanging around?'

'Is that what you think? That I don't want to be here?'

'If you did, you'd take the trouble to talk to us once in a while. That way, you might even find out what's going on as it's bothering you so much.'

'At the moment, between rehearsing all day and performing all night I haven't time to breathe.'

'Only to parade around Ponty Park with blondes.'

'That was one morning.'

'What do you expect us to do? Wait until you can spare a minute or two? Stand in a row by the front door, so you can pat our heads as you walk in and out?'

'Come on, spit it out. Just what is eating you, Eddie?'

'You. That's what's eating me. You with your London ways, your posh clothes, your phoney accent.'

'Damn it all, Eddie, I work on stage. The clothes, the way I talk, go with what I do for a living. Charlie'd soon boot you out if you turned up in his shop dressed like a miner. To get good bookings, I have to look the part.'

'Exactly my point. You do look the part. Would you like me to tell you what it is?'

'No!' Fighting to keep his temper under control, Haydn

walked over to the stove. Lifting the dinners off the saucepans, he paused on his way to the pantry. 'Do you want one of these? Because if you do I'll heat it up.'

'No thanks. I've had the last of big brother's leftovers that I'm going to take.'

'Eddie, please. Can't you see I'm trying? Won't you at least meet me half-way? If I've done something, I'd like to know what. If we talk . . .'

'Talk away.'

'What's the point, with you in this mood?'

'What mood?'

'All right, if that's the way you want it, let's try again,' Haydn said determinedly. 'Been sparring down the gym?' he asked, switching to what he hoped would be an innocuous topic.

'Yes.'

'Fight soon?'

'Palais, tomorrow night.'

'What time?'

'Half-past nine.'

'I'll call in as soon as I've finished the show. I might catch the last couple of minutes.'

'You won't. My opponent will hit the canvas before the first bell sounds.'

'Pretty confident, aren't you?'

'Big heads run in the family.'

'Do you want some tea?'

'I'll get it myself.' Eddie took the kettle from the stove and went out to the washhouse to fill it.

Haydn picked up the milk and sugar from the pantry and carried it to the table, thinking all the while of Jenny Griffiths and how difficult it was to bring her name up in conversation with anyone in the family. He lifted down two cups and saucers from the dresser.

'Playing mother?'

'Eddie, you're not making this easy, and I really do need to talk to you.'

'About what?' Eddie hooked the hotplate open and set the kettle on to boil.

'It's Jane,' Haydn said finally, lacking the courage to broach Jenny' name, thinking that if they could manage to discuss the questions raised by Jane's odd behaviour, it might be possible to bring up Jenny's threats later, when Eddie was in a more receptive mood.

'What about Jane?'

'I think she's hiding something from us.'

'What makes you say that?'

'Something she said.'

'You talk to her?'

'She asked me to teach her to dance.'

'Dance!' Eddie laughed. 'Somehow I can't see you as a dancing master.'

'You've seen me on stage.'

'Prancing from one nude to the other.'

Haydn allowed the insult to pass. 'We were talking about nothing much in particular when we got on to the subject of her family. She said she was an orphan. I asked her if she'd met Phyllis in the workhouse, and she clammed up. Told me where she'd met Phyllis was none of my business, and ran off.'

'That's not surprising.'

'What's not surprising? Why do I get the impression that I'm the only one in the house who doesn't know about her?'

'What's there to know?'

'That's what I'm trying to find out,' he shouted in exasperation.

'She's only the lodger. Who cares what she does?'

'I do, if it's going to get Dad into any more trouble.'

'And what would you know about that? You never went to see him in prison.'

'Because I was working the other end of the country at the time. Eddie, please, I don't want to quarrel with you. Can't you see I'm concerned? Dad told me that Phyllis was in the workhouse. That he feels guilty about her and Brian being there. If Jane was there as an unmarried mother . . .'

'And if she was?'

'If she was, someone must have taken her out. Perhaps we could go and see them and ask them to help get her baby out if that's what she wants. Damn it all, it's not her morals that concern me.'

'That's big of you.'

'Hasn't it occurred to you that she might have done something illegal to get out?'

'Like what?'

'If I knew I wouldn't be asking. But I'm afraid it could be something that could land Dad back behind bars.'

'Whatever she's done, she's living with us now. She told me Dad and Phyllis know her story, and that's good enough for me.'

'Then you do know something about her?'

'Only that she's had a rough time and could do with a little kindness. And seeing as how you're only lodging here for the duration of the show, it really isn't any of your business, is it?'

'Eddie, what's got into you?'

'I've told you. You. Coming back here. Looking down your nose at us. Telling us how to live our lives. Trying to change everything . . .'

'I'm not trying to change anything.'

'No? Then why are you throwing your money around? You tried to buy every round in the New Inn. You're as bad as Beth's bloody husband. Will and I earn good money now. Maybe not quite up to Revue standard,' Eddie mocked bitterly, 'but it's honestly earned, and we don't have to make fools of ourselves tiptoeing around naked girls to do it. We've got our lives sorted, thank you very much. We don't need you, your prying ways, or your damned charity.'

'Eddie,' Haydn reached out and laid a hand on his brother's shoulder. Eddie shrugged it off. Haydn walked away. If he'd stayed in the kitchen a moment longer he would have hit his brother, and given Eddie's prowess in the ring, that wouldn't have done any good. Any good at all.

Haydn lay on his bed in the front room and listened to the

229

kitchen clock chime away the hours. At three he heard the click of a light switch and the creak of a floorboard overhead. Jane was only just going to bed when she had to be up again at five. She hadn't eaten a proper meal all day, and it was his fault. Eddie had said nothing that went on in the house was his concern, but he couldn't help feeling that even if his family wasn't his concern any more, Jane was. After all, they worked in the same place. He'd taken her under his wing, was teaching her to dance, walking her home. But was he taking an interest in her because he had no one else? His father was too wrapped up in Phyllis and Brian to have much time for him – no, that wasn't fair, his father had waited up to talk to him on a Sunday night when he had an early start the next day, and he was to blame for the estrangement between himself and Eddie and, if he were honest, William and Diana as well. He hadn't taken the time to say more than half a dozen words to any of them since he'd been home. He should have left the girls to their own devices last Sunday and spent the day with his family. Was it too late to ask if he could join them next Sunday?

Feeling isolated, lonely and very sorry for himself, he turned over in the bed. This was a repetition of what he'd lived through when he'd left home to go to Brighton. Surrounded by people, and no one to talk to, not about things that mattered. No one? He thought of Bethan, the big sister who'd always tried to make everything come right for him as long as he could remember. If he left the house early in the morning he could walk up the hill and see her before rehearsals started at nine. Bethan was sensible. She would know what to do about Eddie and Jenny, and also about Jane. He punched his pillow and rested his head on it. His last thoughts were of his sister. Serene, smiling, and setting his world to rights.

Haydn was up, washed and dressed early in the morning, but before he emerged from his room at a quarter-past six he'd heard the front door bang shut four times. When he went into the kitchen Phyllis was alone with Brian, who was busily collecting the crumbs from the toast plates and arranging them on his handkerchief.

'Feed the birds,' he said as Haydn lifted him down from the chair he was balancing on.

'Good idea.' Haydn ruffled Brian's curls as he set him on the floor. 'They're probably starving.'

'Straight up the back, and straight down. Scatter the crumbs on the shed step, and no sticking your fingers into the dog pen,' Phyllis lectured him.

Brian's only reply was a deep throaty chuckle as Haydn tickled him before opening the washhouse and back doors for him.

'You're up early this morning.'

'Thought I'd call up and see Bethan. I haven't seen her since the night I arrived.'

Phyllis pushed a slice of bread on to a toasting fork. 'There's tea in the pot if you want some.'

Haydn lifted down a cup, and picked up the pot. 'Do you want one?'

'No thanks.'

'The pot's almost full. It'll go to waste. There's nothing spoiling is there?'

'Just shopping day.'

'That can wait.'

'I suppose it can.' She turned the toast over, and started on the other side.

Haydn poured out two teas, then stood and watched as Brian climbed the steps, one leg at a time, holding on to the walls either side to keep his balance. 'Bethan's right. Brian is a carbon copy of Eddie at that age.'

'So your father and William keep telling me.'

'Except in one respect. He hasn't got Eddie's vile temper.'

'Vile temper? Eddie?'

'You haven't seen it?'

Phyllis shook her head, as she slid the toast from the fork on to a plate and handed it to him.

'Count yourself lucky. You must be one of the few.'

'I know he's a bit on edge at the moment, because he's boxing in a big charity match tonight. A benefit in aid of the hospital. Your father's going, and Will.'

'I'll call in after work. With luck I might catch the last couple of minutes.'

'If you don't, it can't be helped. Eddie will understand.'

'I wish I had the same faith in his understanding as you.' He looked across at Phyllis, her face red from the reflected glow of the fire as she toasted a second slice of bread. Her eyes had something of the same look of contentment he had noticed in his father since he had been home. 'Phyllis, about Jane?' he chanced hesitantly, hoping she wouldn't respond to his questions the same way Eddie had.

'What about Jane?'

Was it his imagination or was she deliberately keeping her head averted? 'Did you meet her in the workhouse?'

'Whatever gave you that idea?'

'Dad told me he felt responsible for you and Brian ending up there, and something Jane said last night –'

'What did she say?' Phyllis broke in sharply.

'Nothing much, that's the point. Just that she was born in the workhouse.'

'A long time before I was there.'

'Of course. Look, I'm just concerned for you.'

'Me, why?'

'Well you and Dad have taken her in and . . .'

'The less you know about Jane the better, Haydn.' Tight-lipped, she eased the second piece of toast from the toasting fork on to his plate. 'Do you want any more?'

'No thanks. Phyllis, I'm sorry if I've upset you. I didn't mean to. All I seem to have done since I've come home is say the wrong thing. I'm beginning to feel like a pantomime villain.'

'Looking at things from Jane's point of view, I can understand why she doesn't want to talk about herself to you, or anyone.'

'Because she has something to hide?'

'Her shame at her poverty. She told you she's an abandoned orphan who was born in the workhouse, what else is there for you to know?'

'What she did before she lived here.'

'She survived, and that in itself isn't easy for a girl in her position. You can't begin to imagine how hard life can be for orphans. I lost my parents when I was fourteen. Fortunately I'd already started work and Rhiannon Pugh offered to take me in as a lodger. If she hadn't, I would have been in the same position as Jane. But I found Rhiannon, just as Jane found us. She has a job and things are going better for her now than ever before.'

'It's the before that concerns me.'

'It shouldn't, Haydn, because it's none of your business.' Her voice was soft, but Haydn sensed iron beneath the velvet exterior. 'And neither should it be your business when you'll soon be moving on.'

'Not until the end of the summer season.'

'Jane is trying to set up a life in Pontypridd for herself, and the last thing a girl with her background needs is a good-looking man fussing over her . . .'

'I'm not after Jane. Not in that way. I'm just trying to be friendly.'

'The friendliest thing you can do for Jane Jones is leave her alone. Don't put ideas into her head that will lead nowhere. She's had nothing but disappointments in her life so far and she's learned to cope. If you give her a glimpse of something she can never have she'll be discontented with her lot until her dying day. Now you wouldn't want that on your conscience, would you?'

Haydn mulled over what Phyllis had said as he turned left at the bottom of Graig Avenue and started the long haul up Penycoedcae Hill. The birds were singing, the air was fresh, the trees were bright green as opposed to the muted, milky green of stage sets and everything around him suddenly seemed startlingly alive and real. He breathed in deeply as he left the snorting horses and rattling milk carts of the dairy behind him. The hustle and bustle on the hill served to remind him that he alone of the people who lived on the Graig didn't have 'decent' employment to go to. Only a rehearsal for a make-believe world. A childish world that couldn't, and never would, really matter to anyone. Least of all the people who moved within its narrow confines.

He walked quickly, but not so quickly as to disregard his surroundings. He hadn't realised just how much he had missed his native hills in London. Even the yellowed scrubby grass at the foot of the black slag heaps was like balm to his country-starved eyes. Half-way up the hill he stopped, leaned on a gate and pulled a cigarette from the packet he always carried in his top pocket. He looked out over the steeply sloping fields he had once tobogganned down on his mother's washboard, remembering the cold rush of air, the crunch of snow as he skidded over it, the feeling of exhilaration mixed with fear – and the beating his mother had given him with a stair rod when she had caught him trying to sneak the damaged washboard into the washhouse.

In the valley far below nestled the village of Maesycoed, the grey stone and redbrick buildings of the school dominating the rows of terraces around them. In another age, another lifetime, he had caught hold of Bethan's hand and walked beside her down Factory Lane to the Infants. Later when they had been promoted to the Junior School they had been entrusted with Eddie and Maud. And, later still he had taken to stopping at the top of Factory Lane to pick up Jenny – Jenny again. There wasn't a memory that didn't include her, except the days he had spent in the Boys' Grammar School before short-time working and the eventual closure of the Maritime put paid to both his own, and Bethan's, dreams of academic success.

A maid dressed in traditional black and white uniform, complete with cap, answered his knock. He wondered if the uniform had been Andrew's or Bethan's idea. He hoped it was Andrew's. He didn't like the notion of Bethan joining the crache and growing even further away from him than she already had.

'Haydn, glad to see you at any time, but this is an unexpected pleasure.' Andrew walked into the hall to greet him, friendly and

234

eager to please as always, and for the first time since Haydn had known him, jacketless, with his waistcoat unfastened and his collar dangling from the neck of his shirt, attached by only one stud. 'Bethan's upstairs, but she'll be down any minute. You'll breakfast with us?'

'I've eaten, but thank you for the offer.'

'Coffee then? Come in.'

Haydn followed Andrew through the hall into the dining room that overlooked the lawned garden. Birds were feasting at a neatly constructed wooden table covered with scraps.

Andrew held out the coffee jug, then remembered working-class preferences. 'Would you prefer tea?'

'Coffee, please. I developed a taste for it in London.'

'What brings you up here at this hour?' Andrew poured the coffee and place it in front of him.

'I haven't seen Bethan since the night I came home.'

'That's understandable. You've been very busy, from what your father and Phyllis have told us.'

'Rehearsing Variety by day and playing Revue all night.'

'You must be exhausted.'

'Not if everyone in Pontypridd is to be believed. Didn't you know that singing isn't real work?'

'You believe them?'

'As I'm the one who's on stage, I'm not allowed to hold an opinion.'

'There's nothing wrong, is there, Haydn?'

'With me?'

'It's difficult to come back to a place like Pontypridd when you've made a success of your career,' Andrew said perceptively.

'You've found that out too?'

'Doctoring's slightly different, but I do know there's no race like the Welsh for putting a man down when they've found him guilty of getting above himself.'

'Then I've been tried and sentenced?'

'Not that I've heard.' Andrew took his customary place at the head of the table. 'But I know Pontypridd people.'

'They never change, do they?'

'And God bless them for it.'

'God bless who, for what?' Bethan appeared in the doorway. She was wearing a cream silk dressing gown that flowed over her swollen figure and fell around her ankles in soft folds. Her dark hair was brushed back, away from her face. She looked like a pale, fragile version of Lady Macbeth. Haydn had a sudden pang of conscience. How could he have even contemplated troubling Bethan with his problems? She had enough of her own, with a house of this size to run, a husband to look after, and another baby on the way while she was still mourning the last one.

'I was warning Haydn that the people in Pontypridd will never change.'

'In what way?' She sat down and Andrew poured her tea without asking if she wanted any.

'You know how it is, sis, everyone assuming I've grown a big head.'

'Now you're on stage.' She made a wry face as she sipped her tea. 'I can imagine. But for someone who has to work late every night, you're up early this morning.'

'It's the only time I could think of coming. I've hardly seen anything of you since I've been home.'

'Whose fault is that?'

'Mine, that's why I'm here. You keeping all right?'

'Fighting fit.'

'You look tired.'

'That's because she won't rest.'

'Andrew, if I rest any more, I'll turn into a cabbage.'

'Never.' He left his seat and kissed her on the forehead. Walking over to the sideboard he picked up the covers from the array of silver chafing dishes. 'Sure we can't tempt you with something, Haydn? Scrambled eggs, haddock, porridge?'

'If I eat now it will go straight to my legs, and I've a full morning of dancing ahead.'

'Anything for you, darling?' Andrew asked solicitously.

'Dry toast, please.'

He passed her a rack. She took a piece and laid it on her plate.

'I know you, Haydn. You wouldn't have left your bed to walk all the way up here if there hadn't been something on your mind. Come on, out with it.'

'There's nothing, Beth, really.'

'Just brotherly concern?' She looked at him over the rim of her cup. 'I don't believe you.'

'Well maybe just one little niggle.'

Andrew frowned at him, clearly warning him off, but Haydn didn't need Andrew's prompting to see just how frail his sister was.

'Is it the family? Dad's ill . . .'

'Nothing like that, Beth,' he reassured. 'Everyone's fine, and just as you told me when I came home, happy.'

'You're getting on with Phyllis? Because if you're not you can stay here.'

'Brian, Phyllis and I get along very well'

'Then what?'

'It's the lodger,' he murmured, hoping he'd settle on a subject that wouldn't concern her too much.

'Jane . . . Jane Jones, isn't it? Phyllis mentioned her last Sunday. She's working in the Town Hall as an usherette?'

'That's right.'

'From what Dad said she's moving on soon.'

'When she's worked her week in hand and can afford to take up lodgings somewhere else.'

'Then what's the problem?'

'It's hard to explain, really.' He racked his brains trying to think of something that wouldn't alarm Bethan, wishing he'd never come. 'Forget it, I shouldn't have mentioned it.'

'This is just what he was like as a boy,' Bethan complained. 'He'd say something like "Now I've done it, Mam will kill me", run off, and leave me to worry and search the house for signs of wreckage.'

'This time it *is* nothing. I can't get anything out of her.'

'Like for instance?'

'What she's done until now. Where she's come from.'

'You think it could be prison?' Andrew joked.

'That could come as a recommendation in our family,' Bethan interposed tartly, thinking of her aunt and her father.

'It could be the workhouse,' Haydn said uneasily. 'I get the feeling she's afraid of something, or someone. She's a nice kid, I'd like to help her, and I wondered if either of you knew any more about her.'

'So that's it? Sir Galahad to the rescue. Well I'm afraid I can't help you. I don't know anything. I've never even met the girl. If there's a mystery there, you're going to have to solve it yourself.'

'As I said, that was only one of the reasons I came. I really did want to see how you were.' He caught Andrew's eye. Bethan was smiling, but Andrew wasn't. He pushed his coffee cup aside and reached for a cigarette.

'You're up and about early.'

'Thought I'd make you my first stop and give you something to brighten your day.' Eddie dropped the small ham and dishes of brawn and pressed tongue on to the counter in front of Jenny. Leaning over, he kissed her full on the mouth.

'It's just as well the counter is between us,' she murmured breathlessly when he finally backed off.

'I won't be able to see you tonight because I'm fighting, you do know that, don't you?'

She nodded as she stowed the cooked meat he'd brought on the cool slab. 'I'd give anything to be there.'

'Girls don't go to boxing matches.'

'Who says?'

'Everyone. Matches can get bloody.'

'And you don't want me to see you getting hurt?'

'I won't get hurt. But the other fellow won't be a pretty sight.'

'I can stand it if you can.'

'My trainer . . .'

'Joey Rees.'

'You follow boxing?'

'Only your fights.'

'He's a bit old-fashioned. Doesn't like women around the ring.'

'How do you know?'

'Because Bethan and Laura Ronconi watched me once when I fought in the booth in the Rattle Fair.'

'You won?'

'I did,' he answered proudly.

'Well, there you are then. Joey can hardly object if I come tonight.'

'But that was different. This is a proper match. The place will be packed out. There'll be talent scouts there . . .'

'I could borrow my father's suit again.'

'Without me to look after you? Forget it.'

'Please,' she begged, brushing her hair out of her eyes. He looked at her and felt as though his heart was melting. He wanted her, enough to take her right here and now, on the shop floor.

'I suppose I could nip out of the shop at dinner time and ask Joey Rees if you can come,' he capitulated.

'And if he says yes?'

'I'll let you know on my way home tonight. But if he's prepared to organise a seat for you, you'd better be on time, sit quietly and not say a word.'

'To see you box, Eddie, I'd do anything.'

'Anything?' he murmured suggestively.

'Anything.'

The shop was deserted. He vaulted over the counter, gathered her into his arms, and kissed her again. The bell clanged above the door, but neither of them looked up.

'First thing in the morning, Eddie Powell? Ach y fi, for shame on you. You too, Jenny Griffiths,' Mrs Richards scolded as she dumped her battered shopping basket on the counter.

'It's a good way to start the day, Mrs Richards.' Eddie clasped Jenny hard before releasing her. 'You should try it yourself some time.'

'You keep away from me, young man,' she shouted as he

dived back over the counter. She picked up her basket and held it in front of her. 'Do you hear me, you stay away or I'll have Mr Richards after you.'

'I'm terrified.' He turned to Jenny. 'See you later.'

'And what do you think you're doing, young lady?' Mrs Richards demanded as Eddie rode away on his bicycle.

'Serving you, Mrs Richards. Have you a list?'

'List nothing. Look at you, going from one brother to another. Unnatural, I call it. And it will come to no good. You mark my words. No good at all.'

Chapter Fifteen

'It's good of you to offer me a lift down the hill.' Haydn followed Andrew out of the house into the coachhouse that had been converted into a garage. 'But really there's no need, I can make my own way.'

'No trouble, I have to go into town.' Andrew opened the doors, pinned them back, unlocked the car and pulled out the crank.

'I'll do that.'

'Be my guest.' Andrew handed it over and sat in the driver's seat.

'I'm the one who should be thanking you,' Andrew said as he negotiated out of the drive on to the narrow lane that led into Pontypridd.

'What for?'

'Not upsetting Bethan.'

Haydn slid back the window, pushed his hat to the back of his head, and rested his elbow on the sill. 'The last thing I want is to upset Bethan, especially now with another baby on the way.'

'And I'm grateful. I'm no Einstein, but it doesn't take a lot of brains to work out that you didn't walk all the way up Penycoedcae hill just to talk about the lodger.'

'As long as Bethan thinks I did.'

'I think you managed to convince her that you're concerned about her and the baby.'

'I am.'

'I know I haven't made a very good job of looking after your sister so far, but from now on I intend to take care of her. I love her, Haydn. Very much.'

Haydn had never felt easy in his sister's husband's company, but there was a quiet dignity in Andrew's voice that commanded respect. 'You've been through a rough time,' he said awkwardly.

'And it looks as though you're going through one now.'

'It's nothing I won't be able to work out for myself.'

'Just answer one question,' Andrew said, changing down a gear as the terraces of the Graig came into view. 'Is Bethan likely to find out about whatever it is that's troubling you?'

'I hope not. Look, is there something I should know about Beth. Is she ill? Is it the baby?'

'After Edmund, we're both worried about this baby, and we'll continue to worry until it's born. But so far there's been no signs to indicate that Bethan's carrying anything other than a normal, healthy child.'

'And Bethan?'

'She's not ill. Weak and tired, yes. She's not resting properly. She hasn't been strong for a while, and the events of last winter really pulled her down.'

'Is there anything I can do?'

'Calling in this morning and telling her you're getting on with Phyllis helped. She worries about the family. Especially Maud in Italy.'

'But there's no need. Dad wrote and told me that when Trevor Lewis saw her last month the tuberculosis was no longer active.'

'And he told Bethan the same thing when he came home, but telling Bethan is not the same as allowing her to see for herself. And I wouldn't risk taking her to Italy, not in her condition. And then there's Eddie . . .'

'Eddie's fighting fit.'

'Fighting being the operative word while he insists on boxing. She's terrified he's going to get hurt.'

'Eddie can look after himself.'

'That's what I keep telling her. And as if Maud and Eddie aren't enough, there's your parents. It's not exactly a straightforward situation, although I agree with Bethan, things seem to have worked out for the best there. Neither one of them was happy when they were together.'

Haydn stared at him in amazement. 'Aren't you worried what people are saying?'

'I've learned the hard way that the only thing to do with gossip is to ignore it. People can say what they like. My only concerns are the health and happiness of those close to me. Nothing else.' He pulled up alongside the fountain. 'This is as close as I'm going to get to the Town Hall on market day.'

'Yes, of course. Thanks for the lift.'

'Haydn,' Andrew stopped him as he opened the door, 'I meant what I said about being grateful for not bringing any problems to Bethan's attention at the moment, but if you want someone to talk to, or if there's anything . . . anything at all you think I can do to help you at any time I'd be honoured if you asked.'

'Thank you for the offer, but there's nothing.'

'But there is something you can do for me,' Andrew smiled wryly. 'Get me four tickets for Saturday's show. The last performance. A box if you can. I'll pay you.' He put his hand in his pocket.

'Pay me if I can arrange it. Last nights are usually packed.' Haydn couldn't resist a dig, after all Andrew's talk about looking after Bethan. 'Thinking of organising a boys' night out?'

'Anything but. I'd like to take Bethan, Trevor and Laura. We haven't seen a lot of them since they've come back from Italy.'

'You two would take your wives to a Revue?'

'Why not? Bethan would watch anything as long as you were in it, and you know Laura. She might be a Lewis by marriage, but she's a Ronconi by birth and they're game for anything. Besides –' Andrew pointed at a poster on a pillar at the market entrance – 'it says there that the displays are tastefully arranged.'

'And you believe that?'

'It's there in black and white. Look, provided you manage the tickets, how about coming out with us for a few drinks and a supper after the show?'

'I'd like to, but it will be the last night.'

'Of course, how stupid of me. Theatrical tradition and all that. Well if you can't manage the tickets, we'll see you on Sunday.'

'You will?'

'Bethan's birthday. The family are coming up for lunch, and Charlie, Alma, Trevor and Laura. They did tell you?'

'Yes,' Haydn lied, wondering if anyone would have got around to mentioning it if he hadn't called at Bethan's.

'Can I take a break today, Mr Horton?' Jane asked as she checked the time on the clock on the end of the wall of the market. Judy and Mandy had told her they would be in the New Inn from one o'clock on, and she had promised she'd try to meet them there. If Mr Horton didn't let her go, she'd have to wait until she went into work at four o'clock to see the photographs and pick up her second five-pound note. The money worried her more than the photographs. She wasn't at all convinced that she was going to see it.

Wilf Horton looked around the hall. Trade had been brisk that morning, although it was now beginning to ease off. Whether his and the other traders' good fortune was due to the school holidays or the warm summer weather that had encouraged people to make a day of it, or whether times were really getting better and the economy of the town was picking up after the depression, he wasn't sure. But he didn't want to analyse the cause too closely in case the upturn in customers and profit didn't last.

'I suppose this is as quiet as it's going to get. Half-hour, that's all, mind.'

'Thank you, Mr Horton.' Clutching her handkerchief in her pocket, which now contained a five-pound note as well as her precious hoard of coppers and silver, Jane raced out through the door and around the corner to the New Inn, to find Judy and Mandy waiting for at the table she had begun to think of as theirs.

'Almost given you up,' Mandy said as Jane sat down breathlessly.

'I can't stop for long.'

'Is that because it's your turn to pay?'

'Of course not.'

'Take no notice of her, she's just teasing,' Judy chipped in.

'No really, it is my turn.'

'Well you'd better take this then, if you're paying.' Judy pushed an envelope across the table. 'Your money's in there as well as the photographs.'

Jane opened it carefully. A five-pound note was tucked into the top of a large brown cardboard folder.

'For God's sake hide it under the tablecloth.' Mandy eyed the matrons who were sipping tea and eating cucumber sandwiches around them.

Jane picked up the first photograph and almost fell off her chair.

'Hard to recognise yourself, isn't it?'

'You've seen them?'

'Merv was that chuffed, he couldn't wait to show us.'

'That's the trouble with the camera, it puts pounds on,' Judy grumbled. 'Skinny little things like you always come out better than the well-blessed like me. But even Merv said he was staggered with the way your top storey developed. His very words.'

Jane flicked through the photographs. There were twelve in all. Half a dozen taken with her naked back to the camera, long strands of black hair streaming over her shoulder and lightly grazing her naked buttocks, as she peeked coyly at a point somewhere to the left of the lens; and six front view, where the only thing fastened was the collar and tie around her neck. The sides of the shirt draped wide to expose her chest, the tie falling midway between her naked breasts, the crook of the hockey stick angled carefully to conceal the flesh-tinted patch glued between her thighs.

'Merv will make a tidy sum out of those.'

'Oh by the way, he asked if you'd pose for him again,' Judy

mentioned casually. 'He said all you have to do is call into his studio to fix a day, but a Tuesday afternoon would be best. I thought somewhere around two would give you enough time before the theatre opens, but then you can always sort that side of it out with him yourself.'

'I'm not sure I'd want to do anything like this again,' Jane said doubtfully, staring at the photographs. At first glance it didn't look much like her, but then someone who took the trouble to study the features would recognise her, even beneath the wig.

'There's a problem?'

'I can't help worrying about what might happen if someone who knew me saw these. It's not as if I'm moving on like you. I live in this town.'

'Who are you afraid of?'

'Well there's my landlady and her family . . .'

'Haydn Powell's family! From the way he behaves they haven't got much to shout about,' Judy countered scathingly.'

'And there's the people in work.'

'The manager and stuffed-shirt Evans. They wouldn't notice it was you if you signed your name and sent them complimentary copies,' Mandy consoled her. 'Look, love, like we said, these are probably going to be sold in Cardiff, not around here.'

'At least you haven't got a family,' Judy said shortly. 'My old man threw me out when he bought a packet and saw his own daughter in the altogether. Filthy old bugger, what did he expect when he kept me and my mother so short we couldn't make ends meet.'

'What's done is done,' Mandy said briskly. 'What can't be altered isn't worth fretting over. Spend your tenner, have a good time, and move on. Life's for living, not brooding.'

'It's also for working, and if I'm going to put this money in the Post Office before going back to the stall I'd better be on my way.' Jane pulled her handkerchief out of her pocket and undid the knot. Counting out three shillings from her sewing money she left it on the table.

'I didn't mean it about paying,' Mandy said, embarrassed that Jane had taken her hints so literally.

'I know, but I wouldn't be happy if I didn't keep my end up.'

'As you insist, but how about having lunch with us tomorrow? Our treat.'

'Can't.' Judy opened her enormous handbag and fished around for her cigarettes. 'We're rehearsing with the new singer, Haydn's replacement, remember.'

'You know Haydn's staying on here in Variety while we go to the Empire in Swansea next week?'

'Someone told me.'

'Roll on, that's what I say. Swansea's much livelier than this place. You can always find a sailor on leave, just hanging about waiting to give a girl a good time.'

Jane left the table.

'Remember Merv's message. Try and call in and confirm the arrangements with him. Before Saturday if you can.'

'You that desperate for two quid?' Mandy asked after Jane had run off clutching her photographs and handkerchief.

'Every little helps. Besides, I like to think we've given the girl a leg up in the profession, as well as lining our own pockets. She has real talent.'

'Perhaps more than us,' Mandy said thoughtfully, remembering Merv's reaction to Jane's photographs, and the way Haydn Powell had been avoiding her and Rusty while still finding time to give Jane dancing lessons and walk her home.

The hall was crowded and noisy. Deafened by loud voices, and reeling from the heat that emanated from hundreds of closely packed bodies, Jenny stood at the top of the stairs and peered through the doors at the rope and canvas ring that had been set up in the centre of the hall she knew only as a roller-skating rink. For all her five feet eight inches she felt small and insignificant, cast adrift in a sea of towering, excited, red-faced masculinity. Clouds of beer and smoke-laden breath drifted over her as she stood on her toes and searched the crowd for a glimpse of William Powell. Eddie had assured her that his cousin would look out for her, but he was nowhere to be seen.

'So you did come. I was hoping you'd have more sense.'

'Hello, Mr Rees,' Jenny murmured uncertainly.

'Stand back here, out of the way,' he ordered, pushing her unceremoniously towards the cloakroom doors. 'You may as well know first as last, I hold no truck with women near the ring. They're nothing but a bloody nuisance, and if I had my way you'd be back home in your mam's kitchen where you belong. But it's Eddie who's the important one here today. He's the only one I'm concerned about.'

'But you told him I could come, Mr Rees.'

'Only because I could see that the bloody fool was set on you being here. If I'd said no, there's no telling what he might have done. Thrown the match, like as not, worrying where you were and what you were up to with that brother of his.'

'There's nothing between Haydn and me,' she protested, lowering her voice. Joey Rees's shouting had attracted the attention of half the men standing around them.

'That's not what I've heard. Well as soon as William Powell gets here, you go off with him. Evan's already here and between them they'll see that you behave yourself. And make sure you stay with them. There's a good few exhibition fights before Eddie's, but I'm telling you now, I'll tolerate no women in my dressing room.'

'*Your* dressing room, Joey?' Eddie ran up the stairs dressed in the grey sports coat he'd worn the day before. He winked at Jenny as William came up to him.

'As long as I'm your trainer, I run your dressing room, and I say no women,' Joey ordered. 'I told you when you started in this business that they take the blood away from where it's needed to win fights.'

'Joey!'

'Don't Joey me.' The old man ignored Eddie's objection and Jenny's blushes. 'I know you better than you know yourself, boy. Time to get off to the dressing room and start bandaging those fists.'

'Don't worry, Eddie. Jenny'll be safe with me.' William clamped his hand on Jenny's arm. His grip was like iron, but she managed a smile as Joey dragged Eddie away.

'You don't think I should be here either, do you?' Jenny asked as William pushed her ahead of him through the throng.

'That depends on two things.'

'What?'

'What you intend to do now you're here.'

'And the other?'

'Why you're out to catch Eddie.'

'Haydn, can you . . .'

'Sorry, Rusty, busy.' Haydn lifted his foot on to a chair and laced his tap shoe.

'With your scruffy little usherette?' She moved in behind him, effectively blocking the exit from his dressing room.

'I'm teaching her to dance.'

'I could have forgiven you if you'd gone off with Mandy, or even one of the girls from the Variety, but a nonentity like her!'

'I'm teaching her to dance,' he repeated.

'I know your dancing lessons. You used to give them to me, remember?' She ran her fingers lightly over his flies. When she tried to unhook the buttons, he caught her hand and held it fast.

'This time it is just dancing lessons, Rusty. She's a kid. She lives with my family.'

'And you're using her to avoid me.'

'If that's what you want to think.' He lifted his foot down from the chair, and turned to face her. She stood her ground. Crossing her arms she leaned against the doorpost.

'Is this your way of saying "Thank you very much, Rusty, but it's over?"'

'It couldn't have lasted.'

'Not for ever, but with loving care we might have made it to the end of the week.'

'I'm sorry. It's the town. It's not like any other.'

'Because it's your home town, and you have relatives breathing down your neck?'

'Something like that. And then there's the business. People talk, your husband –'

'For God's sake Haydn, I've never expected much from you,

249

but I did hope for honesty. Don't play the hypocrite with me. Not now. Not after everything that's passed between us. Like last Sunday afternoon,' she whispered, her voice husky with unshed tears.

Her restraint was more than he could bear. 'Look, we can't talk, not here. Perhaps after the show.' He remembered Eddie's fight. 'Tomorrow. I'll ask Chuckles to give me some time off from rehearsals.'

'You should have asked him last Monday when you decided to dump me.'

'I didn't . . .'

'Then what is this? I thought we had something going between us. Something that deserved more than the "you can dress now and go on your way" treatment.'

'Rusty, what can I say? I am sorry. Truly.'

'Do you know what hurts, Haydn? When I met you I really thought you were different. That you hadn't been corrupted by the "sod the world and everyone else" attitude that infects this whole rotten world of Variety. I thought when you said something you meant it.'

'I did.'

'You might have before we hit your home town.'

'Tomorrow –'

'Forget tomorrow, Haydn. It should be easy enough. After all, you've forgotten everything else.' She eyed Jane coldly as the girl came rushing down the corridor, cap askew, hands full of confectionery for the girls. 'And as a parting gift I'll give you some free advice. Stick to the relatives. You may not like them, but they're a safer bet than waif-like orphans. You've used her to get rid of me, Mandy and whoever else you've been fooling around with, but if I were you, I'd be asking at what price. You may find out it's a lot more than you're used to paying.'

'Trouble?' Jane asked as Rusty retreated into her dressing room and slammed the door.

'Nothing I can't handle. Want a lesson?' he asked abruptly.

'I wasn't sure you'd want to give me one after last night.'

'Last night was then, this is now. You free?'

'Yes,' she answered, wary of his mood.

'So's the stage. Let's go.'

'Keep your head down,' William commanded, as he frogmarched Jenny down the aisle towards the front row of seats where Charlie and Evan were already sitting.

'I'm sorry I'm not invisible,' she bit back sarcastically.

'So am I. Women attract too much attention in a place like this for my liking.'

'Hello, Mr Powell, Charlie.'

'Jenny.' They acknowledged her then resumed their conversation. Their indifference hurt even more than the open hostility of William and Joey Rees.

'I take it you've never been to a boxing match before?' William asked as he pushed her into a seat alongside Evan's.

'No.'

'If you don't like what you see, crawl under your seat. Don't draw any attention to yourself, and whatever you do, don't scream, especially when Eddie's boxing. If you do, you could put him off his stride, and then –'

The voice of the ringmaster boomed through the microphone, drowning out the end of William's sentence.

'And then?' Jenny whispered below the roar of the crowd as the first pair climbed into the ring.

'And then he could get really hurt.' William flashed her a warning look that made her wonder if Haydn had said anything to William about the threats she'd made, if not to Eddie.

Jenny sat through seven sickening, blood-spurting, bone-crunching exhibition boxing bouts, with her eyes closed and her fists clenched in her lap. The only merciful thing about the rounds was their length. Every fight was limited to four two-minute rounds. At the interval William left her with a stern injunction not to move. On his return he dropped a programme into her lap.

'You can read that instead of sitting with your eyes closed. If you hold it up at the right angle, you could even use it to block your view of the ring.'

She flicked through the pages. Tucked away among the advertisements for Goronwy Brothers butchers, Brooks hairdressers, and the Ruperra Hotel, 'home of good beer and boxing', she found brief biographies of the boxers. There was even a photograph of Eddie next to his: bare chested, gloved fists raised high in front of a punchball.

> *Introducing Eddie Powell (Graig, Pontypridd)*
> *20 years of age. 6'2° tall. 12st 10lb of fighting blood and*
> *muscle.*
> *A quiet unassuming boy. Prefers not to talk about*
> *fighting. Born and bred in Pontypridd and under the care of*
> *his trainer and mentor, the well known ex-welterweight*
> *champion Joey Rees.*
> *A gifted amateur who has never lost a fight. On the*
> *brink of turning professional. Is it too much to say that this*
> *boy will put Wales on the map again? That today we have*
> *a champion who will take our minds back to the period of*
> *the late Freddy Welsh, 'Peerless Jim Driscoll', and other*
> *champions who are fortunately still with us – Jimmy Wilde*
> *and Frank Moody.*
> *I venture to say that Eddie Powell will take his place*
> *amongst the champions and share the pride and admiration*
> *that we, in Wales, gave to his predecessors.*

'Without a woman hanging on to his coat tails Eddie could go far,' William commented drily, as he looked over her shoulder at what she was reading.

The ringmaster climbed into the ring. Cigarette packets were stowed away as he spoke into the microphone once more. The crowd roared as the two fighters flanked by their trainers walked the length of the aisle. It was the first time Jenny had seen Eddie in his boxer's strip of red and white silk dressing gown and shorts. Bucket, sponge and stool in hand, Joey took possession of the outside corner in front of Charlie and Evan's seats. The referee, a small wizened ex-lightweight, beckoned to the two protagonists.

He spoke to them, looking for all the world like a dwarf sandwiched between two giants, but Jenny could see that Eddie's attention was fixed on the crowd, not on what the referee was telling him. He was scanning the front rows feverishly, obviously hoping to catch a glimpse of his family – and perhaps even her. Before she could make a move, William held up one hand while keeping the other firmly clamped on her upper arm, effectively pinning her down in her seat.

A hush descended. The fighters went to their corners and shed their gowns. Jenny shuddered when she saw the black and purple sparring bruises on Eddie's chest. She'd made love to him. Knew what it felt like to have him lying naked next to her. She had caressed his face, every inch of his arms, back, thighs – but she knew his body only through touch. The stockroom had been as black as pitch, and the twilight gloom of the copse in Shoni's had been more romantic than illuminating. Next time – and she knew now that there would be a next time – they would make love in the light, so she could kiss every one of those bruises.

Eddie turned his back and there was a sharp hissing intake of breath next to her, as well as a few ribald comments from the men around them.

'He said he fell against a tree in Shoni's,' Joey said to Evan.

'A tree with bloody sharp nails.' William looked down at Jenny's hands.

She was glad when the bell rang a few seconds later. A resounding cheer echoed to the rafters. William's cry of 'Come on, Eddie!' was taken up by dozens of men as the two fighters circled one another warily on the canvas. Dizzy with excitement and fear for Eddie, she sat on the edge of her seat. The scene around her dissolved into a thick grey mist. Only Eddie remained, outlined in sharp relief against a wavering void, his black curly hair and dark eyes shining in contrast to his pale skin. He looked beautiful – strange that word should come to mind; she had never thought of any man as beautiful until now. Beautiful – and with the swollen gloved fists of his opponent raised against him, vulnerable – and her lover.

She flushed in embarrassment, as she remembered the things he had done to her last night. Yet her embarrassment didn't stop her from wanting to repeat the experience. Here Eddie was the centre of attention. Privately he was hers, and she couldn't wait to put her mark on him. Possess him, completely and unequivocally. Love didn't enter into the equation. Not when she remembered Haydn and his rejection of her. It was enough that Eddie was as important as Haydn in his own right, that he was handsome and wanted her. In possessing him she'd be the envy of half the girls in the town. Hostility from Eddie's family seemed a small price to pay for that much gain.

Eddie was the first to throw a punch. It connected with his opponent's jaw. The crowd roared as he closed in. The referee stopped the match and parted them. Seconds later it was Eddie who was reeling, blood pouring into his left eye from a split above his eyebrow. She screamed and gripped William's arm.

'Shut up before he hears you!'

Until William spoke, she hadn't even realised she'd made a noise.

'Damn it all, they've got to stop it. He can't see.' Evan gripped the sides of his chair, fighting the temptation to climb into the ring and stop the fight himself. Eddie bounced from foot to foot, throwing punches blindly as the blood continued to pour down his face.

'He's hurt.' Jenny rammed her fist into her mouth and bit back her tears. 'They have to stop it.'

'There's only a few seconds to the bell. You wanted to be here. Now you are, sit there and shut up. If you'd taken the trouble to get to know Eddie, you'd know he lives for boxing and nothing else.'

She wanted to shout that he cared for her too, but something held her back. Eddie did live for boxing. She hadn't needed William to tell her that. But now she also knew, first hand, the kind of risk he was running. What if he got badly hurt? What if those handsome features ended up misshapen and broken, like those of the old boxers who sold the *South Wales Echo* on the Tumble? Men who could no longer talk, only mumble unintelligibly, so punch drunk no one could understand what they were saying.

The bell signalled the end of the round. Joey was in the ring in an instant. He moved swiftly towards Eddie, who was trembling uncontrollably as blood continued to pour down his face on to the dark bruises that covered his chest.

'Killer Daniels looks out of shape to me,' William shouted to Evan over Jenny's head. 'Eddie should flatten him as soon as Joey sorts that eye out.'

Evan looked to Charlie, who shook his head doubtfully.

'I don't know,' Evan muttered, tight-lipped. 'Daniels has been quick enough on his feet until now. I've never seen Eddie so rattled in an opening round before.'

'That's what comes of bringing bloody women in to watch.' William turned angrily on Jenny. 'Eddie's probably more worried about you watching, than himself fighting.'

'You want me to go?'

'You shouldn't have come, but now you're here the last thing I want you to do is upset Eddie by moving around and drawing attention to yourself. Just remember, Eddie can see and hear your every move from up there.'

Jenny shrank lower into her seat and watched Joey layer lengths of plaster above Eddie's eye. The cut was a long one, and took a lot of stanching. Eddie rinsed his mouth out with water, Joey rammed the gum shield back between his teeth, the bell rang, the referee stepped forward and it began all over again.

William clamped his hand over Jenny's mouth when Killer Daniels's second punch connected with Eddie's jaw. Choking on his fingers she tried to prise them away, but he was too strong for her. Then came Eddie's retaliatory punch, swiftly followed by another, and another. Now it was Killer Daniels's turn to reel. And he did, from one side of the ring to the other, Eddie closing in, hounding him from rope to rope. Raining blows down on his chest, his jaw, and with one final resounding crack, the side of his head. Daniels fell to his knees, then slowly, infinitely slowly amidst a reverential hush that descended over the hall, slumped forward, finally falling to rest face down on the canvas.

The hall rocked as the crowd sent up a deafening clamour. Men were on their feet shouting, waving their arms, clapping, wolf-whistling, cheering. The referee held up Eddie's hand, the ringmaster was shouting something into the microphone that no one could hear. Joey climbed into the ring and put his arm around his protégé's shoulders. But Eddie's attention was fixed on the front row of seats. Disorientated, he turned from one side of the ring to another. William and Evan were on their feet, shouting along with everyone else. He saw them first, then her.

He spat out the gum shield on to the blood-soaked canvas. Joey stooped to pick it up.

'Jenny.' The sound was lost, but she knew he had called out her name. William heaved her to her feet. Thrusting her forward, he propelled her to the side of the ring.

'God knows why he wants you, but he does. And all I can say is you'd better care for him as much as he cares for you. If you don't . . .'

'But I do. I really do care for him.' Jenny looked up through the ropes at Eddie's bruised, battered and bloody face. And with the cheers Eddie had earned resounding in her ears, she believed every word of it.

Chapter Sixteen

It was a long time before the ringmaster succeeded in restoring hush to the hall. Before the applause died, Eddie climbed over the ropes, reached out and extended a gloved hand to Jenny. She clung to his arm, wanting to hold on to him long enough to show his father, Joey – and especially William – just how much he thought of her, but Joey pulled him away. There was barely time for her to register the wreckage on his face before Joey paraded him triumphantly out of the hall. The cut above Eddie's eye had reopened, and blood had trickled through the plaster on to his cheek. His jaw was already beginning to swell, his chest was blotched with red marks, yet his eyes had never shone with more life and there'd been a smile on his mashed blue and bloody lips.

'There'll be some booze put away in the Ruperra on the strength of this tonight,' William yelled after him.

'He's really hurt!' Jenny exclaimed.

'Boxing's not pat-a-ball. And there's no damage there that Joey hasn't seen before and can't fix.'

'But his face . . .'

'Boxers don't stay pretty for long.'

'Can't we go with him?'

'You prepared to try after what Joey said about women in his dressing room?'

'Then what do I do now?' she demanded petulantly.

'Sit and watch the next two bouts. Eddie's turn may be over but the exhibition isn't finished.'

She returned to her seat and watched Eddie's opponent's trainer work on the figure slumped on the canvas. He'd removed Daniels's gum shield, soaked a rag in water and was squeezing it over the unconscious man's lips. After a few minutes he succeeded in raising him to his feet and helping him out of the ring.

The last two fights passed in a blur of movement and noise. Jenny sat and stared at the figures dancing around the canvas. She watched punches being thrown, heard crunch after sickening crunch as they homed in on their flesh and bone targets. But long before the final bell, she knew that Joey Rees and William had been right. A boxing tournament was no place for a woman. Closing her eyes, she clenched her teeth and waited for it all to be over.

'That's it then.' Evan rose to his feet as the final bell rang to a rousing cheer.

'Wonder what Eddie's share of the purse will be?'

'Whatever's left after the referee takes his fee, his opponent gets his cut and the gloves are paid for,' Evan answered William.

'What do you think of your son now?' Joey Rees demanded as he joined Evan and Charlie.

'I think you've done a good job of training him.'

'Eddie tells me you were never that keen on him going into the ring.'

'That was more his mother's sentiment than mine. As long as it's what he wants to do, he comes out on top, and doesn't get too badly hurt in the process, I've no quarrel with him boxing, but when he starts to go downhill . . .'

'That won't be for a long time yet. He's got a great future ahead of him.'

'And not all of it in boxing.'

'Coming back to the Ruperra for a drink?'

Evan looked at William and Charlie who both nodded, making Jenny feel more of an encumbrance than ever.

Eddie emerged from the door that led to the back rooms. He was wearing a long black winter-weight overcoat and dark trilby, on Joey's advice. It was easy to pick up a chill after a match, even in summer.

'Nice clothes,' Jenny complimented him. He reminded her of a darker, more satanic version of Haydn.

'Shilling a week club in Rivelin's. How much did you see of the bout?'

'As much as William would let me.'

'Coming back to the club for a drink, Eddie? There's a promoter I want you to meet. Mr Wallace, important man. He's shipping over champions from South Africa and New Zealand for a tour. Word is, he was impressed by the way you performed. If he's prepared to put you up against his boys it could lead to professional status, the national championship and maybe even an American tour like Frank Moody in '23. After that, who knows? Heavyweight world championship?'

'How long will he be in the Ruperra, Joey?'

'That's not the kind of question you ask a man like Mr Wallace.'

'I'm asking because I'm going to walk Jenny home.'

'There's no need,' Jenny protested, sensing Joey's hostility sharpening.

'I could do with some fresh air,' Eddie insisted stubbornly.

'This is a big man . . .' Joey began testily.

'I'll walk Jenny home for you,' William interrupted.

'As if I'd let you.'

'Please, I'd much rather go alone.' Jenny picked up her handbag from the floor.

'I won't hear of it. I'll see you back in the Ruperra, Joey.'

'If you're prepared to throw away your career, who am I to stop you?'

Jenny braved a smile at Eddie in spite of the pressure raining down on her from all sides. 'I promised Tina and Gina I'd look in on them this week. If I go to the café now, I can walk home with them afterwards.'

'You can go tomorrow night.'

'I told my father I'd work in the shop. Please, Eddie, tonight would be best.'

'I'm still walking you to the café.' He turned to Joey: 'I'll catch up with you in the Ruperra.'

'Just be careful that you do, boy,' Joey replied flatly, staring belligerently at Jenny.

'They don't like me.'

'Only when you're around the ring.' Eddie folded his hand over hers as she took his arm.

'Don't try to soft-soap me. They don't like me, and it's because I went out with your brother before going out with you.'

'That was last year.' He stopped on the corner of Mill Street and pulled her into the jeweller's doorway. 'It is over between you, isn't it?'

'Of course it's over.' She tried and failed to look him in the eye. 'But that doesn't alter the fact that Haydn's your brother.'

'So, you went out with my brother? I was the first one who mattered, wasn't I? You told me nothing ever went on between you two.'

'Not like us,' she broke in quickly, suppressing the sneaking wish that it had.

'My share of the purse was ten pounds tonight,' he revealed as they moved on.

'That's incredible. Ten pounds for just a few minutes in the ring.' The size of the sum momentarily outweighed the magnitude of his injuries.

'And it looks like Joey has got more of the same lined up. What say you we get engaged on the strength of it?'

Engaged! She couldn't believe what she was hearing. She had told Haydn that she would marry Eddie. Now he was asking without any prompting from her.

'It's usual for a girl to answer when a man asks her to marry him.'

'I know. It's just that . . . it's . . .' Tears blinded her eyes for no reason, and she choked on her words. They were crossing the bridge opposite Rivelin's. Beneath the road the river gushed, black and gleaming between dark, mysterious banks. On their right the lights at the back of the buildings in Mill Street ribboned the darkness.

'It's what, Jenny?' He halted and faced her, blocking her path.

'Unexpected,' she mumbled, still unable to look at him.

'After last night?'

'I . . .'

'Will you marry me?' he asked, his voice slurring from the damage Killer Daniels's battering had inflicted on his mouth.

She finally looked at him. His eyes, dark, searching beneath his trilby, stared intently into hers. 'Why are you crying?'

'Because you're hurt. Because . . . just because . . .'

Bending forward he kissed her. A soft, gentle embrace that belied the savagery that accompanied his lovemaking, but she still couldn't help comparing it to the loving caresses Haydn had once given her. She closed her eyes and clung to him. The hem of his coat brushed against her knees, his muscled arms were hard beneath her hands. It took so little to imagine it was Haydn who was holding her.

'You'll marry me?'

'Yes, Eddie, I'll marry you.'

'We'll take rooms. There's no point in waiting. I have a good job, with the prospect of more coming in from boxing purses. We'll soon be able to afford a decent house. In fact we could almost rent one now.'

'Eddie,' she pushed him away from her. 'Let me go to the café.' When he opened his mouth to protest, she laid a finger over his lips. 'I don't want to talk, not now. There's too much to think about and get used to. Call into the shop on the way home. I'll leave the storeroom door open, and I'll wait up, no matter how late you are.'

'Promise?'

'I promise.'

261

'And you will marry me?' he repeated like a child seeking re-assurance.

'Yes.'

They walked the short distance to the Tumble in silence. He kissed her once more before turning on his heels and striding back through the town. She hesitated, her hand on the café door. There was no way she could talk to the girls, not now. She had plans to make, thoughts to put in order. Waiting until Eddie was out of sight, she turned under the bridge and up the Graig hill.

'Where's Jane?' Evan asked as he walked into the kitchen, William trailing at his heels, both of them slightly the worse for drink.

'She ate her meal and went straight to bed.' Haydn put extra cups on the table and poured out three teas. 'I just made a fresh pot. Must have sensed you were coming. Where's Eddie? I tried to get into the Palais, but they said the place was jammed to the rafters. Still, I did manage to talk to the doorman. He told me Eddie won his bout. Did very well, by all accounts.'

'He did.'

'He's not hurt, is he?'

'If he's hurt it's not from any punches that were thrown in the ring,' William said sourly.

'William!' Evan admonished.

'He did do well?' Haydn persisted, sensing there was some-thing he wasn't being told.

'He did, damned well. Got an offer to box a South African champion in Cardiff next month, and depending on the outcome of that, turn professional and tour South Africa and New Zea-land. Joey and Mr Wallace, the promoter who made the offer, reckon he could be taking a crack at the championship within a year,' Evan said proudly.

'Good on our kid.'

'I'm glad for him. I think he feels he's got a lot to live up to with you around.'

'What have I got to do with anything?'

'Don't look so innocent,' William said as he heaped four sugars into his tea. 'Successful older brother coming back from the London stage to star in the Town Hall is enough to make anyone feel second rate.'

'London stage?' Haydn scoffed derisively. 'It was hardly the West End. You should see some of the Empires I've played on the outskirts of London. Dismal is not the word.'

'Eddie doesn't know that, and unlike me he hasn't his dazzling good looks to fall back on for consolation.' William's attempt at humour fell flat.

'The tournament win tonight is all his, Will,' Evan finished his tea. 'No one will ever be able to take that away from him.'

'No, I don't suppose they will.'

'Phyllis gone up?' Evan asked.

'An hour ago. She only waited to give Jane and me our meal, although I've told her there's no need. We can serve ourselves.'

'You know what she's like, always worrying about everyone eating properly. Don't be too late, boys. And tell Eddie to keep the noise down when you come up, Will.'

'Where is Eddie?' Haydn asked as his father climbed the stairs.

'With his lady love.'

'Who is she?'

'Who do you think? Your bloody cast-off.'

'Jenny?'

'He even insisted she come to the Palais tonight.'

'Is it serious?'

'Serious enough for him to turn down the meeting with the promoter in the Ruperra to take Jenny home. You should have seen the look on Joey Rees's face.'

Haydn fumbled blindly for his cigarettes. 'I was afraid of this.'

'Because you want her back?'

Haydn's hands shook as he pushed a cigarette between his lips. He started to talk and it all came out. Jenny waylaying him on the hill, throwing herself at him as soon as they were alone, the threats she'd made about Eddie when he'd rejected her advances. William sat sipping his tea, listening intently to every word.

'Did you tell Eddie any of this?' he asked when Haydn eventually fell silent.

'I tried to last night, but he wouldn't listen.'

'So that was what all the shouting was about.'

'It wasn't about Jenny. I tried to talk to him about other things before building up to what she'd said, but he refused to take notice of anything I had to say, and by then I was afraid to bring up Jenny's name in case he thought I wanted her back.'

'Do you?'

'Before she called me into the shop on Sunday night, I wouldn't have been able to answer that. But after the way she behaved, most definitely not.'

'But when you first came back to Ponty there was still something there?'

'Probably,' Haydn admitted reluctantly. 'Enough to parade the girls from the show around town in an effort to convince her and myself that I no longer cared. She hurt me. It does me no credit to say this, but I wanted to get my own back on her for going out with Eddie after we quarrelled. But when she called me into the shop and tried to kiss me I realised that I didn't have to pretend any more. That if there ever had been anything resembling love between us, it's finished.'

'But she thinks it's still alive?'

'She seems to be where I was before I came back, wanting revenge, but unfortunately it's Eddie she's taking it out on, not me.'

William poured out two more teas, emptying the pot. He took his cigarettes from his pocket, but Haydn tossed his packet to him.

'Have one of mine.'

'No. Earning twice as much as the rest of us doesn't give you the right to take away our pride.'

'I'm sorry, I didn't know I was.'

'Look mate, we know you're doing well. There's no need to rub our noses in it. Things are better than they were when you left. The pits are reopening, Charlie's set himself up fine and he's seen to it that Eddie and I are all right too.'

'I've said I'm sorry, what more do you want me to do?'

'Take one of my bloody fags.'

'But I'm still smoking.'

'Then stick it behind your ear.' Haydn did as he asked. Opening the oven door William pushed a taper into the coals. 'Well, now we know what Jenny's up to, the question is what do we do about it?'

'You've no idea how good that "we" sounds. I've been worrying myself stupid since Sunday. I even went to see Beth this morning.'

'And what did she say?'

'Nothing, because I didn't tell her about it. When I got there she looked ghastly. Andrew said she's not been too well, so I thought better of laying my troubles at her feet.'

'Do you want me to talk to Eddie?'

'Do you think it would do any good?'

William exhaled twin streams of smoke from his nostrils. 'Probably not,' he mused. 'Not if you've already tried and got nowhere.'

'Let's face it, she's got us beaten before we even start. Eddie'll never believe a word I say about Jenny because he hates me.'

'No he doesn't. As I said, he just feels second rate compared to you.'

'So what do we do?'

'Looks like as far as Eddie's concerned, there's nothing we can do except let it run its course. That leaves Jenny.' William ground his cigarette to dust in the tin ashtray on the table. 'I could try appealing to her better nature, always supposing she has one.'

'Do you think she'll listen?'

'No harm in trying.'

'There could be if you try to see her alone. And given what you want to say to her I don't think there is another way.'

'I'll pick my time. When the shop's empty. There's not much she can accuse me of, provided I keep the counter between us.'

'Don't you believe it. After what she tried with me there's no telling what she'll do to you.'

'Is your father in?'

'Hours ago. I hid behind the counter, and sneaked back to open the door again after he went upstairs. You're later than I thought you'd be.'

'Sorry, got talking. Lining up another fight.'

'Close your eyes.'

'Why?'

'Just do it.' She switched on the light and bolted both doors. 'You can open them again now. I just wanted to see you, that's all.'

He blinked against the harsh light of the single, bare light bulb. She was sitting on a box wrapped in a blue flowered eider-down.

'More comfortable than a blanket.' She rose to her feet and opened it out. He looked at her and kept on looking. She was wearing nothing beneath it. 'Thought it would save time,' she murmured, spreading it out on the floor beneath her.

High on success and excitement, he was on her in an instant.

'For once I wanted to see you in the light,' she whispered, tangling her fingers in his curls as his mouth closed over her nipple.

'The sooner we're married, the sooner we'll be able to do this every night.'

'You're insatiable,' she giggled as he stroked the inside of her thighs.

'The purse for the next match could be as high as twenty pounds. If you meant what you said earlier, we could choose an engagement ring.'

'I'll ask my father to give us a party.'

'This is the kind of party I like.' He turned her over and kissed the length of her body as she lay spreadeagled, next to him.

'There's just one thing,' she whispered as he eased his body on to hers.

'What?' he asked thickly, prepared at that moment to promise her anything.

'I wouldn't want to wait too long, before getting married. I'm afraid.'

266

'Of what?'

'Of having a baby. It would kill my mother.'

'I'll talk to your father. Tomorrow.'

Every time William walked up or down the Graig hill that week, he made a point of calling into Griffiths' shop, but no matter how many times he went there in a day, he never found Jenny alone. In the mornings it was full of people rushing to buy their tobacco and cigarettes before work, in the evening it was packed with children running last-minute errands. If her father was there she avoided serving him; when she couldn't, she was polite, cool and distant, not that he expected her to be anything else after the way he'd treated her during the boxing match. Any mention of Eddie or Haydn was met with a curt dismissal in favour of the next customer in line.

When the week passed and Saturday dawned without him making any headway, he went to Charlie and pleaded to be allowed to work in the shop instead of the market. By dint of persuasion, and the invention of a mysterious and fictitious new girlfriend, he managed to convince both Charlie and Eddie that he needed to finish early. Eddie took over the stall, which meant working until after the nine o'clock auction bell, when all the leftover meat on the stalls was sold, whereas he'd be able to pack up at five when the last of the cooked meats had gone from the shop. Even after helping Alma scrub the food trays and clean the kitchen, he was outside Griffiths' shop before seven, a whole two and a half or three hours before Eddie could possibly make it.

He pushed open the door and looked around. It was deserted, the wooden bread tray empty, the enamelled cooked meat tray clean and scrubbed; even the vegetable sacks were only a quarter full.

'Coming . . .' Jenny stepped out of the back room. She was wearing a blue dress, one he hadn't seen before, made from a soft silky material that clung to her slim figure and showed off her full breasts. He smiled, and momentarily forgetting his behaviour during the boxing match she smiled back. Her whole face lit up, and for the first time he understood why both his cousins had lost their heads. Jenny wasn't simply pretty, she was beautiful, with the kind of sensual beauty he could easily imagine naked. Then suddenly he remembered why he was there.

'Eddie asked me to call in and tell you he'd be late.'

'Late? But we were –'

'Going out?'

'As a matter of fact we were.' The smile hardened into a frown. 'What are you doing here so early? I thought you worked the market.'

'Eddie swapped with me.'

'Why?'

'Because I asked him to. Eddie's a reasonable man, provided he's not lied to, or crossed.'

'I know.'

'Do you, Jenny? Do you really?' he asked softly.

'Do you want anything?' she snapped, sensing what was coming.

'Seeing as how we're both at a loose end, I thought we could go to see *Robin Hood* in the Palladium.'

'No thank you.'

'It's in colour and it has Errol Flynn. Now there's a swash-buckler to match even Haydn.'

'I'd rather wait until Eddie finishes work for the day.'

'It could be a long wait, and you're turning down not only Errol Flynn, but the chance to try out another Powell.'

'If you want anything I'll serve you, otherwise please go.'

He put his hands on the counter and leaned forward. 'Take a warning when it's being given. It's not only Haydn who can see through the games you're playing.'

'I don't know what you're talking about.'

'Come on, you can't remember Haydn calling in here last Sunday?'

'I remember Haydn asking me to forget Eddie so we could pick up where we left off.'

He took a deep breath. If he hadn't seen Haydn, heard his version of events for himself, he would have accepted what she was telling him without question. 'You expect me to believe that?'

'Eddie will if I tell him.'

'You think so? You're a cool liar, Jenny, but have you thought what's going to happen when he does find out what you're up to? He will, you know. Sooner or later someone will tell him and he'll believe them, not you. How do you think he's going to feel then? Knowing that he's been taken for a fool by a girl who loves his brother.'

She turned her back and opened the storeroom door. 'I'm going upstairs, Dad.' When she looked around, the shop door was closing. She watched William walk past the window. As she climbed the stairs all she could think of was Eddie and the look on his face when he'd asked her to marry him. She might not love Eddie, but she made him happy. She knew she did. And by marrying Eddie, she'd prove to Haydn that she wasn't one to make idle threats. He and William could say or do what they liked, they wouldn't change Eddie's mind about her. Not now. Not after Shoni's and last night. And she'd show both of them, especially Haydn. In fact she'd show the whole of the Graig on the day she and Eddie got married. And for her, it couldn't come soon enough.

'Note for you, Haydn.' Arthur pushed open Haydn's dressing-room door.

Haydn slit open the envelope and deciphered his brother-in-law's unfamiliar handwriting.

> Thanks for the tickets. Any chance of changing your mind about that quick drink in the New Inn afterwards? Andrew and Bethan.

'Any reply?'

'No. I'll go and see them. I know which box they're in.'

'They look like crache.'

'What do you expect my sister and her husband to look like?'

'Get away, that's your sister? But she's so dark, and . . .'

'Beautiful?' Haydn pushed the note into his pocket, picked up his overcoat and hat and closed the door.

'Going somewhere?' Joe Evans asked as he stepped into the corridor.

'Box.'

'In costume?'

'I've covered my suit, and then again I'm not one of the girls.'

'You'd be locked up if you were. First call in ten minutes.'

'I'll be here to take it.'

'Sure you don't want me to send for your understudy?'

'Very funny. He's got next week, he can do without tonight.'

'From what I hear the girls aren't looking forward to losing you.'

'They'll get over it.' Haydn walked down the corridor and opened the door in the auditorium that was closest to the boxes. Looking down over the stalls and up at the circle he could see that the house was jam packed.

'Haydn! We didn't expect you to come and see us.' Bethan was smiling. She looked happier and healthier than when he had last seen her.

'I came to tell you I won't be able to make it to the New Inn for a drink. There's a party here in the bar afterwards. Why don't you stay?'

'And let my husband loose amongst showgirls?' Laura shook her head. 'If they're anything like the girls on the poster . . .'

'They're a lot prettier,' Haydn said cheerfully. 'But don't worry, I'll warn them you'll scratch their eyes out if they go near Trevor.'

'I'm not sure I'd thank you for that,' Trevor retorted.

'Won't it be a closed party?' Andrew asked.

'No. There'll be a lot of outsiders there. Practically everyone in the cast has invited someone. I've asked Will and Eddie.'

'Are they coming?'

'Will said he might, I'm not sure about Eddie,' Haydn said evasively.

'Well, if you're sure we won't be in the way,' Andrew conceded, 'we'll see you later.'

Haydn looked down and watched Jane showing two men to the front row, programmes on her arm, torch in hand, every inch the experienced usherette. There was an air of quiet confidence about her that wasn't part of her skinny orphan persona.

'Problem?'

'No. That's Jane Jones.'

'The new lodger?' Bethan looked over the edge of the box. 'Pretty little thing.'

'I've never really noticed,' he said slowly, looking at Jane's face as though he were seeing it for the first time.

'Your first week's wages. What you going to do with them, Jane?' Joe Evans asked as he handed over a small brown envelope after the curtain fell on the last house.

'Buy a pair of leather shoes.'

'That can wait a week or two if you've pressing bills to pay.'

'If I can manage it, Mr Evans, I'll get them.' Jane pocketed the envelope.

'Manager's been watching you this week. I don't mind telling you it's not often he's impressed, but you seem to have picked up the job quickly, and in acknowledgement he's agreed to put you up to fifteen shillings and sixpence a week, as of next week. I can't remember the last time an usherette rose to full pay so quickly.'

'Thank you.'

'Don't forget, you're expected to join the cast for a glass of sherry after you've finished clearing up.'

'I won't forget, Mr Evans.'

She couldn't resist checking the contents of the envelope. She permitted herself a small glow of pride. She'd done well for herself in two weeks. She'd worked off most of her debt with Wilf Horton and bought a second lot of clothes. Her lodgings were paid to date, courtesy of her sewing earnings. She now had her wages, which would cover next week's lodging, wherever it was going to be, and a deposit on a pair of leather shoes, and she had a few shillings in her pocket to spare. Without the ten pounds there'd be nothing in the bank, but she consoled herself with the thought that she wouldn't have to keep buying clothes forever. Another few weeks before she could start saving in earnest. But all in all, she wasn't doing too badly for someone who had walked out of the workhouse with one and elevenpence, two workhouse dresses and a pair of clogs.

Chapter 17

By the time Haydn had changed out of his evening suit into a pair
of cream trousers, cream silk shirt and a Turkish tapestry waistcoat that an assistant in a Brixton men's outfitter's had assured
him was all the rage, the party was well under way. He made his
way to the bar, only to find it half empty.

'Everyone's on stage,' Joe Evans told him. 'Manager had the
sets moved to the back, and the tables and chairs from here
carried down.'

Haydn raised his eyebrows.

'I think half the Town Council wants to wave this show off,'
Joe said wryly. 'Beer?'

'And a large whisky chaser.' Haydn remembered that Chuckles
and the cast of next week's Variety had been invited to the send-
off by Norman. After the events of the past week, Babs, Rusty and
Mandy in one room might prove to be a bit much.

Taking his drinks he went in search of Bethan, Andrew, Trevor
and Laura. He found them sitting at a table on the edge of the
stage, talking to the manager and a couple of councillors.

'Our star,' the manager beamed expansively, lifting his brandy
glass.

'That wasn't what you called me last year when I worked here.'

'That's because you weren't one then. Ah, at last, here come the girls.' He approached the chattering group who appeared, each clutching a glass of champagne, compliments of the house. 'I have some people over here who are dying to meet you.'

'Very nice.' Andrew winked at Trevor before turning his head to take a closer look.

'Do you want this sherry in your eye, Andrew John?' Laura enquired.

'If you're offering.'

'Men, they're little boys who never grow up. We're a pair of fools, Bethan. Both of us are going to end up with two babies to look after.'

'They'll be playmates for one another.'

'Are congratulations in order?' Haydn asked Trevor.

'Not for him,' Laura snapped. 'His was the easy part.'

'Want to meet the comic?' Haydn suggested, deciding he'd be on safer ground introducing Billy than any of the girls.

'I can always do with a laugh.'

'Billy, over here,' Haydn called. The comic was still in full make-up and the evening suit he'd worn on stage.

'Might have known you'd be with the most beautiful ladies in the room.' He walked past Haydn and kissed Laura and Bethan's hands.

'My sister, her husband, Andrew. Dr and Mrs Trevor Lewis . . .' As Haydn effected the introductions he saw the usherettes standing awkwardly in a tight cluster on the fringes of the party, each with a glass of sherry in her hand. 'Jane?' he motioned her to join them.

'Someone's lucky,' Avril said. 'That's his sister and brother-in-law. He's a doctor.'

'Haydn probably only wants me to meet his sister.'

'Be careful, my girl. Haydn's not the sort to invite a girl to meet his family unless he's got an ulterior motive.'

'What was that supposed to mean?' Myrtle asked as Jane straightened her cap and walked to where the Johns were sitting.

'I've seen which way the knickers are falling there all week.'

'Come on, the girl's lodging with the family.'

'He walks her home every night, doesn't he? And he hasn't had Rusty in his dressing room once this week.'

'You can't be serious,' Ann laughed. 'Not Jane. She's such a little mouse.'

'Those are the ones who need watching with tigers like Haydn Powell on the prowl.'

'She's right,' Myrtle nodded agreement. 'Don't you remember that West End star last year?'

'Falling star, you mean.'

'Whatever. He was still a pretty star. His girl was the dresser and she looked like the back end of a cow.'

'Men like Haydn are surrounded by beautiful women all day. He knows only too well what they get up to when their men are out of sight. It's my guess he'll take a leaf out of a lot of good-looking men's books. When he settles down it will be with a real plain Jane, and they don't come much plainer than that particular Jane.'

'You really think he'd marry her?' Ann watched as Haydn introduced Jane to an attractive dark-haired woman. There was an odd look on his face. One she hadn't seen before, even when he'd been a callboy. Gentle, almost compassionate; the kind of look that told her Avril just might be right.

'Dance, Rusty?'

The orchestra had returned to the pit by popular request, although they might not have been so eager to comply if it hadn't been for the liberal oiling of whiskies and brandies that had come courtesy of the house.

'Why should I?'

'Old times' sake?'

She gave Haydn a look that told him it would have been more prudent to have remained with Bethan and Andrew.

'You're an absolute rat, Haydn Powell.'

'I know. But go on, admit it. It was fun to be with a rat for a while.'

She glowered at him, but not for long. She began to laugh: a deep throaty chuckle that attracted the attention of most of the

275

men in the room. 'Oh what the hell. I can hardly claim you're the first, and with a husband like mine I don't suppose you'll be the last. Yes I'll dance with you. But the next one, not this.' She went to a side table, picked up two fresh glasses of champagne and handed him one. 'Here's to you, and mud in your eye. May you marry a woman who leads you a long and miserable life.'

'I'd rather not drink to that.'

'Why not? A wife won't stand a chance of curbing the lifestyle of a rat like you. What's the betting we'll bump into each other thirty years from now, remember this night, have a good laugh, walk back to our respective theatrical digs and beds which are being warmed by our current loves, without giving one single thought to the poor souls sitting at home, or in my case another theatre, waiting for us to get in touch.'

'I hope not.'

'You hope you won't be treading the boards in thirty years?'

'No, I hope that I'll regard my marriage more seriously.' He chose his words carefully, deliberately omitting all mention of concepts like 'love' and 'commitment' lest she take them as a further reminder that she had been no more than a passing diversion. Now the passion between them was spent, he wondered what had prompted him to sleep with her in the first place. But since Christmas he could have asked himself that question a dozen time over at the conclusion of a dozen similar, and equally unsatisfactory affairs.

'I don't know of any bride or groom who gets married with the idea of playing around. It's just something that happens. Like scratching yourself when you itch.'

'Then I'll have to make sure I do all my scratching now, before I meet my wife.'

'You can try, but have you ever tried sleeping in advance when you know you're not going to get your full eight hours for a week or two? Like everyone else, you'll mean well when you start out, but you're no different to any other man whose looks and libido outweigh his brains. When the little woman is far away tucking babies into bed and you're sharing a nightcap with a soubrette or the junior lead, you'll forget your good intentions.'

'There's no point in arguing with you, Rusty. Not when it can't be proved one way or the other.'

'Ah, but given time it will.' She laughed again, only this time it was a harsher, more brittle sound.

The band struck the opening bars of 'Begin the Beguine'. He led Rusty on to centre stage. On their left Andrew and Bethan were still seated at their table; behind them Trevor was attempting a foxtrot with Laura. Most of the Revue girls had been propositioned and claimed by the town notables.

'Right, let's show them how it's done,' Rusty said loudly. She began to dance, her exquisite body swaying, keeping time to the music. Haydn took his cue from her. They stepped side by side, commanding more and more space, relegating the other dancers to the wings as they swirled, turned and improvised new and showy steps.

'There's nothing like those two when they get going, not even Fred Astaire and Ginger Rogers.' Judy reached for her fourth glass of champagne.

'Oh I don't know,' Mandy said airily, confident that she could have done as well if she'd been partnering Haydn. 'I think Rusty's a bit past it, don't you?'

'No,' Judy said flatly. 'And neither does Norman. Word is he has both of them earmarked for the West End next winter. A revival of *The Garden of Allah* but if this war goes ahead . . .'

'War, war, war!' Babs complained, as she made her way to the table to refill her glass. 'That's all anyone ever talks about these days.'

'If it does come, it's got to be good for us,' Judy the businesswoman pronounced authoritatively. 'It'll be just like last time. The whole country awash with servicemen in transit and on leave with money burning holes in their pockets. And we all know there's nothing servicemen like better than a good time. If we're good and clever girls and play our cards right, we'll make sure we'll be there to give it to them.'

'You really think it will be like that?' Babs perked up at the thought of men in uniform paying court to her. She looked at

Haydn and imagined him in something dashing. A Captain's uniform, perhaps.

'Yes, and I also think that those two will be in the forefront of it all. Can't you just see them doing that routine in army fatigues?'

'That was quite a display.'

'My dancing partner, Rusty. My sister and her husband.'

Rusty nodded, 'Pleased to meet you,' and moved on, but not before Andrew intercepted a glance between her and Haydn that confirmed his suspicions about the rumours concerning Haydn and chorus girls.

'William and Eddie have arrived.'

Haydn looked up and saw Trevor and Laura locked in earnest conversation with his brother and cousin. To his dismay he also noticed Jenny standing beside Eddie.

'I need a drink.'

'So do I,' Bethan said. 'Something soft like orange juice.'

'Women,' Andrew smiled fondly. 'Give them unlimited champagne and all they want is orange juice.'

Haydn walked around the flats at the back of the stage, but he and Andrew didn't manage to pass unseen. William joined them as they reached the corridor.

'Eddie insisted on bringing her with him,' William apologised. 'I couldn't do anything about it.'

'It doesn't matter.' Haydn buttonholed the barman. 'Could you do us three beers, three large whiskies – ' he looked enquiringly at his companions, who both nodded agreement – 'and an orange juice please, Des.'

'Well, seeing as how it's you, Haydn. Had enough of the party?'

'Not really. It's just getting a bit warm in there.'

'Saw you and Rusty. Saw Babs and Mandy looking on too. Not surprising the temperature's climbed a bit high for comfort.'

'What's all this?' William probed.

'Des likes a good gossip, don't you, Des?'

'No. I just stand back in awe, admiration and envy. I can't keep one woman happy. And look at you, three of them on the go, and not one complaint that you'd notice. What's your secret, boyo?'

'No secret. Just making sure I steer well clear of the altar. Can we keep the bottle, Des?' Haydn put his hand in his pocket and pulled out a pound note.

'Anything to keep you out of my hair.'

Haydn parked himself on a stool, the only seating left in the bar, between Andrew and William.

'Trevor won't be too pleased if he thinks we're getting drunk without him.'

'This isn't getting drunk, that'll come later,' William said earnestly.

'This is just a simple family occasion.' Haydn downed his whisky and topped up all three glasses.

Andrew looked at Haydn. 'Problems?'

Haydn shook his head.

'You can tell me to keep my nose out if you want to. I know what it was like when Bethan and I – '

'It's nothing as simple as a row with a girl.'

'I thought that you and Jenny . . .'

'I used to go out with her. There's been nothing between us for a long time.'

William looked at Haydn. Haydn stared into his glass and nodded. What did it matter who knew? If William told Andrew and everyone else who would listen, it might even get back to Eddie and make the idiot see sense for the first time in his life.

'Jenny stopped Haydn on the hill the other night and asked if they could pick up where they left off.'

'When I said no, she threatened to make a beeline for Eddie. Looks like she's done what she set out to do.'

'Then she's only going out with Eddie to get back at you?'

'That's what the lady said.'

'Have you tried talking to him?'

'Yes. But I didn't even get as far as mentioning her name. If you think you can succeed where I failed, please, be my guest, go ahead.'

279

'Not me.' Andrew rubbed his jaw thoughtfully. 'He knocked me out once, remember.'

'I remember,' Haydn smiled. 'Just before you married Bethan. He made a good job of it too.'

'I wasn't right for months afterwards. When this bottle is finished, please allow me to get the next. If I can't do anything constructive to help, I can at least engineer temporary oblivion.'

'That won't solve anything,' William said.

'No, but it'll blur the edges and numb the pain if I do happen to find the courage to tackle Eddie and he does lash out,' Haydn answered drily.

Music echoed from the auditorium, accompanied by the unrefined tones of Billy's voice: 'I can't dance, don't ask me. I can't dance . . .'

'Where you going?' William asked, as Haydn refilled their glasses, picked up the bottle, and headed for the door.

'Taking the doctor's advice,' he bowed to Andrew. 'Getting drunk. Then I intend to dance with every girl who's willing. I may even make love to a couple. And afterwards I intend to tell little brother that he's walking out with the wrong woman.'

'Haydn, just look at the way Jenny's fawning all over him. It's going to take a lot more than a grand gesture from you to change Eddie's mind about her. Please, leave it to me.'

'What makes you think he's going to listen to you when he wouldn't

listen to me?' Haydn looked from William to Andrew, then in the mirror behind the bar at himself. 'I don't know about you, but at the moment I think we're about running neck and neck in the depths of Eddie's estimation. The cousin who, on his own admission, couldn't have made it plainer in the Palais that he hates Jenny; the brother who once lusted after her, and the rich brother-in-law he calls Cashmere Coat. Which one of us do you think he hates the most?'

'Haydn didn't mean anything by that,' William apologised to Andrew after Haydn left.

'I've learned that insults from the Powells are a kind of in-itiation rite into the family. I hope that if I continue to take them without complaining too much, you may eventually accept me.'

'It's not been easy for Haydn since he's come back. He was looking forward to it, he even wrote to me to tell me how much, but now he's actually here, all he does is moan that nothing's the same.'

'And it won't be ever again, because he now lives in a different world. One foot in both and belonging to neither. I know exactly how he feels.'

'You do?'

'I went to medical school when I was eighteen, and came back at twenty-three to find everything changed. Principally myself.'

'Come to think of it, Haydn has changed more than the rest of us.'

Andrew picked up his pint and the orange juice. 'I should be getting back to Bethan.'

'And I to the chorus girls. I seem to be the only Powell who hasn't got girl problems, and one or two of the right kind would be very welcome.'

Mandy and Judy were holding centre stage with an up-to-the-minute version of 'Dance Little Lady' that brought the Charles-ton into modern times. Billy had handed over the microphone to Haydn, who was down on one knee, singing to the girls, much to everyone's amusement.

'Life on stage seems to be one big party.' A real, or imagined wistfulness in Jenny's voice set Eddie's teeth on edge.

'You think so?'

'It's not all glamour, exotic clothes and good times, Miss . . .' Billy looked at Jenny.

'Griffiths. Jenny Griffiths.'

'I've yet to meet a Jenny who wasn't the essence of loveliness.'

'You were telling us about life on stage,' Andrew broke in hastily as Eddie glowered at the comic.

'It's sheer hard work. And an awful lot of it. Practise, rehearse, practise, and then at the end of the day when all you want to do is fall into your bed, alone,' he nudged Jenny's elbow within Andrew's sight, but thankfully out of Eddie's, 'because you're too tired to do anything except sleep, you have to get out there and perform. Give your all and more because you can't disappoint your audience, even if they are only local shopkeepers on complimentary tickets that have been handed out by the bill-stickers. And you even learn to be grateful for that appalling audience, because the alternative of no audience at all is too ghastly to contemplate. If you don't believe me, all you have to do is ask that one.' He pointed to where Jane had retreated with the rest of the usherettes.

'She's not on stage,' Jenny said sharply.

'Ah, but she wants to be, and she has talent.'

'Jane?'

'Your brother has been coaching her,' Billy informed Eddie. 'Hey, darling,' he waved vigorously to Jane, who, immersed in Mandy and Judy's dancing and Haydn's singing, didn't hear him until the music ended. Just as the orchestra fell silent, Billy put two fingers in his mouth and whistled. 'Here girl,' he commanded as though she were a dog.

'What do you want, Billy?' She sidled over, half expecting a squirt of water from his buttonhole.

'"Something to do with Spring,"' he shouted down to Gustav in the orchestra pit.

'Only if you tear up my poker IOUs.'

'You're on.' He turned to Haydn. 'Do you mind?'

'Mind what?'

'Me dancing with your protégé.'

'I'm not dancing with you. Not with the manager, Mr Evans and everyone else watching,' Jane protested.

'Everyone's had so many glasses of champagne they wouldn't notice if I was dancing with a two-headed octopus.'

'Come on,' Haydn took her arm.

'Hey, this was my idea,' Billy shouted.

'No chance, Billy boy. Jane's my discovery.'

'Good heavens, is that Jane?' Joe Evans peered over the rim of a glass at Haydn who was dancing to the refrain of 'Poor Little Rich Girl' with Jane.

'Talented theatre as well as stage staff.' Trevor pushed his glass towards the manager, who was topping up all the glasses on their table.

'What a party. I can't remember one like it.' The manager carried on splashing champagne recklessly into every glass in sight, forgetting that Norman had only offered to pay for the first two dozen bottles.

The music ended. Haydn stood and laughed as Jane, red-faced and breathless, ran off backstage.

Andrew left the table. 'Lovely party. Thanks for getting us invited, but it's time we were on our way.'

'Nothing wrong with Bethan?' Haydn slurred slightly, on target towards his goal of getting drunk.

'Just past her bedtime.'

'We'll be seeing you tomorrow?' Bethan asked as Trevor helped her on with her wrap.

'Wouldn't miss your birthday for the world.' Haydn kissed his sister's cheek.

'I suppose it is too early to offer you a lift?'

'Yes it is. I'll walk up later with Jane.'

Bethan looked over to the gap between two flats where Jane was hiding with Ann and Avril. 'Bring her tomorrow will you, Haydn. Everyone else is coming, and she can't very well stay at home by herself.'

Haydn walked Bethan, Andrew, Laura and Trevor to the door. He locked it behind him and slowly climbed the steps. The champagne had gone to more than his head. Or possibly it was the dancing. Either way, his feet were dragging when he looked up and saw Mandy standing in front of the shuttered box-office, two glasses in hand, her light green silk gown clinging seductively to her voluptuous curves.

'Goodbye drink?'

'I have to get back to the party.'

'I'm not here to whine, Haydn. Not like Rusty did last week when you told her it was over between you.'

He recalled the ugly scene between himself and Rusty and the thin walls between the dressing rooms, and wondered if anything in his life could be classed as private.

She smiled, biting her lip to stop it from trembling. 'It was fun while it lasted, but I knew I'd never have exclusive rights, not over someone like you.'

'I doubt you'd want to if you knew what I was really like. As Rusty said, I'm a rat.'

'When romance is in the air, a girl never notices what part of the animal kingdom a man comes from.'

He was left with the uncomfortable feeling that he'd heard the line somewhere before. In a play or a film?

'To success, and our separate careers?' She descended the steps and pressed a glass into his hand.

'To success.' He drank, but he had reached a watershed. His stomach revolted at more liquid being poured into it. Even champagne. 'Good luck on the rest of the tour. Got anything lined up at the end of it?'

'Not straight after, but I've been offered pantomime at Yarmouth for the Christmas season. I was there last year. It's *Dandini*. What do you think? Third billing's not bad for a Revue girl?'

'Not bad at all.' Because her face was barely an inch away from his, he bent his head intending to kiss her cheek, but she moved at the last minute and he found himself kissing her mouth.

'Goodnight, Haydn.' Jane brushed past him, descending the steps in company with the other usherettes.

'I'll walk you home,' he called after her, forgetting Mandy's presence.

'I'd rather walk home with the other girls.'

'Goodnight, Haydn,' Avril called blithely. 'See you next week.'

'I'm sorry,' Mandy said tartly as they slammed the door behind them. 'I didn't mean to sour things between you and your little girlfriend.'

Her injured air and patronising tone infuriated Haydn. 'She's not my "little girlfriend". She lodges in my father's house.'

'Really?'

'Is that the only damned word showgirls know?'

'My God, you do love her.'

'What I do, or don't do, is none of your damned business.' He ran down to the door, hesitated when he remembered he had left his coat in his dressing room, then decided he could do without it for one night.

'You don't know everything about sweet innocent Jane,' Mandy mocked as he opened the door.

'What do you mean?' he looked back at her. She was leaning against the wall, smiling maliciously.

'You'll find out in time.' She held up her empty glass. 'I need more of this.'

'Mandy!'

Ignoring him she walked away, her heels tapping in time to the melody of 'Auld Lang Syne' echoing from the auditorium. 'You don't know everything about sweet innocent Jane?' Sometimes it seemed to Haydn as though the whole world knew more about Jane Jones than he did.

Mandy didn't go back to the theatre. Instead she went to the dressing room. Taking an envelope from her handbag, she scrawled 'Love Mandy' across the outside before slipping into Haydn's room. She switched on the light and looked around. The shelf was too obvious. Then she saw the coat hanging on the back of the door.

Haydn caught up with Jane under the railway bridge.

'You didn't have to leave early.'

'I didn't, it was breaking up.'

'Not so I noticed.'

'The manager realised he'd got to the end of the champagne supplied by the Revue company and was paying for it himself,' she laughed.

'You don't do anywhere near enough of that.'

'What?'

'Laugh.'

'I suppose I haven't had much practice.'

'Tough being an orphan?'

She gave him a hard look and he realised he'd hurt her unduly sensitive pride, yet again.

'I'm sorry. I didn't mean to say that. It's probably the drink talking, not me. My sister's invited you to her birthday party tomorrow.'

'I can't go to your sister's birthday party.'

'Why not?'

'It's a family occasion . . . it's . . .'

'She asked me to bring you because she wants you there. You live with us, I'm afraid that means you have to suffer our "family occasions" whether you want to or not.'

'I'd rather not go on sufferance.'

'She couldn't bear the thought of you staying in the house all alone. And we can't have Bethan being upset on her birthday, can we? Especially in her condition.'

'She's going to have a baby?'

'I hope so, otherwise she's carrying a lot of weight for nothing.'

'That's a charming thing to say.'

'That's the drink again. I didn't mean it. We're all hoping it will work out this time. It's not her first. She lost a little boy last winter.'

'Is that why she wants another?'

Her reaction seemed odd to Haydn. He looked keenly at her, not knowing anything about a world where pregnancy was regarded as a disgrace and the harbinger of a woman's downfall. Or that Jane had never met anyone in her short life who'd actually wanted a baby and looked forward to its arrival as a joyful event.

'Do come. We can walk up Penycoedcae Hill together. If the weather's the same as today it will be glorious.'

'I haven't got her a present.'

'Get her one in the post office in Leyshon Street tomorrow morning.'

'Like what?'

'Like a bar of chocolate.'

'Would that be all right?'

'Of course. Have you ever been to a party before?' he asked.
'Not before tonight.'
'I mean a family party. A birthday party.'
She shook her head.
'It's not much different to a family meal. Noisier, that's all.'
'You're sure she wants me to come?'
'I'm sure.' He tucked her hand into the crook of his elbow, and held on to her fingers. She was such an odd, confusing mixture of avaricious acquisitiveness and naivety. It had to be curiosity, and nothing more, that was driving him to get to the bottom of whatever had made her that way.

Although Jane had no mending to do the following morning she was up at her usual time. The cast of the Revue were leaving on the nine o'clock train out of Pontypridd. She'd decided to go down to the station to say goodbye to Mandy and Judy, the first real friends she felt she'd made other than Phyllis. She stopped off, not at the post office, as Haydn had advocated, but at Griffiths' shop, and spent ten minutes choosing between the relative merits of different bars of chocolate before settling on bars of Fry's Five Boys for Mandy and Judy and a shilling box of chocolates for Bethan.

'Someone's birthday?' Jenny asked, as Jane untied the handkerchief she kept her money in.

'Yes.'

'Then you'll be wanting a card.' Jenny pushed a box of birthday postcards towards her.

Jane glanced at the clock and realised she only had ten minutes to get to the station. 'I can't stop now. Will you be open in half an hour?'

'Where are you going in such a hurry?'

Jane didn't stop to answer. She rushed out through the door and down the hill. She could hear the train steaming on the platform overhead as she bought her penny platform ticket. The station was crowded with men who'd come to wave the girls off. Bewildered, she looked around at the sea of capped and straw boatered heads. Fighting her way to the edge of the platform she looked up and down the train. Two porters were stowing the enormous wickerwork baskets that held the props into the guard's van. Norman and Billy were helping Rusty into a first-class carriage. Lower down the train, she spotted a group of girls clustered in front of the third-class carriages, Mandy and Judy among them. She started running, then stopped in her tracks. Haydn was walking up the steps holding a bunch of red roses. He passed by without seeing her and made his way to the first-class carriages, halting in front of the one Norman had helped Rusty into.

'Jane, don't tell me you've come to see us off?' Mandy cried, pulling out a handkerchief and dabbing her eyes with it. 'God, I hate goodbyes.'

'Me too.' Judy purloined Mandy's handkerchief.

'I bought you both some chocolate for the journey.' Jane pushed the bag into Mandy's hands. 'It's Fry's, the kind you like.'

'Don't! You're going to have me crying in a moment.'

'I didn't mean to upset you. You've both been so good to me.'

'And you to us.' Judy hugged her. 'What are we going to do without you to mend our stockings?'

Billy, who'd spotted Jane from the first-class section, walked down the train. Winking at her from the open door, he said, 'If ever you get tired of being an usherette, write to me and I'll take you on as a comic's assistant.'

'Don't, whatever else you do, work for a comic,' Judy warned solemnly. 'They all turn to drink in the end, and as if that's not enough, most of them are born queer.'

Without warning Mandy gave Jane a rib-splitting hug that drove all the breath from her body.

'I'm sorry, Jane. I'm really, really sorry . . .' the rest of Mandy's words were lost in a dam-burst of tears.

'Mandy,' Judy turned impatiently to her friend, 'this is not an audition for *Anna Karenina*. Come on, into the train before you get completely hysterical.'

Mandy fought free of Judy's grasp. She stood on the step of the carriage and looked back at Jane.

'I'm sorry,' she repeated.

'What for?' Jane asked in bewilderment.

'For everything,' Mandy sobbed. 'Absolutely everything.'

'Looks like you're not the only one to come down and see us off,' Rusty said to Haydn as she looked along the train.

'Jane's fond of the girls. You've all been good to her.'

'She's been good to us. Thanks to her my clothes are in one piece for the first time since I started this tour.'

The conductor walked along the train slamming doors. Haydn thrust the bouquet of red roses into Rusty's hands.

'These are for you.'

'You were right yesterday.' She allowed the conductor to close the door, but pulled down the window. 'It was good while it lasted.'

'You know my agent's address. If you ever want to get in touch with me . . .'

'Don't worry, sunshine. When you're up there in the West End with Noel Coward I'll give you a call. You'll need a good head girl.'

'Or co-star.'

'No, darling. My days of topping the bill are drawing to a close. I recognise a rising star when I see one. A falling star always does.'

'Take care.'

His words were lost in a hiss of steam. A minute later there was only a puff of smoke on the platform and when it cleared, Jane looking very small, lost and forlorn.

Chapter Eighteen

'I'd like to have a word with you if I may, Mr Griffiths.' Eddie screwed his cap into a ball, and shuffled nervously from one foot to the other as he faced Harry Griffiths across the counter of his shop.

'Talk away, Eddie.' Harry carried on stacking empty Thomas and Evans pop bottles into a rough wooden crate.

'I'll do that, Dad.' Jenny blocked his access to the corner where the empties were stored. He looked at her and saw in an instant what was coming. Wiping his hands on his khaki overall, he planted both hands on his knees and rose stiffly to his feet.

'Perhaps we ought to go upstairs, Eddie.'

'Thank you, Mr Griffiths.'

Harry opened the connecting door between the shop and the living quarters. A mouthwatering smell of cooking beef wafted down the stairs to greet them.

'I'm sorry, Mr Griffiths, I didn't mean to interrupt your dinner.'

'You're not, boy, Mrs Griffiths is in church. We won't be eating until she gets back. Come in.' He opened a door at the top of the stairs and showed Eddie into a room that would have been considered large if it hadn't been crammed full of furniture. An enormous, stuffed horsehair, brown Rexine three-piece suite dominated the area closest to the window. A heavy oval mahogany table and four chairs upholstered in the same brown Rexine were pushed up close to an enormous sideboard at the opposite end. The overall impression was of gloom; dark shadows interspersed with occasional teardrops of sunlight that had escaped the confines of the thick yellow lace curtains. Upstairs, Eddie found the cooking smell, now mingled with beeswax and washing soda, overpowering.

'Sit down.' Harry pointed at the sofa and Eddie perched on the edge, still clutching his cap.

'Cigarette?' Harry offered the packet, before remembering where he was. His wife didn't allow anyone, not even the vicar, to smoke in her precious sitting room.

Eddie glanced anxiously about him. There were so many highly polished surfaces he was petrified at the thought of dropping ash or scorching something. 'Not right now, but thank you for offering, Mr Griffiths.'

'You wanted to see me?'

'I'd like to marry, Jenny,' Eddie blurted out.

Harry sat in a chair opposite Eddie. The request wasn't unexpected, despite Jenny's assertion that there was nothing of a romantic nature between Eddie and herself. But he could remember Haydn Powell calling into the shop, and the light Haydn had kindled in his daughter's eyes. If Jenny loved Eddie the way she had once loved Haydn, there was no obvious, outward sign of it that he could see.

'I'd like to marry Jenny soon, if I may, Mr Griffiths,' Eddie pressed.

'How soon?' Harry barked, a horrible suspicion forming in his mind.

'We haven't set a date or anything. I know we'd have to get a home together first. Sort out where we're going to live, buy furniture, and all the things we . . . every married couple needs . . .' his voice tailed as he realised he'd given no thought to domestic details. Only to what was going to happen between himself and Jenny every night in the bedroom.

Harry relaxed. At least Eddie hadn't mentioned next week; hopefully that meant things weren't urgent enough to send his wife into a rage. 'You can afford to put a home together?'

'I've saved some money from my boxing purses.'

'Not a very secure job.'

'No, but my position in Charlie's shop is.'

'You're not thinking of turning professional, then?'

'Not until it's worth my while. Because soon, if you give your permission that is, I'll have Jenny to consider as well as myself.'

'At the moment she's my consideration.'

'I know, but I'd look after her, Mr Griffiths. She'd want for nothing, I promise you.'

'I don't doubt it.' Harry capitulated. It was no use fighting any longer. His craving for tobacco was too strong. He pushed a cigarette between his lips, and struck a match. He wanted to ask Eddie about Haydn; if he realised that Jenny had gone out with his brother. Then he remembered Mrs Richards and her endless gossip. The whole of the Graig had known about Jenny and Haydn. There was no way Eddie could have been kept in the dark.

'All I'm asking Mr Griffiths, is that you, and Mrs Griffiths of course, give your blessing to our engagement, and then as soon as we've found a home . .'

'You say you've some money saved. Enough for a house?'

'Not straight off, but certainly enough for furniture. And although we'd start off by renting, I intend to buy just as soon as I can. My father's always owned his own house,' he added proudly.

'And what does Jenny say about all this?'

'She wants to marry me.'

'You've already asked her?'

'Last night, Mr Griffiths. That's when she said I had to come and see you today.'

Harry suppressed a smile. It was the first time the poor lad had spoken in terms of 'Jenny said'. He hoped for his sake it wasn't the beginning of a lifetime of henpecking. He loved his daughter dearly but occasionally, like now, he could see the heavy hand of her mother's upbringing in her.

'Well, I suppose in that case there's nothing to do except bring out the sherry.'

'Harry Griffiths!' His wife stood glowering in the doorway. 'What's that you have in your hand?' she demanded furiously, making no allowances for Eddie's presence.

'Nothing.' Harry squashed his cigarette out on the lid of the packet and pushed the dog end and the ash inside. 'Eddie Powell's just asked if he can marry our Jenny.'

'If that's all right, Mrs Griffiths.' Eddie rose to his feet, his hands still busily scrunching his cap into a creased ball.

'Our Jenny!' Mrs Griffiths glared balefully at Eddie. 'She's far too young,' she snorted dismissively.

'No younger than you were when you married me,' Harry protested mildly.

'That's precisely what I mean.'

'Our Jenny's old enough to know her own mind. She'll be twenty-one next birthday.'

'And how old are you?' Mrs Griffiths demanded of Eddie, ignoring her husband.

'Twenty next birthday.' It sounded better than nineteen last month.

'And how do you think you're going to support my daughter? She's been used to a high standard, you know. We've given her everything a girl could possibly want. She's never had to shift or make do in her life.'

'We've been through all that. Go downstairs and get Jenny, Eddie. Tell her to shut the shop.'

'On a Sunday morning!' his wife exclaimed.

'Ten minutes isn't going to hurt. I think it's time we had a toast.'

Eddie couldn't wait to get out of the room. He ran down the stairs at breakneck speed.

'Just what do you think you're doing? Telling that young man to go downstairs and get our daughter to toast an engagement when I haven't given my permission.'

'Jenny isn't going to need our permission to marry soon, not when she's twenty-one.' He lifted the lid on a Royal Doulton tea-pot that had never been used, and extracted the key to the sideboard from it.

'But . . .'

'There's no buts. Not this time. Our Jenny'll be up in a minute, and if it's what she wants, I can't see how we can stop her. Particularly with this war coming.'

'A war, you, like every other man, can't wait to start.'

'There's such a thing as bowing to the inevitable. Young men will have to go and fight, the women will stay at home, and the threat of separation will be enough for young people to see it as an excuse to hurry up their lives.'

'And there'll be as many mistakes made as last time.'

'Probably.' There was more than a trace of irony in Harry's voice. 'But when a young man's faced with imminent death, he can't see past the sweet young girl in front of him to the old shrew waiting in the wings.'

'Harry Griffiths!'

'Look Mam, Dad,' Jenny walked into the room, Eddie hovering behind her. She held out her left hand. On the third finger a gold band set with two diamond chips glittered prettily as it caught a sunbeam.

'And where did you get that?'

'The jeweller in Mill Street,' Eddie said quickly, wanting to assure his future mother-in-law that it was real gold and diamonds, not a market-stall copy that would peel or turn black.

'Isn't it lovely?' Jenny pushed it under her mother's nose.

'Lovely.' Harry uncorked the sherry.

'Eddie got the jeweller to open up especially for him last night.'

'He was drinking in the Ruperra,' Eddie admitted, trying to make it sound as though he hadn't gone to any great effort.

'Drink a lot, do you?'

'No, Mrs Griffiths. But I do go to the Ruperra every night. I train there.'

'Train?'

'Boxing,' Harry explained succinctly.

She studied Eddie, seeing the bruises on his face and the plastered cut above his eye for the first time. 'So you're the Powell who boxes?'

'Yes, Mrs Griffiths.'

'And just what kind of husband do you think you'll make, going around with a bashed-about face like that?'

'He'll make a marvellous husband.' Jenny linked her arm protectively into Eddie's. 'And his face isn't going to get any more battered than it already is, because he's a splendid boxer.'

Harry lifted a silver tray of small glasses from the sideboard, poured sherry into four of them, and handed them to his wife, daughter and Eddie. 'Well here's to the happy couple.' He held his glass high.

Mrs Griffiths took her glass and held it at arm's length as though it contained poison. 'If it's not too much to ask, do you mind telling us when you're thinking of getting married? I don't know about your family, but in this one we like to do things properly, and that means making plans.'

'We're going to marry the minute we find somewhere to live.' Jenny pulled Eddie close to her; the movement jerked his arm and a little of the sherry slopped over the edge of his glass on to the carpet. Mrs Griffiths noticed and stared pointedly at the mess he'd made.

'I only hope you're going to get enough together to start off within your own four walls. In my opinion it's always a mistake for couples to begin in someone else's home.'

'Your sister started off with your mother,' Harry commented, feeling the need to assert himself.

'Yes,' his wife conceded. 'But it was far from ideal.'

'We'll find somewhere of our own,' Eddie said, drawing strength from Jenny's proximity, 'when the times comes.'

'Well then, let us drink to that time.' Harry raised his glass again.

Jenny looked from Eddie's apprehensive face to her mother's disapproving one. Only her father had succeeded in raising a smile. She looked back at Eddie. He squeezed her hand, but she couldn't bring herself to respond. If only he had been Haydn she would have been sure that she was doing the right thing.

'Doesn't look like Hitler will pull out of Poland,' Trevor said to Andrew.

'Not now. I think the content of the Prime Minister's broadcast is inevitable.'

'This is my birthday,' Bethan reminded them, as Andrew opened half a dozen bottles of beer and distributed them among the men. 'And I won't have any talk of war.'

'But if it comes, Beth, it's going to affect us all,' William protested. 'We'll all get called up.'

'Not today,' Bethan said firmly.

'But next week . . .'

'She's right,' Andrew handed William a bottle and a glass. 'Today the only important thing is Bethan's birthday, and if the ladies all have their sherry and the gentlemen their beer, I'd like to propose a toast to my wife's health.'

Jane sat nervously clutching her sherry on the sofa next to Haydn. She'd never been in such lavishly appointed surroundings, she'd never drunk anything alcoholic, and she'd never felt quite so overawed. This was one situation when she knew that the bluff and bravado she had come to rely on to get her through life was useless. Watching Diana, Laura, Alma and Phyllis, she copied them and raised her glass towards Bethan.

'To Bethan, the best wife a man could have,' Andrew said gravely.

'To Bethan.'

'That's the door.'

'Our Eddie. Late as usual.' Evan was furious with Eddie for disappearing early that morning just as the family were about to walk up the hill to Penycoedcae. Neither Diana nor Phyllis knew where he'd gone, and although Haydn and William had their suspicions they hadn't voiced them.

The maid's heels clipped across the tiled floor of the hall, the door opened and Eddie's voice, accompanied by the low murmurs of a woman's voice, floated in. Suspecting who the woman might be Bethan eyed Haydn, but he appeared to be in deep conversation with Jane. The maid opened the door to the drawing room and Eddie and Jenny stood side by side.

'Sorry I'm late, sis.' Eddie handed her a package. 'This is from both of us.'

'That's very kind of you.'

'Aren't you going to open it?'

She lifted the lid on the small, flat cardboard box. A fine white lace handkerchief was pinned to a square of deep, blue paper. In the centre, fastened by a tiny, dark blue velvet bow gleamed a miniature sapphire bottle of Evening in Paris perfume.

'That's very kind of you, Eddie, Jenny, thank you. It's beautiful.'

'I'll put it with the others.' Andrew relieved her of the package and laid it on the side table that held her presents. 'Beer, Eddie? Sherry, Jenny?'

'Thank you.' Jenny looked around. The room was beautifully proportioned, high ceilinged and grand enough to hold four sofas, three armchairs and an assortment of side tables and cupboards without appearing crowded. Which was just as well, considering the number of people present. Dr Trevor Lewis and his wife Laura were sitting on a small sofa next to the french windows that opened out on to the front lawn, bringing a taste of the glorious summer morning to the assembly. Eddie's father Evan, Brian and Phyllis had claimed the sofa next to them. Alma and Charlie were opposite. Haydn, Jane, William and Diana were piled on the largest couch, and Bethan and Andrew in chairs either side of the magnificent white marble fireplace.

'Jenny and I have a small announcement to make.' Eddie cleared his throat and deliberately avoided his brother's eye as he lifted Jenny's hand. 'We got engaged this morning.'

Andrew was the first to regain his composure. He stepped forward with their drinks. 'Congratulations.' He dumped the glasses on the table that held Bethan's presents, and shook Eddie's hand before kissing Jenny on the cheek. 'Now we have an excuse for another toast.'

'To the happy couple.'

'The refrain echoed raggedly around the room. Haydn fixed his gaze on Jenny, but she refused to meet it, looking determinedly and adoringly at Eddie as she sipped delicately at her drink.

Bethan looked from one brother to the other in confusion. Then she remembered Haydn's unexpected breakfast visit. Was this what had been on his mind? Her heart went out to him. He had been so much in love with Jenny a year ago.

The door opened and the maid crept to Bethan's side. 'Cook sent me to ask if you'd like lunch laid in the drawing room or outside in the garden.'

'It's such a glorious day, we thought it would be nice to eat outside,' Andrew explained. 'We set up a trestle under the chestnut tree, but if anyone objects, say so now.'

'Sounds wonderful to me,' Laura enthused.

'Then the garden it is.'

Trevor slapped Eddie soundly across the back as the maid left. 'Good on you, Eddie.'

His gesture galvanised the others. Evan and Phyllis stepped forward to give their congratulations, and soon Eddie was in the centre of a crowd. Diana hugged Jenny to welcome her into the family. Only Haydn took advantage of the confusion to slip out through the french windows into the garden. He walked over to the trestles, already covered with snowy, white damask linen, that had been set up in the shade of an enormous tree.

'You all right, Haydn?'

He looked down. Jane was beside him, her small face furrowed with concern. She reminded him of an anxious mouse. He smiled, then as her frown cut deeper into her forehead, he laughed. 'Why shouldn't I be?'

Jenny heard the laugh, and looked through the window. She saw no further than that he was happy and with Jane. And she hated him, and Jane – plain and insignificant as she was – for it. If he had shouted at her or Eddie, created the scene she'd secretly hoped for, she would have handed Eddie back his ring without a qualm. As it was, Haydn's reaction only served to make her all the more determined to marry Eddie.

'That was some party in the Town Hall last night,' Trevor said to Haydn as he joined him in the garden.

'If you think that was good, wait until we get to the last night of the Summer Variety.'

'Starts tomorrow?'

'If we can remember the routines.'

'I'm sure it will be wonderful,' Bethan said as she left the house.

'Wish I had your confidence.'

'Have you seen any of the rehearsals, Jane?'

'No,' she answered shyly as Haydn pulled a wickerwork garden chair out for her. 'The rehearsals have all been in the morning when I haven't been working.'

'I suggest Haydn gives us a song from it so we can judge for ourselves.' Andrew sank down the chair next to Bethan's.

'You going to play the piano for him?'

'Why not? I'm not that dreadful.'

'I think Haydn's repertoire is slightly more extensive than "Twinkle twinkle little star".'

'You have a piano?' Evan asked.

'Andrew bought me one for my birthday. He hoped I'd learn.'

'It was the only thing I could think of that she'd have to sit down to do.' Andrew refilled Laura and Diana's sherry glasses.

'He wouldn't listen to me when I told him I was tone deaf.'

'But I believe you now, darling.'

'And rather than send the piano back, he's decided to try and learn himself.

'As my teacher gave up on me when I was eight years old that will give you some idea of the standard I've achieved. But, my "Twinkle twinkle little star" has to be heard to be believed.'

'I think it would be better for everyone present if we took you at your word.'

'Laura can play,' Trevor volunteered.

'Would you like a piano?' Bethan asked. 'I know of an almost new one, hardly played, going cheap.'

'I'd love one, but I have no time to practise. Between running the new restaurant for the family, and cooking this one's – ' she pointed at Trevor – 'meals and doing his mending. And cleaning up after . . .'

'Truce!' Andrew called.

'Music would be nice.' Bethan smiled at Haydn.

'I'll do my best if Laura plays.' Haydn was aware of Jenny watching him. Of an old, familiar look in her eye, which dispelled the final vestiges of hope he'd nurtured, that her threats had been idle ones.

'I love summer,' Diana said as she sat on the grass and leaned back against the tree trunk.

'Don't we all.'

'Make the most of it,' William said flatly. 'It could be the last for a while.'

'Summer will come even during a war.'

'It did in the last one,' Evan murmured. 'Although it didn't always feel like it when the casualty lists came in.'

'Perhaps Hitler will see sense. Even now at this late stage. After what happened to them last time, I can't believe the Germans are any more eager to fight than we are.'

This time Bethan didn't stop Trevor from talking. The mere mention of war – and there seemed to have been nothing but talk of it during the past few weeks – was enough to close a fist of icy dread around her heart. She couldn't bear the thought of her brothers and Andrew leaving. Possibly for ever, as William and Diana's father had done the last time. Trevor's optimistic declaration that it might not come to that was one straw in the wind that she wanted to grasp.

'I'd like to think you're right.' Andrew squeezed Bethan's hand as he gave up his chair to Phyllis and sat at his wife's feet. 'But if Hitler was going to move his troops out of Poland, I think he would have done so by now.'

'The Fascists have been asking for it for a long time,' Evan said, picking up his beer.

'They didn't learn, not even when you tried to punch them on the nose, eh Dad.'

Everyone laughed at Eddie's joke, as much from relief as at any trace of humour it contained.

'Come on, Haydn,' Laura took his hand. 'Let's go and find this piano of Andrew's and give it a bashing.'

She led him through a second set of french windows into the dining room and soon afterwards the melodious strains of 'Where are the Songs we Sung' drifted out into the garden. The maid came out with a tray loaded with condiments and napkin-wrapped cutlery and started to lay the table. Andrew went into the drawing room and emerged with more beer and another bottle of sherry.

'All the latest songs,' Alma smiled as Laura switched to 'Dearest Love'.

'Of course,' Andrew agreed, 'I do know what sheet music to buy, even if I haven't progressed from nursery rhymes.'

'Haydn can really sing,' Charlie observed.

'Can't he just.' Bethan passed Phyllis's glass to Andrew. 'I often wonder where he got it from. Or you, your boxing ability, Eddie. Dad told me how well you did on Friday, and we heard that you've been picked out by a top promoter. Congratulations.'

'We're hoping it will give us enough money to marry.' Eddie laid his arm protectively around Jenny's shoulders.

'You thinking of setting the date soon?' Diana asked.

'As soon as we find a place to live,' he answered with a defiant look towards the dining room, where Laura's voice had now joined Haydn's.

'It'll be nice to have a wedding to celebrate in the family.'

'How about some dancing?' Andrew suggested. 'There's only one rug in the dining room. If you give me a hand to shift the furniture back, Trevor, we'll have plenty of room.'

Evan pulled out the pocket watch that had been his father's. 'Ten minutes to go before the Prime Minister's broadcast.'

'I'll put the radio on.' Andrew rose to his feet. 'If I turn the volume up, we'll be able to hear it from here.

The only sounds that disturbed Chamberlain's voice were the singing of the birds, and the drone of a motorcycle and side-car as it chugged slowly along the lane past the garden. As the broadcast continued, the silence closed in, blanketing, suffocating. Afterwards Bethan felt as though she couldn't breathe. She fumbled blindly for her husband's hand, looking down at her lap lest anyone see her tears.

'There'll be a shortage of miners.' Evan looked to his two older sons, and his nephew. 'Like last time, they'll probably make it a protected occupation.'

'I'd feel a coward if I didn't take my chances along with everyone else.'

'I had no idea you wanted to go, Eddie.' The shock in Jenny's voice was genuine.

'I don't think many men our age will be given the option of whether they want to fight, or not.' Haydn glanced at Will, who nodded agreement.

'All you can do is wait and see what will be wanted,' Evan said curtly.

'Men,' Charlie pronounced dully. 'That's what will be wanted. Sheep to the slaughter, just like 1914. Fodder for the Generals, the trenches and the mass graves.'

There was a grim knowledge and finality in the Russian's voice that none of them dared contradict, not even Alma whose love for her husband had never been so plainly etched in her eyes.

'I don't want to go through another day like this one, ever again,' Bethan said to Andrew as they leaned over their front gate and waved goodbye to the last of their visitors. Evan and Phyllis had been the first to go, driven down the hill in Trevor's car, little Brian's head lolling sleepily against his mother's shoulder. Charlie and Alma, Jenny and Eddie had been next. William, Diana, Haydn and Jane stayed until dusk, making the most of the peace of the garden and Andrew's generous hospitality.

'I'm sorry. To have a birthday on the day war is declared is bad enough, but then to go and have Eddie announce his engagement to Haydn's ex-girlfriend is possibly even worse.'

'There's always been a certain amount of friction between them.'

'Something tells me there'll be more now.'

'Did you have any idea?'

'About Eddie and Jenny?'

She nodded. The war news was too immense, too great. She didn't want to think about that now. Eddie's involvement with Jenny was easier to cope with.

'I saw the way he was looking at her last night.'

'You never said anything.'

'I thought you'd notice. After all, aren't women supposed to be the intuitive ones?'

'Poor Haydn.'

'Haydn will get over it,' he said unthinkingly, 'but I'm not so sure Eddie will.'

'What do you mean?'

He turned the question on her. 'Do you think Jenny really loves Eddie?'

'She must do. Why else would she get engaged to him?'

'Well, you know women better than I do, I hope you're right.'

'You think she's trying to get back at Haydn in some way, don't you?'

'I don't know.'

'But if she is, someone should tell Eddie . . .'

'Tell Eddie what? That we're all paranoid?'

'Concerned for his happiness.'

'Beth, Haydn and Eddie are grown men. They're not going to thank you for interfering in their lives. All you can do is congratulate, smile sweetly and let them both know that you're here for them if ever they should need you.'

'I suppose you're right.'

'You know I'm right. Now,' he kissed her gently on the lips, 'let's leave your family where they are, and celebrate your birthday the way I'd like to. In bed.' He led her away from the gate and across the lawn. The moon shone down, silvering the leaves and the burgeoning fruit on the cherry and apple trees, glinting above the gables of the enormous house she had come to love in the one short season she and Andrew had lived within its walls. She breathed in the scents of the night, and summer. The fragrance of flowers, slowly released into the atmosphere after the heat of the day. Hay drying in the fields, and Andrew's cologne mixed with cigar smoke as he walked beside her.

'It's all going to change, isn't it?'

'He stopped and gathered her into his arms. Her eyes shone feverishly, her face was unnaturally pale and vulnerable in the moonlight. He wanted to shield her from everything unpleasant that the world had to offer, but all he could do was love her. He had never felt the emotion quite so futile and inadequate before.

'The war will alter everything, especially our lives, but never my love for you.'

She had known what his answer would be, but like a child obstinately willing otherwise, she had wanted him to contradict her.

'It's inevitable, Beth. I'd be lying if I told you otherwise.'

'And you'll go away to fight?'

'Let's cross that bridge when we come to it.'

'You'll have no choice. They'll need doctors even more than they'll need soldiers.'

He buried his lips in her hair, breathing in the sweet, fresh fragrance he would always associate with her. 'Someone will have to stay in Pontypridd. The town can't be left without a doctor.'

'There's your father and old Dr Evans.'

'Whatever happens, you must know that the last thing I'd want to do is leave you and the baby.'

'That's if you have a choice. But they won't give you one, will they?'

'No one can answer that. Not yet.'

'I know you.' There was an edge of bitterness in her voice. 'You'll do the "right thing", as you see it. You may not be as anxious to go as William and Eddie, but you'll still go.'

'You haven't mentioned Haydn or your father.'

'Dad's too old. And Haydn has enough sense to know that even those who come back won't be the same men who marched away. He has his career. He'll try to stay out of it.'

'Beth, tonight no one knows anything other than we're at war. Tomorrow the whole country will be sitting down and thinking out exactly what that means, but I don't want to have to do that now. It's a wonderful night, we have each other, we have something very special to look forward to, and I promise you it will be all right this time.' He laid his hand lightly on her abdomen. 'Let's enjoy what we have, while we can, and make some memories that will see both of us through whatever lies ahead.'

Chapter Nineteen

'That didn't go too badly,' Eddie commented as he and Jenny parted company from Charlie and Alma at the foot of Graig Avenue.

'No, Diana and Phyllis were nice about our engagement.'

'Meaning the others weren't?'

'No, silly. Meaning that women are more romantic than men.' She slipped her hand into his pocket and tickled the top of his thigh through the thin cloth.

'Can I come in for a while when we get to your place?'

'My father'll still be in the Morning Star, and my mother will be looking out for us. She was none too pleased at our news.'

'So I gathered.'

She slowed her steps as they passed a shop that had been closed and shuttered for years. On the left was the lane opening that led to Shoni's pond. 'We could go for a walk.'

'To Shoni's, in the dark?'

'There's a moon. And I don't want to say goodnight yet.' There was a huskiness in her voice that was all the persuading he needed. Once around the corner he wrapped his arm around her, cupping her breast with his hand.

'The quicker we walk, the sooner we'll be at the lake,' she teased provocatively.

'I just hope I don't fall in the dark. Not in these clothes. They're almost new.'

'If you take them off, they won't get spoiled.'

'How about you taking yours off first?'

'If you want me to. How about nude swimming?'

'Now?'

'Where's your sense of adventure?' She stripped off her dress and shoes as the lake shimmered into view.

He stood and watched as she folded and piled her clothes neatly on the ground. Turning her back on him she waded into the water. He leaned against a tree, breathing in the fragrance of pond water and dry grass, studying the long, slim lines of her legs, the soft, luscious swell of her buttocks, her narrow waist, her back, half covered by a mass of pale gold hair. Her body gleamed like polished silver in the thick, dusty twilight. She hesitated as the water brushed the top of her thighs.

'Aren't you coming?' She turned to look at him, trailing her fingers sensuously over the surface of the lake. She'd spoken in a whisper, but the sound carried, echoing over the water to the bank. He removed his clothes but kept on his underpants as he followed. She ducked; swimming underwater she emerged behind him, playfully splashing him with water that flowed over his skin like warm silk. He tried to seize her, but she slipped from his grasp.

'Isn't this wonderful. I feel marvellous and incredibly alive.' She kissed his neck, rubbing the full length of her body against his back.

'It's wonderful, but I'm not a fish. How about we get out and finish what you've started on firm ground.'

'Eddie, you're the most unromantic man I know.'

'I'd rather not drown if it's all the same to you.'

Confident of his arousal and his need for her, she swam around him, moving her hands lightly over the contours of his body. 'How about we get married?'

'I've asked you.' He grabbed her wrists, successfully holding on to them this time.

'I mean sooner, rather than later. I'm tired of all this sneaking around. I want to sleep beside you all night, every night, wake up next to you in the morning.' She couldn't see his face. Darkness had fallen, suddenly and totally, transforming the outlines of the trees and bushes into black shadows. She didn't even have to close her eyes to imagine him as Haydn.

'All right.'

'If I find a place we can move into, you'll marry me right away?'

'Tomorrow.' He picked her up and carried her to the bank.

'You mean it?' He set her down on a grassy slope. The sharp edges of twigs and coarse-leaved weeds dug into her back, but she was unaware of the discomfort. Uppermost in her mind was Haydn's rejection, Will's mocking offer of a trip to the pictures, and the need to make Eddie hers before he, or someone else, changed his mind.

'I wouldn't have said it if I didn't.'

She rose to her knees and buried her face between his thighs. A man was so different, so very different from a woman.

'I'd marry you right now, Jenny.'

'Tomorrow will do, Eddie.' She moved back and slid her hands down the inside of his legs.

'It can't come soon enough for me.'

Those were all the words she wanted to hear. She lay on her back and prepared to receive his embrace.

'Take me out to supper after the show.'

'Everyone's going out, Babs,' Haydn said. 'Together.'

'But not everyone's sitting next to you.' She snaked her fingers along his shoulders and into his collar.

'Babs . . .'

'The Revue girls have gone. You're left with little old me. But that's not so bad. You do remember the good times we had in Brighton, don't you?'

'Yes. But as I've told you, this isn't Brighton. I live here. This is my home town.'

'All the more reason for us to have fun. Rusty and I compared notes, and we both agreed, when it comes to lover boys, you're the best.'

'You talked to Rusty about me?'

'We talked to one another about you. Rusty admitted that she was lucky to entice you between the sheets. After all, she is almost old enough to be your mother, and . . .' Babs pursed her lips and raised her eyebrows, 'a lot more experienced. But then she did say what you lacked in practice you more than made up for in enthusiasm. She also said no one can fondle a woman's nipple the way you can.'

The one thing Haydn had always been squeamish about was the chorus girls' habit of publicly discussing their sexual adventures in frank, and often crude terms. He'd learned to forget the mores drummed into him during his puritanical, chapelgoing Welsh upbringing and listen in silence. But Babs's revelation that she and Rusty had compared his sexual prowess left a bad taste in his mouth. Suddenly he saw himself through their eyes. A young man with a body they could take pleasure in and make use of, the way some men used whores.

'Babs, do me a favour?'

'Anything,' she purred seductively.

'Go now, before I'm tempted to say or do something we'll both regret.'

'If I go, you'll be left without a woman in your life.'

'That's the way I want it.'

'Not you, Haydn. You're not cut out to be a monk.'

'I think you've just given me reason to join their ranks.'

'Not you, sweetie.' She reached out but he dodged, avoiding her touch. 'It's no good setting your sights on Helen. She's engaged. And he's richer than you.'

'I know. I worked a London Empire with him. Good comic, nice chap.'

'Haydn . . .' she made another grab for his crotch but he was too quick for her. Opening the door he bundled her out into the corridor.

'You bastard, Haydn Powell. Think you can use people and

drop them just like that! Well I'm not just anybody, you know. I'm special. I'm going places, I' . . .' she stormed into her dressing room and slammed the door.

'What the bloody hell is going on back here?' Chuckles stood in the main corridor looking down towards the dressing rooms. He saw Haydn standing in his open doorway and guessed. 'Damn and blast it, man, do you have to go upsetting the girls ten minutes before the curtain goes up?'

'Not me,' Haydn asserted innocently. 'Just a bad dose of pre-performance nerves.'

'And I'm a monkey's uncle.' Max Monty poked his head out of his dressing room, scratched at his armpits and hopped about like an ape.

Haydn went into his dressing room, closed the door, and took out the bottle of brandy he kept in his bag. He'd had the same bottle for months. Wary of hard liquor he usually only opened it on the rare occasions visitors called in after the show. He'd seen too many performers take a 'tot' to steady their nerves, only to come a cropper on stage afterwards. But just this once he needed a boost. Pulling the cork with his teeth he poured a small measure into a metal beaker.

'I smell brandy.' The door opened and Max came in.

'You're incorrigible.'

'And don't you just love me for it?' Max said, deliberately camping it up.

'Sometimes.'

'Ooh good. Now batty Babs has gone, does this mean I'm in with a chance?'

'No, you idiot.'

'Shame, you would be a welcome addition to our ranks.'

'Thanks, but no thanks. Mind you,' Haydn downed his measure and poured out another for Max, 'with all the woman trouble I've had lately, I'm seriously considering taking up another hobby. Something harmless like fishing.'

'You poor soul.' Max held out the empty cup. 'More?'

'Don't you ever buy your own?'

'No, because I'd drink it, and I know it's bad for me before a show. Besides I don't want to end up a drunk, and other people's meanness is my way of checking my weakness.'

Haydn refilled the beaker, but stoppered and stowed away the bottle afterwards.

'Missing Rusty?' Max asked as Haydn checked his make-up in the mirror.

'Not really. It couldn't have lasted.'

'Not with her husband waiting in the wings. I've heard he's an absolute brute. But I know you Welsh boyos, for all this talk of fishing you've got to have at least one female around, otherwise vital parts will shrivel and die. Who's going to be the lucky lady this time? The gorgeous Helen?'

'She's engaged.'

'Rusty was married.'

'We're just friends.'

'Oh oh, I've heard that one before.'

'This time we really are.' Haydn dipped his comb into Vaseline and ran it through his hair.

'I know – it's Jane, isn't it?'

'Don't be silly, she's only a child,' Haydn said irritably.

'A child who has the most horrendous crush on you. If you weren't so wrapped up in chorus girls, you'd have seen it already.'

'She's my father's lodger.'

'And plain, and nice, unlike your last half a dozen lady loves, or at least the half a dozen I know about. Probably a bit too skinny for your taste too. You always have rather tended to run to voluptuous – '

'Five-minute call for Mr Powell – five-minute call for Mr Haydn Powell. Five-minute call for Miss Bradley – five-minute call for Miss Babs Bradley.'

'There you have it, old son. The top of the bill. The most important cog in the wheel, or is that the other way round?'

'You shouldn't have had that second brandy.' Haydn left his chair, straightened his open-necked shirt and the garish garland of artificial flowers around his neck. 'I look bloody ridiculous in this get-up.'

'Don't we all, sunshine, but you know Chuckles. He always has gone a bundle on all things Hawaiian.'

'I'm too tired to teach anyone anything right now.'

'I didn't expect it, Haydn. Not on your first night. I just wondered if you wanted anything from the kiosk. I'm getting the girls' ice creams.'

'And no doubt you'll be doing their mending, and running their errands just as you did for the Revue girls.'

'If they want me to.'

'And charging them too?'

'Only for mending. The manager's made my pay up to what the other usherettes are getting, so things aren't quite so desperate as they were. Is there anything I can get you?' she repeated, uneasy with his mood. He'd often been short with her, but never downright aggressive.

He stared at her and she coloured, conscious that she was wearing a new black dress. One that fitted her better because it hadn't come off Wilf Horton's stall, but new out of Leslie's Stores. She'd bought it that morning along with two more sets of underclothes, stockings and leather shoes. She'd also bought a green sprigged summer dress and straw hat like the ones she'd borrowed from Diana, because everyone had said they'd suited her, and a bottle of lavender water for Daisy who worked in the toilets by the fountain. It had meant taking three pounds out of the Post Office, but she'd paid Phyllis a final week's rent with the last of her sewing money, and Wilf Horton with her wages. It was a good feeling not owing anyone anything. She had money in the bank, wages coming at the end of the week, and all the clothes she needed. She didn't have to put up with anything from anyone, especially moodiness from Haydn.

'I won't be able to walk home with you tonight either; the cast are going out for a drink after the show.'

'That's all right, I didn't expect you to.'

'Damn you! Don't you expect anything from anyone?'

'No.'

'What is the matter with you?'

'Haydn.' She stepped into his dressing room and closed the door behind her. Knowing how thin the walls were, she lowered her voice. 'I know there's something wrong . . .'

'And you're going to tell me not to take it out on you?'

'No, not to let it affect your performance. I overheard Chuckles apologising to someone in the auditorium for the opening number. There's a man no one's ever seen before sitting next to him. One of the girls said she thought it was an impresario from London.'

'And Chuckles didn't tell me?'

'Perhaps he was afraid of rattling you more than you already are. You've been odd since you came in tonight.'

'In what way?'

'All sorts. Sometimes it helps to talk things out, then if you're lucky you can see them more clearly. When I was small and had no one to talk to I used to sneak into a big room that had a mirror in it and talk to the mirror.'

'You suggesting I should talk to myself?'

'No, but William perhaps, or your father. He and Phyllis were really good to me when I went to them with my problems.'

'And you think I have problems?'

'It's obvious, Haydn. Yesterday you couldn't stop looking at your brother and Jenny. Not that I blame you. She is very beautiful with all that long golden hair, and . . .'

'And you think I'm in love with my brother's future wife?' He made a resolution to watch his movements carefully the next time he found himself in Jenny's company. If Eddie could hear Jane now, he'd lay both of them out.

'I heard that you two were inseparable before you went to London.'

'Did you?'

'I know it's none of my business . . .'

'No, it isn't. But I'll tell you something for nothing. If I was going to fall in love, Jenny Griffiths would be the last person on my list. I happen to think she's bad for Eddie, that's all. And he won't listen to me, and –' he realised he'd said far more than he'd

313

intended – 'and the whole thing is a bloody awful mess,' he finished miserably.

'Not necessarily. If Eddie really loves her perhaps it will be all right between them,' Jane said, wondering what Haydn had meant by 'bad for him'.

'You think she'll change because Eddie loves her?'

'Yes. Not that I know very much about it, but if anyone loved me I'd try very hard to become whatever they wanted me to.'

'I'll give you a piece of sound advice. Don't change for any man. None of us are worth it, and you're just fine the way you are.'

'No I'm not. I'm skinny and ugly, and an orphan and no one will ever want me,' she said seriously, neither soliciting nor receiving sympathy for what she saw as a plain statement of fact.

'We want you. In fact I heard my father say this morning after you left the house that he didn't know what we were going to do without you. I think he has it in mind to ask Diana if she'd mind you moving into her room so Brian can have his back. That way you can stay until I leave, then you can have the lodger's room.'

'Your father really said that?'

'Yes, but don't go letting on that I told you.'

'I promise I won't.'

'I'm sorry I was foul to you when you came in.'

'Sometimes it helps to shout at someone.'

'You never do it.'

'No,' she smiled grimly. 'But I've often been the one shouted at. You get used to it after a while.'

'You did have a rough time before you came here, didn't you?'

'Not that bad. If it will help, I could ask Des to make you a cup of tea or coffee.'

'You really going to get the girls ice cream?'

'Yes.' She jumped to her feet, realising they would probably have given up on her by now.

'I'd like a cold orange juice. Do you think you could manage that?'

'Yes.'

'Get yourself one while you're at it, and come back here and drink it with me?'

'If there's time.'

'I wanted you to be the first to know.'

Haydn struggled to focus in the strong light of the back kitchen after the darkness that had shrouded the hill.

'The first to know what, Eddie?' he slurred, staggering on his feet. Two shows, not much in the way of food, plus a long discussion with a visiting producer who worked for the BBC, and who thanks to Jane's warning was leaving Pontypridd reasonably impressed with Haydn's talents, plus several beers followed by brandy chasers and a long warm walk up the hill didn't make for coherent thinking.

'Jenny and I went to see the vicar of St John's this evening.'

'Tony Pierce?'

'St John's is Jenny's church. He's calling the banns next week. We're getting married next month.'

'You know what you're doing?'

'You saying I don't?'

'I wouldn't dare.' Haydn swerved and fell into a chair.

'Jenny . . .'

'Jenny's your girl, Eddie. You're welcome to her.'

'What's that supposed to mean?'

'Absolutely nothing. There's nothing between Jenny and me. There was, but it's over.'

'You're drunk.'

'Guilty,' Haydn agreed amiably.

'Just as long as you continue to remember that it is over between you and Jenny.'

'Why wouldn't I, when I've got the pick of the chorus to choose from. Ripe, luscious pieces, just begging for it.'

'You disgust me,' Eddie said abruptly as he left his chair and walked out of the room.

'That's all right,' Haydn called after him. 'I disgust myself. So at least we're agreed on one thing.'

The weeks before the wedding passed in a blur for Jenny. She felt as though she'd climbed aboard a runaway bus. Against all logic she still expected Haydn to step out in front of her at any and every turn, and carry her off to some quiet, peaceful paradise where they could make love all day long and not trouble themselves with the boring, mundane trappings of life like houses, furniture, clothes and food. Every night she went to bed and pictured the miracle that would save her, and every morning she woke only to be dragged into town, and occasionally Cardiff by her mother to purchase things for her 'bottom drawer', every item of which was designed to show the Powells that their Eddie was marrying way above his station into a very superior family indeed. And when she wasn't in town with her mother, or having her wedding dress fitted in Gwilym Evans', Eddie walked her to the woods behind Shoni's and the place that had become special to them. Once there she closed her eyes, imagined the past year away and relived the time when the copse had been hers and Haydn's.

Eddie made love with open eyes but she kept hers closed, fantasising that it was Haydn touching her, Haydn who whispered her name, Haydn who'd be waiting at the altar when she finally wore the long white satin frock that had become her mother's one obsession. Day after day dawned, passed, and little that was real permeated her trance. She shopped, made love to Eddie, served behind the counter, all actions blurring into one. Nothing she did touched her, except late at night after Eddie brought her home. Then she hid in the shop and waited for Haydn to walk up the hill with Jane. It was only then, when she saw them together, that she felt something. An acute pain that wrought an almost unendurable anguish.

'I pronounce that they be man and wife together.'

The Reverend Tony Pierce, resplendent in white surplice over black cassock had said the words. Jenny was wearing the frock and holding the flowers her mother had taken such pains over. Eddie's plain gold band was on her finger – the band Haydn had handed him – the band Haydn had touched. Diana, her only bridesmaid, helped her with her veil. She turned to face the church full of people. Her family and Eddie's in the front pews. Everyone except his mother, who had refused to come, paving the way for Phyllis to attend, leaving those few people who hadn't suspected the relationship between Evan and Phyllis in no doubt of the state of adultery and sin they were living in. Jenny forced her lips into a smile, a spurious imitation that actually hurt the muscles in her face. The organ began to play, Eddie took her arm, led her down the steps and to the left into the vestry, Diana, Haydn, her parents and Evan and Phyllis trailing behind. People were smiling and nodding – her uncles and aunts, her cousins, the customers from the shop – but all she could see was the look on Haydn's face as he had handed his brother the ring. It had been a look of pity. The same look she remembered him bestowing on William when his dog had died all those years ago. Haydn might have loved her once, but if he had, one thing was clear: he didn't love her any more and now it was too late.

'Even nervous brides have to sign the register.' Someone pushed a pen into her hand and she signed because there was nothing else to do. Eddie, his father and hers had preceded her. A joke was made, everyone laughed. Diana kissed her, Evan kissed her, even Haydn brushed his lips briefly against her cheek, making her aware of Eddie's grip tightening on her arm.

Back down the aisle, the organ still resounding to the rafters. Outside the church, standing in the porch while William took a photograph with a borrowed camera. Down the steps at the side of the church, into the hall below, where her mother had arranged for a wedding breakfast to be laid out.

'Stop right there, both of you. Turn around. Perfect.' Andrew John took a photograph. 'If the rest of you stand behind Eddie and Jenny, I'll take another.'

She continued to smile vacuously as Andrew used up all the film in his camera.

There was a gramophone. It played dance tunes after the meal of sandwiches, cake and salad had been eaten. She and Eddie danced, but not for long.

'Bride and groom ready?' Andrew John was there again, looking incredibly handsome in a tailored suit that fitted far better than Eddie's off-the-peg ensemble bought for the occasion. It was the first he had owned that hadn't belonged to someone else before him.

'Dr Lewis said we could change in his house, remember?'

She looked blankly at Eddie.

'You do want to go on honeymoon?'

Everyone laughed again.

She obediently followed Eddie through the door and over the road to Trevor and Laura Lewis's house where Eddie changed in the spare bedroom. She was led into Laura and Trevor's bedroom and fussed over by Laura and Diana. They squirted lavish applications of Evening in Paris and talcum powder over her, exclaiming with delight at the tailored pale grey costume her mother had sniffed at because the colour wouldn't stand up to everyday wear. Then back over the road to stand in front of the church while relatives showered them with confetti.

More kisses for the bride. Evan, Trevor, her father, William – in a daze she went to Haydn. Eddie, no longer at her side, was kissing Bethan and Diana goodbye. Oblivious to William's close proximity, she grasped Haydn and kissed him, pushing him around the corner of the porch, out of sight of most of the guests. She refused to release him, even when he tried to thrust her away.

'Jenny?' Eddie stepped past an embarrassed William, gripped her neck and yanked her away from Haydn with a force that stung. He frogmarched her to Andrew John's car and pushed her unceremoniously into the back.

'Sure you haven't married the wrong Powell?' he hissed in her ear.

She stared at him blankly, uncomprehendingly, as the car careered down the hill and drew up outside the New Inn.

'Good luck, and enjoy your honeymoon.' Unaware that anything was wrong, Andrew lifted the two small suitcases out of his boot and handed them to a porter who had walked down the steps to meet them.

'Why don't you come in and have a drink with us?' Jenny pleaded, suddenly nervous at the thought of being alone with this strange, dark and glowering Eddie.

'Thanks for the thought, but Bethan gets very tired in this heat. I'd like to take her home.'

'Thank you.' Eddie held out his hand.

'For what?' Andrew asked, taken aback by the gesture after all the antagonism Eddie had shown towards him.

'For this.' Eddie looked up at the New Inn. 'And for driving us down in the car.'

'Least I could do for a brother-in-law.'

They both stood and watched Andrew drive away, then, with a sinking heart, Jenny followed Eddie up the steps and into the hotel.

'It's eleven o'clock in the morning, I feel stuffed full and I haven't got to be in work for a couple of hours.'

'Lucky you,' William and Diana grumbled as they passed Haydn on their way out of the church hall.

'I assumed you both had the day off.'

'Wyn's sister is looking after the shop for me,' Diana explained, 'but I promised I'd be back as soon as I could. She hates leaving Wyn's father for any length of time.'

'And Charlie wants to get back from the stall to Alma. The shop's busier than the stall now on a Saturday. Eddie certainly knows what day to get married on,' William complained as he followed his sister down the hill.

'Which leaves us.' Haydn offered his arm to Jane. 'Want to go for a walk before the matinée?'

'I'd like that.'

'Shoni's?'

'I've never been there.'

'In that case it's time you saw it.'

'I will have time to go back to Graig Avenue and change out of this frock afterwards?'

'Of course. I've got to change myself.'

319

'But you don't have to be in the Town Hall until half an hour after me.'

'I promise to give you plenty of time.'

They walked slowly up the hill, Jane carrying her straw hat. Her hair had finally begun to grow, and although to her chagrin it was as straight as rats' tails and much the same colour, Diana had succeeded in coaxing it into fairly respectable waves in honour of the occasion.

'It's odd to think of Eddie living in Griffiths' shop,' Haydn said half to himself as they passed the corner of Factory Lane. 'When we were kids, we used to dream of living in a shop. All the sweets you could eat, biting off the corners of the bread, cutting slices of cheese whenever you wanted to. We used to think Jenny was the luckiest girl in school.'

'I think she's lucky now. Your brother obviously cares for her very much.'

It was on the tip of Haydn's tongue to ask if Jane thought Jenny cared for Eddie, but he didn't. Only he, William and Eddie knew what had happened, and it was best left that way. Besides, the last thing he wanted was to destroy Jane's romantic illusions. 'I doubt he would have married her quite so quickly if he'd known there was a shortage of places to rent. I've a feeling Jenny's mother doesn't relish the idea of him moving into her house.'

'They'll soon find somewhere. Jenny told me she's put their name down with every landlord in Pontypridd, and with the war on, men are going away, and some wives back to their mothers.'

'I suppose you're right. Although it still doesn't feel very much like war to me. If it wasn't for the newspaper headlines, and the evacuees coming into town, I wouldn't believe it.'

They left Llantrisant Road and walked up the lane.

'It's pretty here. You'd never guess you were so near houses. It's like real countryside.'

'Like Church Village?'

'A bit. Although the fields there are more orderly, if you know what I mean.'

'Regimented?'

'Was that a scream?'

'It's coming from the direction of the pond. Kids are probably swimming there. Pity I didn't think. We could have gone home and brought our bathers.'

'It's the girls.' Jane put her hand over her mouth as she glimpsed three of the Variety chorus diving into the water from the bank, stark naked.

Haydn burst out laughing. 'There's no need to run away. I'm sure none of them has got anything you haven't.'

'All the same, I'd rather not view what they've got in your company.'

'Come on, you've been working in the Town Hall for a while. You should have learned by now that chorus girls aren't normal. They're used to men looking at their bodies, and they think nothing of flaunting them.'

'But those aren't Revue girls, they're Variety girls.'

'It doesn't make much difference; today's Variety girl is only a poorer version of tomorrow's Revue girl,' he murmured, quoting one of Rusty's favourite maxims.

'Isn't that the mouse of an usherette with Haydn?'

'If you ask me she's not all that mousy,' Babs said angrily, eyeing the new green frock and waves set in Jane's glossy brown hair. 'They're always together these days.'

'His brother was getting married today. She lives with the family, so they probably invited her.'

'Then why aren't they both in church?' Babs demanded.

'There's nothing between them,' Helen said kindly. 'Haydn told me Jane has no one. He sees himself as an older brother.'

'That's how he might see himself, but I'm not so sure about her.' Babs looked at Jane's flat chest and scrawny figure and climbed out of the water. Pushing out her breasts, she posed on the diving rock and shouted. 'Haydn, coo-ee, over here! Come and join us.'

'Not today thanks, Babs.' He led the way on to the opposite bank and round the lake. 'Cigarette?' he asked Jane, reaching for the packet in his pocket.

'I've never tried.'

'Do you want to?'

'I don't think so. If I liked it I'd want to buy some.'

'And you're saving?'

She nodded, grateful that the girls were now behind them. 'What for?'

'Nothing, really. Just putting money by in case I lose my job.'

'I don't think the Town Hall's going to let you go in a hurry.'

'You never know. Anything could happen.'

'It's time you stopped looking over your shoulder. Dad and Phyllis will never put you out, not while they've got a roof over their heads. Diana's fond of you. Brian adores you.' He sat on the bank that overlooked the stream at the top end of the lake. Jane would have preferred to walk on, out of earshot of the cries of the chorus girls.

'How much longer has the Variety got to run?' she asked, eyeing the bank next to him.

'Another three weeks. Here,' he took off his jacket and spread it out on the grass.

'I can't sit on that, it's too good.'

'Of course you can. Pity I haven't got my coat. The weather's been so warm lately I'm not even sure where I've left it.'

'What are you going to do when the Variety finishes?'

'I've signed up for a run Chuckles has managed to get an angel to underwrite.'

'An angel?'

'A fairy godfather who has more money than sense, and fortunately for us, enough of it to back a show. If we're lucky it will survive in the provinces and go to the West End. I hope it does. I'd like to do things the right way round for a change, instead of taking up the provincial runs from the West End stars.'

'I hope it works out the way you want,' she said, not quite understanding all the ins and outs of Variety.

'Thank you, kind lady.' He pushed his hat to the crown of his head and leaned back on his hands. 'Here,' he took the carnation Harry Griffiths had clipped to his buttonhole and handed it to her. 'Sweets to the sweet, as they say,' he murmured as she took it from him. Their fingers touched. He looked into her eyes and saw something that had eluded him for a long time. A loving intimacy born out of innocence. The kind he had once enjoyed with Jenny before chorus girls with their sophisticated, maneating ways had entered his life. Putting his fingers beneath Jane's chin he lifted her face to his, and kissed her.

Chapter Twenty

'I didn't mean that to happen.'

'I'm glad it did.'

'I'm not. You deserve better than a rat like me who can make love to three girls in one week.'

'Four?' she looked up at him, mischief glowing in brown eyes streaked gold by the sunlight.

'Listen Jane, you can't rely on me, I'm here today, gone tomorrow. Different town, different theatre, different girl every week. I'm not even fit to be around someone decent like you. In a couple of weeks I'll be moving on, we may never see one another again.'

'You'll be here long enough to make some memories.'

'Memories aren't what you need, Jane. You need someone steady, who'll always be there to care for you.'

'I don't want caring from someone steady.' She slipped her hand into his. 'Just another kiss from you.'

'Don't you understand . . .'

'I understand. You're trying to tell me that you're sorry you kissed me because you won't be in Pontypridd much longer. Well, I'm not sorry. I liked being kissed by you. If I didn't I would have thumped you right where it hurts, just as I did the first boy who tried to take liberties with me.'

'Were there any others who dared to try to "take liberties" after him?' he asked, smiling at the old-fashioned expression.

'No.'

He started to laugh.

'What's so funny?'

'You are. The thought of a girl as pint sized as you thumping anyone is hysterical.' He glanced at his wristwatch. 'Come on, if we're going to change before the first performance it's time to make a move.' He rose to his feet and offered his hand to help her up. She took it, and held on to it as they walked away.

'Then it's all right?'

'What's all right?'

'You'll consider kissing me again before you leave?'

'I mean it, you deserve better.'

'And if I don't want better?'

'It can't possibly go anywhere.'

'Who wants it to go any further than this?' She stopped. Lifting her head and standing on tiptoe she raised her face to his. Wrapping his arms around her, he bent his head and kissed her again. She tasted of spring, of youth laced with the bitter tang of foreboding. He sensed this was one impulse he was going to regret. But none of the presentiments of impending disaster stopped him from doing what they both wanted until the sun beating down reminded him that they had jobs to go to.

Eddie followed the porter who carried their bags upstairs, into the bedroom Andrew John had booked for them. Pushing aside the net at the window, he looked out over Market Square. It was teeming with Saturday shoppers. It felt most peculiar to be here in the middle of the day with no work to go to, and nothing to do until it was time to eat later.

'Is everything satisfactory, sir, madam?' The porter hovered in the doorway.

'Fine, thank you,' Eddie nodded, then he remembered. Delving into his pocket he pulled out a sixpenny bit.

'Thank you, sir, madam. We hope your stay with us will be a

325

'pleasant one.' He closed the door behind him, and Eddie walked across the room and locked it.

'Eddie, no. Not in the middle of the day. Everyone will know what we're doing.'

'Would you rather do it with my brother?' he asked bitterly.

'No, not ever. And not with you in the middle of the day.'

'Well you've no choice in the matter. You've said I do, and that's it, madam. And while we're talking about obeying, you can start forgetting all about Haydn, right now. No matter what you did with him once, it's over, and it's not going to happen again. Not if you want to remain in one piece.' He crossed the room, pulled her to him and began to unbutton her jacket.

'I told you, I've never done anything with Haydn. It's over between us. I'm sorry for what happened at the church. I just lost my head. I wasn't thinking straight. Eddie . . .' She backed away, trembling, afraid of the strange light in his eyes.

'You're nothing but a bloody tease . . .'

Eddie's outburst was interrupted by voices echoing in the corridor outside. Jenny went to the only chair and sat on it, legs demurely together, hands resting in her lap. The pose of the lady drummed into her by her mother.

'Over here!'

'No. Everyone in the hotel has probably guessed we've just got married.'

'So what? There's a first night for everyone.'

'Exactly, a night not a day.'

'Time and place have never stopped you before.'

'Well they're stopping me now.'

'Why? Because we're married? Is this what it's going to be like from now on? You've caught me, you've got the ring on your finger, and now you're going to kiss my brother behind my back and make me beg every time I feel like having a bit of fun?' He was so angry he failed to see how close she was to tears. 'Bloody hell! No wonder the gym's so full of men getting away from their wives. I thought, really thought, you were different. Prancing around Shoni's without a stitch on, kissing every inch of me, all that talk about wanting to sleep beside me every night. Then that night you – '

'There was no one there.'

'There's no one here now.'

'They're just outside the door.'

'So what are you saying? That you can only drop your knickers and open your legs in the dark in Shoni's?'

'Have you got to be so crude?'

'You never thought I was crude before.'

'That's because you weren't.'

'But now you've hooked me I'm crude and not good enough for you any more. And Haydn is? Well I'll tell you one thing Mrs *Eddie* Powell. You haven't got your father here,' he rammed his finger into his chest. 'Your mother may have pushed him out of her bed and relegated him to the box room, but I know my rights. I married you, and that means I can have you, any time anywhere I choose.' He caught her by the shoulders and threw her on to the bed. Then the tears came, a dam-burst that soaked her cheeks and quenched his rage. Furious with himself for allowing his temper to surface, and with her for provoking him, he turned his back and looked out of the window.

At that moment the irrevocable permanence of what he'd done hit home. Right or wrong, he'd made his choice, tied himself to Jenny and was stuck with her. As the marriage service said 'till death us do part'. The muffled sounds from the corridor, her ragged breathing interspersed with sobs closed in around him, crushing, unbearable. He wanted to scream and shout. To run from the room and her, as fast as he could. Soft shoes shuffled over the thick carpet outside the door. There was a knock. Grim faced he walked from the window to open it. A bellboy stood there holding a silver bucket containing a champagne bottle set in ice, and a tray with two glasses.

'Compliments of Dr and Mrs John, sir,' he murmured looking at Jenny's tear-stained face.

Eddie took the tray from him.

'Would you like me to open it for you, sir?'

'No.' Eddie kicked the door closed. This time, Jenny noted with relief, he didn't lock it.

'Aren't you going to open it?' she asked timorously, wishing that once, just this once, he'd tell her he loved her.

'Doesn't look like we've got anything worth celebrating.' He set the tray down on a side table.

'Eddie, I'm sorry. But I can't go to bed with you, not now in the middle of the day. Imagine if we had and that boy had come with the champagne?'

'We would have asked him to leave it outside the door and he would have. This is a hotel. They're used to coping with life.'

'I'm sorry I'm not.'

'So am I.'

There was a barbed edge to his voice that she didn't know how to begin to soften. She left the bed, went to the wardrobe and removed a coat-hanger. Opening her case she proceeded to hang up the few things she'd brought. It would only take her a few minutes, but she had to do something to stop the voices in her head from screaming that she had married the wrong man.

Before she'd emptied her case she heard the door opening. She whirled around to see Eddie, with his hat and jacket on.

'You're not going out?'

'Why shouldn't I? There's nothing to keep me here.'

'I never knew it could be so warm at this time of night,' Jane observed as she and Haydn walked up the Graig hill at the end of what seemed like a marathon of three shows.

'It won't last.' Haydn stopped and removed his lightweight jacket. He'd found his coat, and left it where he'd found it, hanging on the back of his dressing-room door. Slinging his jacket over one shoulder he loosened his tie and unfastened the collar on his shirt. 'Winter'll soon be here and then we'll be wanting more of this.'

'I suppose we will,' she agreed, remembering last winter and how cold she'd been scrubbing the workhouse yard and steps.

'If the weather holds tomorrow, we could go to the seaside.'

'The seaside!' Even in the subdued lighting of the street her eyes glittered with excitement.

'Which do you prefer, Barry Island or Porthcawl?'

'I don't know.'

'I prefer Barry myself. Most people say the fair is better in Porthcawl, but Barry is the first holiday place I remember going to, so I've always liked it best.'

'Wouldn't it cost an awful lot?'

'The train fare isn't that much. Make it my treat, and we'll get Di and Will to come with us.'

'I'll go only if you let me pay my way.'

'I said, my treat.'

'I won't come otherwise.'

'All right, be independent.'

'I will.'

'We'll have to take blankets, food, buckets and spades, and bathers,'

'Bathers?'

'There's no point in going to Barry if you don't go swimming, girl.'

'What do you mean you haven't got a pair of bathers?' Diana looked at Jane in amazement.

'I've never been swimming.'

'And I've only got one pair, unless . . .' she opened her wardrobe door and went rummaging in the bottom.

'What are you looking for?'

'Trying to see if Maud left a pair behind. I couldn't swear to it, but I think she was even skinnier than you.' Diana fussed around throwing out various odd shoes, bits of ribbon and crumpled handkerchiefs. After five minutes she emerged with what looked like a child's hand-knitted swimsuit. 'Do you think you could get into this?' she asked doubtfully.

'I could try.' Jane lifted the skirt of the cotton frock she'd put on that morning, kicked off her bloomers and struggled into the suit.

'Let's have a look.'

Jane pulled her dress over her head and Diana gazed critically at her.

'I think you're just the right side of decent.'

'I've put on weight since I've come here,' Jane said, studying herself in the mirror. She'd filled out a little, although Merv could still quite rightly say that she didn't have a lot upstairs, she reflected, thinking wistfully of Judy and Mandy's figures, and wishing that they hadn't told Merv where she worked. Haydn's kiss had changed her whole outlook on life. All of a sudden money didn't seem as important as some other things. She'd burnt Merv's photographs in the stove in the early hours of the morning, at the same time promising herself that she'd never, never go to his studio again, no matter how much he offered her.

'Is it comfortable?'

'Not too bad.'

'Then I'd wear it and pack your underclothes into a towel. That way you don't have to change on the beach. You can always dry and dress yourself under the skirt of your dress easier than you can undress. Right, let's go. Sooner we make a move, the sooner we'll get there.'

'Train leaves Barry Sub at half-past nine,' William announced through a mouth full of toast and dripping.

'You're coming, aren't you Phyllis?' Diana asked. 'Because I'll feel awful if you don't, seeing as how it's my day to cook.'

'Evan and I are coming.' Phyllis wrapped cheese and pickle sandwiches in brown paper.

'This is a great idea of Haydn's.'

'Where is he, Will?'

'Clay piping his shoes out the back. He's dug up a blazer from what looks like the props department of a pierrot show. I'm not sure I want to be seen with him.' William finished off the last piece of toast in one bite.

'One bucket and spade.' Evan walked in from the garden with a battered tin spade and bucket in one hand and Brian in the other.

'Sandwiches.' Phyllis thrust them into her shopping bag. 'But we haven't any drinks.'

'Don't panic, we'll pick up a couple of bottles of pop and some biscuits in Griffiths' shop.'

Caught up in the air of excitement, Jane dashed around with the others. Phyllis put a tin of scones on top of the sandwiches, then packed a layer of Diana's home-made biscuits on top of the scones. William produced an old cricket bag and packed two blankets and the rolls of towels and underclothes into it. Evan pushed the bucket and spade on top. Diana found a couple of balls and made room for them. Checking the strength of the sun by standing in the back-yard, Phyllis ran to get a large floppy-brimmed cotton hat for Brian that the boys protested made him look like a girl. Then just as the others were ready to leave, she decided she needed her cold cream as well.

'If we don't go now, we'll miss the train,' William shouted impatiently.

While Diana strapped Brian into his pushchair, Evan wrote out a note for anyone who might call. Laying it in the centre of the kitchen table he called, 'Ready?'

Diana picked up the food. William took the cricket bag, Phyllis pushed the pushchair and they went out through the front door.

Jane ran on ahead to Griffiths' shop to save time. She bought bottles of orangeade and lemonade as her contribution to the holiday, then on impulse asked for a box of chocolates.

'You going out for the day?' Harry asked.

'To the seaside.'

'Then it'll be boiled sweets or wine gums you'll be wanting, love, not chocolate. It'll melt in this heat.'

Settling on a quarter of each, Jane ran out and caught up with the others.

'We've picked a good day,' William said, looking up at the sky.

'Always is a good day on workmen's club outing.'

'I didn't know they were going today,' Haydn took the bottles from Jane.

'Showing your age,' Will shook his head. 'Too old to be taken on the outing and too young to join and drink with the men.'

'You a member?'

'Not yet, but I'm working on it.'

'Do you remember how it always used to rain on Sunday School outings when we were small, and never on club?' Diana laughed.

The platform on the Barry Sub station was crowded with men in short-sleeved shirts, women in cotton dresses, and boys and girls carrying buckets and spades. William and Haydn stood poised when the train came in, and by dint of judicious elbowing they managed to commandeer the door to a carriage. Standing one either side, they helped Phyllis and Brian in first, Evan with the pram, then Diana and Jane.

'Perfect.' Diana fell into a corner seat next to Evan and Phyllis.

'Who said you can sit there?' her brother demanded.

'I did.'

He looked at the bench seat opposite. He hated sitting with his back to the engine; besides, Jane had commandeered one window seat, Haydn the other.

'Sorry,' Jane jumped up when she saw him frowning. 'You can have this seat if you like.'

'He most certainly can not.'

'Why not, if the lady insists?'

'It's supposed to be gentlemen who give up their seats to ladies,' Diana informed him tartly as he took Jane up on her offer. 'Sometimes I wonder if you'll ever grow up.'

'He hasn't changed since he was six years old and pulled the communication cord because he wanted a wee.' Haydn took the centre seat so Jane could take his.

'I most certainly did not,' William contradicted indignantly.

'First I've heard of this.' Evan looked from Haydn to William.

'We were going to Creigau. Auntie Megan took us there so we could pick primroses for Mothering Sunday.'

'Brave woman.'

'That's what the guard said when he came down the train to collect the five-pound fine.'

'Did Megan pay it?'

'He took one look at us six children and her black dress and let her off, but it was touch and go for a while.'

'Is that the train starting?' Jane asked as the whistle blew and the engine gathered steam. She looked out of the window. 'Where's that?' she asked excitedly as they chugged past the Maritime colliery alongside a row of houses.

'Woodland Terrace,' Haydn informed her. 'That's Maesycoed, and up there is the school we all went to.'

'One day it will have a plaque on the wall to commemorate the fact,' William teased. 'Haydn Powell, Revue artist and singer sat and didn't learn his lessons here.'

'Sandwich, anyone?' Phyllis opened the bag.

'We haven't left Ponty yet, woman,' Evan said.

'I thought if they had their mouths full they'd stop bickering.'

Everything was new to Jane. The sound of the engine, the sensation of travelling at speed, the scenery. The only times she had ever gone anywhere with the orphanage they had walked, and the transfers between orphanages and workhouse had been via a tattered old charabancs. She exclaimed over everything, finding magic in the most mundane of landscapes. Excitement mounted as the minutes ticked closer to journey's end where the sea beckoned. Just as she's seen it on the posters on the wall of the station. Barry Island! Even the name conjured up images of *Robinson Crusoe*.

Jenny read the notice on the bedroom wall.

'ALL ROOMS HAVE TO BE VACATED BY 10 A.M.'

'We'd better pack before we go down for breakfast.'

'Not much to pack.' Eddie picked up the pyjamas Jenny had laid out for him which he hadn't worn, as he hadn't bothered to undress when he had come in drunk at two in the morning. Fortunately the crowd he had fallen in with hadn't known that it was his wedding day, but they had known about his success in the exhibition bout, and luckily for him they'd been prepared to celebrate it.

'I suppose not.' It was strange they were married, man and

wife. They had slept together in that bed, but because of their quarrel they had remained each in their own half. The bottle of champagne still stood on the table, untouched, the dinner Andrew and Bethan had paid for uneaten. After the lonely hours she had been shut in the room with nothing to do, Jenny almost looked upon the walls around her as a prison.

'We'd better get breakfast while they're still serving it.'

'Yes, I suppose we'd better,' she echoed dismally, following Eddie through the door.

As the hills gave way to softer, more rounded contours, William sniffed the air. 'I can smell the sea.'

'In your imagination,' Diana retorted.

'Big Water!' Brian cried, pointing out of the window.

Jane looked and saw mud flats and a dirty brown expanse of water, a little like a sluggish river, only wider.

'That's the sea?' Dismay was evident in Jane's voice.

'It's the sea, but it's not the beach,' Haydn reassured her. 'That's further on.'

Jane left her seat. Standing at the window she watched the water roll past. Little wicker gates painted brown and cream came into view, alongside a line of straggling fencing. Evan and Phyllis began collecting their things together. The train drew to a long, slow halt. Finally it jerked and juddered to a standstill. William heaved down the window, opened the door, and picked up the cricket bag. Clutching her bag of sweets Jane followed out on to the platform.

'Beach first?'

The others walked on briskly. Jane didn't even try to keep up with them. She wanted to stop and look. Everything was so different from the valleys: whiter, cleaner, even the air was crisper, tangy with a fizz not unlike that of bubbling lemonade.

'You've never been to the seaside before, have you?' Haydn enquired perceptively.

She shook her head, gazing at the length of the promenade and the expanse of yellow sand beyond, littered with thousands of picnicking families. And beyond them the sea, blue and brilliant twinkling with a myriad dancing sunbeams.

'Or on a train?'

'You must think I'm a real country bumpkin.'

'No, just checking, so we can organise you a day worth remembering.'

'I thought you'd be back for Sunday dinner.' Mrs Griffiths opened the door to the flat on top of the shop. 'One of your family dropped your case around yesterday, Edward.'

'No one calls Eddie, Edward, Mam,' Jenny protested.

'Was it my cousin William?' Eddie asked for the sake of something to say.

'Probably, I didn't see him. Mr Griffiths took it. He put it in your room, Jenny,' she said abruptly with an air of disapproval. 'And if the weight of the case is anything to go by, you're going to have problems making room for your husband's things in your wardrobe.'

'We'll manage, Mam.'

'It will only be for a little while, Mrs Griffiths. A week or two at the most until we find a place of our own.'

'Yes, well, that's what you said when you started looking four weeks ago.'

'We will find one, and soon, Mam,' Jenny said insistently. 'Come on, Eddie, I'll show you my room.'

Eddie followed Jenny out of the passage into her bedroom. Set at the back of the house it looked down over the smoking chimneys of the coke works. Furnished with an enormous, old-fashioned bedroom suite and double bed which left as little room for manoeuvring as the living room, the atmosphere was every bit as stuffy and uninviting. Jenny opened the wardrobe door. Pushing her clothes to one side, she removed a couple of spare hangers.

'You can have these. And I emptied the two bottom drawers in my chest for you on Friday night.'

'Thanks.'

335

'I'm sorry about last night, Eddie.' She reached out to him. 'Why don't we go up Shoni's as soon as we've eaten?'

'Eddie, Jenny, the meal's on the table. When you've got a place of your own you can do as you like, but while you're living in my house I expect you to keep to my hours.'

'Coming, Mam.'

'Shoni's?'

'I have to go down the gym.'

'Please, Eddie, I want to make it up to you.'

'I work there every Sunday.'

'Can't you give it up now?'

'We need all the money we can get. Besides, Joey's generally there on Sunday afternoons, and I get in a bit of training.'

'Can I come with you?'

'No.'

'Jenny!'

'Don't keep your mother waiting, Jenny,' he said coldly.

'Do you know this is the first time Jane's been to Barry Island,' Haydn said as they walked down the white concrete steps that led from the promenade on to the uncomfortably warm sand of the beach.

'Then stick close to Uncle William, I'll teach you everything you need to know.'

'Like how to get sand in sandwiches, and soak your clothes in salt water?' Diana suggested.

Evan and Phyllis were all for sitting where they were, but William insisted on walking until they found what he called 'the ideal spot' which, Jane discovered, wasn't anywhere near other people. Given the packed nature of the beach, which was pitched somewhere between Ponty park on a Whitsun and Ponty market at Christmas time, the task seemed impossible. Eventually they found a patch of sand that met William's exacting specifications. Not too close to the water to be damp, and not too close to the wall to be in the path of newcomers walking down from the promenade.

Diana and Evan spread the blankets. William and Haydn dug

deep holes with Brian's spade, much to his annoyance, and buried the bottles of lemonade and orangeade up to their necks so they'd stay cool. As soon as they'd finished Diana and William whipped off their clothes to reveal their bathers and ran down to the sea, while Phyllis and Evan lay back on the blankets and watched Brian play with his bucket and spade.

'Come on you two,' William shouted from the foreshore, 'it's swimming time.'

'I don't suppose you've swum before either?' Haydn asked Jane.

'You know what it's like on a farm, Haydn,' Phyllis broke in quickly. 'Never any time for anything, and certainly not for trips down Ponty park to the pools, or the beach.'

'Well she can paddle now.' He grabbed her hand.

'Let me get my dress off first.' She removed it and, folding it carefully, laid it next to the towels.

He looked at her in amazement. He'd always thought of her as a skinny little thing, but he hadn't realised just how undeveloped her figure was. Or was it that he was used to chorus girls? That must be it. He was so accustomed to seeing the shape of show-girls, he'd forgotten that females could come in different sizes. Realising he'd been staring, he looked down to see Phyllis watching him. Embarrassed, he seized Jane's hand and pulled her behind him down to the sea.

She hung back as small, white-crested waves, brown and muddy with churned-up sand, crashed over her toes.

'It feels peculiar. I think I'm sinking.'

'If you keep walking you won't sink.' He raced ahead and threw himself into the water.

'It's Haydn Powell!' Jane heard the cry taken up by half a dozen girls.

'It looks like him, but it can't be.'

'It is, you know. I saw him last night.'

The boldest of the group walked up to Jane, who stood shivering uncertainly in the cool breeze that was blowing in from the sea. 'It is Haydn Powell isn't it?'

She looked helplessly to William and Diana who were wading towards her.

'People are always mistaking him for Haydn Powell,' William said, flexing his muscles. 'His name's Dai Evans. He's a delivery boy from Treorchy. Now look at me, I'm actually Clark Gable's younger brother.'

'Eddie please don't go,' Jenny begged as she watched him pack the strip he used for sparring into a holdall.

'You want to stop me training?'

'No, but . . .'

'But? You don't want me to bring home the boxing purses that'll buy us a place of our own?'

'I'm sorry, Eddie. I really thought I'd find us somewhere.'

'Well you didn't, and until we have somewhere, don't expect me to sit around in this dismal bedroom listening to you shouting "not in daylight".'

'Eddie, I've said I'm sorry. We only married yesterday . . .'

'As if I'm likely to forget it.'

'What do you expect me to do all afternoon?'

'Whatever you normally do on a Sunday.'

'I can hardly go down the café on my own.'

'Why not?'

'Because we got married yesterday. If I go down there by myself people will talk. They'll say there's something wrong between us.'

'Then they won't be far wrong, will they?' He picked up his bag and walked out.

Chapter Twenty-One

'This is beautiful.'

'There's better seaside places.'

'There can't be.' Jane, like Haydn, had left her shoes with Evan and Phyllis, but with the sun scorching down she'd followed his example and covered up. They were paddling side by side in the shallows, Haydn with his trousers rolled above his knees and his shirt flapping in the breeze; Jane with her frock unbuttoned over her damp swimsuit. He took her hand as they splashed past the last of the bathers, and picked their way over the carpet of gravel that marked the boundary between the popular stretch of sands and the deserted far end where black rocks cropped up, straggling jaggedly down to the sea.

'I spent the winter season in Brighton. You should see the pier there, it's huge. It has its own theatre as well as penny arcades and tea rooms.'

'I've seen pictures of piers. Aren't they built right over the sea?'

'Unfortunately yes. We opened this season on Weymouth pier. For the first week we had nothing but spring storms. We went out every night praying the orchestra would play loud enough to drown out the sound of the waves crashing beneath us.'

'Wasn't that scary?'

He rolled his eyes. 'Frightfully!'

'You look as though you're auditioning for a toff's part.'

'Even a miner's son can aspire to playing an Earl.' He climbed on to the rocks. 'There's a natural seat here,' he called down, extending his hand. She stepped up, sat beside him and looked back along the beach. It was like an illustration from a children's book. Babies playing in the miniature, white-crested waves that broke on the fringes of the sea. Middle-aged men and women solemnly swishing their ankles in foot-deep water, licking at ice creams that dribbled over their hands and wrists; the women's dresses tucked high into their knickers, the men sporting knotted handkerchiefs on their bald spots. Further up the beach, older children were busy with buckets and spades, digging deep holes and building elaborate sand castles decorated with seaweed and shells. Matrons dressed for church, sat stiffly on hired deckchairs, frowning disapprovingly on pairs of lovers entwined in one another's arms on old army blankets. And in the distance the white concrete glare of the promenade, alive with diminutive figures clad in brilliant white and pastel summer outfits; towering above them, the ramshackle wooden buildings and rides of the funfair, its infectious music drifting in snatches on the breeze.

'The rides have started early,' Haydn commented as faint, high-pitched screams of delight carried towards them. 'I don't suppose you've been to a fair either?'

'No.' She looked out to sea, thinking that nothing could have prepared her for this. The clear, sparkling brilliance, the sound of the waves interspersed with the chatter of a thousand day trippers, and above all the smell: a salty, fishy, tangy fragrance mixed together with stewed tea, sickly sweet candy floss, sticky, sugary rock and frying onions from the sausage and chips stands.

'Then you're in for a treat.'

'How expensive a treat?' she asked, wondering if the half a crown she'd brought with her would be enough.

'To you, nothing.'

'I told you I pay my own way.'

'I earn more than you.'

'That doesn't mean I'll allow you to treat me.'

'I thought you agreed to be my girl until the end of the season.'

'Girl, not sponger.'

'Accepting a couple of rides won't compromise your independence.'

'I prefer to use my own money.'

'I refuse to argue on a day like this. Come on,' he helped her down from the rock.

'What's over there?' she asked, pointing to a row of small wooden cottages.

'Chalets. You can rent them by the week.'

'It would be heaven to spend a whole week in a place like this.'

'I wouldn't know, but I can imagine. No work, no stage, nothing to do except this all day long.' He looked over his shoulder to check that no one was close. Twining his fingers gently in her hair, he pulled her head towards him and kissed her, more slowly and thoroughly than he had the last time. As the length of his body burned against hers, she felt as though she was melting, fusing into one with him, the sun, the sand, and the sea.

'The others will be wondering where we are.'

'Let them wonder.'

'They'll suspect.'

'I can live with that if you can.'

'I wish it could be always like this.'

'You and me?'

'Not you and me, silly,' she replied quickly, mindful of his warning that he would soon be gone, and not wanting to spoil a moment of the time he was prepared to give her by being too demanding. 'This! The day, the beach, the sun and those chalets. I'd like to live in that one over there. The pink one on the end, not just for now and the summer, but all the year around.'

'Pretty bleak, cold and damp in winter.'

'I wouldn't care. They must have fireplaces. I could build a fire and . . .'

'No chimneys,' he pointed out logically.

'This daydream is mine not yours. Don't upset it; if I want to imagine a fireplace in that chalet I will.'

'Am I allowed to visit and sit by this hearth of yours?'

'For tea on Sunday, if you're good.'

'Well this Sunday, it's time to go and eat. Not tea and crumpets, but pop and sandwiches.'

'And then we'll have to go?' There was such a crestfallen expression on her face he couldn't resist hugging her again.

'Not for a few hours. But if you want to look at the fair we'll have to leave the beach fairly soon.'

He felt more content and at peace with himself than he had done for a long time as he walked Jane back to the others. She was so naive, trusting and inexperienced. It was almost as good as being in love and courting for the very first time.

'Again!'

'Absolutely not. You're getting ruined.' Phyllis lifted Brian from the roundabout that boasted a bright blue cockerel among its wonderfully weird bestiary. He'd taken a shine to it the moment he'd seen it. Evan had paid for his first ride, but his reluctance to leave his new-found wooden friend had prompted Haydn, William, Diana and Jane to pay for another four.

'Please?' Brian looked up at his mother with enormous eyes that looked all the larger for the touch of sunburn on his round cheeks.

'No. My arm is tired from waving to you every time you go round.'

'If you come with Dad and Mam now, I'll buy you a stick of rock to eat on the train on the way home,' Evan bribed him.

'You really want to go?' Haydn asked.

'Brian's worn out. If he doesn't have a nap soon he'll start whining, and if we go now we can be home when Charlie and Alma come up for tea.'

'But don't let us stop you from staying as long as you like,' Phyllis urged them. 'I'll make a pie that can be eaten cold.'

'Don't cook,' Haydn said. 'We'll stay until dark so Jane can see the fair lit up, and buy fish and chips to eat on the train.'

'The fair won't be lit up tonight, boy.'

'Why not?'

'We're at war. Blackout, remember.'

'I keep forgetting.'

'If it never gets any worse than it is now, I won't be sorry,' Phyllis said softly.

'I'll take the bag.'

'Leave it in the station, Uncle Evan. I'll pick it up when we get in,' William offered.

'I intended to.'

Placated by the promise of rock, Brian waved goodbye and trotted off happily between his parents.

'Right, ghost train first.' William dropped a piece of seaweed he'd been carrying down Diana's back.

'And the shooting gallery.'

'And the penny arcade.'

Diana and William knew the fair inside out. Every time there'd been a few shillings to spare, their mother, Megan, had taken them to either Barry or Porthcawl. Familiarity with the layout enabled them to race from amusement to amusement at breakneck speed. But Jane refused to be hurried. She lagged behind, content to be a bystander, to watch others enjoy the rides and try their hand at the roller-ball and shooting galleries. Haydn finally collared Will and Diana at the cakewalk and arranged to meet them outside the fish and chip bar at dusk. Free to wander at Jane's pace he led her into an arcade where she fed a penny into the laughing policeman. When the grotesque clown-like figure had chortled his last, he rolled a penny into a miniature waxwork model of a barber's shop encased in glass. A door opened to reveal the barber wielding an axe instead of a razor. A customer's head was severed, rusty stains dripped down the smock of the victim, the door closed, but not quickly enough. Jane saw the figures sliding back into their opening pose so the drama could be re-enacted as soon as the next penny was dropped into the machine.

'I prefer the laughing policeman.'

'Try, "What the Butler Saw".'

'Why?'

'My grandmother thought it too risqué for us when we were kids, so it's probably all a sweet young thing like you can take.'

'You're forgetting I've seen Revue.'

'Two numbers. We kept the best ones for when the usherettes went out.'

He followed her from one machine to the next, and later from one sideshow to another, all the while watching the expression on her face change from delight to confusion at the peculiar mix of fantasy and tawdry illusion.

'Where to next?' he asked as they emerged from an exhibition that included a bearded lady and a mermaid. 'Miniature world inhabited by dwarves? Or the boxing booth?'

'I'd prefer to take one last look at the sea.'

'If it's money . . .'

'I have lots.' She held out her hand, showing him the three sixpences she had left from her half-crown. 'I just want to see what the beach looks like now the sun's setting.'

The noise of the funfair grew fainter as they walked down the promenade towards the steps that led to the sands. Men, women, and even a few children, sat huddled under blankets in the shelter of the sea wall below them.

'Better to be down and out in a seaside resort where there's a chance of earning a few bob cleaning up around a stall or passing out a few deckchairs, than in a workhouse back home,' Haydn said as they descended to the beach.

'I had no idea so many people didn't have a home to go to.' She looked at them and wondered why she hadn't found the courage to run away from the workhouse sooner.

'Not all of them are homeless. Some are just here for one or two nights. Especially the families with children. If you can't afford a chalet, camping out on the beach is the next best thing. The railway return for two or three days isn't that much more than a day trip.'

'And the others?'

'I hope for their sake they find somewhere better to go before winter.' He looked back at the fair. 'I haven't seen this place so crowded in years, but then I suppose people want all the good times they can get before the war begins to bite. I only wish you could have seen it all lit up. Now that is a sight worth seeing.'

344

'It will be lit up again when the war finishes.'

'Strange to think we're at war. In a few weeks when it all gets organised, probably no one will be allowed to walk along here.'

'Why?'

'Beaches will be out of bounds, lest the Germans try to land spies on them. Though pity help the spy who tries to creep in on this coast. The Welsh are a suspicious lot, even of people they've lived next door to for years.'

Dusk rose from the ground, thickening the twilight and turning the sand a cold, silver grey. The sun was sinking low on the horizon, its dying rays smudging the line between sea and sky tinting it a subtle, velvety shade of red-gold.

'The water looks like the powdered ink we used to mix in school.' Jane stepped on to a peninsula of sand that a few short hours ago had been a magnificent castle, complete with driftwood drawbridge and pebbled battlements. The sea washed around her, lapping over her feet on its inexorable journey over the sands.

'You're going to get your shoes wet.'

'They're old ones.' Wilf had been right. The oilcloth hadn't worn well.

'That's the last turret gone,' Haydn observed as a wave surged into the moat and undermined the remaining hillock of sand.

'But there'll be more tomorrow.'

'Not as many as today. There'll only be the local children and those lucky enough to be staying in the chalets to build them. But if the sun shines we'll come again. And next time we won't give our costumes to my father to take home early. There's nothing like moonlight bathing.'

'You've done it?'

'Not here. In Torquay, and over in Shoni's when we were kids. My mother used to put us to bed, then go to chapel meetings, and in summer we'd creep down the stairs and sneak out through the front door. My father never missed us. He was always in the kitchen with his nose stuck in a book.'

'The water must have been freezing.'

'No. It's warmer at night than in the day. I'll bring you back here next week and prove it to you, or better still, take your bathers to work tomorrow and we'll call in Shoni's on the way home.'

'As long as you go into the water first.'

'Coward.' He led her away from the sea. Holding her close he pulled her to the ground. They knelt facing one another, the sand cool beneath their legs, their lips warm as they kissed.

'You were right earlier; it would be wonderful if this could last.' He looked towards the end of the beach. 'There's a light on in your chalet.'

'It's not mine yet.'

'When it is, can I live there with you?'

'For as long as you like.'

'I think I'm falling in love with you, Jane Jones.' He hadn't intended to say the words, but he meant them. For the first time since Jenny.

'I fell in love with you the moment I saw you.'

'Are you serious?'

'You were on stage, singing . . .'

'Then you fell in love with the stage me?'

'Only for a little while, before I got to know the real you.'

'And now?'

'Only the real you. The one who's with me now.'

When he looked around again, the outlines of the stragglers on the beach had darkened to black silhouettes, against a rich, deep, navy blue sky.

'I told Will and Diana we'd meet them at dusk. We should go.' He dusted the sand from her legs as they rose to their feet. 'Hungry?'

She shook her head.

He lit a cigarette. 'Well I am.'

'Move along there! No one allowed on the beach. Move along there!' A row of tin-hatted air-raid wardens were rousting out the vagrants sleeping in the shelter of the wall.

'Out, that cigarette!' one of them ordered Haydn. 'Don't you know there's a war on? Every light, no matter how small, is an infringement of blackout regulations.'

Tempted to protest that the Germans weren't likely to see one cigarette even if they had been flying overhead, Haydn thought better of challenging the man, and dropped it into the sand.

'What, may I ask, were you doing on the beach, sir, miss?' A policeman accosted them as they reached the promenade.

Jane began to tremble and Haydn wrapped his arm around her shoulders.

'Looking at the sea,' he answered.

'Make the most of it, while you can. There's no saying how much longer the beaches will stay open. Now if I were you I'd get home quick.'

'I feel as though the war has started,' Haydn said bleakly, straining to see the way to the fair through the blackout.

'What gives between you and little Miss Muffet?' William asked Haydn as they left the girls at the Ladies on the station.

'Nothing.'

'You two haven't half been doing a lot of sneaking off for "nothing". With what you've got in the Town Hall I'd never have thought you'd go for a plain Jane.'

'She's not plain.'

'Ay ay.'

'Ay ay, what?'

'Come on, Haydn, it's got to be love if you think Jane's pretty. She has a figure like a scarecrow with the straw taken out.'

Haydn gave William a look that cut even through the darkness.

'Sorry. I had no idea it was serious.'

'It's not.'

'If that's so, then why are you looking at me like that?'

Eddie had never been much of a one for the pub or drinking, but after he cleaned the gym that Sunday night he stayed on in the Ruperra. He joined Joey and a few of the boys for a pint which became two, three, and ultimately he lost count of the number. If he'd had his bedroom in Graig Avenue to go back to, he probably would have left when the walls and floors of the pub began to waver around him. As it was, he remained seated next to Joey, getting caught up in round after round of pints; it seemed a better option than walking into the Griffiths' flat and facing Jenny's mother. He imagined her sitting in the overfurnished, stuffy living room knitting and listening to the radio with the same disapproving look on her face she'd worn when he'd left.

He couldn't help thinking the clock back to this time a week ago. He'd rushed up the hill as soon as he'd finished in the gym, knowing that Jenny would be waiting for him in the storeroom. There hadn't been a day between his proposal and yesterday when they hadn't made love. But apart from the kiss in the church he hadn't touched her since the vicar had declared them man and wife. Was this what all the half-humorous, half-serious warnings married men directed at single ones were about? That once a woman had a man's ring on her finger it spelt the end of sex?

He'd wanted to marry Jenny because she was pretty, and unlike one or two of the other girls he'd gone out with, hadn't minded taking her clothes off. He'd seen enough of his parents' marriage to know the damage that a frigid woman could inflict on a man, and had promised himself that he'd never get caught in that trap, no matter how attractive the woman. Yet here he was, one day after saying 'I do' at the altar, more lonely and frustrated than he'd ever been.

'Penny for them?' Joey asked.

'My thoughts aren't even worth that,' he said sullenly, emptying the pint glass in front of him.

'I'll grant you they look miserable enough from where I'm sitting. Married life disagreeing with you?'

'It's not a bed of roses.'

'I tried telling you to stay away from females, but you wouldn't listen. I've yet to meet the boy who does. Mind you, I didn't expect you to look quite so glum so soon. Jenny problems?'

'Mrs Griffiths problems,' Eddie hedged evasively.

'Is it true about Mrs Griffiths?' Glan Richards whispered, as he looked around the bar which was almost deserted; the landlord only opened illicitly for the gym and card school regulars on a Sunday evening.

'She doesn't turn into a witch and ride a broomstick at night, if that's what you mean.'

'I didn't think she did,' Glan said impatiently. 'Is it true she doesn't allow Harry into her bed?'

'How in hell do you expect me to know that?'

'You're living there, aren't you? Does he sleep in the box room?'

'You know he does. Mrs Evans opposite told everyone on the Graig that years ago.'

'Well does Mrs Griffiths ever go in the box room?'

'Not that I've seen, but then I only moved in this morning.'

'I think it's true,' Glan reflected. 'After all, Harry always looks miserable. As if he doesn't get enough "you know what".'

'You want to know something, Glan,' Eddie rose unsteadily to his feet. 'After you're married, sex isn't the only thing you think about.'

'Go on!' Glan stared at him in disbelief. 'In that case I don't think I'll ever get married.'

'That's just as well, seeing as she'd have to be pretty desperate to take you on.'

'Jenny's in bed.' Mrs Griffiths clutched her candlewick dressing gown close to her ample figure and eyed Eddie suspiciously as he staggered up the stairs. 'She tried waiting up for you, but she gave up in the end. Which is hardly surprising, considering the hour. Try not to wake her when you go in.'

Eddie was about to say that now Jenny was his wife, he'd do as he damned well pleased in their bedroom, but the look in Mrs Griffiths' eyes decided him against it. She stepped back as he loomed towards her. Banging clumsily into the wall he tried to open the bedroom door towards him before he succeeded in stumbling into the room. A bedside light was burning. Jenny was lying on her side turned away from him, a book propped up on the pillow in front of her.

'You're late.'

'So what? I'm a grown man, it's a free country, I can do whatever I please.'

'As Mam says, you're married now, and married people have to make sacrifices.'

'Seems to me I've done nothing but make bloody sacrifices since I walked out of church with you yesterday morning.'

'You went down the gym tonight.'

'Only because I want to get enough money together to get us out of this . . .'

A banging on the wall interrupted him mid-flow.

'Now you've woken Mam.'

'I doubt your Mam ever goes to sleep. Most vermin are nocturnal.'

'Eddie!'

The banging started up again and they both fell silent.

'Why do I get the feeling she's got a glass pinned to the wall so she can listen to every word we say.' He sat heavily on the end of the bed and untied his bootlace. When one boot fell with a loud thump to the floor, he began on the other.

'I took a walk up Leyshon Street this afternoon.'

'That must have been nice for you.'

'I saw some rooms.'

'Oh yes.'

'They weren't bad. One down, one up, in Mrs Edwards's house.'

'Old Mrs Edwards?'

'Her son's signed up for the army and her daughter's married. She's going to have trouble making ends meet once he goes and she said we can rent them off her for ten shillings a week.'

'Ten bob? You can rent a whole bloody house in Leyshon Street for that!'

'If you can find one. Come on, Eddie, there's only her in the house, it would almost be as good as having our own place.'

'Ten bob's more than we can afford.'

'You agreed to pay Mam fifteen.'

'But that included food.'

'Eddie,' she laid her hand on his arm. Her touch was enough to make him forget everything except his frustration. Leaning towards her he fumbled with the neck of her nightgown.

350

'Eddie, not now,' she hissed, conscious of her mother the other side of the wall.

'Not now! Not bloody ever.'

'Eddie . . .'

The banging started again.

'It's all right, Mrs Griffiths,' he bellowed. 'Your daughter's saving her virtue for the worms, just like you.' He picked up his boot.

'Where are you going?'

'Out.'

'At this time of night? Eddie . . .'

'When you find a place at a price we can afford, and you're prepared to carry on where we left off before yesterday, let me know.' He picked up his bag and stuffed into it the contents of the drawers and the few things in the wardrobe that were his, before storming out of the room and down the stairs.

'You moving back in?' Evan asked as Eddie walked through the door carrying a case.

'For tonight,' he growled.

Evan smelt the drink on his son's breath. 'If you come into the kitchen I'll make you a cup of tea.'

'Aren't you on your way up to bed?'

'No,' Evan lied. 'Just checking on Brian. I thought I heard him crying. Jane moved in with Diana yesterday so he's back in his old room.' He led the way into the kitchen and set the kettle on the stove to boil. 'Trouble?' he asked quietly.

'Seeing as how no one in this house was all that keen on the idea of me marrying Jenny, you'd like that, wouldn't you?'

'No.'

'I know you thought of her as Haydn's girl.'

'He told me before you got engaged that there wasn't anything left between them.'

'But you had to ask?'

'We were talking about something else at the time.'

'Like what?'

'Like me, and Phyllis and your mam, if you must know.' He spooned tea into the pot.

'Oh Christ, what's the use. It's not really Jenny,' Eddie said angrily, loath to divulge the whole truth to his father. 'It's her bloody mother.'

'I can imagine.'

'No you can't. I came back from the gym tonight, and before I could even get into bed with Jenny, she started banging on the wall.'

'Perhaps she's scared of what you'll do to her daughter in your condition.'

'You saying I'm drunk?'

'Aren't you?'

'I suppose I am,' he conceded miserably.

'If Mrs Griffiths is a problem, you could try moving in here.'

'With Jenny?'

'If Haydn moved upstairs with William, you and Jenny could have the front room.'

'It wouldn't work. Not with Haydn living here as well.'

'The only problems between Haydn and Jenny are in your head.'

'I don't know what's the matter with me.'

'You're probably still coming to terms with everything happening so quickly.'

'It seemed like a good idea to get married when Jenny suggested it. With the war and everything . . .'

'You're not thinking of joining up?'

'Not me. Not until they send for me.'

'Then what did the war have to do with it?'

'I don't know,' Eddie said illogically.

'Seems to me that now the deed is done, you've two choices. Give up as your mother and I did, or make the best of it.'

'There's no best to make of anything in the Griffiths' house.'

'Then look for a place of your own, as you said you would.' Evan handed him his tea.

'We have.'

'Obviously not hard enough.'

'She said she found somewhere in Leyshon Street today. Rooms in Mrs Edwards'.'

'And?'

'And I was angry and said a lot of things I shouldn't have.'

'Stay here tonight. Think about what you want. Go for a walk with her tomorrow. If you talk it over between you, you should be able to sort out something.'

'You think so?'

'For both your sakes I hope so.' Evan was exhausted; it had been a long day at the beach and he had to be up early to get a cart out first thing in the morning. If Eddie had been in a receptive mood he might have tried saying more to him, but in Eddie's present contentious frame of mind there seemed little point. He looked back as he reached the door. 'You do love her, don't you, son?' he asked seriously.

'I suppose so.'

'In marriage there's no "suppose so". It's either yes or no, and that's something I learned the hard way.'

'I married her, didn't I?'

'Then it wouldn't hurt once in a while to tell her you love her.'

'Is that what you did with Mam?'

'No, but that's what I do with Phyllis. All the time.'

Chapter Twenty-Two

Despite the deafening din of the alarm clock rattling in the biscuit tin next to his bed, William woke slowly and sluggishly. He reached out to switch it off. The first sensation his sleep-numbed brain registered as he silenced the noise was the skin across his shoulders, tight and burning from too much sun; the second was of a body lying next to him. Suddenly wide awake he turned swiftly and saw Eddie lying on his back, eyes open, staring at the the ceiling.

'What are you doing here?'

'What does it look like?'

'Jenny had enough of you already?'

'No,' Eddie answered shortly, leaving the bed and pulling on his trousers.

'If I'd got married on Saturday, I wouldn't have shared a bed with you last night.'

Ignoring his cousin, Eddie picked up the remainder of his clothes from the floor, pushed his bare feet into his boots, opened the door and clumped down the stairs. It was early, half-past three. Monday morning was baking and slaughterhouse morning in Charlie's. William and Charlie took the slaughterhouse and he and Alma saw to the baking in the kitchen at the back of the shop. A full day, and he doubted that he'd had more than an hour or two of sleep. He felt foul, and because of the strict regime his trainer usually insisted on wasn't sure why, although if he'd asked his brother or his cousin they would have diagnosed the classic symptoms of hangover. After washing, he finished dressing in front of the range in the kitchen. William joined him, but neither bothered with breakfast. There'd be time enough for that when the first joints were baking in the shop's ovens.

Irritated by Eddie's close-lipped silence, William couldn't resist a gibe. 'Going to call in and kiss your wife good morning?' he asked as they left the house.

'The old witch might put a spell on me.'

'Her mother?'

'You recognise the description.'

'What's she done to you?'

'Not much, just wouldn't stop banging on the wall when I went back there last night.'

'Back there? Eddie, don't tell me you went down the gym the night after you got married?'

'Got an important fight lined up in a month. And Jenny didn't seem to mind.' It was convenient to blame the row between himself and Jenny on her mother. Half-truths were easier to remember than outright lies, and he'd have suffered any torments gladly rather than tell Will or anyone else in his family what had really triggered the argument between himself and Jenny last night.

'Is that what she told you? She didn't mind? God, you've a lot to learn about women.'

'I've got nothing to learn about *my* wife that you can tell me.'

'Look mate, you're gunning for the wrong enemy. I'm on your side. Cigarette?' William held out the peace offering.

'Everything would have been fine if it hadn't been for her damned mother interfering.'

'Pity you didn't have the sense to pick an orphan like your brother.'

'Who's he added to his string now?'

'Jane.'

355

'Jane? In the house Jane?'

'I don't know of any other.'

'She's not Haydn's type,' Eddie declared emphatically, tightening his fists at the thought of Jenny wanting to kiss his brother barely an hour after she'd married him.

'That's what I'd have said, but you should have seen them together in Barry Island yesterday.'

'You went to Barry Island?'

'All of us. Your father and Phyllis as well.'

'And you didn't think to ask me?'

'You expected us to knock you up from your wedding night in the New Inn to invite you to Barry Island?'

'You could have.' Eddie couldn't help thinking that a trip to Barry Island would have been infinitely preferable to spending the day arguing with Jenny, and eating Mrs Griffiths' Sunday dinner in the uncomfortably warm, oppressive atmosphere of the Griffiths' living room. But then Haydn would have been there and, if William was to be believed, with Jane. But would he have stayed with Jane, if Jenny had been there? Questions seared through his mind, inflaming raw and bleeding jealousies. Did Jenny still love Haydn? Did Haydn love her? Had Haydn made love to her behind his back since he'd been home, despite all the denials?

'What's the New Inn like?'

William's conversation maddened him like a nagging toothache. 'You've been in there,' he said.

'Not to stay. I've never had the money.'

'It's like I expected it to be. Full of puffed-up flunkeys and overpriced drinks.'

'Not a good idea of Beth and Cashmere Coat's, then?'

'Good enough. You sure about Haydn and Jane?'

'They kept disappearing. It wasn't so obvious on the beach because Jane can't swim. Someone had to stay with her, and you know me and Di.'

'Out with the ferries.'

'Not quite that far. But when we got to the fair your father and Phyllis took Brian home early and Haydn told – didn't ask, mark you – told us that he'd see us at the chip shop at dusk. Then off he marches arm in arm with Jane.'

'You think it's serious between them?'

'How should I know? Haydn says not, but then you know your brother; since he's come home he's played his cards close to his chest.'

'But you think there's something in it?'

'Diana saw him kissing her. What amazes me is that with all that delectable crumpet going begging in the Town Hall, he picks out a girl who looks like Olive Oyl. But then looks aren't everything, or so all the old, ugly women keep telling me. Not every man can be as lucky as you with Jenny. Now there's a looker for you.'

'That's my wife you're talking about.'

'As if I didn't know. Between you and Haydn I never got a chance to put my oar in, not even in school. Not that I'd want to now,' he added swiftly, realising what he was saying, and who he was saying it to. Marriage certainly did change a man, and not for the better if Eddie was anything to go by. A couple of days ago he could have said almost anything to him, and Eddie would have shrugged his shoulders and laughed. Now holding a conversation with him was like trying to walk on a carpet of eggs. 'I know the first rule of self-preservation: married ladies are out of bounds.'

'You didn't think so last spring,' Eddie reminded him acidly.

'That particular married lady had a husband who was too old to appreciate her. You're not old, you're also handy with your fists and I'm an abject coward. I hereby declare that Jenny's entirely yours, and I promise not to even cast as much as a glance in her direction. Look, we've got a couple of minutes to spare,' he said as they drew close to Griffiths' shop. 'Why don't you nip in and make it up with her?'

'No.'

'This is one time you shouldn't dig your heels in. Go on, Eddie, it'll blight your day if you don't. I'll wait for you.'

'You really think I should?' Eddie slowed his step.

'If I had a wife like Jenny, and we'd quarrelled, I'd be crawling back on my hands and knees, begging forgiveness.'

'Even if it wasn't your fault?'

'What's fault got to do with anything when the stake is sleeping in her bed as opposed to mine?' William leaned against the wall of the small shop opposite Griffiths' and lit a cigarette, watching as Eddie crossed the road and walked round to the side door in the yard.

Eddie tried the storeroom door; it was open. Had Harry left it open, or had Jenny come down last night and opened it, hoping he'd come back? He stole through the shop and crept quietly up the stairs. Jenny's bedroom was closed. He turned the knob and went in. She was lying curled on her side, her face wet with tears, her blonde hair spread out in a silken spray on the pillow next to her.

'Jenny?' he whispered. 'Jenny . . .'

Her eyes flickered open, heavy and hazy with sleep. She looked at Eddie for only a moment before closing them again, but her mouth curved upwards into a lazy, loving smile. 'Haydn . . .'

'It's your husband, not your lover!'

'Eddie! Oh my God, Eddie!'

'What's going on here!' Mrs Griffiths slammed open the bedroom door, her face shiny with cold cream, iron curlers in her hair. 'I thought you left last night. If you've come back to hurt my daughter . . .'

'Hurt her!' White shock paled Eddie's face as he started to laugh. 'She's not worth bloodying my fists.'

'Eddie!'

William heard Jenny's hysterical screaming as Eddie latched the yard door behind him.

'What happened?' he asked, running to catch up as his cousin walked on down the hill. 'Look, I'm sorry,' he murmured, chilled by the bleak look on Eddie's face. 'I should have kept my mouth shut. I was only trying to help . . .'

'It doesn't matter,' Eddie said in a cold, dead voice. 'It really doesn't. Nothing matters any more.'

358

Charlie was waiting for them outside the slaughterhouse on Broadway, a side of beef balanced on his broad shoulders.

'You're late.'

'Lazybones here wanted to stay in bed and cuddle his wife,' William explained, glancing sideways at Eddie.

'There's two pigs ready gutted waiting to be carried to the shop.'

'We're there.'

'Thanks,' Eddie murmured as they walked through the huge double doors.

'For what?'

'Not letting on to Charlie where I slept last night. Not that he won't latch on soon enough.'

'Think nothing of it, mate. After all, it's not as if it's permanent. Is it?' he dared to ask as Eddie moved on ahead of him.

Alma had already lit the stoves, so all that had to be done when they arrived at the shop was the cutting and preparing of the carcasses into joints ready for cooking. Eddie set to work, but he did so mechanically, preoccupied with thoughts of Jenny and Haydn. He allowed the oven doors to swing wide as he lifted the heavy roasting and baking trays in and out of the stoves, and much to Alma's annoyance he also poured away the water the hams had boiled in, and drained the fat instead of keeping it for her to use in making pork pies. Both of them were glad when six o'clock finally came and he left her to carry on with baking the pies, pasties and croquettes while he opened up the shop for the early customers. Even then, every time the bell rang he looked up fearfully, half expecting, half hoping to see Jenny in the doorway. Wondering what he would say to her if she did actually materialise.

The early trickle thickened to a mid-morning rush, but Jenny still hadn't put in an appearance by midday when Charlie and William came in from the slaughterhouse.

In silence he toyed with the meat baps Alma had cut for him, pretending to read the paper so he didn't have to contribute to Charlie and William's discussion on the war news and who in the town was likely to get called up first, or see the looks Alma and Charlie exchanged when they thought no one was looking; looks that reminded him of just how close a man and a woman could be. He wondered what Jenny was thinking now. Was she too afraid to confront him? Probably. And then again even if she did come, what could she possibly say that he'd listen to? What excuse could she have for refusing to make love to him in the night and calling him by his brother's name, in her bedroom the following morning?

William and Charlie finished their meal and left to do the rounds in the new van. The day lagged on, the piles of meat and cooked pies diminished and there was still no sign of Jenny. But he couldn't stop looking out for her, right up until the moment Alma pushed the bolts home on the door.

Whatever problems he'd faced before, he'd tackled them square on, settling most of them with his fists. But this was one situation he couldn't fight his way out of. He could hardly punch Jenny – or for that matter her mother – on the nose. Neither could he help thinking of Harry Griffiths and the miserable celibate life he led under his own roof. Well, he'd show Jenny. He'd told her he wasn't like her father. If she was giving what was his by right to Haydn, then he'd just have to find someone else. Someone who could remember his name, and wasn't too particular about wedding rings.

By the time everything in the shop had been washed down and cleaned ready for the morning he'd thought of a hundred and one excuses for not going up the Graig hill and confronting his wife. He'd said all that he had to say. There was nothing for him there. He'd already packed and taken everything that was his out of Jenny's bedroom. She wouldn't be expecting him. And then again maybe she didn't even want him any more. Maybe she was with Haydn right now – making love this very minute? Then he realised he was being irrational. How could she be, when Haydn was on stage in the Town Hall?

Nor would Phyllis be expecting him. After all, hadn't his father told him to make amends with Jenny? He'd left the house that morning before Phyllis had come downstairs, and he doubted that either his father or William would tell her he'd been there. That left the gym. His training was more important than ever now. It offered a way out from Pontypridd, and away from Jenny. He could buy himself tea in a café – not Ronconi's, William or Diana might be there – but one of the others. Egg and chips was filling and cheap enough. And after his training and a few pints he'd go home – to Graig Avenue. If Jenny had gone looking for him there, Phyllis or his father would know about it, and if she hadn't, he would shrug his shoulders and say he hadn't expected her. That way he'd save face. That was the most important thing of all at the moment: impressing on everyone that what had gone wrong wasn't his fault, that it was a case of wife turned brother's whore. More than any man except a saint like Harry Griffiths could possibly put up with.

'I saw you skulking in the bushes with your little usherette.' Babs propped herself in the open doorway of Haydn's dressing room.

'We weren't skulking, we were walking.' Haydn stared at her in the mirror as he continued to smooth greasepaint on to his face.

'She's a bit of a come-down for a man like you, after what you've been used to.'

'I'd say I was going up in the world.'

'With a plain Jane like that?'

'Who was it said, "Beauty is in the eye of the beholder"?'

'A woman who had nothing going for her.'

'We are feeling more than usually bitchy today, aren't we?'

'You're not even going to deny it, are you?'

He turned sideways on his chair and faced her. He loathed scenes, particularly the hysterical, emotional traumas Babs was adept at engineering, but this was one row he was going to have to suffer sooner or later. And with yesterday fresh in his mind, he decided it may as well be sooner, for both his own and Jane's sake.

'What I do, and the friends I choose to do it with are no concern of yours, Babs.'

'Friends! Is that what you are with that little nobody?'

'Lay off the hair shirt, it doesn't suit you. It was good between us while it lasted, let's leave it at that.' He was conscious of using the same hackneyed lines he'd spoken to Rusty. Was that a sign that he was now more a native of the theatrical world than the normal? What would come next? Speaking only scripted lines? Hugs and kisses all round, and calling everyone 'Sweetheart' or 'Darling' like Chuckles did, when he couldn't remember their names?

'That wasn't what you said to me that first afternoon after re-hearsals, or the Sunday you dragged me into the bushes in the park.'

'We lunched in the New Inn.'

'After you got what you wanted. I haven't forgotten it, even if you have. If you felt then that it had been "good between us while it lasted" why did you take my knickers off?'

He felt conscience-stricken and ashamed. What could he say to her? That he'd been bored and she'd been an attractive diversion? That Rusty wasn't enough for him? That he'd wanted to show off his collection of girls to the town? Every one of those replies would have held a certain amount of truth.

'What was I to you?' Cold anger was now liberally laced with tears of righteous indignation. 'If you'd left me for Helen I wouldn't have liked it, but I could have consoled myself with the thought that she had longer legs, bigger tits, a nicer bum and glossier hair than me. But Jane . . .'

'We're friends, not lovers. Perhaps I'm tired of playing around, Babs. Have you thought of that?'

'Tired of playing around? Tired of sleeping around, you mean! Not you, Haydn. I may be a chorus girl, I may make my living out of showing off as much of my body as the Lord Chamberlain will allow, but please, give me credit for some intelligence. I've slept with you. Night after night for six weeks. And here . . .'

'Keep your voice down,' he pleaded, sensing an unnatural silence outside the door.

'Why the hell should I when you're spinning me lies? Me, who's given you everything a girl has to give, and now when I could be carrying your baby . . .' She slumped dramatically to the floor and burst into noisy, theatrical wails.

He stared at her in horror, remembering his father; his parents' sterile marriage.

'That's shut you up, hasn't it? What have you got to say about "it was good while it lasted" now?'

'Are you pregnant?' His voice was leaden.

'Serve you bloody well right if I am.'

'Babs . . .'

'I'm not some stupid country bumpkin. I know enough to make you pay all right. Every last penny it's going to cost me to raise your bastard, and every penny I would have earned on stage while I'm carrying it. I've got talent. Ask around, everyone says so. I was destined for great things before this happened. Chuckles wanted me for the West End. And now it's all gone out of the window . . .'

The tears came again. He shut the door, and held her in his arms. All the while he stroked her hair, and murmured trite, meaningless reassurances, he breathed in the smell of her powder and the harsh, astringent scent she was wearing and wondered how he could have been so stupid as to fall for the oldest trick in the book.

'Five-minute call for Mr Powell! Five-minute call for Mr Haydn Powell! Five-minute call for Miss Bradley!'

He looked into the mirror, seeing Babs and himself – together. Her greasepaint smeared on to his costume shirt; his rouge was smudged. He had to repair his make-up, tell her to do the same. Then they had to go out on stage. Smile. Perform. Put on a show. Afterwards they'd have to talk, and make decisions. What was the worst possible scenario? That he'd marry her and live out the rest of his life in some crazy theatrical production of her making, where there'd be no audience other than themselves. He shuddered at the thought.

'Haydn . . .'

She was calmer. But he wasn't egotistical enough to believe that it was anything he'd done. The five-minute call had a sobering effect on every professional.

'We have to get ready.'

'And after the show?'

'We'll talk.'

'Promise?'

'I promise.'

She left, he returned to his make-up mirror and set about layering on the gloss. And the worst that could happen if he refused to marry her? She would take him to court and sue him for maintenance for herself and the child. He'd have to economise, set aside a portion of whatever he earned each week for his baby. His son – or daughter! He suddenly saw beyond the concept to the being he had unwittingly created. A child he had given the worst possible start in life. A mother he didn't even like, let alone love.

'Well?' Jenny looked apprehensively at her father as he walked into the shop and shook the rain from his coat.

'Five bob a week.'

'You managed to knock Mrs Edwards down, then?'

'It wasn't difficult. She was just trying it on.' He opened the door into the hallway, slid his soaking umbrella into the stand, and hung his hat and coat on the end hook, away from all the others. The weather had taken a turn for the worse. Rain had begun to teem down late that afternoon at a rate that made up for the six-week drought, and showed no sign of abating. Puddles had collected in the potholes on the hill and Harry's shoes and socks were completely sodden. 'You can move in right away. Her son leaves on the early train tomorrow for Cardiff. She said you can bring your own furniture, but as the place is furnished already I thought you'd probably want to leave it for a while.'

'It would be more sensible to move in and use Mrs Edwards's furniture, wouldn't it?'

'To start off with, I think so.'

'Eventually of course, when we get a place of our own, we'll have to buy things.' Her heart beat faster as she remembered the previous night, the anger etched into Eddie's face. Had he returned to his family and told them what a sham his marriage had turned out to be? Would he talk to her, much less allow her to persuade him to move into Mrs Edwards's house? He'd suggested she look for a place, but had he meant it? And then this morning . . . She shuddered, unwilling to even consider the consequences of calling Eddie by his brother's name. She had to see him, persuade him to move in with her, and quickly. Then she would show everyone how she could be the perfect wife. She didn't think who exactly the 'everyone' she wanted to show, were.

'You do want to live with Eddie, don't you Jenny?'

'Of course, Dad.' She crossed her fingers behind her back.

'It's not just your way of trying to get back at your mother after the fuss she created last night and this morning? Because if it is . . .' his voice trailed away awkwardly as embarrassment set in.

'I wanted to marry him, Dad. We've just had a sticky beginning, that's all.'

He cleared his throat, thinking back to his own wedding night. The one and only night he had slept with his wife, with disastrous consequences that had dogged the whole of his married life. The only good thing that had come out of the entire bitter, humiliating experience had been Jenny. He couldn't help wondering if a similar situation now existed between his daughter and her husband. The prospect was too miserable to contemplate. It didn't have to be like that between a man and a woman. He knew because there'd been others who'd been more of a wife to him than his own, especially Megan Powell, William and Diana's mother. Perhaps that's why he had such a soft spot for Eddie.

'Dad,' Jenny took his arm. 'It was just Mam last night banging on the wall, that's all. And this morning, it was just a stupid misunderstanding.'

'You sure?'

'I'm sure. When we have our own place we'll be all right. I'll go up to Graig Avenue and see Eddie now. Tell him to go to Leyshon Street tomorrow after work. She did say we could move in straight away?'

'Tonight, but I told her tomorrow will do. I'll carry your cases up for you.'

'It will be all right, you'll see,' she reassured him, trying not to think of the look on Eddie's face when she'd woken that morning.

'Here, Eddie, take a look at these.' Glan Richards walked to the corner of the gym where Eddie was skipping at high speed.

'What you selling now?' Eddie asked warily. Glan rarely offered anyone a free look at anything.

'Something that a newly married man like you needs to give him inspiration.'

'I don't need inspiration.'

'No? Then what you doing down here, wearing yourself out when you've a corker like Jenny keeping your bed warm at home?'

'That's enough!' Joey Rees shouted. He'd been too far away to hear exactly what Glan had said to Eddie, but he knew his protégé well enough to read the change of expression on his face. Another word to Eddie, and Glan would be wearing his smile on the wrong side of his head, and he preferred to keep his boy's talents for the ring. 'This a gym or a gossip shop? Eddie, you've had enough for one night. Go home and thank Jenny for sparing you. Tell her that if she keeps you at this fitness level she'll be spending that South African boy's purse at the end of next month.'

Joey watched Eddie hang up the rope and sling a towel around his neck. Was it his imagination, or was the boy off colour? He'd certainly been troubled about something last night. Perhaps it was Jenny. Marriage took a bit of getting used to, and he hadn't helped by being so hard on him. He'd pushed Eddie to the limit from the minute he'd walked in.

'See you same time tomorrow, Joey.'

'Make it a bit later if you like. We've got plenty of time before the big fight.'

'Just trying to make sure I win.'

'You will.'

Eddie followed Glan into the changing room. Making a beeline for the back, Glan was soon surrounded by a huddle of boys, who pored over the postcards he handed out with a suitable appreciative chorus of sniggers and titters. Ignoring them, Eddie went straight to his locker. He'd grown out of pin-ups when he was sixteen, probably as the result of exposure to the real thing.

'Take a look?' Glan shouted above the sea of heads.

'No thanks, I'm going to wash.' Eddie went to the men's room. Filling a sink with cold water he splashed it over his face, then delved into his American cloth bag for the metal soap-dish that contained his own bar of Lifebuoy soap. The soap in the gym was dark green, multi-purpose washing soap that Joey bought in bulk from the laundry suppliers's. It stank of grease and carbolic, a heavy cloying smell that lingered on the skin for days. Stripping down to his underpants, he washed himself and put on his trousers. Looking over his shoulder to check no one was watching, he took a small bottle of men's cologne out of his bag. Not thinking about why he was doing it, he tossed drops liberally over his neck and chest, hiding the bottle before buttoning on his shirt. He Vaselined his hair and walked to the mirror to check his appearance, in case – just in case – Jenny was waiting to waylay him as he walked up the hill, so she could see what she'd turned down for Haydn. Pushing his kit into his bag he returned to the locker room to put on his socks and shoes. The crowd in the corner had grown, as had the noise they were making.

'I haven't seen this one before.'

'She's just a kid.'

'Tell you what, I wouldn't mind finding a kid like that in my bed.'

'Go on, you dirty old man. She only looks about twelve.'

'Look at those eyes. Twelve or not, she knows what's what.'

'And what she's got may be small, but it's all there.'

'Come on Eddie, a look will cost you nothing,' Glan coaxed. Eddie had a good job as well as boxing purses, which meant that he had more money to splash around than most of the gym's patrons. Although Glan had never actually sold him anything, he lived in hope. He held up a stack of postcards. 'Merv's latest.'

'And you're flogging them at a quid for twelve.'

'Tell you what,' Glan walked over to Eddie's locker and whispered, 'seeing as how it's you, and your need is greater than most, just being married and all, I'll knock off my commission. Seventeen and six. How's that for a bargain between mates?'

'It's great to know what friendship's worth, especially when Merv gives you five bob in the pound.'

'How do you know?'

'Because he offered me the job first.'

'You can at least take a look.'

'That's a girl from the Revue,' one of the boys shouted excitedly. 'I saw her on stage.' He thrust a pile of postcards into Eddie's hands. 'That one there, look.'

Eddie did just that. There was something familiar about the peroxide blonde. Stage right, on a pedestal? He cast his mind back to the Town Hall and the blue-lit stage, thick with billowing smoke. For once Glan's sales pitch had hit somewhere near the truth. The girls were new. Merv must have persuaded the Revue nudes to pose for him when they were in town.

He flicked through the cards in a tired, desultory fashion. Jenny with her natural beauty had far more to offer than the overblown, over-made-up blonde – but then, he had to remind himself, that had been the old, pre-marriage Jenny. And no photograph had ever had the same effect on him as a glimpse of the real thing. A silk-clad knee, or a button undone half-way down a blouse with the promise of more to come, had more power to excite him than a full-length nude, even the live ones on stage in the Town Hall. He handed the cards back to the boy who'd given them to him.

'You've got to see this one. Just look at the hair.'

'It's not the hair I'm interested in.'

'That's a wig. They were all wearing them in that scene in the Revue.'

The boy pressed another card on Eddie. It featured a different girl: shorter, smaller, and thinner than the last, although her face was still covered with a mask-like layer of make-up. Her lips were drawn into a cute bow, her eyebrows arched into fine lines. But there was something else. Something in the face that reminded him of someone. Someone he knew ... He looked again. Half child, half woman, small breasts, much smaller than Jenny's, he noted, taking satisfaction from the fact.

'She has that effect on you, doesn't she?' Glan nudged. 'Makes you want to look, and keep on looking. Though I'm not sure why. She hasn't got as much to offer as the other two. Must be the eyes, I suppose. She seems to be looking straight at you. All I know is I wouldn't mind a couple of hours alone with her.'

'Got any more of this one?'

'Here, six back shots, six front.' Glan pushed them at Eddie, sensing a sale. 'As you can see, a very tasty little piece.'

'Very,' Eddie said drily, seeing a way to get back at Haydn without even lifting a finger. 'I'll take these four. Five bob do it?'

Chapter Twenty-Three

'Thought I'd come backstage, admire my great brother and offer firewater to revive his jaded spirits.' Eddie plonked a bottle of beer on to Haydn's cluttered dressing shelf.

'Thanks, but if you don't mind I'll leave it until after the second house. It'll go down a treat once I know I'm through for the day.'

'Suit yourself.' Eddie opened a second bottle he was carrying, using a gadget attached to his pocket knife.

'To what do I owe this honour?' Haydn asked, hoping Babs would stay away until after the second house, as he'd asked her to.

'I can visit you, can't I?'

'Any time. It's great to see you. It's just that I thought you'd be busy.'

'I'll never be too busy to talk to you, big brother.'

'Glad to hear it,' Haydn replied cautiously, wondering what was coming next. 'How's married life?'

'You know of any reason why it shouldn't be a bed of roses?'

'None.'

'There you are then.'

'Been down the gym?' Haydn asked, noticing the bag at Eddie's feet.

'Keeping my hand in. You know how it is. Can't let anyone else aspire to the title of the most promising up-and-coming fighter in Wales. How's life with you?' Eddie raised his eyebrows as giggles resounded through the wall from the adjoining dressing room.

'Can't complain.'

'Bet you can't. Which one is it now?'

Before Haydn could answer Eddie's barbed question, knuckles rapped at his door.

'Come in.'

'It's only me.' Jane stuck her head around. 'Sorry, Haydn, didn't know you had Eddie with you.'

'No need to be sorry, I don't bite.'

'I know you don't,' she smiled. 'The girls want ice creams. Do you want anything?'

Haydn shook his head. 'Want anything, Eddie?'

'No thanks.' Sitting on the stool he propped his feet up on the wall and proceeded to drink the beer he'd brought. 'She's come a long way in a few short weeks,' he commented after Jane left.

'I suppose she has.'

'William said you two are quite friendly.'

'We are.'

'You stuck to her like glue in Barry yesterday.'

'Only because she's never been there before. She's a nice kid.'

'Like everyone else, I'm wondering what plain Jane's got that's put all the crumpet in there – ' Eddie inclined his head towards the dressing room next door – 'in the shade.'

'They're probably the reason I spend what little free time I have with Jane. What you see is what you get with her. There's no false layers to dig through, of make-up or anything else.'

'You think she's honest?'

Haydn didn't like his brother's question. 'There's something innocent about her that reminds me of the way we used to be when we were kids.' He turned to the mirror to check his make-up.

'And that's why you walk her home every night?'

'There's a few reasons, like we finish work at more or less the same time, and we go the same way.'

'I'm surprised she doesn't stop off in station yard.'

'What do you mean?' Haydn whirled around.

Eddie put his hand into his inside pocket. 'Take a gander at these.' He flung the photographs he'd bought on to the cluttered shelf below the mirror. 'Bought them in the gym tonight. Glan was flogging them for the usual pound a dozen, but I managed to knock him down to six bob for those four. I think I did rather well. New girl and all that. But I don't mind telling you she was the last one I expected to see posing for Merv. Still, what can you expect from a workhouse girl?'

Haydn reached out and picked up the photographs. The topmost one was a study of a brunette, ludicrously long hair cascading down over one shoulder, carefully arranged to give maximum exposure to her naked back. But there was no mistaking the features beneath the wig. Pouting lips, enormous eyes, thin cheeks. His mouth dried as he turned it over and stared at the one underneath: a full frontal view that left nothing to the imagination above the waist and very little below it. 'Workhouse girl?' he echoed dully, unconsciously reiterating Eddie's last words.

Eddie had wanted to see Haydn hurting, he'd gambled on William being right about Haydn being infatuated with Jane, but he felt no jubilation on seeing Haydn's pain. The triumph of getting his own back on a brother who still figured largely in his wife's thoughts, and possibly even in her bed, disintegrated as he witnessed an anguish cross Haydn's face that told of more than infatuation. All the resentment and envy he'd accumulated over Haydn's past with Jenny dissolved in a wave of shame and disgust with himself for what he'd done.

'Workhouse girl?' Haydn repeated.

'I shouldn't have said anything. I promised not to.'

'You knew all along she was from the workhouse?'

'William said you were keen on the girl. I had no idea it was serious. If I had done, I wouldn't have bought the photographs, I wouldn't have come here.'

'You would have let me find out from someone else?'

'No . . . Yes . . . I don't know! How was I expected to know you thought that much of Jane? You've never talked about her. Never said a word.' Eddie tried to ease his guilt by shifting some of the blame on to his brother's shoulders. 'And it's not as though you were about to marry her, or anything.'

'No?'

'Look, if you were thinking about going that far, then it's just as well you found out about her now, before it's too late.'

Haydn turned over the last photograph Eddie had given him. He looked at all four for a moment before laying them face down on the shelf. It was no use. He could see her still. Smiling face transformed by greasepaint into a doll-like mask, blatantly naked body, posed like a Revue trouper's. 'Tell me what you know about her.'

'I promised – '

'All the promises in the world won't make any difference now. Not after these.'

Since childhood Eddie had been a fighter, possessing a physical strength and agility that had soon outstripped Haydn's advantage of age. As a result, he had never been afraid of his older brother – until now. There was an iciness in Haydn's unnaturally calm composure that he found terrifying. If he'd been shown pin-up photographs of Jenny he would be smashing his fist into something by now. The door, Merv's face, Glan for selling them . . .

'She never told me about herself. I'd appreciate it if you would.'

'She came into Charlie's one morning. It was early. We'd only just opened up. She was wearing a workhouse dress. One of those grey flannel things, and she had clogs on her feet. She looked rough, as though she'd walked the streets all night. She didn't have much money, and she was hungry so I gave her a pasty. The following Sunday Diana introduced her as the new lodger.'

'Five-minute curtain call for Mr Powell. Five-minute curtain call for Mr Haydn Powell. Five-minute call for Miss Babs Bradley.'

Haydn looked into the mirror. He picked up a stick of flesh-coloured greasepaint and applied it to his chin and nose. Puffing

373

powder on his face, he coated his lips with a lurid red. Every move seemed to be taking place in slow motion, as though he were underwater.

'That's all I know, Haydn.'

'Then why did she make you promise not to tell anyone?' Haydn was looking at his own face in the mirror, yet all he could see was Jane posed shamelessly in front of the camera. He looked down. The sales legend on the back of the cards leered up at him: 'Want to see more, apply to this box number care of Pontypridd Post Office.'

'More?' Was she working out of Merv's back room instead of station square? Warmer, cosier and easier money than sewing for the chorus.

'I'm not sure, but I think there might be something fishy about the way she got out of the workhouse.'

He didn't even hear what Eddie'd said. He'd been a fool to think that Jane was special, someone he could care for. She was no different from any of the showgirls he'd slept with, except physically. Plain Jane! The ugly duckling who worked among swans. But her ugliness hadn't stopped her from behaving just like every other woman he'd met. She was out for Jane Jones. No one else. Out for what she could get, and perfectly capable of using any man stupid enough to say he loved her. His first impression had been the right one. She'd do anything to earn a quick shilling or two – or better still, a pound.

'Three-minute curtain call for Mr Haydn Powell.'

'I'd better be going.'

'Give my regards to Jenny.'

'You haven't seen her?'

'Not since we waved you off to the New Inn. I wish you happiness, Eddie. I really do.'

'I know you do.'

'There never was anything between Jenny and me except puppy love. And there never will be, not now. You do know that, don't you?'

'I do now.'

Haydn closed the door behind his brother. Straightening his bow tie, he slipped on his jacket and checked his image one last time in the mirror.

'Two-minute call for Mr Powell.'

He picked up the photographs and held them in his hands ready to tear them in two, then, thinking better of the idea, he slipped them into the inside of his jacket. Opening the door of his dressing room he stepped out in front of Helen.

'All right, Haydn?'

'Raring to go.' He led the way down to the wings. Holding out his arms to Helen and Babs, the three of them walked out on to centre stage in front of the chorus line-up seconds before the curtain started to rise.

'One . . . two . . . three.'

Haydn came in at the beginning of the third bar. The girls joined in the chorus. They danced side by side, smiles nailed to their faces. Only Haydn's eyes stared blankly out into the black void that cloaked the audience. He was playing musical comedy for all he was worth, because if he allowed himself to stop play-acting and face reality, even for a moment, they would have to bring the curtain down.

I hoped to catch you on your way up.' Jenny was standing outside the shop, the 'Closed' sign on the door behind her. She was shivering. The rain had brought with it a drop in temperature, and it had been a long wait. She'd been too nervous to sit in the comparative comfort of the shop once darkness fell, lest she miss Eddie in the blackout. He paused in front of her. He hadn't said anything, but then neither had he ignored her and walked on. Summoning all the courage she could muster she forced herself to continue. 'Eddie, about this morning, I'm sorry. I was half asleep . . .'

'And half asleep you wanted Haydn, not me?'

'I didn't know who was there.'

'In your bedroom?'

'Eddie, please. You've been so foul to me since we got married . . I didn't mean that,' she cried as he went to walk on. 'Please,

375

it's you I married, not Haydn, and I don't want to argue with you here in the street.'

'You have no choice. I seem to remember your mother saying something this morning about never allowing me over her door-step again.'

'She doesn't have to. I rented those rooms I told you about from Mrs Edwards. I'm moving into them first thing in the morning. I was hoping you'd move in with me.'

'At ten bob.'

'We knocked her down to five.'

'Who's we?'

'My Dad. He heard the row last night, said it was as much Mam's fault as yours. That you couldn't be expected to live in our house the way things are.'

'That was good of him.'

'Eddie.' She stretched out her hand and brushed an imaginary speck of dust from his jacket. 'Please, give me one more chance. We can even go there tonight if you want to. Mrs Edwards will probably be asleep by now, but she said we could move in right away, and if you don't want to go there, I think Mam's in bed. There's the storeroom . . .'

'The storeroom? For an old married couple like us?'

'We will make an old married couple, won't we?'

'Ask me again in fifty years.'

'Then you'll move to Leyshon Street?'

'I'll think about it.'

'Eddie, I'll do anything . . . anything you want.' She wondered whether or not to tell him she loved him. It wouldn't be true, but did that matter? Lies or truth, love couldn't be that important to him. He'd never once mentioned it, even when he'd suggested marriage. 'Eddie, I want to sleep with you. You know I like sleeping with you. It just didn't seem right with people around, that's all.'

'Mrs Edwards will be in the house.'

'She's deaf and besides she wouldn't walk into our rooms, not the way Mam walked into mine this morning.'

'And Haydn?'

'He hasn't said more than a few words to me since he's been home, and even then it was to tell me what I already knew. That it's over between us. That he doesn't love me any more, if he ever did. Eddie, you knew you were the first. I swear to you on my life, there hasn't been anyone else.'

'I suppose I've got nothing to lose by giving it one more go.'

'Then you'll go there tomorrow? To Leyshon Street after work?'

'I'll be there.'

'I'll have your tea on the table.'

'I hope you can cook.' Turning his back, he walked on.

'Eddie?'

He looked back.

'You do know the number of the house?'

'I know the number.'

She watched until his shadow merged with the others on the hill. Rubbing the cold from her arms she opened the door and went into the shop.

Jane finished her work, unpinned her usherette's cap and went into the Ladies to comb her hair. As soon as her hair had grown long enough to hold iron wavers she'd bought a set, although she hadn't had a good night's sleep since she'd taken to wearing them in bed. But the look Haydn had given her the first time he'd seen her hair crimped was worth every minute of the nightly agony.

She pinched her waves, looked sideways in the mirror, dabbed essence of violets on to her wrists and behind her ears and added a touch of pink lipstick to her mouth.

'Dancing lesson?' Avril asked, walking in behind her.

'If Haydn's not too tired.'

'He never seems to be too tired for you, love.'

'You think so?'

'No doubt about it.'

'Thanks, Avril.' Jane finished primping and made her way to the dressing rooms. All the rooms were silent and all the doors

377

closed except Haydn's. Babs was with him, but outwardly oblivious to her presence he sat, slumped in front of his dressing mirror, his eyes glazed, a bottle of whisky and a metal beaker on the shelf in front of him. Wary of Babs, Jane hovered uneasily in the doorway. She hadn't seen Haydn drink anything stronger than an occasional glass of beer before; never whisky, and never alone like this. He lifted his eyes and saw her in the open doorway. She started guiltily, as though she'd been caught spying.

'As you're busy, I'll walk on up, Haydn.'

'I would if I were you,' Babs advised icily. 'He's pissed as a newt, and no good to any woman in his present state. I'll leave our discussion until tomorrow, Haydn.' Gathering her gloves and handbag from the chair, she stalked out.

Jane waited until she heard the outside door closing. 'Aren't you going to change out of costume?'

'Want some?' Ignoring her question, he filled the metal beaker and pushed it along the shelf towards her. He lifted the bottle and drank heavily. Wiping the dregs on the sleeve of his jacket he smeared it with red and flesh-coloured greasepaint. 'You don't want it?' He picked up the beaker and drained that as well. 'Of course, I should have remembered. You don't drink. You don't do anything naughty, do you, Jane? You play Miss Goody Two-Shoes without a script. Don't drink, don't smoke, don't play around with men. A complete little innocent who knows nothing of the alley-cat morals of the average chorus girl.' He left his chair and slammed the door, sealing them in together.

'What's the matter? I've never seen you like this . . .' Her voice faltered as he swayed threateningly towards her, the bottle still in his hand.

'You've never seen me like this, because I've never been like this before.'

'Haydn, after yesterday – '

'Yesterday? Are you referring to the sweet adoring look you gave me when you said you loved me? You've got talent, Jane. Not looks,' he qualified gravely, shaking his head as he fell back on to his chair, 'but talent. It was a fine performance. Had me fooled. And I'm a pro who's played with the best.'

'I meant every word.'

'I'm sure you did – at the time. But then you seem to have had difficulty in differentiating between the truth and lies before. Lived on a farm in Church Village, did you? A poor little orphan girl who was taken in by kind people who knew your mother?'

She covered her mouth with her hand.

'You can forget the stories,' he went on mercilessly. 'Eddie told me the truth.'

'But he . . .'

'He promised? Don't blame him, it just slipped out. We Powells aren't good at keeping secrets. Not used to lying. Too bloody honest for our own good, that's us.' He loosened his bow tie as he refilled the beaker.

'Haven't you had enough?'

'Probably.'

Silence fell between them, the absolute silence she associated with the empty theatre: an echoing mustiness redolent with the odours of stale sweat and greasepaint.

'I am an orphan.' Her words fell softly into the stillness. 'I was born in the workhouse. They told me my mother's name was May. She found a job on the outside when I was six weeks old and she ran away. I don't blame her.'

'Because you did the same?'

'Yes. That's why I asked Eddie not to tell anyone about the workhouse uniform I was wearing the first time he saw me. I did live in Church Village, in the orphanage, but I had to leave there when I was sixteen. The only place that would take me was the workhouse. I was there for two years before I was offered a job as a live-in skivvy in a dosshouse. It was even worse than the workhouse, so I went.'

'To Phyllis?'

'Before this – before the theatre – she was the only friend I had.'

'You think you've made friends in this place?' he sneered.

'Some,' she answered defiantly, 'but none as good as Phyllis. We used to talk to one another when the staff weren't around.

379

She told me what it was like on the outside. She was kind, that's why I went to her for help when I had no one else to turn to.'

'And she didn't disappoint you?'

'Neither did your father. They didn't have to take me in, but they did, after I told them the truth. I knew it was a risk for them, that's why I told them everything.'

'Everything?' He pulled the photographs from his jacket and flung them at her. They fell in an untidy heap at her feet.

She fell to her knees and snatched them up.

'It's a bit late for that. I've seen all there is to be seen.'

'He said they wouldn't be on sale in Pontypridd, only Cardiff. That no one would see them . . .'

'Merv?'

She nodded, too mortified to look him in the eye.

'And you believed him? What else did he tell you? And what else did you do for him besides pose for these?'

'Nothing. I swear it, Haydn. Nothing.'

'As I said before, you're good.'

'You don't understand,' she insisted fiercely.

'I understand, only too well.'

'Do you? Do you know what it's like to live in the workhouse? To have to rely on parish charity for everything? To own nothing of your own. Not a penny piece, not even the clothes on your back?'

'But you own your own clothes now, don't you, Jane?' He reached out and fingered the cloth on her bodice.

'I earned them, fair and square and honestly with the one and only thing that I can call my own. My body. Posing for these means that I have savings in the bank. Savings are my security. If I lose this job, if Phyllis and Evan put me out on the street, it won't matter. I can live on *my* money – for months if I have to.'

'Don't worry, you won't have to scrimp and save. Not you. It's a short step from those – ' he flicked at the photographs she was holding – 'to station yard.'

'I'm not a prostitute.'

'Not yet.' He drank from the beaker.

'When I left the workhouse I made myself a promise that I'd never go back there, whatever it cost me.'

'There's decent, honest work around if you look for it.'

'I've found it.'

'With Merv?'

'Once with Merv. To earn enough to open a bank account.'

'And the next time you want something?'

'I'll save for it.'

'Wouldn't it be easier to strip off again?'

Unable to bear the contempt on his face she turned her back on him. A ten-pound note fluttered before her, falling to her feet.

'Strip!'

'No.'

'Sorry, I forgot, experienced people cost more.' A five-pound note landed on the one that lay on the floor. 'Strip!'

'No!'

'Why not? I'm offering more than Merv.'

'Haydn, please . . .'

'You want more? I've run out of ready cash, will you take a cheque? It will be honoured, you have my word.'

'No, Haydn. Not for you. Not ever.' Tears coursed down her cheeks, he could see them glittering in the lamplight. But he was used to tears. The thought crossed his mind that she could have put on a better display. When Babs cried her tears were accompanied by harsh, rasping sobs. He lurched out of his chair. Wrapping his arms around her, he kissed her: a whisky-laden, vicious, savage embrace, totally unlike the gentle caresses of the day before.

'There's nothing of you. I could crush you, right here and now.'

'Haydn, you're frightening me, let me go . . .'

'"Let me go",' he mocked. 'Why? You're a whore, I'm a customer. You don't shout "let me go" to customers, Jane. You're nice to them. You give them what they want. After all, they're your livelihood. And I'm making you an offer you're not likely to get again in a hurry. Name your price, I'll pay. And I can be a lot more generous than Merv . . .' Losing his balance, he grabbed the front of her dress. It was the new, button-through summer black she'd bought in Leslie's. The buttons popped beneath the strain and scattered over the dusty floor. She screamed, terrified of the stranger he'd become. The cries reverberated into the emptiness.

'It's a bit late for wailing, Jane.' Haydn slumped against the wall, and for the first time she realised how drunk he was. 'There won't be a man in Pontypridd by the end of the week who hasn't seen everything you've got to offer.'

'I only did it once.'

'And you did it for money. Just like the girls in the Revue.'

'That doesn't make them worse or less than any other woman.' Fear turned to anger, giving her a strength she hadn't known she possessed. 'You worked with them, you earned your money the same way. By selling what you've got. if I'm a whore then so are you.'

'You can't buy twelve nude photographs of me in a gym for a pound.'

'Only because no one would want them, except Max or Billy. You've been lucky, Haydn. You've had good breaks, and you've a family behind you who'll always take you in, and give you food and a bed when you need it. Well my family is that ten pounds, and it was the only way I could see to get it.'

Clutching her torn dress she walked towards the door.

'Where are you going?'

'To get a needle and thread. Despite the names you've called me I'd rather not walk around the town this way. Not even in a blackout.'

'I loved you. I was prepared to . . . prepared to . . .'

'Prepared to what, Haydn?'

'Look after you,' he mumbled miserably.

'The way you looked after Babs and Rusty and Mandy? I don't need that kind of looking after.'

'I thought, really thought you were everything they weren't. That's why I loved you.'

'If you thought I was nothing like them, you don't know me or them. You've never taken the time or trouble to get to know any woman except between the sheets.'

'That's not true.'

'Isn't it? Well one thing's for certain, whoever you thought you cared for doesn't exist. No one could live up to what you want, Haydn. You want a saint. A sweet pure, innocent saint to be at your beck and call, and tell you how wonderful you are. Well not even a saint would have turned down an offer like the one Merv made me, if she had the threat of the workhouse hanging over her head. I'm not a bad person. Just desperate enough to do what it takes to keep myself alive and in one piece.'

'Then I wish I'd met you before you became that desperate.'

'There was no before. This is me. The way I am.'

'Why didn't you come to me if you needed money?' he begged. 'I would have given you whatever you needed.'

'No you wouldn't have. Because when I posed for those pictures you didn't even know I existed.'

'I did. Damn it all I did . . .'

'All right, supposing I had asked you, Haydn? What then? You would have just handed over the money and expected nothing in return? I want to stay honest. Pay my own way. Be beholden to no one.' She wrenched open the door.

'Jane . . .'

'You don't have to worry I'll be out of the house first thing in the morning. I have enough money to take lodgings elsewhere now.'

'You don't have to go.'

'Yes I do. Eddie's seen those photographs.'

'How do you know?'

'You said they were on sale in the gym. It can only be a matter of time before they're in the pubs and someone else sees them. William, or your father.'

She left. Haydn heard her go into the girls' dressing room next door, presumably to repair the damage he'd done to her dress. He fell to his knees. Gripping the stool with both hands he willed the room to stop revolving around him. When he caught sight of himself in the mirror he was horrified. His suit was creased, heavily stained with dust and greasepaint. It would need cleaning and pressing before the show tomorrow. He leaned on the shelf and peered in the mirror. Through bloodshot, bleary eyes he studied his paint-smeared face. The red from his lips had streaked his chin. The blue from his eyes had run half-way down his cheeks and nose. He picked up a jar of cleanser and a wad of cotton wool. Ten minutes later, with his face clean, and dressed in his own clothes, he felt only marginally more human. At that moment he would have offered almost anything to anyone who could have magicked away the effects of the whisky. He'd been a bloody fool. He'd seen enough people on stage drink themselves out of sanity and a career to know what an overdose of booze could do. Hearing movement, he opened his door.

'Jane.' He reached out to her, but she shrugged off his touch. 'Some of those things I said. It was just the shock of seeing you in those photographs. And because I care . . .'

'If you'd really cared you wouldn't have said them.'

He stood in front of her, blocking the narrow corridor, forcing her to face him.

'Jane, we have to talk.'

'If you're sober enough you'd better lock up.'

'You'll wait? Walk up the hill with me?' When she didn't answer he lost control again. 'In God's name talk to me.' He caught her by the shoulders and shook her. 'Jane . . .' In that precise instant he knew why he was so angry; why he'd got so drunk. Photographs or no photographs, he still loved and wanted her. He knew then that he could never have left her behind when he moved on at the end of the season. He needed to be with her, now and always. Bending his head, he kissed her. Moments later he was reeling against the wall, in agony from a sound slap across his face and the force of her knee hitting his groin.

'Oh no you don't, Haydn Powell. I think too highly of myself to become just another name on your list of conquests.'

'I love you.'

'No you don't.'

'I do. I've just realised how much.'

'Love to you is a roll on a dressing-room floor, and because you've seen those photographs you think I'd be only too happy to take your fifteen quid and roll. Well, I may be a worthless tramp, but I can live in hope that one day a man worth having will tell me that he loves me, and mean it. Enough to put a ring on my finger. And if that happens, he'll be entitled to get himself a virgin, not one of your cast-offs. Let me pass.'

'Not like this, Jane . . .'

She kicked him again, but he stood his ground. 'If it's marriage you want, I'll marry you.'

'You'll change your mind in the morning.'

'I won't. I swear it.'

'I've had enough of your swearing for one night, Haydn. If you care for me at all, just let me go. Please, just let me go.'

He sat in the dressing room for a long time after she went, listening to the rain spatter against the window pane as he tried to sort out the mess of his life. Eventually he rose to his feet and lifted down his coat from the back of the door. It was then he found another set of photographs in the pocket: a full set this time, twelve as opposed to the four Eddie had given him. He barely glanced at them before dropping them into the bin along with the others. He lit the edge of one with his lighter, standing back and watching as the blue and yellow flames licked around the edges, curling the paper and consuming every trace of that other Jane.

Chapter Twenty-Four

'It's clean, tidy and I expect my lodgers to keep it that way. No visitors, no food allowed in bedrooms, all clothes and personal possessions kept in cupboards, no pictures or photographs on display. Those are the rules and I warn you now, I don't stand nonsense from anyone.'

'No, Mrs Morgan, I can see that.'

'And I won't tolerate any smart alecs, girls or boys in my house either. Rent's eight shillings and sixpence a week, paid in advance every Friday night. That includes breakfast and a good hot meal every evening except Sunday when it's at one, prompt. I do no washing other than bedlinen. Sheets and pillowcases changed every Monday morning, lodgers expected to strip and make up their own beds. The front and back doors are locked every night at ten. I expect everyone to be in at ten minutes to that hour.' She folded her arms across a bosom that reminded Jane of an overstuffed bolster.

'Ten is going to be a bit difficult, Mrs Morgan.'

'Why? No girl of your age should be out any later.'

'I work in the Town Hall.' Jane saw Mrs Morgan's expression change from distaste to disgust.

'You're a showgirl?'

'An usherette. We have to clean up after the last show finishes.

Generally I can't leave until half-past ten, sometimes eleven, and if we've been particularly busy, occasionally even later than that.'

'Then this isn't the house for you, young lady. If you'd told me where you worked when you stepped through this door, it would have saved me a lot of time and trouble.'

'I'm sorry, Mrs Morgan.'

'So am I.' She shut the door on the bedroom Jane had caught barely a glimpse of. 'There's some in this road that'll take theatricals, but I'm not one of them. I don't hold with riff-raff showing off on stage, prancing around half naked, putting ideas into people's heads and encouraging them to stay out until all hours. And I'll have no one coming into this house and wanting to eat meals in the middle of the night, either. Unchristian and unnatural, that's what I call it.'

'Which houses in this street take theatricals, Mrs Morgan?' Jane ventured timidly, wondering why she hadn't thought of Variety lodgings. The chances were that a house that took in artistes wouldn't find anything to object to in an usherette.

'You can try Mrs Thomas in Number thirteen,' Mrs Morgan sniffed as she showed Jane the door. 'She's not too particular who lives under her roof.'

'Mrs John.' Harry Griffiths bustled round the counter and set a chair out for Bethan. 'There was no need for you to come down. If you'd sent your list in, I would have delivered your goods as usual.'

'I haven't come about my order, Mr Griffiths. I was hoping to see Jenny.'

'She's packing.'

'Packing?'

'Haven't you heard? But then, how could you. They only decided late last night. They've taken rooms in Leyshon Street.'

'No, I hadn't heard. That's wonderful.' She was surprised by the news. Phyllis had told her only that morning that Eddie had moved himself and all his belongings back into the bedroom he'd shared with William, on Sunday night.

'I'm sure Jenny would love to see you.' He opened the connecting door and called out to his daughter.

'Please don't bother, Mr Griffiths. If she's busy . . .'

'Coming, Dad.' Jenny came down the stairs and handed her father a cup of tea.

'Mrs John's called to see you.'

'Please Mr Griffiths, call me Bethan.'

'Won't you come up?' Jenny invited her politely, hoping that Bethan hadn't called on account of anything William or Haydn had said.

'Thank you, I would like to, if I'm not disturbing you.'

'Would you like tea?'

'Only if you're having some yourself.'

'It's already brewed. As you can see, my father likes a cup at this time of day. I'm sorry my mother isn't in,' Jenny prattled as she led the way up the stairs. 'She's gone to see my aunt.'

'Actually it was you I was hoping to see. Your father told me that you and Eddie are moving to Leyshon Street.'

'Today.'

'That's really good news.'

'We were lucky to find rooms of our own so quickly. Please sit down.'

'I feel a bit foolish now.' Bethan sat in the chair nearest the window. 'You see I couldn't help but notice that things weren't going too well between you and Eddie – '

'It was trying to live here,' Jenny interrupted. 'My mother's not the easiest person to get on with.'

'Neither is Eddie. He has a talent for rubbing people up the wrong way. That's why I was going to offer you rooms in our place. I talked it over with Andrew, and he agreed.'

'That's very good of you Bethan, but it's a bit far up the hill.'

'Well if it doesn't work out in Leyshon Street and you need a stopgap you know where to come.'

'Thank you.'

'I didn't come here to pry, Jenny. Only to help if I could.'

'I wondered what the family would think of Eddie moving back into Graig Avenue the night after our wedding.'

'We thought the obvious, that you two had problems. And if there's anything we can do to help, you only have to ask.'

'That's kind of you,' Jenny said mechanically.

'Being married takes a lot of getting used to. I loved Andrew with all my heart when I married him, but there still came a time when I felt I couldn't live with him. Now we have a good marriage, but only because we've both learned to talk every little detail out before it becomes a problem.'

'But you're so happy!' Jenny exclaimed.

'Yes we are. But believe me, it wasn't always that way. Sometimes I think it's hard to live with someone all the time. No matter how much you love them there's bound to be times when you irritate one another, and then again, as I just said, Eddie's not always the easiest person to get along with. But he does love you, Jenny. Very much. You only had to look into his face at my birthday party to see how much.'

'You think so?'

'I know so.'

'The problems between Eddie and me are all my fault.'

'I don't believe that for a minute. I've grown up with Eddie's temper. But he doesn't always mean what he says when he's angry. Still, you must have found that out by now.'

'He thinks I love Haydn,' Jenny ventured. A wave of relief swept over her, as though the mere mention of Haydn in some way lessened her infatuation.

'Perhaps that's understandable,' Bethan answered cautiously. 'After all, you were Haydn's girl for a while. But I'm sure both you and Eddie thought very carefully before taking your marriage vows. No one makes those kinds of solemn promises unless they believe they can keep them.'

Jenny heard her own and Eddie's voices echoing back from the church: 'Love, cherish and obey – till death us do part.' Bethan was right: she had made promises. The most solemn ones of all, and they shouldn't be too difficult to keep now she knew for certain that Haydn didn't want her. Eddie had every right to expect loyalty, love and devotion from her. He might not have said the words, but as Bethan had said, he must love her. Why hadn't she realised that before? He had made so many sacrifices for her. Ignoring her past with Haydn, taking her to the Revue, risking and attracting the mockery of his friends. Buying her chocolates when romantic gestures of that kind were totally alien to his masculine nature. And when he made love to her, hadn't she forgotten everything and everyone else after the first few caresses when she'd tried so desperately to imagine him as Haydn?

'I'd better be going.'

Jenny stared at Bethan, stupefied. She'd forgotten her sister-in-law was with her.

'Would you like some more tea?' she asked.

'I can't, I'm afraid. Andrew's outside.'

'Why didn't he come in?'

'He had a call to make, and he insisted on waiting. He's overprotective, won't let me go anywhere on my own, not in this condition. Bethan patted her stomach, and smiled. 'Men! Where would we be without them?'

'I don't know.' Jenny was suddenly very envious, not of Andrew but of the deep, honest, open love he and Bethan shared and their coming baby. At that moment she resolved to do everything in her power to build the same kind of trusting marriage with Eddie. She only hoped it wasn't too late.

'What do you mean she's gone?'

'What I say.' Phyllis dropped some toast on to a plate and handed it to Haydn. 'She was up and out through the door before William this morning. Packed everything she owned into two carrier bags and left. Wouldn't listen to reason. Just said that . . . said . . .'

'Said what, Phyllis?' Haydn urged as her voice tailed away.

'Nothing that concerns you.'

'She said she wouldn't tell anyone where she'd be staying so you wouldn't get into trouble, didn't she?'

'What are you driving at?'

'I know Jane's from the workhouse. That she ran away from a dosshouse.'

'She told you?'

'Not willingly. I met someone yesterday who'd seen her in a workhouse uniform,' he admitted, blurring the truth. 'Then I confronted her. She didn't want to tell me anything, but I forced her.'

'Forced her? Haydn, what happened between you two?'

'What do you expect? We had a blazing row.'

'I tried to warn you that you'd end up hurting her. Jane's not like other girls, at least not the kind you're used to. Someone with her upbringing takes life more seriously than most. If you said or did anything . . .'

'I was drunk. I can't remember half of what I said. I'm not proud of myself, but after seeing . . .' He halted mid-sentence. There was no way he could bring himself to tell anyone, not even Phyllis, about the photographs. 'I thought she was hiding something,' he finished lamely.

'Like what?'

'I don't know, that was the trouble. I was worried about you, Diana, Will, and especially Dad. Knowing what effect prison had on him last year.'

'You thought Jane was a criminal? That your father would hide a criminal?'

'I didn't know. That's the point, Phyllis. I didn't know and no one in this house would answer my questions. Not you, not Dad, not Jane. What was I supposed to think? The last thing I wanted was for anyone to get into trouble.'

'And when you heard she'd been in the workhouse you thought she was an unmarried who'd abandoned her baby?'

'Not after I got to know her,' he muttered, too ashamed to admit that the thought had crossed his mind.

'How well did you get to know her?'

'Enough to want to see her again. Do you know where she's gone?'

Phyllis shook her head. 'The last thing she said was that she was tired of being afraid of everyone she met. You don't think she could have gone back to the workhouse?'

'She said last night that she'd do anything to stay out of the place.'

'I hope you're right,' Phyllis said fervently. 'Because if she does, they'll take everything off her, even her clothes.'

He was out through the door before Phyllis could say any more. He didn't know where he was going. He only knew he had to find Jane and tell her, soberly this time, that he loved her and wanted to marry her.

'Ten shillings a week, hot meal after the show . . . that's a bit steep for you, isn't it, love?' Mrs Thomas was tall, thin, and had a smile that displayed a full complement of teeth set like subsiding tombstones. She'd catered for travelling theatricals for years, but she'd never thought of usherettes. Now one was actually standing in her hall asking for a room, she wished she'd considered theatre staff when she'd first gone into business. They didn't earn as much, but they'd be a sight more dependable, and a few shillings less a week would be small sacrifice to set against a bed that never languished empty.

'I've been paying seven and six,' Jane explained.

'Well then, tell you what I'll do. Seeing as how you don't mind taking that small room at the top of the house, we'll call it seven shillings. But you help me to carry out the supper dishes every night. You don't have to wash them, my girl will do that in the morning. I don't like to keep her up late to wait on the guests' supper table when she has to be up at five to see to the stove and the fires.'

'If you're sure about it, Mrs Thomas, I'd be happy to help out.'

'Then that's settled. My legs aren't what they used to be, and I could do with another pair of hands around the place. My husband used to do a lot of the heavy work, but since he passed on it's been a bit of a struggle. There's only me and the girl and she's not getting any younger either.'

Jane glanced into the room next door where 'the girl', who looked to be on the wrong side of sixty, was making up a bed.

'You'll be bringing your case?'

'I have everything I need in these for tonight.' Jane held up the carrier bags. 'I'll get the rest later.' She crossed her fingers, hoping her new landlady wouldn't pass comment on how little she had.

'Well then, you can move in right away. Breakfast is from eight to ten every morning, those are the hours that suit the theatre people best. If you want yours any earlier you can get it yourself in the kitchen. The girl will serve you. Supper is after the show. Eleven, most nights. Here's your keys. Front door, and room. Don't forget about the supper dishes.'

Her purse lighter by seven shillings, Jane walked up the two flights of stairs that led to the attic rooms. The bed was soft, clean and inviting. Propping her carrier bags on an enormous chest of drawers that filled one wall, she lay down and closed her eyes, meaning to rest for just a few moments, but she was asleep in a minute. The night had been long and wakeful, and she had spent it trying to recall exactly what Haydn had said to her. Each and every vicious word.

As Haydn reached Temple Chapel a black car slowed in front of him. The passenger door opened.

'Lift?' Andrew John asked.

'Thank you.'

'Going into town?'

'I suppose so.' It would be as good a place to start as any. He remembered Jane saying something about a woman called Daisy who worked in the Ladies by the fountain. Then he realised that was the one place in town he couldn't walk into.

'You don't know where you're going?' Andrew asked as he slid the car into gear and moved off.

'Not really. Andrew, you work in the workhouse, don't you?'

'The Infirmary part. You're not thinking of admitting your-self?'

'Not this week. Look, if someone ran away from there . . .'

'Ran away? Over ten-foot walls?'

'Supposing someone got taken out by an employer, and the employer turned out to be a slave-driver, and then they ran off.'

'This someone wouldn't be Jane Jones by any chance?' Andrew enquired shrewdly.

'If it was, you wouldn't tell anyone?'

'No.'

'She's terrified of being taken back.'

'After seeing the way the pauper's wards are run, I can understand that.'

'So what would they do if they caught her?'

'Haydn, where have you been? Don't you read the papers? There's a war on.'

'What's that got to do with anything?'

'Everything. Money and manpower are needed. And in vast quantities. One girl less in the casual ward isn't going to upset the parish guardians. In fact on the contrary, it will be one less mouth for them to feed.'

'Then they're not looking for her?'

'Put it this way. If they came across her and found out that she was keeping herself, and not breaking any laws, they'd be only too happy to leave her where she is.' He stopped the car outside the main gates of the workhouse. 'So you can walk back up the hill and tell her no one's looking for her. If she's worried about setting the record straight, I'll put a word in the right ear, and get her crossed off the books.'

'You can do that?'

'Don't you know doctors are miracle workers? You want to tell her?' Andrew prompted when Haydn made no move to leave.

'I only wish I could.'

'You've had a quarrel and she won't talk to you?'

'We've had a quarrel and she's gone. Left the house this morning.'

'Don't tell me a woman's actually run away from you. The great, good-looking, all singing, all dancing Haydn Powell?'

'I suppose you think I had it coming to me?'

Andrew suppressed a smile. 'No more than any other man, myself included. Wasn't it Oscar Wilde who said, "Each man kills the thing he loves." I'm not sure I'd go quite that far, but we certainly do seem to know how to hurt women. And how to play the indignant fool when they've decided they've had enough, and leave us.'

'Beth did it to you, didn't she?'

'You remember? I deserved it at the time, and my blood still runs cold every time I think of how close I came to losing her. You love Jane?'

'Yes.'

'Then you'd better find her and tell her so. And don't worry about the records in this place, I'll set them straight.'

'Or crooked?'

'Depends on your point of view.'

Haydn opened the car door. 'Do you know what's so strange? Admitting to myself and everyone else that I do love Jane. I thought I'd never say it to any girl, and mean it.'

'None of us ever does.'

Haydn made his way down to the Tumble in a daze, trying to think himself into Jane's mind and work out where she could have gone. She'd have to find somewhere to live. The question was, where? Pontypridd was teeming with lodging houses, and there was scarcely a house on the Graig that didn't let out at least one room. She could have gone to one of the usherettes, but other than knowing that they walked home via Mill Street, he hadn't a clue where any of them lived. Then in a sudden burst of inspiration it came to him. A hard-working conscientious girl with an exaggerated sense of loyalty like Jane would never leave the manager of the Town Hall in the lurch. She would turn up for work tonight. All he had to do was make sure she didn't leave before he apologised and explained how much he loved her. And then if she forgave him . . . if she agreed to get engaged . . . Engaged!

He looked around. He was outside the New Theatre. There was a jeweller's on the corner of Mill Street. He patted his pockets: by some miracle he had his cheque book.

'That's the smallest we have, sir.'

Haydn held it in the palm of his hand. A diminutive plain gold band set with a single diamond. Unpretentious, and perfect. Like her.

'I'll take it.'

'It's the smallest, sir, but unfortunately not the cheapest.'

'I'll still take it.'

'And if it doesn't fit the young lady, sir, we can make adjustments.'

'That's good to know.' Haydn wrote out the cheque, pocketed the box and left the shop. He'd done something positive, something he hoped would help show Jane just how much he valued her. Now all he had to do was while away the hours until the theatre opened. Perhaps if he went there now, left a note . . .

'Eddie, we need change.' Alma held up a ten-pound note.

'Times must be getting better. When I first started helping Charlie out on his stall we never saw anything bigger than half a crown.' William carried two enormous platters of sliced ham out of the kitchen and set them down behind the counter.

'Copper and silver, Eddie,' Alma reminded him.

Eddie removed the apron he wore over his overall and left the shop. It was a short walk down Taff Street to the bank, and it was a glorious day. Good to be outside and in the fresh air.

'Haydn?' Jenny waylaid him outside the dress shop next to the New Inn. His feelings for Jane didn't stop him from casting an admiring eye. She looked stunning. Beautiful and elegant with her pale gold hair knotted into a chignon on the nape of her neck, her lips gleaming with the lightest touch of pink lipstick. She was wearing the same grey suit she'd worn as her 'going away' outfit, with a shopping basket hanging somewhat incongruously on her arm.

'Sister-in-law.' He went to tip his hat then realised he'd left the house in such a hurry he wasn't wearing one.

'Haydn, I must talk to you.' She pulled at his sleeve in an attempt to draw him out of the flow of pedestrian traffic.

'I'm not talking to you again without Eddie around.'

'It's not what you think. Please, couldn't we go somewhere? Somewhere public, like Ronconi's where everyone can see us. What possible harm could there be in that?'

'A lot, if people see us and talk.'

'Haydn, you don't understand me. I have to tell you something, about Eddie and me. I really want to make our marriage work . . .'

Eddie saw them as he passed the entrance to Market Square. He didn't look at their faces; he didn't have to. There wasn't another man in Pontypridd with hair as blond as Haydn's, or another suit like the Howell's special that Jenny was wearing. Rage erupted. The street, the sky, the buildings whirled in a bizarre kaleidoscope of crimson fragments. Clenching his fingers into fists he moved towards them. Jenny saw him first. The smile died on her lips as she looked into his eyes. Haydn stepped back, but not far enough.

Jenny screamed as Eddie's fist connected with Haydn's jaw. Haydn flew backwards, crashing into the central display window of the dress shop. Glass shattered beneath his weight, flinging him into a chaotic jumble of jagged splinters and smashed dummies. He landed on his back, one leg twisted beneath him, his body a broken and bloody mess. Men came running, one or two of them in the blue and silver livery of the New Inn. Jenny's scream died in her throat as people started shouting to one another. There was a cry for a telephone call to be made for an ambulance. Numbed and shocked, she reeled towards the figure on the ground.

'You did this, sonny?' A policeman stepped between her and Eddie. She forced herself to look at her husband. His face was ashen, drained of every vestige of colour.

'You did this?' the policeman repeated.

'He did.' A woman wriggled through the thickening crowd. 'I saw it all. He did it.' She jabbed her finger into Eddie's chest. He didn't even flinch.

'You'd best come with me.' The policeman took his arm. Eddie wrenched it from his grasp.

'Haydn! That's my brother. Why isn't anyone helping him? I have to . . .'

The policeman was joined by another. Between them they succeeded in restraining Eddie.

397

'We've found a doctor, we've sent for an ambulance. It'll be here soon.' The man who spoke was wearing a porter's cap.

A woman unlocked a wooden door at the back of the shattered window. Eddie watched someone step through it and move towards Haydn. He was carrying a brown leather doctor's bag. Kneeling among the broken glass, he bent over Haydn's head. The crowd pushed forward, pressing around the policemen who had trapped his arms in elbow locks. He could hear the whispers . . .

'It's Haydn Powell.'

'Go on, it isn't.'

'It is, I'd know him anywhere. I saw him in the Town Hall.'

'Someone's husband got him, by the look of things.'

'Probably deserved it too from what I've heard.'

'Eddie,' Jenny floated into view. An arm was wrapped around her shoulders, supporting her. 'Eddie?'

He saw her, heard her speak, but would allow nothing to distract his attention from the lifeless figure on the ground.

'You know this young man, Miss?' one of the policemen asked.

'He's my husband.'

'His name?'

'Eddie Powell. That's his brother Haydn.' She turned to the window, watched as the ambulance men crunched their way over the carpet of broken glass. One of them accidentally jarred the window-frame. A thin spear of glass trembled and plunged downwards. A gasp tore through the crowd, the doctor looked up and swung his case over Haydn's chest. The point pierced the leather, shuddered and fell harmlessly to the side.

'The sooner we get him out of here, the better. Move him carefully now. That's it, gently . . . gently.'

Jenny heard the Cardiff accent and realised the doctor was Trevor Lewis. She stepped forward as the stretcher was eased out of the display case. Haydn was swathed in red blankets, his fair hair matted with congealing gobs of blood that were already turning black, his skin masked with a red that sparkled with the glint of glittering shards.

'He's dead!'

The man holding her strengthened his grip.

'We hope not, Miss,' one of the policemen said flatly. 'For your husband's sake, as well as that poor sod's.'

'Looks like this fell out of his pocket.' The woman who'd opened up the window handed the policeman a small, bloodied leather box. He opened it. Both Jenny and Eddie saw the ring nestled on the background of deep red satin. A solitaire engagement ring.

'He was showing it to me. He'd just bought it. For Jane.'

Eddie couldn't look Jenny in the eye. Holding out his hands, he allowed the policemen to handcuff him and lead him away.

Chapter Twenty-Five

'You're late,' Joe Evans said curtly as Jane ran up the stairs ten minutes before the doors were due to open.

'I know. I'm sorry, it won't happen again.' She dashed down the corridor to the office, shaking her headdress free from her pocket as she went.

'Sorry to hear about Haydn, Jane,' Avril commiserated with her as she walked through the door. 'Bet the family are upset.'

'Not as upset as the manager and Mr Evans, or Chuckles and the girls when they found out that they've got to go on tonight with Max playing leading man *and* comic.'

'Haydn's not performing?' Jane looked from Myrtle to Avril.

'You don't know?' Ann, who was quicker than the others, asked. 'About Haydn,' she continued in response to the blank look on Jane's face. 'His brother attacked him.'

'Eddie?'

'It was awful,' Myrtle chipped in. 'I saw it. Well, some of it,' she qualified. 'I was over the road, in front of Woolworth's at the time. Heard the crash then everyone went running to see what had happened. And there he was, lying on his back amongst all that broken glass in the dress shop window. There was blood everywhere. Well, I took one look and thought, that's it. He's a goner. Even the ambulance man who carried him out said he wa

400

more dead than alive. If that nice young Dr Lewis hadn't been drinking in the New Inn, there's no saying what would have happened. He did something to stop all the blood pumping out of him –'

'That brother of his should be shot, hitting him through a plate-glass window like that,' Myra interrupted. 'Soon as Mr Evans heard about it, he got Chuckles and drove him up to the Cottage Hospital. Babs said they told them it could be months before Haydn's fit to work again. That's if anyone offers him a tour with all that damage to his face. One thing's certain: he's not going to come out of this as pretty as he went in, and that's always supposing he comes out at all.'

'Stop it, Myra,' Anne ordered sharply, watching Jane. 'Last I heard, he's going to make it.'

'Two minutes to opening.' Joe Evans popped his head around the office door. 'Come on, what's got into you girls tonight?'

'Jane didn't know about Haydn, Mr Evans,' Myra explained as she picked up one of the sheaves of programmes laid out on the desk.

'Bad business.' Joe Evans shook his head.

'He is going to be all right, isn't he, Mr Evans?' Jane asked. 'You must know. Avril said you went to see him this afternoon.'

'When I was there he was in a different kind of theatre to the one he's used to. They were trying to stitch his head back together.' He squinted at her. 'But you must know all this, you live with the family.'

'I moved out this morning.'

The footsteps of the first patrons coming up the stairs echoed into the office.

'We've got a theatre to run.'

'I'm sorry, Mr Evans.' She pinned on her cap.

'Your programmes.' He heaped a pile into her arms. 'There's notices everywhere, but you'd better warn those who bought their tickets beforehand that Haydn's been replaced. If they don't want to stay they can get a refund at the box-office.'

She nodded, all she was capable of doing.

'Come and see me between the houses. I'll telephone the Cottage Hospital to see if there's any better news.'

'Mr Evans.' She hesitated in the doorway. 'You will tell me if the news is the other kind?'

He was about to utter a platitude, when he looked into her eyes. 'I'll tell you whatever they tell me.'

'Thank you, Mr Evans.' She squared her shoulders and walked away.

'You're bloody lucky he wasn't killed, Eddie.' Evan Powell sat opposite his son in a cold, comfortless cell in the basement of the police station. 'I've always said that temper of yours was going to be the death of you some day, but I never thought it would be the death of Haydn too. What on earth possessed you?'

'It doesn't matter, Dad, not now. Tell Haydn I'm sorry . . .'

'Tell him yourself.'

'He really is going to be all right?'

'He won't be singing for a while. Or appearing on stage. His right leg's broken and his face looks like it's been marked out for a jigsaw pattern, but Andrew said the break is a clean one and the scars on his face should fade eventually. Until they do he'll just have to put on a couple of extra layers of make-up.'

'I didn't mean to hurt him. I just went wild.'

'Because you saw him with Jenny?'

'Yes.' Eddie walked to the barred window, set high against the ceiling. The light had faded, dusk was falling, and all he could think of was that if it hadn't been for chance, and Trevor Lewis's quick actions, this day could have been his brother's last.

'Jenny said they were just talking. Haydn had bought a ring for Jane.'

'I know that now.'

'Well I've said all I've come to say. And that look on your face says everything I want to know. It's one hell of a way to learn a lesson, but I know that you'll think twice about hitting any man outside of the boxing ring again. Come on boy, time to go, your wife's waiting.'

'I can leave?'

402

'Andrew paid the bill for the damages at the shop. Haydn's been interviewed in hospital and he's not willing to press charges, and your Uncle Huw has persuaded the sergeant to drop the charge of affray. You're lucky and free.'

Eddie picked up his jacket.

'But before you start work tomorrow, you go and see your brother in hospital and square everything with him. You boys mean a lot to me. Both of you. I won't have you splitting up the family. Not after all we've been through.'

White, strained and still wearing the same costume that she'd worn into town that morning, Jenny sat waiting in the foyer of the police station. She watched through an open doorway as the duty officer returned Eddie's personal possessions, and gave him the form to sign for them. Evan patted his son on the back, and gave her a tight smile as he passed her on the way out.

Eddie walked slowly towards her, cap pulled low over his face, jacket slung over one shoulder.

'Eddie, I'm sorry. We were only talking.'

'I know.'

She followed him outside into the yard. 'He wants to marry Jane.'

'So I've heard.' He turned to face her. 'Go on back to the house.'

'Leyshon Street?'

'Whichever house you want.'

'You won't be coming home tonight?'

Home! A place he'd never even been to and she called it home! 'I won't be there. Not tonight.'

'Tomorrow?'

'I'll be in touch.'

'Eddie, I'm your wife. You can't avoid me for ever.'

'I have to see Haydn.'

'Tomorrow then.'

'Perhaps.'

'They wouldn't let me see Haydn, so I asked if you were here.'

'And I am. Come in Eddie.' Andrew dropped the pen he'd been using to write up medication records. 'Sit down.'

'He is going to be all right, isn't he?'

'Barring accidents he's going to be fine.'

'I thought he was dead.'

'Dead people don't bleed that much.'

'Please, I need to know the truth. How bad is it?'

'There's no damage done that can't be cured by care and time. It was fortunate that Trevor was idling away his time in the New Inn. He stopped the bleeding before it got to the dangerous stage. Most of the serious cuts are to the back of his head and will eventually be hidden by his hair. We've X-rayed him, there's no skull fractures. The wounds to his face are fairly superficial, and should heal soon. But, there's still the broken leg, a bad concussion, and shock of course. He'll probably be here for a few days.'

'But he will live?'

Andrew thought he'd never seen such a mixture of guilt and misery on a face before. 'He'll live,' he repeated as he left his chair. 'But as you obviously aren't convinced, you'd better come with me.'

'Now?'

'I can't think of a better time if you're going to sleep tonight. But I warn you, he's not a pretty sight. Definitely a case of looking worse than he is.'

Haydn was in a single-bedded side ward. That in itself worried Eddie, as he could see a room lined with what seemed like dozens of beds up ahead. That had to mean Haydn's condition was more serious than that of the other patients. A nurse who was sitting with him rose when Andrew entered. He picked up the chart at the foot of the bed and signalled for her to go outside.

'A few minutes, Eddie,' he said as he followed her out. 'And be careful not to tire or upset him.'

Haydn was lying on his back. From what little that could be seen of his face beneath the copious layers of bandages, his eyes were closed. Eddie crept up to the chair.

'Haydn?'

One red, swollen eye opened, then more slowly the other.

'Haydn, I'm sorry . . .'

'So am I, mate.' The bandages moved slightly as Haydn attempted a smile, but he abandoned the gesture. It was too painful, even though the effect of the anaesthetic hadn't quite worn off.

'You see, I thought . . .'

'I love Jane, not Jenny,' Haydn mumbled through swollen lips.

'I know that now. Andrew says you're going to be all right.'

'It's useful having a doctor in the family.' Haydn was having trouble focusing. Everything was blurred, including his brother; if he hadn't known him better he would have said he was crying. 'When I get out we'll go to the New Inn, your treat. Me, you, Jenny and Jane. You're a lucky sod, kid. You've a good career in the ring ahead of you, and a wife who loves you.'

'You think so?'

'She may not know it yet, but she will. People do funny things.' Haydn's voice grew faint. Eddie had to bend forward to catch what he was saying. 'They conjure up a soul-mate and fit the first person who comes along into their idea of a dream lover. I tried to do it with Jane before I saw who she really was. I think Jenny did it with me after I went away. But I'm the dream and you're real, Eddie . . . you're real . . .'

'That's enough.' Andrew walked into the room and replaced the charts. 'It's time the patient slept.'

'See you, Eddie.' Haydn's eyes were already closing.

Eddie went into the corridor. He sank into the nearest chair and buried his face in his hands. He was still sitting there a few moments later when Andrew passed.

'Come on, time we both went home. I'll give you a lift.'

'I could have killed him.'

'You could have, but you didn't. Try remembering that.'

I hope you don't mind me calling so late, but I've come to see how Haydn is.' Yesterday Jane had lived in this house, today she was hovering at the front door wondering what kind of reception she'd get, uncertain as to whether or not Haydn had told his family about the pin-up photographs – or even worse shown them.

'He's going to be all right,' Phyllis said as she ushered her through to the kitchen.

'You've seen him?'

'We all have.'

'And I've just left him.'

Jane only just managed to conceal her surprise at the sight of Eddie sitting at the table. After what Myra had said she'd expected him to be in jail.

'Tea?' Phyllis asked the room in general.

'No thanks, I'm swimming in the stuff.'

'Pity they don't have beer on tap in the hospital.' William winked at Jane.

'You'll have tea, won't you?' Phyllis asked Jane as she set the kettle on to boil.

'No thank you. I only called to find out how Haydn is. First night in new digs, the landlady will be wondering where I am.'

'You've found a good place?' Phyllis pressed, hoping for the address.

'It's fine, and the landlady is really nice.'

'And you'll come and see us?'

'I'll keep in touch,' Jane replied ambiguously.

'If you're set on going, I'll walk you. I could do with a breath of fresh air,' Evan offered.

'No,' Jane said quickly. 'It's not far, and I'll enjoy five minutes' peace and quiet. The Town Hall can get a bit hectic.'

'You could go and see Haydn if you like. Visiting's every Wednesday and Saturday, but if you time it when Andrew John is around, he'll let you in for a few minutes.'

'I won't be able to visit. It's just that the girls in the Town Hall were worried, so I said I'd come up and ask how he is. Everyone will be pleased to hear he's going to be all right.'

'He won't be back on stage for a few weeks yet.'

'Give him our best wishes.'

'Our?' Phyllis asked.

'All the staff.' Jane opened the door.

'I'll see you out.' Phyllis walked Jane to the front steps.

'And I'm for bed. Don't stay up too late, you two.' Evan closed the kitchen door behind him.

'You all right, nipper?' William asked as Eddie slumped over the table.

'Would you be if you were me?'

'There's no permanent harm done.'

'That's not the point.'

'Look on the bright side. While you carry on packing punches like that, the Nazis aren't going to set their sights on Ponty.'

The kitchen was very still after everyone had gone. Eddie sat staring into space, trying not to think about what might have happened. It was no use. Every time he closed his eyes an image of Haydn lying lifeless and covered in blood amongst the debris of the shop window came to mind. Pacing to the range he saw a copy of the *Pontypridd Observer* on Evan's chair. An advertisement on the front page caught his eye.

WELSH GUARDS

Volunteers required now for the WELSH GUARDS. *Age 20-35. Height 5ft 9ins or over. Men can present themselves for enlistment at all Recruiting Centres. Enquiries will be answered at all Police Stations.*

Men registered to be called up under National Service, but not already called, may enlist now in the WELSH GUARDS.

Enlistment on normal engagement, or for the duration of war.

'You can't run from me. I'm your wife.'

He couldn't run from Jenny while he stayed in Pontypridd, but there was one way of avoiding her, and all his problems, for the duration.

He opened the drawer in the huge old oak dresser that dominated the wall opposite the window and extracted a long, flat cardboard box. Inside he found what he was looking for: a pen, writing paper and envelopes.

'What you doing?'

'Getting clean clothes.'

'What time is it?' William tried to decipher the numbers on the clock without much success.

'Too early to get up. Go back to sleep.' Eddie found the bag he'd carried from the shop the night before and hadn't unpacked. Backing softly out of the door he tiptoed downstairs. He washed, shaved and changed in the washhouse. Picking up his bag again, he realised that he'd find no use for half the things in it once he was in uniform. He took it into Haydn's room, switched on the light and emptied it out on to the bed. He repacked his towel, shaving kit, Post Office book, boxing gloves and strip. He felt a momentary pang of regret for the match with the South African that he wouldn't be fighting, but then, after what he'd done to his own brother he wasn't sure he wanted to enter a ring ever again. A grim smile crossed his face as he realised the strange sentiments he was carrying to war.

He left before dawn. The things he'd left behind were in a neat pile on Haydn's bed. Two of the letters he'd written were on the kitchen table, one addressed to Evan and the other to Charlie. William would take Charlie's down. Another rested in his pocket. The hill was in darkness, but his eyes became accustomed to the blackout long before he reached Griffiths' shop. He stopped and posted the envelope through the door. Walking on, he stood on the hill for a few moments looking down at the dark shapes of the Maritime and the workhouse.

He reached the station just as the first pale light of dawn touched the eastern sky.

'You're up and about early, Eddie,' Dai Station commented as he walked into the booking hall.

'Couldn't sleep. When's the Cardiff train due?'

'Five minutes. Fight lined up?'

'The biggest one of all, mate,' he answered before running up the steps to the platform.

'You're not going to get a better offer, boy.'

'I know and I'm grateful.'

'Think about it, Haydn. What else could you possibly do until your leg mends?' Chuckles pressed insistently, very much on the producer's side. He'd been responsible for inviting the producer down to see Haydn perform in Pontypridd, and the least he could do was ensure that the man succeeded in his aim of putting Haydn under contract, and incidentally compensating him for having to replace his leading man for the remainder of the Summer Variety run. 'There isn't a show that will consider a leading man, or for that matter a chorus boy, with a broken leg and facial scars like yours.'

'I know.' Haydn shifted restlessly on his bed. Six days in hospital was six days too long. He was stiff, irritable and bored witless. Not one of his letters to Jane had been answered. On reflection – and he'd had a lot of time for reflection – he didn't blame her for not writing after some of the things he'd said. It was just that he couldn't stop hoping that she'd take pity on him in his present state. The other girls had. He'd been showered with chocolates, magazines and kisses from the chorus and every usherette except the one he wanted to see. But it wasn't just Jane. It was the war. Eddie had joined up and William and Charlie were both talking about volunteering. And all he was capable of doing, all he'd been offered was . . .

'It'll practically be your own radio show, son,' the producer said persuasively. 'There'll be others, of course. Four singers in all, two men and two girls, but you'll be the linchpin and I'll personally see to it that you're given a free hand. You'll have a secretary to sift through the requests from the troops, but you can pick and choose your songs from whatever comes in, and perform and arrange them any way you like as long as you keep the audience happy. And from what I saw of you on stage, that seems to be second nature.'

'We've talked to the doctor. He's agreed that you can leave with us tonight.'

'Tonight?' Haydn looked at Chuckles in disbelief.

'He said there shouldn't be a problem, provided you carry on your treatment in London. You'll get the best possible doctor, help with dressing – '

'But we have to leave in an hour,' the producer interrupted, checking his watch.

'If I agree to go with you, there's one thing I want you to know . . .'

'That you intend to join up as soon as you're back in one piece? Don't look so surprised,' the producer said irritably. 'It's what everyone is threatening to do these days. But don't worry, boy. You won't be needed. By the time that leg heals it'll all be over.'

'There's also someone I'd like to see before I go.' Haydn looked at the clock. Eight! Jane would be in the Town Hall. He wouldn't even be able to climb the stairs with the plaster cast.

'We have to get back to London before morning, and that means leaving as soon as we've eaten. I've no time to waste shilly-shallying.'

Haydn looked up to Andrew in the doorway.

'I can pack your things and bring them here.'

'Sounds like a conspiracy.'

'I can't see you getting a better offer in your present state of health.'

'Have I got time to dress?'

'You can have as long as it takes us to dine in the New Inn. We'll pick you up afterwards. Don't worry about accommodation or anything. Everything will be sorted for you, including a doctor to keep an eye on those cuts and that leg.'

Andrew brought not only Haydn's case but also the entire family. Suddenly there seemed to be no time left for anything. Diana and Phyllis sat ripping the seam open on the right leg of a pair of his trousers. William ate the last of the chocolates the Variety girls had sent in to save him the trouble, and Evan, Bethan and Phyllis tried to ask sensible questions about the job, but didn't get very far because Haydn was too abstracted to listen to what anyone was saying. Knowing that there was absolutely no chance of Jane walking in still didn't stop him from hoping.

'They've just pulled up outside.' Andrew pushed a wheelchair into the room. 'Right, if you ladies leave, we'll get what's left of his trousers on, then you can say goodbye.'

Diana, Phyllis and Bethan left. William and Evan helped him on with his clothes; Andrew handed him his hat.

'This,' Andrew produced a letter from the pocket of his white coat, 'is for your new doctor.'

'Thanks, not just for this but for everything.' William and his father had gone out into the corridor. He could hear Diana and Bethan laughing at something William had said. 'I have one more favour to ask.'

'Ask away.'

'You remember what I said that morning you gave me a lift?'

'About Jane?'

'Will you see she gets these?' He thrust a note he'd managed to scribble in the bathroom and a small box into Andrew's hand. 'I told her if she doesn't want to keep the ring she can give it back to you.'

'You want me to send it on?'

Haydn shook his head. 'If there's no letter, just write and tell me what she said.'

'I'll do that. And Haydn,' Andrew offered his hand as William wheeled him out. 'Good luck. I hope it works out for you.'

'For him!' William exclaimed indignantly. 'Why shouldn't it? He's going to have a cosy studio to sit in, girls flocking around him, not to mention money in his pocket. It's the poor Taffs like me and Charlie who'll be left with all the dirty work in this man's war.'

'That's because poor Taffs like you were born without brains.'

'Talk to you at the end of the war, mate, about who's got brains.'

Haydn forced a laugh. They were his family, the people he cared for most, only this time it wasn't he who was leaving them.

Next time he came home they wouldn't be here. First Eddie, soon William and, he looked at Andrew and Bethan, eventually, even the men who had a lot to stay for.

'Be seeing you.'

'That a cue for a song?' Diana asked.

Everyone laughed.

'Not this time,' Haydn called back as William wheeled him to the waiting Bentley. 'But maybe next.'

Andrew handed the box and the letter to Jane at the stage door. He didn't have time to stay, and she didn't have time to say more than 'Thank you.' She put the box into her pocket, opened the envelope and walked slowly up the stairs, reading it as she went.

> *Dear Jane*
> *I'm sorry I had to leave before seeing you. I love you, and I want to marry you. I understand now that it's not for me to forgive you, but for you to forgive me. I hope you can.*
> *Please write. Phyllis will have my address.*
> *All my love, now and for ever.*
>
> *Haydn*

Chapter Twenty-Six

'I hate it when the autumn run ends and the pantomime starts. It's the first sign winter's arrived.'

'Never mind the birds migrating, the panto's started,' Avril laughed.

'Birds? What birds do we see in here?' Ann asked. She moved out of the office as Arthur grated back the bolts on the door. 'That's the end of peace and quiet. Last performance of any show always brings them out in droves.'

Jane picked up her programmes and followed Ann into the auditorium. Two theatrical seasons had come and gone since she had bulldozed Joe Evans into giving her a job, and with it her diffidence. She took her station at the back of the auditorium every bit as confident as Ann and Avril, selling programmes, directing people to their seats, giving out change, tearing up ticket stubs. It was second nature to her now. Soon it would be Christmas and a New Year and a new decade, 1940 and still no sign of the war abating.

The orchestra's discordant tune-up notes melted into the opening bars of the overture. The lights faded, darkness closed around her, just like the very first time she had visited the theatre with the orphanage. There was the same sense of expectancy – of something about to happen – of people holding their breath. The curtains began to rise, slowly, infinitely slowly, and there it was. A moonlit garden, but not the one Haydn had danced in the first time she'd seen him on stage.

A man and a girl emerged from the wings, singing, they waltzed to centre stage. But the man was short and dark, not tall and fair, and although he sang well, he didn't sing as well as Haydn. Time had moved on to a different garden and a different hero.

Angry because she'd allowed herself to think, and remember, she moved back behind the last row. The problem was, everything always came back to Haydn. The wonderful times she'd spent in Barry and Shoni's, and the most miserable, when she'd swallowed her pride and gone to see him at the hospital only to discover he'd left the night before. Until that moment she hadn't really believed there would be a time when he wouldn't be there. And Dr John hadn't helped by giving her that expensive ring and the letter. She'd kept the letter, slept with it under her pillow every night since he'd given it to her eight weeks ago, but she'd given the ring back to Dr John. If it had been a cheap one she might have been tempted – but it hadn't.

She promised herself that if Haydn wrote again she'd answer him. But days turned into weeks and nothing had arrived, although he knew she could be contacted through the theatre. Once or twice she'd picked up a pen, but every time she looked at a blank sheet of paper she saw his face, dark and angry as it had been when he'd flung the photographs at her. In the end it had been easier to allow time to pass and do nothing. Easier – except at times like this when the darkness of the theatre closed around her, affording privacy to think, and remember – things that were better forgotten.

She looked out over the shadowy heads of the audience. When she had started working in the Town Hall she hadn't been able to imagine a time when she would want to leave. Now all she could think of was change. She burned to move on as so many others had done, and were doing.

The Summer Variety had gone, taking with it the chorus girls she'd come to regard as friends. When they'd left she'd missed them all, even Babs, who'd married Chuckles suddenly and very unexpectedly. Since then there'd been no time to exchange more than passing pleasantries with the casts of shows that flitted in and out of Pontypridd within a week. Then Myrtle and Myra joined the WAAF. They'd tried to persuade her to go with them, but the manager had pulled a face and she had agreed to stay until the New Year. The way things were going he'd have no more time for socialising in his office. Joe Evans was leaving on the first train out of Pontypridd on Monday morning. Two of the stagehands had already left. William and Charlie had called into the theatre to kiss her goodbye. Change – all change – and it had made her restless, given her the urge to become a part of it.

The singing stopped and the curtain fell on the opening number. The orchestra struck up again as the short dark man moved out on to the apron. She closed her eyes and listened.

'Fare thee well . . . till I can be beside you once again my love . . . Parting is such lovely sorrow . . .'

Another voice joined in: 'We can dream about a sweeter tomorrow . . .' She turned clumsily, hitting her torch against the wall.

She blinked, wondering if she was dreaming, Haydn was there – but a different Haydn, dressed in khaki, his blond hair gleaming in the darkness, his cap in his hand.

'Ssh . . .'

He smiled charmingly at the woman who had hissed at him. 'So sorry, madam.' Gripping Jane's arm he pulled her out into the corridor. The door clanged noisily behind them.

'You didn't send the ring back?'

'I did. I gave it to Dr John.'

'You did?' The smile died on his lips. All the way up in the train he'd been dreaming of what he'd say to her, what she'd say to him. The kiss they'd exchange when she flung herself into his arms. He hadn't bargained on Andrew trying to play Cupid.

'I didn't want to give it back, but it was so expensive.'

'Oh Jane, what's that got to do with anything?'

'I didn't want you to think you could buy me. Not after ..
after ...'

'Have we got some talking to do. Come on.'

'I can't go anywhere. I have to work.'

'Not tonight. I've seen Joe, he's covering.'

'Looks like you got your knight, Jane.'

Ann and Avril were standing in front of the confectionery
booth smirking like a pair of fat cats.

'Without his armour and charger,' Avril laughed.

'And with a limp.'

'Right, there's enough witnesses.' Leaning heavily on his stick,
Haydn bent his good leg and extended the other with difficulty.
'This is the nearest I can get to kneeling. Will you marry me?'

'But you said – '

'No buts. Yes or no?'

'Your uniform? You're in a show?'

'Jane, do you ever give a straight answer to a straight question?'

'Are you in a show?'

'You could say that.'

'You've joined up?'

'They've given me a seventy-two hour pass. For the last time
will you marry me? If it's yes we'll get a special licence first thing
in the morning.'

'Yes.'

Using his stick he clambered awkwardly to his feet and kissed
her.

'Let the poor girl up for air,' Avril protested.

'Come on, there's people around here.' He offered her his arm.

'Don't forget to leave the unsold programmes and the money,'
Joe shouted from the office.

Jane handed them to Avril.

'And take tomorrow off,' Joe offered generously.

'Thanks, she will, and the day after that,' Haydn called back.

She tore the band from her hair as she helped him negotiate
the stairs.

'There's one more thing that needs settling. A special licence takes forty-eight hours to clear. I only have a three-day pass. I don't suppose you'd consider honeymooning before the wedding?'

'Where?'

He looked across the blackened square towards the New Inn. 'You know me, always optimistic.'

'You booked into the New Inn?'

'I booked Mr and Mrs Haydn Powell into the New Inn.'

'Can we stay there until you have to leave?'

'I was hoping you'd say until we have to leave.'

'We?'

'I have a room in London. It's not much, but it would be a lot better with you in it.'

'I promised the manager I'd stay until January.'

'You're about to make a promise to obey me.'

'I'm not sure I can hold to that.'

'I'm not sure I'd want you to – all the time. I like a girl with a bit of spirit.' He wrapped his arm around her and kissed her again.

'In that case you won't be able to complain that you didn't know what you were getting.'

'I know exactly what I'm getting. I love you, Jane Jones.'

'Jane Powell.'

'Mrs Powell. Let's go and see exactly how much can be packed into seventy-two hours, shall we?'